Give Me Butterflies

Also by Jillian Meadows

Wreck My Plans

Give Me Butterflies

A Novel

JILLIAN MEADOWS

AVON

An Imprint of HarperCollinsPublishers

GIVE ME BUTTERFLIES. Copyright © 2023 by Jillian Meadows. Excerpt from WRECK MY PLANS © 2023 by Jillian Meadows. Bonus epilogue copyright © 2025 by Jillian Meadows. All rights reserved. Printed in the United States of America. No part of this book may be used or reproduced in any manner whatsoever without written permission except in the case of brief quotations embodied in critical articles and reviews. For information, address Harper-Collins Publishers, 195 Broadway, New York, NY 10007.

HarperCollins books may be purchased for educational, business, or sales promotional use. For information, please email the Special Markets Department at SPsales@harpercollins.com.

Avon, Avon & logo, and Avon Books & logo are registered trademarks of HarperCollins Publishers in the United States of America and other countries.

Originally published as *Give Me Butterflies* in the USA in 2023 by Jillian Meadows.

FIRST AVON TRADE EDITION PUBLISHED 2025.

Interior text design by Diahann Sturge-Campbell

Stars illustration © Negro Elkha/Stock.Adobe.com
Butterflies illustration © ulucsecda/ Stock.Adobe.com
Whisk with mixing bowl © Made by Made/thenounproject.com

Library of Congress Cataloging-in-Publication Data has been applied for.

ISBN 978-0-06-341616-1

24 25 26 27 28 LBC 5 4 3 2 1

To the chronic apologizers: let that shit go.
Don't apologize for things that aren't your fault.
Don't apologize for things you don't regret.
And definitely don't apologize for who you are.

We delight in the beauty of the butterfly, but rarely admit the changes it has gone through to achieve that beauty.

MAYA ANGELOU

Dear Reader,

Give Me Butterflies is intended for adult readers (18 or older), as it contains explicit language and explicit, on-page sexual content.

While I wrote this book intending to make you smile, there are a few subjects addressed in it that may be upsetting for some readers. If you are affected by any of the following topics, please proceed with caution.

- Grief from the loss of a sibling and mention of cancer
- Reference to past emotional and verbal abuse and gaslighting
- Emotionally distant and verbally abusive parents
- On-page anxiety symptoms and anxiety attack
- Brief mentions of alcohol and drugs

Give Me Butterflies

Chapter 1

Millie

I'm a generous person who made a dreadful mistake, and that old man in the white Skechers is making me pay for it.

I held the door for him as he walked into Maggie's Bakery because, apparently, I have a weakness in my heart for the sweet-grandpa type. But he betrayed me by ordering the last almond croissant from one spot in front of me in line, and I've never had such horrendous thoughts in my life.

There are two things I require to have a successful first day of the week: any form of caffeinated coffee and an almond croissant.

Both of those things were essential today because impostor syndrome is a real bitch, and caffeine and an almond croissant would have given me the sugar rush I need to distract me from it.

The living fossil across the coffee shop takes a bite of that buttery, flaky croissant, and I want to fight him for it.

Put us in an arena to battle for the last one. I bet I could beat him.

Or maybe not. He has a hint of muscle under that brown sweater vest.

"We have to learn to make croissants at home," I mutter around a bite of my consolation blueberry muffin, my eyes laser-focused on the Croissant Crook. "I can't live like this."

Lena waves her rainbow-tipped nails in front of me, pulling my attention back to her caramel eyes. "Stop staring daggers at that poor man." She grabs my face and squeezes my cheeks until my lips pucker out. "Eat your muffin. Raise your blood sugar a little so you can bring back nice Millie."

The grinder whirs behind the counter, refreshing the espresso aroma around us as I reluctantly nibble at the muffin. My leg bounces under the table, giving away the anxiety that's been running through my veins all morning.

Lena notices, and her foot nudges mine until I meet her gaze. "Don't worry about your week. You're going to walk in there with your head high and show them you deserve the department director position."

I resist the urge to roll my eyes. Anyone with anxiety knows that someone telling you not to worry is about as helpful as a hangnail.

Today is my first chance to participate in a meeting that Calvin, my freshly retired boss and previous head of the entomology department, would normally attend. While he's off vacationing with his wife, enjoying the life of a man without job obligations, I will be attending the meeting with the heads of every department at the Wilhelmina Natural Science Museum.

And then tomorrow, I have an interview for Calvin's position.

My leg twitches restlessly under the table again just thinking about it.

"I wish I could put you in my pocket and bring you with me," I tell Lena, taking a sip of my Americano. "You can coach me through the day and remind me how amazing I am."

"You've got this. You don't need me, although being your personal Polly Pocket sounds like a blast." She purses her bright red lips and perches her chin on her fist. "Can you get me the beach house with the dolphin and sea turtle? I've always wanted that one."

"Of course." I take another bite of my muffin, hoping it will settle my whirling stomach.

"Will it be the back pocket or the front? Because your cute ass would be way more comfortable."

I can't help but laugh. "Definitely the back. You'll need the bigger pockets for all those accessories you're requesting."

* * *

MY FLATS SQUEAK on the buffed floors as I walk into the Wilhelmina Natural Science Museum, trying my best not to spill the rest of my Americano while I readjust the large bag on my shoulder. The skies are gracing us with a cloudless summer day in Washington, and the bright entryway sparkles in the sunlight streaming through the large windows. Octavius, our massive fossilized *Quetzalcoatlus*, hangs from the ceiling, its broad wings and sharp teeth suspended over the museum's visitors as they enter.

Eleanor waves from her circular reception desk, her round cheeks lifted in a grin. "Good morning, Millie. Love your dress today. Looks like something I would've worn in the seventies," she says, standing to peer over the counter.

"Thank you." I set my coffee on her desk and turn in a slow circle, letting her scan the vintage dress with small butterflies on the collar. "Lena and I took a break from our *Gilmore Girls* marathon this weekend to visit one of our favorite resale shops," I tell her as I come to a stop. "I found it hidden behind a thick rack of old jeans."

Eleanor nods as she sits back down. "That sounds like a wonderful weekend."

"It was," I say with a smile. "How was yours?"

"Honey, I don't think I've told you about my new book boy-friend," she whispers with a mischievous glint in her eyes.

I taught her the term "book boyfriend" a few weeks ago when she was gushing about the hero in her historical romance. She has a book club with some other widows in her neighborhood, and I love to get recommendations from them. Their standards of men are top-tier.

She launches into her weekend read and has me laughing about the audacity of the brooding duke and his love affair with a scullery maid until she suddenly stops.

Her eyes flare behind her glasses.

"Well, you better get to your meeting. I don't want you to be late." She's a little too eager as she nudges my coffee cup toward me. "Don't worry, I'll tell you all about the duke next time. You've got places to be."

"Okay." My gaze narrows as she waves her hands in my direction, clearly shooing me away. When I have everything balanced again, I spin toward my office.

But I smack right into a wall of muscle, and the scent of sage and soap invades my senses.

Two big hands wrap around my arms to steady me, and my coffee cup is crushed between our bodies before it splatters to the ground.

"Oh, dear . . ." Eleanor squeaks behind me, but there's a satisfied lilt to it.

A sigh of defeat leaves my lungs, and I drop my forehead to the crisp white shirt before me. *A moment of silence for the spilled coffee at my feet.* My sanity will be hanging by a thread without that Americano.

Liquid seeps through my dress and into my bra, snapping me

back to the reality. I pull away and find a dark stain covering the top of my dress. So much for making a good impression this morning.

My eyes are reluctantly drawn to the gray tie in front of me. Planets run down the line of fabric, and a little splash of coffee stains the blue of Neptune.

Shit. Pins and needles creep up my spine. I know for a fact that this tie belongs to a man with a gorgeous face, but his permanent scowl ruins the appeal for me.

I swallow, trying to wet my dry throat. There's no hiding from this run-in, so I plaster on my brightest smile and muster the courage to look up.

Past the tie, up the strong column of throat, over the short, trimmed beard, and into . . . stormy blue eyes behind black-rimmed glasses.

My stomach drops at the crease between his dark brows and the tense line of his mouth.

Dr. Finn Ashford has glowered at me every time we've made eye contact, but this time is the most severe.

All the air seems to vanish from the museum as I realize how wrong I was. The scowl doesn't ruin the appeal for me at all. The director of the astronomy department is still more attractive than should be legal for a man with his general demeanor.

Our lives are a wealth of opposites. My job delves into small, up-close discoveries right under our feet, while his focuses on enormous, faraway things humans may never reach.

We are microscopes versus telescopes. Smiles versus scowls. Warm versus frigid.

Was there ever a chance for us to find common ground?

Goose bumps skitter up my neck as his breath moves the hairs that have escaped my braid. He seems to remember his hands are around my arms and quickly drops them, making me stumble back a step. He spreads his fingers wide, flexing them by his sides before shoving them in his pockets.

The distance allows me to take a deep breath and let the replenished oxygen fill my lungs. "Sorry," I mutter, looking at the coffee on his tie.

"Yeah." He lowers his head and rubs his fingers over Neptune like he can brush away the stain.

His clipped tone makes me grind my teeth together.

The nerve of this guy. The *audacity*.

"This isn't *all* my fault," I say, my pulse quickening with irritation. "You're the one hovering so close that you could've given me a back massage while you were there."

His scowl remains, but his gaze jumps to my hair, my cheeks, and then my mouth before it snaps back to my eyes as he clears his throat. "Shouldn't you be working instead of chatting with Eleanor about dukes and secret affairs?"

That raises my hackles, and my usual conflict avoidance turns to dust in the wind as I spit the first thing that comes to mind. "Shouldn't you be rewatching *Star Trek* so you have something educated to say at work today?"

A ghost of a smirk flashes across Finn's mouth before he can contain it. It's the most positive reaction I've ever gotten from him.

I think it would be a point in my column if we were keeping score.

His jaw works as he narrows his gaze. "I'm more of a *Star Wars* guy, actually."

My laugh turns to a very unladylike snort when I try to stifle it.

That would be a point for him. Damn it.

Finn crosses his arms like he's preparing for battle. "I need to speak with Eleanor. I could already be done with that if I hadn't had to wait for you two to finish talking."

I fold my arms over my chest to match him and meet his eyes. Having to crane my neck to look at him probably makes me less intimidating than I'd hoped, but I mirror his facial expression and body language anyway. "Oh, please. Do forgive us *women* for being *friendly* to each other and asking about our weekends. Not everyone can barge through the doors like Kylo Ren, with a cape floating behind them, and glower at every person who crosses their path."

This time, he has to bite both lips to hide his amusement, but I still get a peek at it. "Have you been watching me walk in every morning?" He tilts his head and arches an eyebrow.

I choke on my breath, and I hate that this is another point for him in a battle he's unaware of.

A few people shuffle past us to start their workday, quiet murmurs echoing through the wide halls of the museum, but our eyes stay pinned on each other. We are two opposing officers waiting for surrender or blood.

His gaze drops to my mouth for one small blip before it snaps back up. "May I speak to Eleanor now, or do you all need to continue analyzing how handsome the duke is?"

I guess it's blood, then.

A growl sneaks out of me, and I clench my fists like a toddler, feeling no shame in it. I don't know who pissed in his Cheerios this morning, but he should be taking it out on them instead of me.

"Absolutely. Be my guest," I grind out through clenched teeth, waving him forward.

He bends to grab my coffee cup and gives me a crisp nod before stepping past me to Eleanor's desk.

* * *

THIS HAND DRYER is no help. My green dress still has a dark stain running over it.

Anxiety fills my stomach with a familiar queasiness, dissolving the courage I had built up for this meeting. How can I be taken seriously looking like a barista's hand towel?

The minimal confidence I'd had is now in a puddle of coffee on the floor.

I look back at my reflection and groan at the sight of my cheeks, which are still pink from my run-in with Finn.

Every time I have been in the vicinity of that man, I've left wondering what the hell I did to deserve the looks he directed my way. During my first week at the museum, I held the elevator for him while he stalked toward it looking at his phone. When he finally glanced up, his navy eyes searched my face and the empty elevator behind me.

He stepped back with a scowl and mumbled, "I'll get the next one."

A few weeks later, Calvin and I were in his office going through plant orders for the butterfly vivarium, when in walked Dr. Black Hole with another scowl. He adjusted his glasses and glared my way. "I need to speak with Calvin privately," he said, his attention dropping to his phone while I picked up my things. I had to turn sideways to slide past him in the doorway while he stood there like a statue, unable to move out of my way.

As the memories flood my mind, I have the sudden urge to curse him. He deserves some retaliation for the way he's made me feel.

May *his* coffee spill all over him today. May his socks get wet the next time it rains. May his window never roll all the way up, so it makes an annoying whistling sound as he drives for all eternity.

The soft knit sleeves of my sweater brush over my arms as I tug it on and button it up to cover the coffee stain. Then I inhale a deep breath and watch my cheeks deflate in the mirror.

Mustering pep talks for myself is not my strong suit. Lena is much better at finding the right words. But when I try to channel her confidence, my mind is a blank sheet of paper, with no hint of inspiration for what to fill the page with.

My phone dings with a text, and I pull it out of my bag. I click to open the message and find a crooked selfie of my mom holding a black-and-white duck in our family group chat.

Oaks Folks

Mom: Alfred says good duck today, Millie!

Mom: *It's a pun on the word "luck." Not an autocorrect.

Tess: That's so ducking sweet.

Fabes: Dad is snickering from the kitchen while he reads his texts.

Fabes: He's been writing a response for five ducking minutes.

Dad: Haha. Ducking cute.

Mom: Millie, are you there? Alfred is waiting for a ducking answer.

Chapter 2

Finn

*W*hat the hell was I doing?

My phone screen fades to black, erasing the background image of my nieces, because I've been staring at it for so long. I'm sure I meant to do something productive. Was I going to answer an email? Check in with Gabriella?

I press the button on the side of my phone to reveal the image of Avery and Eloise again, grinning at each other while ice cream drips down their chins.

The view of them is way better than the one that surrounds me.

Every seat in the conference room is full of chattering people, except for the empty one beside me. No one has dared to take it. They're all avoiding me like the plague.

This meeting could've been handled in a mass email, and I'm sure my irritation is written blatantly across my face.

A rush of air glides against the back of my neck, trailed by a familiar vanilla-and-lemon scent.

The chair to my right slides away from the table, and Millie Oaks drops into it with a huff. Her auburn hair dances as she jerks her seat forward, placing a notebook covered in insects and a sparkly orange pen down on the table.

I shove my phone back in my pocket.

Millie smooths her dress and opens the notebook, keeping her chin tipped up like she's determined not to look my way. Her fingers flow over a clean sheet of paper as she writes the date at the top, followed by a heading in swirly, precise handwriting.

It appears she found a sweater to cover the coffee stain. Admittedly, I feel bad about the spill. I was probably standing too close, but my curiosity was piqued when she and Eleanor were talking about a man being charming and grumpy. By the time I figured out they were talking about a book, I had taken a step back, but it wasn't far enough to avoid her collision of chaos.

I glance back at her notebook, where she has drawn two small ladybugs on the side. Then she moves her pencil to the very bottom of the page and smoothly writes,

Eyes on your own paper, Grumpy Spock.

A scoff bursts out of me before I can stop it. That feels like a dig after I told her I wasn't a *Star Trek* fan. I preferred the Kylo Ren comparison.

Her pink lips curve in a satisfied grin before she grabs her notebook and angles her chair away from me.

The door swings open, and Sharon, the museum director, and Reva, the education specialist, step through.

"Good morning, everyone. Are we ready to get started?" Sharon lays a binder down on the table and slides on the glasses that hang around her neck. Her short gray bob swings around her face as she waves to everyone until her eyes land on Millie. "Oh, most of you probably know, but this is Millie from entomology."

Millie shifts in her seat and grins around the room in greeting.

"She's joining us since Calvin is off relishing his retirement in Costa Rica." A few murmurs of envy filter through the room.

Millie turns and settles her notebook in front of her on the table. She has doodled small flowers to cover the words she wrote for me, and for some reason, disappointment settles in my chest.

"Okay. First order of business is our annual summer camp next week. I'm going to let Reva start with that." Sharon leans back in her chair, letting Reva take the lead.

"I hope you all are feeling ready for our little scientists to come visit." She folds her hands in front of her with an excited grin. "As you know, kids will be here Monday through Friday, visiting different departments in the museum. You should all have a copy of the detailed schedule in your inbox, but I brought printed ones to talk about today." She passes the stack of schedules to her right.

I take a paper and hand the rest of the stack to Millie. When she tries to grab them, her soft fingertips graze the back of my hand, and she flinches so much that she drops the papers, sending them fanning out across the table.

Reva continues as I help Millie gather them back into a pile, barely containing the grumble threatening to vibrate through me. "We have a few crossovers happening, as you can see on the schedule. Engineering and astronomy are going to build rockets together, and entomology and local ecology are taking a field trip. Hopefully, you've met up with those other departments to make specific plans."

I tune Reva out a little, distracted by the wavy hair falling out of Millie's braid and the bones in her left hand shifting smoothly as she writes.

The soft, musical sound of her voice snaps me out of my daze. "Yes, we will be keeping the kids very busy." Her eyes jump around the room. "We have some butterflies that should be emerging next week, so the kids will get to see that." She wrings her hands over her thighs. "We have some sprouts to make a pollinator garden in front of the museum. And then a field trip on Thursday to Stafford's Pond."

Everyone's attention moves to the paleontology director as he begins discussing their camp plans, but my focus stays on Millie. She fidgets with the pen in her lap and chews on her plump bottom lip.

My skin prickles as the sudden urge to say something ripples through me, and my brain loses control of my body. I lean toward her and allow myself a small inhale of the vanilla-and-lemon scent wafting from her hair before I whisper low in her ear, "Are you nervous?"

Millie yelps as she jumps a few inches out of her chair, and her head slams into my nose with a crunch.

Fuck.

I immediately cover my face and duck my chin to take a deep breath. My nose burns and throbs as I press my hand under it.

No blood, but I'm going to be sore.

When Millie turns her face toward me, her eyes are narrowed and her lips are pressed into a flat line. She mouths, "Asshole."

"No," I whisper, shaking my head.

Her brows snap together. If looks could kill, I would be a pile of bones at this point.

I narrow my eyes. "I meant—"

"Finn, did you have something to add?" Sharon's question startles me as she glances between us like a principal who just caught her students smoking in the bathroom.

"No. Millie and I were discussing our camp plans." I try to sound as convincing as possible, donning my best poker face.

"Oh, great. I would love to hear them." Reva smiles encouragingly.

Well, shit. It's the share-with-the-class that is every misbe-having student's worst nightmare. I can confirm it still sucks at thirty-four.

As I search for something to contribute to the conversation, I glance at Millie and find her biting her lips like she's trying to contain her laughter at my expense.

I want to laugh. It's right there, the smile pushing against my cheeks to find the humor in our predicament. But I rein it back in with my signature frown instead.

I've avoided this woman for months because something about her sunshine-bright personality makes me want to turn the other way.

She's glowing all the time, illuminating everything around her, and the blazing light feels like a third-degree sunburn for a man who has been in the dark for too long.

* * *

By the time I make it back to my office, I have two missed calls from my mother.

I reluctantly press her name on the screen and she picks up after the first ring.

"Finneas, it's so nice of you to call me back." Her voice has a bite to it that makes me roll my eyes. This conversation needs to end quickly if I have any chance of remaining pleasant.

"Well, I have a job."

"Yes, I remember," she brushes off. "Listen, will you be joining us for dinner Friday? I have sent a few invitations about the party we are hosting, and you haven't responded. I need to give the ca-terers a count. It's not polite to wait this long to reply."

Polite. Does she even know the meaning of that word?

I would rather get a root canal than go to a fancy dinner party with my parents' friends.

"We won't be there, Mom. It's not a good environment for us." This tactic doesn't usually work with her, but I keep trying anyway.

"Yes, son. I remember that your *therapist* told you to set *boundaries*." She says "therapist" and "boundaries" like they are mud stains tracked into her pristine house. "But you don't need boundaries like that with me and your father. We are your parents, for crying out loud. I think the whole idea of someone telling you what to do is ridiculous."

"A therapist does not tell me what to do." A steady throb pounds through my skull. I remove my glasses, set them on my desk, and press my fingers between my brows. "We discuss what might help me move forward in life with the greatest level of mental health."

There's a long pause. A manipulative pause. And I know she's searching for the tender spots to dig her fingers into, forcing me to give in.

"Finneas, you never come home anymore, and your sister . . ." She fades out with a delicate sniffle. I hate that this immediately washes me in guilt. She found the spot she was looking for.

The words "your sister" will make me comply because I don't have the capacity to discuss Clara with her and she knows it.

"Fine, Mother. I'll be there. Alone."

Chapter 3

Millie

*D*on't worry about it, sweetie." My dad's deep voice emanates through the car's speaker. "Your interview is going to be great."

I turn on my blinker and guide my 4Runner onto the main road I take to the museum. Usually, I would walk to work, but I didn't want today's humidity to make my hair any frizzier before my interview.

"Oh, Dave," my mom says, her reminiscing tone cutting in. "Do you remember when she saved all those caterpillars that the chickens were going after? I still have nightmares about when they got loose in the house and I found one on my pillow."

I wince. "Thanks, Mom. That was a sweet memory to bring up."

"I think about that day all the time. I was very grossed out but so proud of you," Mom coos. "Have been since the day you were born."

The car's brakes squeak as I pause at a stoplight. "Well, hopefully, you'll still be proud of me after I try to convince a board of directors and a few department heads that I deserve this job."

Dad hums thoughtfully. "If you need me to come down there and talk some sense into them—"

"No," I interrupt. "I definitely don't need you telling anyone to hire me. I trust their decisions."

Mom sighs. "You say the word, and we'll be on our way. We'll round up your sisters too." The thought warms my heart. They would totally do it. Abandon the family farm and drive an hour just to stand up for me.

"I appreciate it, but I really want to get this job all on my own. Not because my parents made a ruckus in the museum," I tease.

"Okay, sweetie. Don't worry about anything and remember how special you are," Mom reminds me.

I roll my eyes. "Thanks. I'll be sure to tell them you said I am *special.*" My blinker ticks through the car as I turn into the museum parking lot.

"And we are always proud of you," Dad says firmly.

A smile tugs at the corners of my mouth. "I love you both," I tell them before grabbing my phone from the console to end the call.

As I press my thumb to the screen, the phone slips from my fingers and drops below my feet with a *thud.* "Shit," I spit out, leaning down as far as I can to grab it while keeping one eye on the pavement in front of me. I slam on the brake when an SUV rolls into my path, and a sharp crack splits through the quiet car.

That sounded suspiciously like my phone screen.

"Fuck." Let's see how many more curse words this morning can pull from my lips. I glance up once and see the SUV's brake lights, so I duck my head, lift my foot from the brake pedal, and slide my phone out from under it.

The silence in my car ends with a loud *crunch*, and my forehead knocks into the dashboard as I collide with the car in front of me.

"Shit. Fuck. Damn it," I growl, aggressively sliding the gearshift into park and rubbing my hand over my forehead to calm the ache.

Of all the mornings.

How is a woman supposed to impress in an interview with this kind of start to the day?

I raise my head a centimeter at a time. Just as the hood of my car comes into view, my stomach drops as my eyes land on the other driver.

He's doing his Kylo Ren impression, storming toward me with a scowl so tight that he might crack his teeth. His dark hair blows with the force of his steps as fury oozes off him, permeating the parking lot.

Those eyes are the fiercest I've ever seen them, glaring lasers through my windshield like I'm the enemy force he's been sent to obliterate.

I have now spilled coffee on him, smashed his nose, and just *literally* run into him with a moving vehicle.

Those lasers might be deserved.

Finn plants his feet on the concrete at the front corner of my car and crosses his arms over his chest. He waits silently, nostrils flaring with every breath.

I lift myself the rest of the way up, and his eyes land on my face. His features don't shift at all, giving me no inkling of whether he knew who was in this car. Gripping my phone between my shaking fingers, I push open my door, get out, and snap it shut with my hip.

Smoothing out my black pencil skirt, I walk unsteadily on my heels to meet Finn at the front of my car. His violent-thunderstorm eyes are raging as they scan my face, shoulders, and quickly down my body before they pop back up.

My stomach curls into knots as I reach him. "I'm so sorry. I was talking to my parents. They were wishing me good luck on my interview this morning. But I dropped my phone accidentally." My flustered babbling hasn't changed his expression in the slightest. "I heard the screen break." I show him the crack running through the middle of my phone. "But when I looked down to grab it, I guess I bumped into your car."

"You guess?" he rumbles, raising an eyebrow. "I'd say you definitely did."

I expel a long breath as I flick my eyes toward his car and take in the deep indentation with a dark scratch across it.

"Maybe you should go back to walking to work. You appear to be out of practice with driving." His lips lift in a minuscule smirk, and he seems to bite the inside of his cheek to stop it.

Heat spreads through my veins as I straighten my spine. "Now who's watching who arrive at work in the morning?" My hip pops to the side as I cross my arms over my chest. "And these heels would be miserable to walk to work in."

Finn's assessing gaze trails down my skirt and bare calves until he reaches my royal purple heels. His throat works on a swallow before he murmurs, "Impractical."

I don't bother to respond as I step around him, walking between our cars to investigate the damage. Hiking up my skirt, I bend to run my fingers over Finn's smashed bumper.

Well, shit. I don't know much about car bumper repairs, but I'm guessing that'll be an expensive fix.

Finn lets out a loud, exasperated breath behind me. I stand and face his hard scowl and dark eyes.

"I'm so sorry. I'll pay for the damages," I mumble.

His eyes narrow. "Instead of just paying for a new phone screen, you've put yourself in a position to pay for two ruined bumpers as well."

"It's called a mistake," I sass, dropping my hands to my hips. "We lowly peasants make them sometimes." I point my chin to an empty spot beside us. "If you'll let me park right there—"

"That happens to be the space I was pulling into." Finn tightens his arms over his black tie with tiny astronauts, pulling his shirt's midnight fabric taut across his shoulders.

"Okay," I huff. "I will go find a different spot, and then we can exchange insurance information."

Finn grumbles something under his breath as he looks down at his watch. His eye twitches before he says, "I don't have time for that this morning. You'll have to find me later."

Then he turns on his heel and prowls back to his open car door.

* * *

THE MARBLE FLOOR sparkles as I hustle through the museum toward my interview. My momentum is creating a breeze that I'm hoping will cool the sweat coating my skin.

I've been a wreck since my literal wreck twenty minutes ago. I didn't have a spare moment to process my thoughts before the interview because the event in the parking lot has shoved itself to the forefront of my mind.

Why didn't I just let the phone crumble to bits?

It would've been better than feeling flustered and frazzled. No one wants to walk into a job interview like this, least of all a woman in a scientific field dominated by men, where I'm already analyzed on a different level.

I was the only woman in the entomology department at my university, so I constantly struggled with being dismissed as a scientist. One college professor presented a stag beetle to our class and announced, "I'm sure Millie won't want to hold this one, but I know the rest of you will."

Condescending jerk.

Like my gender meant I couldn't handle touching an insect. In an act of feminist defiance, I started a stag beetle habitat in my dorm room that weekend.

Until I got caught by the resident assistant and had to donate them to the same professor who embarrassed me. At least I got the satisfaction of one biting him on the way into its enclosure.

They never bit me, Dr. Hibbard.

Most people thought I would change my mind about insects. That I would wake up one day and start screaming when I saw them, like the token blonde in a cheesy horror movie.

Instead, I graduated with a 4.0 and a job lined up at the National Butterfly Center. The patronizing little comments whispered behind my back didn't stop me. They only fueled my fire to prove I belonged.

I pause in the hallway outside the interview room and force a deep breath while my stomach churns—the first sign of my impending anxiety spiral.

Sweeping my hands over my hair, I try to control the frizz and will my hands to stop shaking. Oxygen swirls in my lungs as I slowly inhale, vowing to leave all the events of this morning right here in the hallway on my exhale. Once I step inside, there will be no more thoughts of fender benders and angry coworkers. This is a fresh start for the day, and it's imperative I forget everything else.

One more deep breath out, and I grab the door handle.

I pull it open with all the false confidence I can muster, and my gaze immediately lands on navy blue eyes.

In a sea of eight people, those twin flames are all I can distinguish for a moment.

My knees go weak, and I stumble over the threshold but manage to stay upright. Finn's gaze narrows, and he tilts his head. His lips kick up arrogantly on one side, almost like he's looking forward to what's about to happen.

Chapter 4

Finn

A colorful spiderweb of galaxies floats across the dome of the planetarium overhead, and I'm lost in the view, swooping through star clusters light-years away.

From my seat at the main control screen, I click a few spots to bring me to Clara's favorite view: the Butterfly Cluster on the tip of the Scorpius constellation. The planetarium delivers me fifteen hundred light-years away, and the small group of stars comes into focus with a vague butterfly shape.

Sometimes, when there are no programs scheduled in the evenings, I like to visit the planetarium by myself. The butterfly formation is hard to see, but that never stopped my sister from enjoying it.

She used to say, "When you work hard for something, you have more appreciation for the end result."

It started one night when she was trying to convince me that my middle school math homework would be worthwhile one day. Then I got to use the line on her when she was complaining about nursing school.

But the first time I brought her into this planetarium a few years ago, she asked to see this star cluster. When I told her I could barely see the butterfly shape, she lectured me to try a little harder, promising I'd appreciate the view in the end.

Years later, I'm appreciating the hell out of this view because it reminds me of Clara, and her memory brings me a sense of peace that has been hard to find lately.

Between the parking lot situation and sitting through five interviews throughout the morning and afternoon, I've had a long day, and I'm forcing myself to relax here this evening before I need to get home.

The interviews ended an hour ago, and we have two great contenders. Millie's passion and enthusiasm for her job were contagious, and the entire panel thinks she would be a fantastic department director. But the other applicant's work experience and motivation would be a good fit for the position as well.

Sharon is going to think through a plan for choosing between the two of them, but after the shitty start to the morning, I hope Millie left feeling like she did fine, because she did.

God, the flare in her eyes when she walked into the interview and saw me sitting there was so satisfying. The man she called an asshole yesterday and crashed her car into today is one of the people deciding on her promotion. *Priceless*.

After she recovered from her initial shock, though, she did a good job. She was relaxed and conversational, and it seemed like the entire panel was hanging on her every word.

Me included. Unfortunately.

She avoided looking my way for almost an hour, but when it was my turn to ask a question, she was forced to pull her gaze to mine. And I loved watching her plaster on a big smile despite probably seething on the inside.

The door to the planetarium squeaks open, and Rachel pops through the gap. The wide smile on my assistant curator's face is visible in the light from the stars overhead.

"Thought I might find you in here. Need anything else from me before I go?"

I click a few controls on the planetarium. "No. I think everything is good for today."

The room darkens as I shut everything down and walk toward Rachel. She helps me flip the last few switches by the door, and I follow her out, squinting as the bright hallway lights hit my eyes.

"How did everything go getting ready for camp next week?" I ask as we walk through the front doors of the museum and toward the parking lot.

"Great. I got plans settled with engineering about our rocket building, and I nailed down the supplies I need to pick up tomorrow."

"Awesome. Sorry I was in interviews all day, but I should be free the rest of the week."

We reach the misshapen bumper of my car, and Rachel winces when she sees it. "Shit. What happened?"

I shove my hands in my pocket and survey the damage. "Fender bender on the way to work this morning," I grumble.

Honestly, it doesn't look as bad as I thought. In my frustration this morning, it seemed terrible, but in the dim evening light, it's not too severe. Millie emailed her insurance information to me this afternoon, but I haven't decided whether I'll do anything with it yet.

"What a way to start your day," Rachel says, backing away toward her own car.

"Yep," I mutter, turning to unlock my door.

As I drop into my seat and start the car, a small grin forms on my lips at the memory of Millie's bright pink cheeks this morning. And the way her green eyes turned fiery when she sassed me about watching her walk into work.

Then, *fuck me*, my next memory is dangerous. The perfect view of her curves in that tight black skirt as she bent over to check the bumper flashes through my mind.

I bite the inside of my cheek to stifle the image.

She is my colleague. I'm on her hiring committee, for crying out loud. I need to be completely professional. Not checking out her ass in the parking lot.

On my drive home, a sign for Maggie's Bakery snags my eye, and I remember Millie's coffee cup from yesterday. I've never been there, but if her emotional reaction to spilling it a few days ago was any indication, it must be some good coffee.

Maybe I should try it tomorrow morning. Just to see if it's worth her dramatics.

Chapter 5

Millie

*T*he cushions dip beneath me as Pepper, my spoiled rescue pup, hops up next to where I'm sprawled out on the couch. She plops down beside my head, scooting her white muzzle into my neck until I give in and pet her.

I've been in this exact position since I got home from work this afternoon. Laid out on the couch, attempting to decompress after the highs and lows of my jumbled emotions today.

The interview went okay, I think, other than the constant distraction of Finn in the room. I put dedicated effort into not looking his way, but I could feel his gaze on me like a hot poker, searing into my skin.

They had a few tricky questions, but I feel good about how my answers sounded. I shoved my swirling anxiety aside enough to at least *sound* like I had the confidence to be the head of the department.

A set of keys jangles outside the front door before Lena pushes it open. She kicks it shut behind her and drops her bags to the floor with a loud *thump*.

"What are we having for dinner? I'm so close to hangry I could just eat a fork," she says with a groan.

I met Lena in college, at a coffee shop where I'd gone to study for my Shakespearean literature final, not knowing they were hosting an open mic night. The urge to study disappeared when I ended up completely distracted by my future best friend's performance. Lena's dark curls and smoky eyes were stunning under the dim spotlight as she spent five minutes reciting a ghost story she'd memorized, with character voices and enthusiastic movements. She jumped across the stage and threw her body on the ground in a death scene at the end that had everyone riveted.

After she stood from her fake death and bowed, she walked right over to the table where I sat alone with my notebook and laptop and dropped into the empty chair.

We've been best friends ever since.

"Want to relax, order takeout, and watch *Gilmore Girls*?" I ask, without moving an inch from my position.

She pulls off her black shirt, leaving her standing in the living room in a sparkly red bra and leggings. "Fuck yes. Those kids took it out of me today. My feet are sore, and I want to live in pajamas forever."

Lena is an elementary school art teacher during the school year and leads art classes at the Wilhelmina Community Center during the summer.

Tilting my head, I narrow my eyes in suspicion at her bra. "Weird choice for work."

She shrugs. "It was my only clean option. But now it's time to get out of it. Freedom is so close." She struts past me toward her bedroom door.

"Free the tits," I call, fist in the air.

"Honestly, getting out of this thing will probably solve all my life problems," she shouts from her bedroom. "Maybe I'm not hangry—I'm booby-trapped."

Once we're both braless and in pajamas, with Thai takeout

in our hands, Lena and I sink into our cozy sectional, curled up with weighted blankets and glasses of sparkling water. Plants cover every surface and hang in the windows of our living room. It's our little jungle oasis, hidden from the rest of the world.

"How did your day go?" Lena asks over her box of chicken pad Thai.

I recount the parking lot events, and Lena's eyes grow wider with every detail until she can't stay quiet anymore. "Mills. That's wild." She sets her food down and faces me. "Dr. Black Hole is in charge of whether or not you get a promotion?"

I swallow my bite. "He's not in *charge* of it, but he is one of the people on the committee, yes."

Lena lets out a squeal of delight. "This is perfect. Do you think you could take a picture of him for me?" Lena pleads with sad puppy eyes. "I need a visual when I'm examining this story. The way you're describing him, he's giving hot-professor vibes."

I adamantly ignore the fact that she is a little bit right in her imagery and roll my eyes. "Yeah, sure. Next time he's frowning at me, I'll tell him to hold that pose while I snap a photo for you."

"Wonderful. Thank you." She pats my leg. "Now tell me about the interview."

* * *

THE HEAVY CLOUDS outside give the museum a dark, introspective mood as I run through the doors the next morning. I hurry past Eleanor and the gift shop manager with a quick greeting and wave—too late to visit.

I rush down the entomology hallway, past the display room, the archive collection, and laboratory rooms, and stumble into our office. As I pass my assistant curator Micah's desk and round mine, my eyes land on a coffee cup with Maggie's logo printed on the side, sitting atop a green Post-it with neat handwriting.

I'm sorry about your coffee.

—F

Setting my bag on the ground, I pick up the cup. The warmth of its contents seeps into my fingers as I turn it around to check the label.

Americano with vanilla syrup and half-and-half. Exactly the way I like it.

My brows stitch together. He must've noticed my order when he threw my cup away Monday morning.

I take a tentative sip, and the earthy, sweet taste is absolutely perfect on my tongue.

Confusion prickles in my mind. This is an odd gesture, especially for the man who has grumbled and glared at me every moment since we met. The sharp change from yesterday feels a bit like whiplash.

With a flick of my computer mouse, I wake the monitor and open a new email.

TO: Finn Ashford
FROM: Millie Oaks
SUBJECT: Coffee

Good morning,

I arrived at my office to find a coffee on my desk. The note is signed by "F." Would that perhaps be you? I've spilled coffee on so many people this week, so I'm not certain it's from you.

If it was not you, then this is awkward, and please disregard.

If this coffee is from you, thank you. It's delicious.

Sincerely,
Millie Oaks
Curator, Entomology Department

I read through it a few times to make sure it seems like a standard thank-you email. It passes my inspection, so I click send before I can overthink it.

To my surprise, his reply arrives a few minutes later.

TO: Millie Oaks
FROM: Finn Ashford
SUBJECT: Re: Coffee

Hello Millie,

I am guilty of delivering coffee to your desk this morning. I had hoped to catch you in person, but Eleanor said you weren't in yet.

Maggie's is not my usual coffee stop, but I enjoyed my own coffee from there this morning. Is there anything else you recommend?

My next episode of *Star Trek* is starting now. I must boldly go where no real astronomer has gone before.

Best,
Finn Ashford
Director, Astronomy Department

I reread his email three times, startled by the humor in it.

Apparently, this is friendly Finn—a side of him I've never met. This Finn jokes about my sassy comments and delivers coffee to me as an apology.

Bringing the paper cup to my lips, I grin behind it before taking a sip. I picture his tall, brooding form standing in the line at Maggie's with the intent of buying *me* a coffee. His scowl is still in place as he orders it, but there's something oddly endearing about the pinch between his brows and the way his lips turn down at the corners.

With a shake of my head, I try to clear the disorienting image and focus on a natural reply.

TO: Finn Ashford
FROM: Millie Oaks
SUBJECT: Re: Re: Coffee

Finn,

You cannot go wrong at Maggie's. It's out of this world! 😉 They could serve me anything and I would eat it, but my personal favorite is the almond croissant. There is no better way to start the morning than with a coffee and croissant from Maggie's.

Is your nose okay? And have you had your car looked at? I'm still so sorry about that.

I'm glad you're getting those episodes in before the camp kids get here next week. They're expecting you to teach them something.

Have a good day,
Millie Oaks

That should be good. I sound normal. Butter-on-toast normal. So normal, I'm borderline boring.

Send.

TO: Millie Oaks
FROM: Finn Ashford
SUBJECT: Re: Re: Re: Coffee

Millie,

I'll have to make a trip back to Maggie's for an almond croissant.

My nose is no worse for the wear. I'm pretty sure it was crooked before you smashed it, so if you notice a slight lean to it, don't blame yourself.

My car will be fine. I got a closer look at it, and it may not even be worth taking it in.

You don't have to apologize about the car. Accidents happen to everyone.

—Finn

I narrow my eyes at the screen as I read the last line of his email. "Accidents happen to everyone?" Is he serious? Yesterday he couldn't even speak an entire sentence without being rude, and now he's just brushing the whole thing off like it doesn't matter? What's changed since then?

My shoulders deflate when I realize *exactly* what has happened since then. My job interview.

Is this a peace offering because I did so terribly that he's trying to soften the blow when I find out I didn't get it? What if this is a ploy to lure me into a state of complacency before he robs me of my dream job?

His possible motives swirl through my mind until I can't think straight anymore. Eyeing the coffee cup, I sigh before taking the last sip and dropping it into the trash beside my desk. I lift my shoulders and let out a sharp breath. I already lost myself to one manipulative jerk in my lifetime, and I refuse to do it again. No matter how good the coffee is.

Chapter 6

Millie

"Craft kits are done." Micah smiles wide as he steps into the lab room with a laundry basket full of paper bags in his arms. His long sandy-blond hair is tied in a bun, and the green camp shirt we designed with our favorite insects on the back adorns his broad shoulders.

I jog over to him and peek at the binocular craft kits he and Emil put together for the camp kids today. "You're a lifesaver." I stand on tiptoe and kiss him on the cheek. "One-hour countdown until the kids get here."

"Good. Plenty of time to dig into my breakfast." Micah nods, depositing the basket on a table before pulling a thermos and something wrapped in a beeswax cloth from his bag. He squats in a kids chair in the center of the room. "Emil made it fresh right before I left." He grins at his breakfast with greedy eyes as he unwraps it, and the smell of onion and garlic lures me over.

"You lucky bitch." I lean my elbow on his shoulder and inhale the delicious smells of his egg, bacon, and cheese sandwich on an everything-seasoned bagel. "That looks divine." I pull out my phone and snap a picture of Micah devouring his first bite with what I can only describe as an orgasmic expression. I add the picture in our group chat with Emil.

Millie: Where's mine? Also, I didn't know someone could get this kind of pleasure from a bagel sandwich. I'm feeling extremely single right now.

Emil: Micah, glad you like it, love. 🖤

Emil: Millie, I'll send an extra one for you tomorrow.

Lena: Can I DoorDash it? Do you deliver? I'm only a few blocks over!

Micah holds his half-eaten sandwich out for me, and I practically dive at it to steal a bite.

***

"I THINK THIS piece goes right here," a seven-year-old instructs me while I kneel next to a table, helping Oliver and his brother Noah put together a butterfly-life-cycle puzzle. They were the first kids to arrive, and admittedly, I'm already a little sick of their arguing.

"No, you're wrong." Noah swats his brother's hand out of the way.

"Okay, boys, I think it's time for a new activity." I point them in the direction of a few insect habitats along the wall.

The exhibit room has short tables through the middle, and the outer walls are covered in plexiglass habitats for a variety of insects. Tall, back-lit display cases bring out the bright colors of the insects, moths, and butterflies we're showcasing.

The boys' eyes widen, and they jump up to run along the row of habitats until they reach the biggest one.

Walking to the front of the lab room, I smirk as Micah explains to a mother that we cannot keep her daughter from touching any dirt while she's here. He smiles patiently while the woman goes on a tirade about how her daughter is wearing a brand-new dress.

When I glance down the hallway to check if anyone is approaching, my mouth pops open at the sight before me.

Finn Ashford walks toward me with calm confidence, wearing a pair of black slacks and a black dress shirt that makes his tan neck and face practically glow.

If there was ever a time to snap a secret picture for Lena, this is it. He looks like he's been plucked right out of a men's fashion magazine and set here in front of me.

Damn. He may be an asshole, but he's the kind women drool over.

And he *is* an asshole . . . right? If there were an asshole checklist in my brain, he's definitely checked off some of the requirements.

But bringing me coffee and joking in emails aren't on that list. He's deviated from it, and it's confusing me to my core, leaving me completely unsure of his intentions.

My eyes follow the line of his starry galaxy tie, and I realize he has a little girl holding each hand.

I momentarily forget how to breathe and have to blink a few times to clear my vision.

But the image stays the same as I track my gaze over him again. Broad shoulders, black fabric over sculpted biceps, rolled-up sleeves, strong forearms, and—yep—those are children.

Finn has kids?

How did I not know this?

My focus jumps to his left hand instinctively.

No ring.

When I look back up, his eyes connect with mine, and he gives me a small grin. Maybe it doesn't even count as a grin so much as a flicker of his lips, but it does something bizarre to my equilibrium.

He's not supposed to *grin* at me. That's not on the checklist either.

I plant my feet firmly to steady myself and wave. "Hello, girls."

The little girl tucked behind Finn's right leg looks down at the ground as she drags her feet. Meanwhile, the other girl is already smiling, bouncing toward me.

"Morning, Millie." The sound of my name in his deep timbre melts my mind like ice cream on a summer day.

"Finn." It's all I can come up with while my brain recovers.

I squat to the girls' level to greet them. "Welcome to camp! We're so excited to have you. I'm Ms. Millie." I smile, grabbing the stack of tags and Sharpie out of my back pocket. "What are your names? I'm going to give you each a name tag."

"This is Avery." Finn tips his head toward the shy one before crouching next to her. Avery's round cheeks are still pointed to the ground, showcasing her raven hair in a smooth, neat ponytail.

Her navy eyes look up at me through her dark lashes. "Hello."

"Hi, Avery. I'm so happy you're here."

The other girl reaches out her hand, and I take it as she says, "I'm Eloise!" Her lighter brown hair is in wild waves around her face, her eyes perfectly matching Avery's and Finn's.

"Well, it's nice to meet you, Avery and Eloise. We're going to have so much fun together." I make their name tags and pass them out. Avery puts hers carefully near her collarbone, and Eloise sticks hers sideways, right over her stomach.

"If you go inside, to that tall guy over there"—I point in the right direction—"that's Mr. Micah, and he is showing everyone our tarantula, Terrence."

Eloise drops her lunch box next to me and makes a mad dash

for Micah, but Avery grabs Finn's hand again and looks at him with a frown.

"Do I have to go?" she whispers.

Finn's eyes turn the softest I've ever seen them, creasing along the edges as he gives Avery a small grin. "Yes, *piccola*. I know you're going to have fun, and I'll see you in astronomy this afternoon." He settles his hands on her shoulders, and I stand and turn slightly to give them some privacy.

Hearing Dr. Black Hole comfort his girls is warping my impression of him.

Avery sniffles but gives Finn a hug and walks right past me toward the table with the abandoned puzzle. His eyebrows draw together as he watches her.

"Don't worry—she'll have a great morning," I try. "We have so much planned, she won't have time to miss you."

Finn stares at Avery like he's in a daze, his lips a flat line. He looks to Eloise, who's giggling as Terrence climbs up her arm. "Can you try not to split them up, if it's not too much trouble? They need each other sometimes."

"Yeah, of course."

He does one more scan of his girls before he turns slowly, almost like it pains him to do so, and walks back down the hall.

* * *

"How OLD ARE you, Ms. Millie?" Elijah asks, tugging on my hand while we walk toward the front of the museum.

"Twenty-nine."

His head droops. "My mom said I can't have a girlfriend if she's more than one year older than me until I'm an adult."

A laugh snorts out of me. "Your mom sounds like a smart woman. How old are all of you?" I ask the herd of children around me.

Avery is holding my other hand, with Eloise beside her, while Oliver and Noah walk in front of us.

We've had a few hiccups this morning, including Oliver pulling Adrian's hair because of a dispute over the best pizza topping. We also had a close call with a butterfly after Noah tried to whack it off his shirt in the vivarium.

Despite all that, it's been a success. The kids loved seeing the monarch butterflies emerge from their chrysalises, and our binoculars turned out perfect.

"Eight," Oliver shouts at the same time Noah says, "Seven."

"We're both five because we're fraternal twins," Eloise informs us, pronouncing "fraternal" perfectly, like she's done it a thousand times. "Mama said having twins in your belly makes it reeeeeeally big because there are two babies in there." Eloise holds her hands out in front of her. "Like as big as that table!" She points to the front desk where Eleanor is sitting and waving at us.

"Is it fun having a twin?" I ask the girls. "I always wanted to be one. I thought sharing secrets would be amazing."

Surprisingly, Avery answers first. "Having a twin is the best. I never have to be alone." She gives me a small smile, but it doesn't reach her eyes.

Eloise puts her arms around Avery's shoulders and says, "It *is* the best thing."

The kids come to a standstill under the *Quetzalcoatlus* fossil and lean their heads back to stare at it. A chorus of questions starts, and luckily, Micah steps in to answer them the best he can.

As I watch Avery smile timidly and Eloise grill Micah with questions, my mind wanders to Finn.

Is he the one who put Avery's hair in that sleek ponytail and helped them pick out their clothes this morning? Eloise's shirt has a little astronaut figure being held up by planet-shaped balloons, while Avery's has a peace sign made of flowers.

I've been telling myself Finn is a scowling, rude grump, but something about the coffee delivery and the emails and the way he spoke to the girls this morning has me admitting to myself that I might not have the whole picture.

Micah reaches the end of his dinosaur knowledge, so we shuffle the kids outside the main doors of the museum and line them up on the sidewalk.

"Okay, everybody," I call, cupping my hands around my mouth. "If you sit down in your spot, Mr. Micah and I will bring each of you a plant, and then we can help you find a good place in the soil to put it."

Paisley shouts, "Do you have gloves for me? My mom said not to get dirty." She smooths the tulle of her purple dress.

"Your mom sent you to the wrong camp, then," I mumble to Micah before calling louder to the kids. "We don't have gloves, but we can wash our hands after. Trust me, it's going to feel so good to dig your hands in there and get some dirt on them. That's my favorite part."

Paisley's curled lip says she doesn't believe me.

Micah and I make our way around to all the kids, passing out yarrow, bee balm, and penstemon seedlings. Aside from Paisley, everyone seems excited to get dirty. Even Avery is on her knees in the flower bed.

I crouch between Eloise and Avery to get them started. "Where should we plant your seedlings?"

Chapter 7

Finn

The sound of laughter from the front of the museum draws me toward my office window, and I peer through the glass to find the camp kids crawling around in the flower beds. Eloise is smiling from ear to ear while she digs a hole in the soil. Even Avery is grinning as her hands move through the dirt.

Millie's on her knees between them, placing a small potted seedling in Avery's hands, and they work together to free the sprout. I glance at Eloise, and she must have her hole the way she wants it because she sits back on her heels and brushes her hair off her face. When she pulls her hands away, she has smears of dirt along her cheeks and forehead.

I huff out a quiet laugh.

The temptation to go spy on the girls has been eating at me all morning. But they look happy—so much more content than I was expecting them to be in a new place, surrounded by strangers.

Millie and Avery have their plant free of its container, and they lower it to the hole together. They loosen the roots, carefully pull soil back around the seedling, then high-five each other when the job is complete. Turning to Eloise, they burst out laughing at the sight of the dirt all over her face. Millie laughs with her whole body, her head thrown back and shoulders shaking, and I can hear her even from thirty feet away and through a building.

My rib cage constricts as I watch Millie rub her hands on her jean-covered thighs before brushing the dirt from El's face.

Ave and El have been through so much for their age that occasionally I forget they're only five years old. Eloise is so lighthearted and carefree that sometimes she seems unaffected, but Avery's tender heart is more somber than her sister's. So seeing her face light up right now makes my own smile dance across my lips.

* * *

A HERD OF loud children walks into the main astronomy room, laughing and talking the whole way. Avery and Eloise have their arms looped together, and Millie tries to corral a wandering little boy back into the group.

"Uncle Finn," Eloise calls, pulling Avery along with her as she runs to me. Two little bodies crash into my legs, and I crouch to hug them tightly, inhaling their summer-sun smell and feeling their warm cheeks against mine.

"Did you girls have a good morning?"

"It was the best," Eloise squeals in my ear.

"That's good. Now you get to build some rockets with me," I say, getting one last squeeze of my girls before I encourage them to walk to where Rachel is waiting to greet everyone.

The other kids rush past me before Millie reaches where I'm standing, hands in the back pockets of her jeans and little strands of hair framing her flushed face.

She tilts her head. "I've been trying to figure out all day how I missed that you had kids. But it's Uncle Finn, huh?"

"Yeah, I tried to come up with an epic uncle name, but it turned out 'Finn' is way easier for babies to say." I run a hand through my hair. I've learned that it's best to clear up any possible confusion, even if it makes things awkward. So I explain, "I guess I do have kids, though. They are my sister's girls, but she passed away a few months ago."

With a deep sigh, Millie pulls her hand from her back pocket and sets it on my forearm. I'm sure it's supposed to be a comforting gesture, but it has the opposite effect. It makes my heart stutter, and my lungs feel twice their weight. "I'm so sorry." She drops her hand and slips it back into her pocket.

Silence threads between us, as it usually does after this news.

Then Millie does me the biggest favor she could. She changes the subject. "I want a completely random name when my sisters start having kids. Not that they're popping out babies anytime soon, but it's fun to think about." She shrugs with a grin. "Like 'Cookie' or 'Sparkles' or 'Bubbles.'"

I try and fail to stifle the loud, hearty laugh that barks out of me, and the whole room goes quiet. Probably everyone in the entire museum is frozen, mouths wide-open and hands midair, like they're so shocked by the sound that they have no idea how to handle it.

But as I release my laugh into the air, it feels like I'm shedding a layer of weight that's been clinging to me. The lightened load is refreshing and unfamiliar.

As my laughter settles, I meet Millie's wide eyes, her lips parted in surprise like she doesn't even recognize me.

"I've never heard you laugh," she whispers.

Before I can respond, Rachel and the kids start talking again. Hopefully, the whole museum gets back to its regularly scheduled programming. Millie beams at me like she's broken the code to get inside my heart's vault, and I can never admit that it's because her aunt names sound like stripper names.

* * *

"DID YOU BOTH brush your teeth?" I ask Ave while I run a brush down her hair. She turns her head and opens her mouth for me to see her sparkly clean teeth.

The girls deserved an ice cream date after their first day of camp. Nonno Lorenzo used to take Clara and me out for ice cream after our first day of school every year. Even when we started college, we were never too cool for an ice cream trip.

Eloise holds my phone up with the video poised to play. "Do I start it?"

I nod, laying down the brush and separating a section of Avery's hair at the top of her head. Eloise hits play, holding the phone to her chest as a woman's voice explains how to start the French braid.

Avery has been requesting them for a while now, and I've been trying my best to master them. The basic braid with the ends of her hair is simple enough, but French braids are proving much more challenging. My big fingers have trouble holding on to her smooth hair. The braid usually ends up too loose or crooked, with a few chunks missing, but Avery is a good sport and always tells me she loves it.

Eloise, on the other hand, hides from having her hair brushed, and I only force her into it about once a week. She's a great hairstylist's assistant, though.

As I get to the end of the braid, Eloise pauses the video and hands me the hair tie from her wrist. The braid is lopsided again, but she nods like it's the best one she's ever seen.

"Did you get your teeth brushed?" I ask Eloise as I finish wrapping the end of the braid.

"Mm-hmm." She drops my phone and jumps into bed.

I narrow my eyes. "El, did you really? Let's see 'em."

She opens her mouth, and I'm hit with the smell of ketchup. *Gross.*

I toss the covers off her. "Young lady, get your booty to that bathroom and brush your teeth."

She sulks away, and I slide into the middle of the bed so the girls can sit on either side of me. They had matching twin beds when we moved their furniture in, but they never wanted to sleep in them and would always end up in mine. So I switched out their twin beds for a bigger one where they could sleep together.

After a few minutes, Eloise bounces back in with minty breath, chattering about Despereaux and Princess Pea from our bedtime story. The girls cuddle in close, their heads on my shoulders while I read the last few chapters, Avery's tiny hand gripping my arm the whole time. Soft, deep breaths echo from each side of me as I finish the book.

Bedtime is the hardest part of the day. Ave and El are tired, and they miss their mama the most in the evenings. I haven't skipped bedtime once since they started living with me, but that's as much for me as it is for them.

My heart aches every night as I'm tucking the covers around them, brushing kisses across their cheeks and telling them I love them.

The first night they stayed here, Clara's cancer had taken a turn for the worse, and she had just been admitted to the hospital. Ave and El slept in my bed, purring like little kittens with their warm bodies curled into my sides. I lay awake all night, tears dripping out of my eyes, thinking about everything my big sister might miss.

There was a mourning period for months before she was gone. She and I had time to talk about what she wanted for the girls so that I could be the best possible parent to them. But the adjustment from fun Uncle Finn to full-time Uncle Finn has been harder than I expected.

With my grandparents gone and no support from my parents, it's just me trying to dig out of this hole of grief, while also trying to help Avery and Eloise out of theirs.

Sometimes it feels like my heart has been shattered into a million little pieces. They're lying on the floor, the sharp, jagged edges cutting anyone who attempts to help me pick them up. And I try as hard as I can to put them back together, but every time I think I've got a piece settled into the place it belongs, everything crumbles again when I reach for another fragment.

Therapy for all three of us has been helping, and Dr. Kline reminds me constantly that everything we're feeling is normal. But I get to see their smiles and hear their laughter, and it destroys me that Clara is missing it. I'm living her life, trying to do the best I can. Trying to make her proud. Trying to make Ave's and El's lives everything she wanted.

She deserved this more than anyone I know. I would have given up anything to trade places with her.

Holding my breath, I slide out from between the girls, trying to scoot as carefully as possible. Once I'm free of their clutches, they roll toward each other, Eloise's head landing right beside Avery's. I pull my phone out of my pocket and take a picture of them.

When I make it downstairs, I'm greeted by a mess of chicken nuggets, macaroni and cheese, and green beans on the counter. The green beans weren't a hit tonight. Apparently, I cooked them too long, and in Eloise's words, "They tasted like the sandbox at the playground."

I made a mental note to keep an eye on her the next time we're at the park because I had no idea she was tasting the sand.

Before the girls came to live with me, I was getting takeout almost every night. So teaching myself to cook has been a big adjustment. I'd love to be able to cook with more variety, but I'm still trying to get the hang of some simple things. Last week I managed to burn every single grilled cheese, so my track record isn't the best.

Gabriella, the girls' nanny, knows it's not my forte, so she helps during the day as much as she can. She leaves homemade lasagna and chicken Parmesan in the fridge sometimes, and I could kiss her for it.

Once I get the dishwasher going and the food put away, I grab a beer and step out the back door. The chilly evening breeze brings goose bumps to my arms, prompting me to start the gas fire. The flames dance into the dark, and I drop onto the outdoor couch.

As I tilt my head back, letting my eyes search out the few stars I can see, a lone howl resounds through the night from a neighborhood dog.

The heartbroken cry for a friend rings through my ears, and something about it echoes into my soul. My heart seems to perk up and call back, *Me too, buddy.*

And for the first time, I realize that buried under the feelings of grief and loss might be a staggering loneliness that I've spent way too long ignoring.

Chapter 8

Millie

I've been haunted for the last twenty-four hours by my conversation with Finn yesterday. He told me something devastating about losing his sister, and Avery and Eloise losing their mother, and I couldn't wrap my head around the right thing to say in response.

Then my anxiety went into overdrive, making my hands clammy and my heart pound in my chest, so I changed the subject to something silly, as though I was trying to distract a kitten with a shiny object.

And while the sound of his deep, rumbly laugh has been replaying in my mind ever since, I have an overwhelming fear that I said the wrong thing, and I want to fix it.

The camp kids are spending their day with prehistoric life and engineering, giving us a chance to reset before they come back to entomology tomorrow. So I cross the museum to a department I rarely visit: astronomy.

Midway down a hallway of offices, I reach Finn's open door. He sits at his desk, a dove gray dress shirt stretched across his back and shoulders as he hunches toward his computer screen. His lips move as he reads silently from the monitor. When he doesn't turn my way, I let my eyes snoop around his office from the doorway, greedy for this tiny glimpse into his brain.

One wall of his office is floor-to-ceiling bookshelves filled with what looks like mostly textbooks. On his desk sits a framed picture of him beaming as he holds a swaddled baby in each arm. There are two drawings on the wall near his bookshelf. One is a stick-figure woman in a dress, holding two little girls' hands, and the other looks like a row of planets with faces floating in a starry sky.

Finn's chair creaks, startling me from my prying. "Good afternoon, Millie." He turns and meets my eyes.

Something yanks on my heart when he says my name, like an invisible thread pulling between us, tugging me slowly toward him.

"Dr. Ashford." My pulse hammers a little faster at the full force of his attention, but he's not scowling today. His eyes are brighter than usual, and his mouth is set in a neutral line. He looks . . . *normal*. "Are you busy?"

"Not at all. Come in," he says, waving me toward a chair in front of his desk. The plush cushion dips beneath my weight as I settle into it. Finn leans back, clasping the arms of his chair and making his shirt stretch tight across his chest. His tie looks like the surface of the moon, splotched with different shades of gray.

I drag my eyes back up and attempt a confident smile. "I wanted to apologize. I'm worried I made a mistake, and I haven't been able to stop thinking about it."

He raises a brow. "Are you apologizing for spilling coffee all over my tie?"

I narrow my eyes. "I've already apologized, even though it wasn't just my fault. And I wouldn't say coffee was 'all over' you. There was a barely visible speck on the edge of Neptune."

"Well, Neptune is very sensitive." He sighs, and a fluttery feeling creeps into my belly. "You must be here to apologize for smashing my nose in the middle of a meeting, then." He steeples his hands under his chin.

That memory has me straightening in my seat. "That was justice after you mocked me for feeling nervous."

He drops his hands and leans forward, brows pinched in concern. "I wasn't mocking at all. It was a failed attempt to check on you. I'm genuinely sorry if I sounded heartless."

My throat feels like the Sahara Desert as I try to swallow what he's telling me. I chew the inside of my lip. "I guess the monologue you were forced to give about Pluto was punishment enough."

He chuckles, and the deep sound rolls over my skin, leaving tingles behind. "I do feel passionately about Pluto. He spent years in the planet club and then was suddenly exiled. I worry about him."

He grins. *Grins.*

Am I in the right office? Does Finn have an identical twin, with the same gorgeous face, but without the grumbly personality, and I've actually found *him* this morning?

"If you're not here about the coffee and the nose incident, you must be here to apologize for the bumper."

Heat rushes to my cheeks, and my molars grind together. Seems he's just going to bring up every single embarrassing thing I've done in his presence. "You'll feel my apology when that insurance claim goes through," I sass.

Silent laughter plays in his eyes as they graze over my warm cheeks.

Sitting up straighter, I try to get back to the real business of why I'm here. "I came by because I wanted to apologize for my response when you told me about your sister. I feel like I didn't say the right thing."

His brows furrow. "You didn't do anything wrong, and it's not quite as fresh now, so it hurts a little less to explain to a new person." He lifts a shoulder in a small shrug. "It's our reality, and I'm getting used to being up-front. Your response didn't bother me at all."

A little of my swirling anxiety loosens in my chest knowing that I didn't completely ruin our professional relationship with my fumbled words.

Finn leans back in his chair to continue. "It has been six months since she passed, and the girls have been with me full-time since a few months before that." His chest heaves as he sighs. "I should've warned you ahead of time about Avery and Eloise in case something comes up while they're at camp this week. This is actually their first time away from me or Gabriella, their nanny, since Clara passed."

My heart aches. Those two little girls have been through so much, and it doesn't seem fair at all. "They had a great day yesterday. They were talkative and laughing, and I wouldn't have known they were going through something like this if you hadn't told me."

"That's good to hear." He nods, a deep line creasing between his brows as he looks down at his hands. "I know it's hard to find the right things to say sometimes, but you did great." A smirk flashes over his lips. "And you made me laugh, which is the best medicine, right?"

I shake my head, remembering his unbridled humor. "I didn't know those names were *that* funny."

He laughs suddenly, just like yesterday, and it has the same startling effect on me, completely ripping the breath from my lungs. His eyes shine brightly as he winces to confess, "It's because it sounded like you were picking out a stripper name."

Oh my god.

A giggle snorts out of me. And then another, until I'm dropping my forehead into my hand as laughter fills Finn's office.

"They were good names, though," he says. "Maybe not for your nieces and nephews, but in case the entomology thing doesn't work out."

"I'm so embarrassed," I mutter as I lift my head and try to calm my laughter.

His bright eyes snag mine, and my smile slowly fades. As we watch each other over his desk, the heat in my cheeks spreads to my neck. The air settles heavy through the office.

He adjusts his glasses and sparks crackle in the space between our gazes. My heart thumps suddenly with a whisper that says this could be *more*.

More than coworkers. More than I had planned.

The sensation is so foreign and unexpected that I shove it away like it's about to sting me.

I've been fighting to be taken seriously as a scientist since day one, and I can't hinder my chance at my dream job to become more than coworkers with Finn. He could literally be the swing vote that I need for my promotion. And I can't have everyone thinking I got it because of a relationship with him.

My brain draws a nice, long coworkers-stop-here line in the sand.

I clear my throat and stand, smoothing my palms down my jeans. "I'll definitely take those names off the aunt list and come up with some better options." I twist my hands, anxious for a way to escape this conversation without my heart tugging me any closer to Finn.

But he completely ruins those plans when he says, "Thanks for the chuckle. I've lived a lonely life the last few months, and laughing with a friend is nice."

Finn brushes his hand through the line I just drew, leaving no trace of its existence.

A friend. We can be friends. I'm friends with Micah and still work alongside him every day.

I draw a new line in the sand and label it Friendship—Do Not Go Past This Line.

Seriously, Millie. That's the boundary.

* * *

MY PHONE DINGS with a picture from my dad while I'm reading in bed that night. I click to open the image, revealing the pumpkin patch on the farm, which is currently a giant field of dirt with little sprouts sticking up.

Oaks Folks

Dad: Baby pumpkin plants. They'll be ready for our family pumpkin-carving contest in a few months.

Fabes: You guys can try to beat my octopus carving from three years ago, but you will fail.

Tess: I'm still saying I slayed with my Zendaya carving last year.

Millie: That Zendaya one was pretty badass. Zendaya octopus this year?

Mom: <picture of Dad on a tractor> Doesn't my farmer look sexy on his tractor?

Fabes: Ew. Mom, I live with you guys.

Dad: Maybe we're trying to motivate
you to flee the nest, Little Bird.

Fabes: You sure didn't want me gone when
I was helping you plant that pumpkin field.

Millie: Come live with me and Lena.
There are no tractors here.

Fabes: I'm going out, anyway.
I have a date tonight.

A flurry of texts pours in after that, asking for more information, but Fable never responds to any of it, so I give up and put my phone back on my nightstand.

I get through a few pages of my book before my phone chimes again, and I snatch it up.

But my smile falters when I see the name. My hands shake as I swipe to open the message.

Kyle: Just thinking about you.
Staying out of trouble?

I hold my breath, trying to stop my heart from panicking. Kyle hasn't contacted me in months—since a few weeks after I finally found the strength to leave him.

But seeing his name on my screen is what I imagine an arrow to the gut would feel like. It's sharp and sudden and it burns through my whole body.

I haven't been in any trouble. *He* was the trouble I got away from.

Slowly, I force a deep breath through my lungs. I pull oxygen in and count to five before letting it out again. Then I turn off my phone.

* * *

PEEKING AROUND THE person in front of me at Maggie's, I count the almond croissants left. I'll get one unless this fancy business-man is about to order five. The sound of the espresso grinder fills the coffee shop, and the nutty, earthy aroma surrounds me. I inhale a deep breath through my nose, hoping the caffeine will transfer right into my respiratory system this morning.

Sleep was slow to come last night after the message from my ex. It would've been great to fall asleep smiling about my goofy family, but instead, my brain went down a Kyle spiral that had me picking at my cuticles and tossing in bed.

After barely sleeping, I woke to another message from him, sent at 2:17 a.m.

> **Kyle:** Haven't heard back from you. Where are you?

My soul was a wasteland after I left him. Just dusty soil where he had ripped every flower out from the roots and left no life. No color.

It has taken every day of the last six months to rejuvenate that soil and breathe life back into it. I'm finally discovering who the real Millie is, and I hate that I'm faced with having to interact with him again.

The man in front of me finishes his order and moves to the side as Maggie struts out from the back with a tray of fresh almond croissants. She winks when she sees my big eyes.

"How many are you having this morning?" She slides the tray

into the display window, her signature overalls and apron dusted with flour.

I tilt my head, debating. "It might be a two-croissant morning."

She smiles and puts two from the new batch into a bag for me and then leans her hands on the counter, her arms covered in intricate, colorful tattoos.

"Maggie, you're a miracle worker." I open the brown bag and close my eyes as I sniff the freshly baked pastry.

A barista delivers my coffee order, and I pay for my breakfast. As I'm closing my wallet, a sweet voice shouts, "Hey, Ms. Millie," from behind me.

I turn around to find Eloise waving me over to their table, her untamed hair flying back and forth as she almost falls out of her seat. Avery and Finn are sitting with her near the window, and he looks too big for the table, hunched over between the girls like the Beast trying to eat dinner across from Belle.

As I approach, Finn stands and pulls an empty chair from the table next to theirs, pushing it into an open spot. "Join us."

"That's okay." I shake my head. "You all enjoy your breakfast. I don't want to intrude."

"Please," Eloise begs, pulling my wrist toward her.

Finn flashes me a secret smirk that I can't quite interpret.

My body and brain war against each other, clashing over whether joining their breakfast is a breach of the line.

But Avery makes the decision for me when she stands from her seat and pulls me toward the empty one, and I drop into it.

I start unpacking my first croissant and smile at the girls. "Having a good morning?"

Eloise nods emphatically. "Uncle Finn said we can have breakfast here instead of at home."

I lean over and whisper, "That's because this place has the best breakfast treats."

As we eat, Eloise tells me about how they had to go out for dinner last night after Finn burned their food so badly that the smoke alarms were going off. I give them a few sneak peeks into what we're doing at camp today, then show them a video my mom sent this morning of two baby otters swimming with their mama.

But throughout my conversations with the girls, my eyes keep dragging back to Finn. He's quiet most of the time, brushing crumbs from Eloise's cheek and comforting Avery when she spills her milk. Every movement seems natural. He's so comfortable with them, and they seem completely at ease with him, teasing him and making him chuckle at their versions of the stories.

And the sinking suspicion creeps into my bones that I don't think I can keep filling in that asshole checklist.

Finn has pretty much burned it, leaving me with nothing but ashes.

***

JUST AS I'M about to leave the office on Thursday evening, I receive an email from Sharon and almost trip over my chair getting to my desk to read it.

TO: Millie Oaks
FROM: Sharon Glass
SUBJECT: Second Interview Request

Good afternoon, Millie,

After careful consideration, we have narrowed down our pool for the entomology director position to two final applicants.

The board of directors and I feel that the best process

moving forward will be a trial week for each applicant, followed by a second interview.

I have attached a separate document detailing the dates of your trial, as well as the responsibilities you will oversee during that week. There will be a slight delay while I attend a convention, so you will have four weeks to prepare for your time in charge of the entomology department.

During that week, you will be giving a tour of the butterfly vivarium to the interview committee. We expect to spend about thirty minutes with each applicant there, and we hope to hear your unique insights and knowledge throughout that time.

We heard some great ideas from you in your interview, and I look forward to seeing what else you share with us.

If you have any questions, don't hesitate to email me or stop by my office.

Thank you,
Sharon Glass
Wilhelmina Natural Science Museum Director

Nausea settles in the pit of my stomach as I reread the email. While I dreamed of being handed the position easily, I know logically that isn't how this works. I want to be the person for the job, but if I'm not, I'm reluctantly glad the committee is taking the time to make the right decision.

A small stab of betrayal pierces my heart when I realize Finn probably knew about this. Maybe that's what prompted the coffee and the kind emails. He felt sorry for me.

I *don't* want special treatment to get this job. I want to earn it fair and square because *I* am the right choice, and *I* am the badass scientist who deserves it.

Four weeks feels so far away right now, but maybe it will give me the opportunity to focus and nail down exactly how I want to present myself for the next interview. Hopefully it will be enough time to snuff out the insecurity zinging through my veins, and I will be able to prove to all of them how much I deserve that job.

Chapter 9

Finn

Well, fuck.

I've spent a week and a half trying to erase the image of Millie bent over my bumper from my mind. The way that tight skirt showcased every curve has stolen way too many of my thoughts.

But here she is, hands on her knees as she laughs heartily, searing the view into my brain all over again.

I try my best to be a fucking professional, and I don't stare at my coworker's perfect ass in those tight jeans.

. . . for more than a few moments.

I wait for a break in the laughter, hoping Millie or the woman beside her will notice I'm here to pick up the girls from their last day of camp. But when neither of them looks my way, I clear my throat.

Millie pops her head up, wiping tears from her sparkling green eyes as she turns to me.

My breath catches. She's shockingly beautiful, uninhibited and happy, and it takes me a second to remember what I'm doing here.

"Hey, Finn."

As soon as my name leaves her lips, the other woman turns so fast that her hair whips her cheek. She scans me with dark eyes from my face to my shoes, mouth wide-open and eyebrows almost to her hairline.

Millie reaches over and snaps the woman's jaw shut. "This is my friend Lena. I'm sorry she doesn't have manners." She narrows her eyes in her friend's direction.

I reach my hand out to Lena, and she takes it eagerly. "Finn Ashford. I work in the astronomy department."

"Oh, I know who you are." She eyes me with a sly smirk, then points to Millie and mumbles, "I want you to know I was right. And if you don't want him, I'll take him."

Warmth hits my cheeks as Millie splutters for a beat. She shakes her head before steering Lena away from us, forcing her farther into the room.

"Sorry about that." Millie bites her bottom lip to stop the embarrassed smile spreading over her face.

Before I can tell her not to apologize, Eloise and Avery squeal from across the room and run to collide with my legs. Lena follows them over and hands me two small canvases.

Avery untangles herself from me and stands on her toes to see the navy-and-purple painting. "Ms. Lena showed us how to paint butterflies. Can we put them on the mantel?"

"Of course. They're beautiful," I say as I kneel next to her.

Eloise points to her orange-and-black butterfly. "I painted orange because that's my favorite color."

"I love them. They'll be perfect in the living room." I kiss my nieces on the forehead before I stand.

Lena has her palms on her cheeks as she watches us, nudging Millie with her elbow.

Millie smacks her shoulder and hisses, "Stop it."

"Are we still making pizza tonight?" Avery asks, tugging on my shirt with sad puppy eyes that always seem to have the power to bend me to their will.

My brain has been so scattered lately that I completely forgot this promise. "Sure, Ave. We need to stop at the store on the way home, though."

Eloise cheers with excitement, and my heart warms at the fact that these two keep believing in me. Even after so many failed meals, they truly trust me all over again the next day.

"You know who makes *the best* homemade pizza?" Lena asks, wiggling her brows up and down.

With wide eyes, Millie opens her mouth like she might be able to stop whatever Lena is about to say.

But she's not fast enough.

"Millie does," Lena says with a beaming smile.

A scarlet blush burns Millie's cheeks. Lena grins, completely shameless, but I can't deny that I like where this is going.

Do I think I can make pizza with my kitchen record lately? Probably not, if I'm being honest. I managed to cook our spaghetti into mush the other day and made a roast chicken that resembled jerky. I'm not too proud to ask for help in the name of pizza.

Millie wipes her hands down her face and looks at me seriously. "I'm sorry."

"Don't apologize," I say, tilting my head. "It just so happens we could use a hand if you want to come."

A battle seems to play out in her eyes as she weighs what the right answer is. Finally, she sighs and admits, "I don't want to intrude."

"You're not. I could use the help. I've ruined our dinner twice this week already." I look down at Ave and El, who are pleading to Millie with the most convincing puppy eyes I've ever seen.

Lena doesn't miss a beat. She kneels in front of the girls and says, "Millie makes the best homemade crust. It's the most delicious thing I've ever eaten."

Avery and Eloise resort to jumping up and down, begging Millie to make pizza for us.

Raising her eyebrows, she puts her hands on their heads and smiles. "Okay, okay. I'll make you the best pizza of your life." She grabs Lena's arm and pulls her up. "You're done," she snaps firmly before shoving her away.

"Enjoy your pizza, girls," Lena calls over her shoulder.

Millie faces me and mouths, "I'm sorry," shaking her head.

I give her a stern look that I hope conveys my seriousness when I say, "Don't apologize." I pull out my phone and hand it to her. "Give me your number, and I'll text you my address. Then you can tell me what I need to pick up from the store."

Chapter 10

Millie

"You and the girls totally teamed up against me!" I yell into the speaker end of my phone. If I weren't driving down the road, I'm sure people would be able to hear my voice echoing through my car as I scream at Lena.

"They did play right into my plans, didn't they?" she croons.

"The next time *you* like someone, I'm going to make sure they know about that time you threw up all over that woman's lap—the one buying you drinks at Barkeep's." I pause at a stop sign as I enter Finn's neighborhood. "Not that I *like* Finn. But you know what I mean."

Lena's dark chuckle drifts through the phone. "Sure. Keep telling yourself that." She lets out a dramatic sigh. "I'm devastated I won't be there. I only saw him for, like, three minutes with those girls, and I was already swooning."

My knuckles turn white as I squeeze the steering wheel. "No one is supposed to be swooning!" I shout as my GPS directs me to turn right.

"Are you the swoon police?" Lena asks, giggling through her words. "Because you might end up needing to arrest yourself. Watch out for that."

"Ugh," I grumble through my tight jaw. "You are the worst

best friend in history, and Micah has just been promoted to your previous position."

Her loud laugh fills my car right as I slam my finger down on my cracked screen to end the call.

I scan the modern houses and cozy cottages until my navigation system tells me I've arrived. Parking in front of the dark-green, two-story bungalow, I check the house number and turn off the car.

The coppery taste of blood hits my tongue, reminding me of how aggressively I've been chewing on my lip. Flipping down the mirror, I use a napkin from the glove box to stop the bleeding.

My mind can't process the fact that I'm going to his house. This isn't like randomly running into them at Maggie's. There's something intimate about being in another person's space, learning how they fold their towels, seeing their favorite coffee cup drying in the kitchen, and getting a glimpse at how they organize their fridge.

Did all his condiments expire three years ago? Does he let everything mold in there before he throws it away?

Once the blood has stopped, I let my eyes wander over the house beside me. Plants surround the wide porch, with massive ferns in hanging pots and flowers lining the walkway up to the wooden steps. Two spruce trees tower over the yard like a grand welcome. The golden evening sun is still blazing in the sky, but a warm glow of light radiates through the windows.

The inviting homeyness tugs at that invisible thread in my heart, pulling me toward the house.

Taking a deep, steadying breath, I run my clammy palms over my jeans and look around the car. My trusty twenty-year-old 4Runner still smells like sunscreen and the pool from my years of driving to and from high school swim practice, and I close my eyes to let it soothe my nerves.

I will have to get out of the car eventually, but I take a moment to give myself a small pep talk. Pretend Lena's in my pocket telling me how amazing I am.

Damn it. *No.* I'm mad at Lena right now.

When I gather my nerves and step out of the car, a soft click sounds from Finn's house. I snap my eyes to his porch.

He stands in his open doorway, arms crossed over his chest as he leans against the frame. I've never seen him in anything other than work clothes, but this evening I have the immense privilege of witnessing what he looks like in jeans. The way they're hugging his muscular thighs is almost obscene. His black T-shirt is stretched across his chest and shoulders, and his bare feet and glasses add to the relaxed ensemble, making me a little light-headed.

As I walk up the stairs, electricity crackles through the air between us, buzzing and snapping as I draw closer. When I look up, his lips are curved in a warm smile, and it distracts me enough that I stumble up the last step.

I'm fully prepared to fall. Just crash at his feet like, *here I am in typical Millie fashion, falling all over you.*

But two large hands grab my upper arms and catch me before I hit the porch's wooden slats. His palms meet my bare skin, and the electricity from the air mainlines straight into my body through his hands—a powerful jolt I'm not prepared for.

"What am I going to do with you, Millie?" Finn smirks as he stands me up straight.

Put your fingers through my hair and kiss me? Slide your hands down to my waist and pull me toward you.

Shit.

Oh my god.

No, Millie.

The line! You aren't *crossing it.*

Quit thinking like a lady starved for an orgasm. You can handle that yourself later.

I plant my feet firmly back under me and practically jump out of his grip, needing to derail my brain. I will not have *those* thoughts in this man's presence. That is so far past appropriate it might as well be in another world.

"I keep crashing into you," I say, smoothing out the nonexistent wrinkles in my jeans as I attempt to rein my hormones back in.

"I don't mind," he replies smoothly. "Come on in." He motions for me to walk through the door first, and Avery and Eloise run into me in greeting.

Avery pulls my arm until I crouch in front of her, and she whispers in my ear, "Uncle Finn was worried you couldn't find our house."

I look up at Finn, but he's fiddling with Eloise's hair and not paying attention. "I was a little nervous, so I was driving slowly."

She nods, squinting at me like she totally gets it.

Eloise grabs my hand, pulling me into the living room. "Uncle Finn was helping us make spaceships," she says, dragging me to a corner littered with Legos. "And this is where we color." She points to a child-sized table cluttered with crayons and open coloring books.

Avery plops onto the midnight-blue couch that has no less than fifteen stuffed animals piled on one side. She holds up a small moose. "This is Moosey." Then she picks up a giraffe. "And this is Giraffey."

A smile blooms on my lips at their name choices. "Nice to meet you, Moosey and Giraffey."

"And, Millie," Eloise says, drawing my attention away from the animal introductions. She stands in front of the brick fireplace and points to a black vase with intricate gold designs on the sides. "That's where Mama is now."

Realization hits me, and my eyes burn as tears rise to the surface. Framed images sit on either side of the urn, of a stunning woman with raven hair and blue eyes. The picture on the right was clearly taken after she had gotten sick—the deep, dark circles under her eyes a stark contrast to the girls' bright faces as they smile at her. Another was taken in happier times—the girls coming down a slide with their mom, laughter on everyone's faces. Behind the framed pictures are the butterfly canvases from this afternoon.

Avery and Eloise have already jumped to the next thing, trying to pull me toward the Legos, but my heart is snagged on the sweet and devastating mantel.

My gaze meets Finn's where he's standing behind the couch. His fingers dig into the back of it as he looks at me with a quiet grin that seems to say, *Welcome to the chaos.*

Chapter 11

Finn

"Alexa, play pizza music," El calls toward the speaker.

Somehow Alexa understands what she wants, and soft Italian music starts drifting through the kitchen. Avery and Eloise cackle with laughter on either side of Millie while they knead their pizza dough on the counter, flour flying in every direction.

I didn't expect having Millie here to be so unsettling. Walking through the house and watching the girls show her every detail was unnerving. I feel like I'm opening a door into our world, and I don't know if I thought through all the side effects.

And hell, no matter how hard I try, I haven't been able to stop myself from checking her out. Her white shirt is slightly lower cut than what she wears to work, and my eyes keep straying to the creamy skin there, like they have a mind of their own.

"Come here, Finn," Millie says from across the kitchen island. "You didn't think I was going to do all the work, did you?" She smiles at me as she scoots El over to make room next to her.

I slide between them, and Millie drops a chunk of dough in front of me. The flour puffs up into the air, landing on my black shirt and glasses.

"Oops," she says, observing the spots on my lenses. She puts her delicate hand on my arm and leans toward me on her tiptoes.

My heart speeds up. I watch her perfect mouth as she puckers her lush lips and gently blows the flour from my glasses.

When her breath runs out, she looks into my eyes with a startled expression, and I stare back at the glittery, golden flecks in her deep-green irises. I let my gaze fall to the freckles sprinkled across her nose and cheeks, and my fingers itch to touch them.

She sucks in a breath as she seems to realize how close we are and drops back onto her heels. "Okay." She shakes her head. "The first thing you're going to do is spread it out like this." Millie uses the tips of her fingers to press her dough away from her gently, while I try to copy her movements with my own. "Then you're going to bring that far side up and fold it over, followed by a ninety-degree turn, and repeat."

She dusts her hands where my black apron sits on her hips and waits for me to start.

"I have to be honest. I have no idea what you did there," I say, turning to give her a sheepish grin. I was too distracted watching the graceful movements of her fingers and the smooth way she rolled the dough around. It's hard to concentrate on kneading when I'm soaking in every detail of *her*.

She leans over my workspace, her waist brushing against my forearm, and does the first step for me. "This isn't rocket science," she teases. The sweet, lemony scent of her hair fills my senses, distracting me all over again. "Now, pull that side over and fold it in half." She lifts her hands, waiting for me to follow her instructions. I try to mimic her movements, and I guess I do it right because she cheers, "Good job! Almost as good as Avery and Eloise."

The girls burst out laughing and clap their hands, sending puffs of flour everywhere. Millie smiles and bumps her hip into mine. "Keep at it. You've got to do that, like, fifty more times."

I try to get in a groove kneading the dough, while Millie is working with skilled confidence next to me, but I'm not getting as much done as I should be. Our arms bump against each other, and she leans in front of me to guide Eloise on my other side. A light dusting of flour covers her hair, and she keeps swaying her hips and humming along to the music.

It's all so distracting, and I'm fighting as hard as I can not to notice.

But it seems like a lost cause.

Once the dough is rising and I've cleaned the kitchen from our flour bombing, I lean back on the counter, observing the girls on either side of Millie at the kitchen island.

"My favorite princess is Elsa," Eloise announces, unsurprisingly. She's been obsessed since the first time she watched *Frozen*.

"Ooh, I've been loving 'Into the Unknown' lately." Millie nods. "Lena and I like to dance to it."

Eloise says, "Alexa, play 'Into the Unknown,'" and immediately jumps from her stool. Millie and Avery turn around in their chairs to face Eloise as she waits through the piano introduction and the siren call before putting her hand to her ear.

Her little voice echoes around the kitchen as she sings along to the first line with a dramatic flair. When the beat hits, she stomps her foot in sync with it and continues through the first verse, twirling with her arms flying in every direction.

As the chorus starts, Millie surprises me by dropping from her stool and joining Eloise. They both spread their arms wide and throw their heads back, belting out the lyrics.

They light up the whole damn house in a matter of seconds. The music rings through the air like a call to action, willing me to give this critical moment my full attention.

Millie and El spin in circles while they sing, and I'm breathlessly fascinated. Here is a woman I barely know, dancing around my kitchen with my niece, completely unembarrassed.

They hold hands and sing right in each other's faces like they're starring in their own Broadway show.

The crowd would be going wild for their enthusiasm.

When the last chorus begins, Millie reaches for Avery, and my heart skips when Avery accepts her hand with a timid smile. She steps up beside Millie and watches her for a few beats before her quiet voice joins theirs. Her movements are shy, but she beams up at Millie, trying to copy her dance through the rest of the song.

My chest tightens, as though someone has taken hold of it and *squeezed*. Something about watching them together is so . . . right that it leaves me breathless.

The song ends too soon, and an ounce of sadness trickles through me. I could've watched the three of them for hours.

Little does Millie know, I've memorized every word of that song—not that she would ever catch me singing it. Our kitchen sing-alongs are a secret between me and the girls.

"Uncle Finn loves that song," El announces as she crashes back into her stool. "He always sings it with us."

Well, fuck. That lasted five seconds. Little snitch.

"Does he, now?" Millie looks like a wolf on the scent of her next meal as she slowly turns my way. "We could've used another dancer."

I snort. "Never gonna happen."

"We'll see about that. I have some potent powers of persuasion," she boasts, and the sultry tone of her voice sends a hot thrill up my spine.

I'm failing so fucking badly at keeping her in the coworker column.

My eyes suffer from a disorder that makes them constantly follow her. My mouth is inflicted with something similar that forces me to grin every time she does. And now my brain is affected by the raspy tone of her voice, producing forbidden images of other places she could use it.

I hastily turn back to the sink, looking for something to distract me from the intimacy and the smiling and the dancing and the teasing.

Women have been the furthest thing from my mind since the girls moved in. When Clara started getting sick, I had been with a woman named Angela for about six months. We had just started talking about moving in together when Clara needed more help with the girls. While I was picking up Ave and El from school and visiting my sister in the hospital, Angela was angry that I wasn't spending that time with her.

"You have too much baggage," she'd said.

As though my perfect nieces, who were going through the biggest devastation of their lives, were extra bags I was going to carry around for eternity.

At the memory of that comment, my fingers clench around the wooden spoon I'm washing. Am I doing something wrong here? Should I let someone new be this involved in the girls' lives? We're allowing her into our world, and they're laughing and dancing together now, but Millie could decide tomorrow that she's over it.

Chapter 12

Millie

Oaks Folks

Millie: <picture of homemade cheese pizza> Made pizza tonight and thought of you guys! I miss you all!

Mom: Looks great, sweetie.

Mom: Is that a child's hand in the corner of the picture?

Tess: Yeah, Mom, she had a secret child and never told you.

Dad: That's your mother's worst nightmare. Don't scare her before bed.

Fabes: But for real, whose tiny hand is that?

*T*he sound of the girls' giggles pulls my eyes from my phone, and I click it off, placing it on the table. They climb the steps of the swing set while Finn and I sit on their back patio, watching the sun dip behind the horizon.

"How did you get into entomology?" Finn asks, dropping his last pizza crust on the plate in front of him.

"Well, I was raised in an outdoorsy family, so insects were always a part of our lives," I say, taking a sip of my water and studying him over my glass. His legs are spread wide in his chair as he holds a beer bottle on his thigh.

A sprinkle of flour still clings to his black shirt, and it gives me a flashback of his tan forearms working as he folded and pressed his pizza dough. It was embarrassing how quickly my heart rate escalated to the beat of a hummingbird's wings.

Before I can get flustered again at the memory, I continue, "I grew up on a farm, and I was always the bug girl in our family." The rest of my words pause on my lips as I realize maybe he's asking me about this as a post-interview question. I don't want that to be the case. I want him to just be interested as a friend, but I'm not sure about the meaning behind it. Should I be answering this as a potential promotion opportunity or as a friend having a drink on a patio?

"What kind of farm did you grow up on?"

I glance at him, and he's looking right at me, the warm glow from the string of lights overhead making his eyes shine. He looks genuinely curious and not at all like someone giving me a job interview. So I let my shoulders relax.

"We have a corn maze and pumpkins in autumn, pick-your-own berries in summer. And my favorite part is in the winter when my parents dress up as Santa and Mrs. Claus for a few events, and we light up a path through the farm for people to drive through. We sell vegetables at the farmers' market, and we have chickens, goats, horses, ducks, a barn cat, and a farm dog. Oh, and a lone donkey." I laugh to myself. "It's a lot. But it's my favorite place in the world."

He nods. "That sounds like a kid's dream. Do you get to go there often?"

"The farm is in Fern River, only about an hour from here. I go once a month or so for the weekend." I take another sip from my drink. "Do you see your parents often?"

"As rarely as I can." He sighs, shaking his head. "We have a complicated relationship. I take the girls over there occasionally, but we don't ever enjoy it, honestly."

"I'm sorry," I whisper, my heart aching at the lack of support he seems to have.

"Millie," he starts, putting his hand over mine on my armrest, inviting my eyes to his. "Don't feel like you should have to go through life apologizing for things you didn't do. Sometimes you don't even need to apologize for things you *did* do. And you absolutely don't need to apologize for my shitty parents." His warm, calloused hand is only there momentarily before he pulls it away.

I nod in a daze, startled by the sincerity and concern in his tone.

It's true. I apologize way too much, but sometimes when I say "I'm sorry," what I actually mean is "I'm sad for you."

Finn continues, "My parents have never been proud of my choice to work in astronomy. It took me a while to realize I didn't have to bend to their will. As a kid, I wanted to make them happy—make them pay attention to me—so I told them whatever they wanted to hear. I said I would be a lawyer, like my dad, but that was never me. Even now, they would love to see me drop everything I'm passionate about to attend law school and work for my dad."

I would be devastated if my parents weren't proud of me or didn't support my dreams. I grew up in a house where we could pursue every single thing that sparked our interest. My childhood bedroom was filled with jars and boxes of insects, and my mom *still* takes the time to send me a picture of any insects she finds because she knows I'll try to identify them for her.

"Shortly after Clara was diagnosed with pancreatic cancer, she had me over to talk about her will." He downs a drink of his beer. "She said she wanted me to take the girls. Their dad has never been in the picture, and we both knew our parents would be awful caregivers for them. It had to be me," he says with a shrug. "Clara was already so sick that I started looking for a house to buy that night." He rubs a palm across his jaw. "My parents threw a fit, of course. In their eyes, they have more money and a bigger house, and they've already raised kids. But, as it is, they can't even find the time to be good grandparents to the girls."

"They're the ones missing out," I say, a flash of protectiveness burning in my chest.

He nods and solemnly whispers, "Yeah."

I tuck my feet under myself and turn in my seat to face him. "So, how did you end up in astronomy?"

"Promise not to laugh?" he asks, a small smirk on his lips like he knows I might not be able to stop it.

"I don't know if I can ever make you that promise."

"Fair enough." He sighs. "It started when I was ten and watched *Star Wars* for the first time with Clara."

A strangled laugh bursts out of me. "Wait, wait, wait." I hold up my hand. "Did you fall in love with astronomy or Princess Leia in the sexy gold bikini?"

His deep, heavy chuckle rolls over my skin. "Is it that obvious?"

"That outfit was hot," I agree.

He shakes his head with a grin. "Well, from then on, I was that kid with their room covered in everything space related—constellation posters on my walls, sheets with astronauts, planets hanging from the ceiling in my room. My mom hated it. It didn't fit the aesthetic of her house, but my grandparents kept buying me anything they found. My nonno Lorenzo moved here from Italy around that time, and he barely spoke English. He couldn't even read the books he got me, but he could tell they were about space." He smiles wistfully. "He would bring me to the museum at least once a month. It opened my mind to all the possibilities out there and gave me something to be excited about."

"Your grandfather sounds wonderful."

He takes a big swig of his beer to finish it off. I try not to get distracted by the way his Adam's apple rolls with his swallow. I also try not to notice the way he licks his lips after he pulls the bottle from them.

But I fail miserably.

He sets his empty bottle on the table and turns to give me a small grin. "Thanks for dancing with the girls tonight. It was great to see them smile and laugh. You even got Ave out there, which is a feat."

"I had a blast," I say as the girls run toward us.

Avery slides a plastic box of cookies on the table to Finn. "Can we have a cookie now?"

"Definitely," he says, prying open the grocery store bakery packaging to pull out a chocolate chip cookie for each of us.

I try to take a bite as the girls run off with theirs, but the cookie is way too hard, so I move it to the side of my mouth and use my molars to break through.

"I have to tell you something," I say around the inedible chunk of dessert. "You know, because friends are honest with each other."

He looks over at me with an eyebrow raised.

"These cookies suck."

"I worked hard on these," he jokes, his brows pinching as he surveys his cookie.

"Well, you need some help, then. I don't know how the girls are eating them."

Finn huffs out a laugh. "Guess you'll have to teach us how to make some better ones."

My brain stumbles on his words. Is he inviting me over again? I've been hanging on by my fingernails to the appropriate side of the friendship line tonight, fighting as hard as I can not to enjoy this evening *too* much. But there's still an invisible thread attached to my heart, yanking me over the line every time our eyes connect.

I cross my arms over my chest and give him a stern look. "That depends on what kind of cookies you like. Because if you want oatmeal raisin, this is officially the end of our friendship. I'll never make those atrocities."

Finn narrows his gaze. "I'm offended. You think *I* seem like a person who eats oatmeal raisin cookies?"

"Maybe that's why you scowl all the time," I say with a shrug, and his glare darkens. But that expression from him doesn't seem so ominous anymore, and it makes my heart skip for an entirely different reason than it used to. "What kind of cookies do you and the girls like?"

"Chocolate chip, obviously. Snickerdoodle, and the girls love anything with icing."

"Oh, I can teach you to make all of those."

His brows perk up. "Next Friday, then?"

The words catch me off guard, even though our conversation has led us right here. He's really inviting me again, all on his own. It's not Eloise bringing me over to their breakfast or Lena shoving me into their pizza night. *He's* asking, and it feels more significant than anything else he's said to me.

It's an invitation for more. More friendship. More time spent together.

And I have to admit to myself that I like the sound of it.

"Deal," I tell him.

The girls lie down in the grass, pointing to the sky as a few stars twinkle out of the darkness, and I realize I should let them get to bed soon.

I stand to gather the plates, but Finn stops me with a hand on my arm. "I'll get those."

His chair scrapes the stone patio as he rises to stack the plates himself. He nudges my arm with his firm chest, leaning across the table and steadying himself with a palm pressed between my shoulder blades. The pressure of it sends warmth to every lonely corner of my body. It's hard to breathe with him this close, his sage-and-soap scent everywhere around me.

When he straightens, I look up to scan his face, and that thread tightens between us, pulling me closer like I have no control over my own body. The air buzzes as we watch each other in silence, and his navy eyes drop to my mouth. His focused attention makes me lick my lips.

Eloise's shrill cry startles me from my trance. Finn drops his gaze, and his hand leaves my back as he sets the plates down. Eloise reaches us, crying that Avery's elbow hit her nose.

I take a deep breath and try to calm my racing heart as Finn drops to his knees, rubbing Eloise's back.

"It's okay, *piccola*. You know, Millie hit me in the nose the other day too," he says, winking at me over her shoulder.

Avery wails, "It was an accident. I was pointing to the stars, and I bumped her." She runs to me, and I squat to catch her as she buries her face in my neck, her tears wetting my skin.

She came to *me*, trusting that I could offer her comfort. I run my fingers through the tips of her hair, and my lips part in surprise when she calms down.

I look over her shoulder and see Finn watching me over Eloise.

We're mirror images of each other, crouched on the ground, consoling the girls.

My stomach dips with a swooping sensation like I'm at the top of a roller coaster about to tip over the edge. I'm seeing the world from a new perspective before I career over the side, into the unknown.

Chapter 13

Finn

The rumbling blender grates on my nerves when I walk into Maggie's in a daze, exhaustion slowing my steps. Eloise woke me early this morning in a rare bad mood, storming through the house and slamming doors because she couldn't find Moosey, her favorite stuffed animal.

I file into line behind a woman with auburn hair. It's not Millie, because this woman is about a foot taller, but her hair color still brings Millie's face to my mind.

The last two weeks have passed in a haze of Fridays.

Saturday through Thursday are fine, routine, plain.

But Fridays are golden because Millie's there.

She came over to make us chocolate chip cookies the Friday after pizza night, and then she taught me how to make chicken Alfredo last Friday. She even made a few vegetables that the girls warily took a bite of. Millie supervises and directs me through each recipe from what I now refer to as *her* barstool.

She has done all the puzzles the girls own, colored every single time they've asked, and prompted more dance parties than I can count. Millie demanded I order some dress-up clothes for the girls, and they sang with delight when the package arrived, then did a fashion show of every outfit combination.

But despite all the good things her friendship has brought us, tension still burns through my body like a sparkler every time she's around.

When she accidentally bumped her hip against mine in the kitchen last week, I almost choked on my piece of garlic bread. Even the slightest brush of her fingers as I handed her a drink felt like flames licking my skin.

I force myself to shove those feelings into a trunk and fasten the lid tight when she's around because I don't want them to interfere with our friendship.

But when I shut the front door every Friday as she drives away, I let myself peer inside the trunk.

And what I discover is a yearning for *more*.

More time together.

More laughing.

More giving in to this gravitational pull toward her.

Just *more*.

"Sir? Excuse me. Are you ready to order?"

The barista's voice breaks me out of my musings, and I snap my attention to her, pushing away my thoughts of Millie so I can order my breakfast.

When my coffee and bagel are ready, I grab them from the counter and turn to leave. But I stumble over my feet as I spot another splash of auburn at a table near the window, and this time I know who it is. My heart pounds heavily in my chest like it's attempting to escape my ribs and soar toward her.

Millie's hair is coppery sunshine in the coffee-shop lighting, making my fingers ache to run through it. As I step in her direction, I will my eyes not to drop to the smooth skin revealed by the open buttons at the top of her green blouse, but it's like a siren's call, luring me toward the spot. My gaze follows the path of freckles over her collarbones and down into the vee of her shirt.

Desire trickles through my veins the longer I stare, wishing I could feel that skin against mine. Let her warmth burn beneath my hands and—*crash.*

Somewhere in the bakery, a plate smashes to the ground, and the sound of shattered porcelain snaps me from my daze. I clear my throat as I force my eyes back above her neck. "Good morning." My voice is huskier than usual as I approach her table and ask, "How are you?"

"I'm great," Millie says, glancing around the coffee shop. "Simply debating why there are so many people here this morning. Everyone is finding out about this place, and I selfishly want to keep it a secret." She narrows her eyes at me. "Have *you* been telling people about Maggie's? Posting about it on some kind of Princess Leia fan board?"

Her teasing makes me grin. It feels like an honor to be close enough that she has ammo for making fun of me.

"I would never do that," I tell her. "I'm as addicted to this place as you are."

"Good. I'm glad I brought someone over to the dark side with me." She pins me with a sharp look. "But you're the only one allowed. And the girls, of course."

"Honored, we are," I say, giving my best Yoda impression, and her twinkling green eyes dance with delight.

She waves to the empty chair beside her. "Want to join me?"

I nod and take a seat. "Was it a muffin morning?" I ask as she picks apart the pastry in front of her.

"One of these people must've stolen the last almond croissant." She shoves a bite angrily into her mouth. "I need to learn how to make them."

"You, Millie Oaks, can't make something?" I tease, taking a sip of my coffee and opening my bagel.

"Ha. Ha," she says with a scowl. "The process is so long, and I need a standing mixer to blend the dough together better. They keep turning into puddles in the oven." She shakes her head and crumbles another bite of muffin between her fingers.

I nod like I get it. Like I really have some understanding of croissant-making logistics. "How was your weekend?"

"Standard, I guess. Multiple pots of coffee, chicken tortilla soup with an entire bag of chips and salsa, and a few rounds of Catan."

"I haven't played that game in forever." I sigh, taking a bite of my bagel. "One of the many hobbies that fall by the wayside when you suddenly have kids."

Millie raises her eyebrows. "You should come to game night sometime. Lena, Micah, Emil, and I try to have it once a week."

The idea of going out and leaving the girls in the evening makes my hands clammy. What if they need me and I'm not there?

"I know it's hard to schedule stuff like that," Millie says comfortingly. "But we'd love for you to come. Bring the girls if you want. We even have some kids' games and Legos for when Lena's niece and nephew visit."

The bell over the door dings behind me, and Millie's eyes snap toward it.

"That sounds—" I start, but I'm cut off when her hand shoots out to grab the knot of my tie. She hauls me to her, burying her face in the side of my neck, and I'm frozen in shock, completely unable to process normal thoughts. Millie's smooth skin is touching mine, and I'm surrounded by her vanilla-and-lemon scent.

"Sorry," she whispers. "There's someone over there I don't want to see me." Her warm breath against my neck is like a heater on my skin, melting my tense muscles.

Don't be sorry at all. This is exactly where I want you to be.

Fuck. I can't say that to my coworker. Instead, I whisper, "That's okay. Did they see you?" My lips accidentally brush the shell of her ear, and her breath hitches.

"Don't think so. I saw him right as he walked through the door." She holds firmly to my tie like it's keeping her from falling over a cliff.

He. My body moves of its own accord like the need to protect her is instinctual. I slide my arm across the back of her chair and turn my body toward hers until Millie's knees nestle between my spread thighs.

"Is this okay?" I ask, hoping it feels like a refuge and not a cage.

"It's perfect," she breathes, her soft lips brushing across my neck as she speaks. I barely manage to hold in the groan that claws its way up my throat.

Strands of her hair wave when I breathe, and the contact of our skin has my heart beating out of my chest. I close my eyes, focusing on every hypersensitive spot connecting us—my rough beard scraping against her delicate skin and her shoulder pressing into my chest.

"Are you okay?" I whisper. I want to wrap my arms all the way around her, but I settle for lazily rubbing my thumb in a circle on her shoulder blade.

"It's my ex-boyfriend," she says with a sigh. "I could write a novel to answer your question, but the short version is, he wasn't great to me."

Rage seeps through me like an ink spill on clean paper, and I have to force myself to ignore it and stay where I am.

My entire hand splays across her back, and I pull her closer as she mumbles, "It's mostly fine. I just don't want to have to talk to him. He has texted me a few times recently, and I didn't want to respond. So I guess I'm hiding like a coward."

I circle my hand over her soft shirt to suppress the urge to punch this guy. "You're not a coward. You don't have to respond to anyone you don't want to, ex-boyfriend or not."

She nods and lets out a long breath. Her grip loosens on my tie, but she doesn't move away. "Sorry about this."

God, if there was *ever* a time she shouldn't be sorry, this is it. "Don't apologize. Stay as long as you need. I'm perfectly comfortable."

I could stay like this for as long as she'd let me.

She huffs a quiet laugh against my skin. Footsteps echo behind us, and her shoulders tense, so I smooth my hand on her back again until she relaxes.

When the bell above the door chimes, Millie lifts her eyes to look around. She must not see him, because she moves back slowly until she meets my gaze.

"Thank you." Her cheeks are flushed, freckles dancing over her rosy skin, and her eyes shine like morning dew on deep-green moss.

"No problem at all." My gaze drops to her full mouth, a mere breath away, and my lips tingle with the desperate temptation to taste hers.

Millie's tongue darts out to lick her lips, and it's agonizing to watch. That trunk full of feelings is leaking in my chest, threatening to drown my entire system.

"Millie." My voice is so deep and scratchy that I almost don't recognize it.

Her attention dips to my mouth for an instant before she jerks back into her seat. "We should probably get to work," she whispers, avoiding my eyes.

Suddenly realizing that I've tilted halfway to her seat, I take a deep breath and force myself all the way back into my own, trying to cool the heat coursing through me.

"Sounds good," I choke out, even though it doesn't. I'd rather stay here with her.

We both sling our bags over our shoulders, and I follow Millie out of the coffee shop. Under the gray morning sky, she scans the sidewalk and street like she's checking to make sure her ex is nowhere in sight.

I've never even seen this asshole, but I hate him.

Quite a few people are downtown this morning, walking in and out of shops and cafés. I shift to Millie's other side, near the street, and put my hand on her back to begin our walk toward the museum. I drove to Maggie's, but I'll walk with her, just in case she runs into *him* again.

"Are you sure you're okay?" I ask.

She sighs. "We broke up, like, six months ago, and I'm definitely over him. He has the sex appeal of a wet paper towel and the personality of a rock you keep stubbing your toe on."

I snort a laugh. "Oddly specific."

"I've had a lot of time to think about it," she grumbles. "I'm getting back to normal, though. I can finally look in the mirror and see myself. My natural wavy hair, my favorite clothes, and my genuine smile. I'm not the version he criticized and altered into what he wanted. And I feel so"—she pauses to look up at me—"peaceful without him." She tilts her head up to the sky like she's asking the universe, "So why do I panic when I see him or get a text from him?"

I touch her fingertips and pull her to a gentle stop under an antique store awning. She turns to me and doesn't try to pull her hand away, so I keep my fingers lightly against hers. "Toxic people will do that to you. Your brain can completely shut down around them to protect itself from those awful memories. But you don't owe him anything. Not a text, a conversation, or even a glance. He made you feel like you weren't good enough. Like you had to change for him. But you don't have to change for anyone."

Her lips press into a thin line. "You're right."

"Well, for the record, my therapist is right." I wince. "And it's still hard to remember that advice myself half the time."

Millie slides her fingers up my forearm, determination etched across her brow. "We deserve better than that."

"Yeah, we do." Our eyes lock, and on the busy street, surrounded by loud conversations and rumbling motors, our gazes are connected by an invisible, unbreakable force. It feels like we just unlocked a new phase of our relationship, and I'm not sure what it is, but I *want* it.

Fuck. All I do around her is *want*.

One side of her lips kicks up, and she lets her hand slip from my arm. We walk for a few minutes in comfortable silence before I ask about our Friday plans. "Are we still on for snickerdoodles tomorrow?"

Millie jumps a few steps ahead of me to turn around and walk backward. Her eyes sparkle with mischief. "Making cookies, we are. Be there, I will."

Chapter 14

Millie

Fucking Kyle. Maggie's is supposed to be a safe place. He doesn't live or work near here. So why the hell was he so close? There are plenty of coffee shops on his side of town. But instead, he shows up at my favorite place and derails my entire day.

My anger must be palpable because Micah steps in front of me, his sturdy shoulders towering over mine before he stoops to meet my eyes.

He's built like a solid brick wall, and I could probably punch him and he wouldn't even flinch. But he's like Ferdinand the Bull—intimidating on the outside and a soft, gooey cinnamon roll on the inside.

"Can I take these babies from you?" He gently removes my clenched fingers from today's shipment of butterfly chrysalises.

Once they're safely in his hands, he breathes a sigh of relief. He sets the tray on a cart before guiding me over to the bench against the lab's wall. "What's wrong? Steam is practically blowing from your ears."

With a weary sigh, I tell him everything that took place this morning while he listens, covering my hand with his when I start picking at my nails anxiously.

"Wow, Mills. That's a lot to go through before eight o'clock in the morning."

"I know," I groan, leaning my cheek on his arm. "The universe really said, 'You think you're doing okay? Try this.'"

He chuckles softly and nods. "Finn is right, you know? Kyle deserves absolutely nothing from you."

The events of this morning have had my relationship with Kyle playing on a loop in my head. Being with him was like a strangling fog that I couldn't find my way out of. I was searching for lights or people or anything to guide my way, but he was shielding my eyes the whole time. I had to blindly crawl my way out and hope I'd find solid ground under me once the fog cleared.

"I need a distraction," I say, lifting my head. "Let's have a game night tonight."

"I'm in." He smiles. "I'll text Emil."

***

Oaks Folks

Mom: Got an email that Christmas pajamas are on sale. I chose my two favorites. You all can vote on your choice for this year's family Christmas pajamas.

Tess: It's summer.

Mom: Hence why they're on sale.

Dad: No onesies this year. I'm too old to get in and out of those.

Mom: Okay, here are pictures of the options. Christmas cookies that say "Let's Get Baked" or dancing turtles dressed as Santa.

Fabes: Mom. Let's Get Baked? Really?

Mom: What? Look how cute the cookies are.

Tess: Somebody else tell her.

Dad: I vote turtles.

Millie: Getting baked refers to being under the influence of something, most likely weed, Mom.

Fabes: I vote Let's Get Baked.

Tess: Same.

Mom: I didn't know that. Not those.

Mom: Here's a picture of another option: light blue with candy canes.

Fabes: MOM. Zoom in on those candy canes.

Dad: Those aren't candy canes, honey. They're dicks.

Fabes: 💀

> **Millie:** Honestly, Mom. What website are you on?

> **Tess:** I still vote for Let's Get Baked.

* * *

"Em, can you hand me that vodka?" Micah waves from the corner of my kitchen, eyes focused on the tumblers in front of him while he mixes the drinks for game night.

Emil grabs the bottle and holds it behind his back with his lips puckered toward Micah. "Payment, please."

Micah leaves his position in front of the counter to reach his arm around Emil, dip him back, and kiss him as he steals the bottle.

"Thanks, love," he murmurs before he turns to fill the tumblers.

Emil lifts a hand to fan his face.

"Damn. I need a boyfriend," I mutter into my cranberry vodka. The charcuterie board I've put together is not as flawless as I've seen on the internet, but it's about to get destroyed by all of us anyway. It's hard to make it look perfect when everyone keeps sneaking off with grapes and cheese.

Lena sits at the dining table, whispering to a new game-night attendee next to her. Diego is an intern at the community center where Lena works this summer and is here through an exchange program from Spain. His brown eyes stare into Lena's, completely enthralled by whatever she's saying.

"Which game are we playing first?" Micah calls through the house.

"Anything but Scrabble," Lena proclaims.

Emil smiles brightly. "I'm always up for kicking your asses at

Scrabble." As a literature professor, he wipes the floor with us every time. We have a three-year-old's vocabulary compared to him.

I pick up my phone where it's charging in the kitchen, and my shoulders slump when I see Finn hasn't answered the text I sent him this afternoon.

> **Mille:** I know it's late notice, but we're having a game night if you and the girls want to come. We are starting around six, and we have pizza, snacks, and drinks. Here's our address in case you can make it.

Chills snake down my spine every time I think about his lips brushing my ear this morning. The warm assurance of his strong hand along my back while his body surrounded mine, keeping me safe. The rumble of his deep voice coasting over my skin.

As much as I want to melt into the memories of Finn, I'm still adamantly trying to avoid those exact kinds of thoughts about him. I try to remind myself every day that things can't get any more complicated with him. I've toed the line of appropriateness for weeks now, but I've never crossed it.

And I have managed to snuff out the urge to talk about my job with him, but the words still burn on the tip of my tongue.

How was my interview?

Can you tell me anything about the other applicant?

What can I do better next time?

Micah calls from the table that it's time to start, shaking me from my thoughts of Finn, and I abandon my phone to join the game of Clue.

* * *

"KNEW IT," I whoop in victory, slamming the cards down and smiling as I look around the table of losers. "Colonel Mustard, you tricky bastard."

Lena tosses her cards and crosses her arms. "Emil, look at her paper. What is she writing down?"

I snatch up my secret weapon before anyone can see the notes. "You'll never know," I yell, running to the trash and tearing the paper into tiny pieces.

A soft knock rattles against the door, and once the last bit of evidence floats safely into the trash can, I walk to answer it. I expect it to be the pizza guy, but when I open the door, Finn, Avery, and Eloise stand atop our Come Back With Tacos doormat.

"We didn't know about the taco rule." Finn winces.

"That's okay. Friends are the exception." Embarrassment colors my cheeks at how massive my smile is, but I can't seem to contain it. I crouch to hug Ave and El. "It's so good to see you."

"Is it still okay that we came?" Finn's brows pull together as I stand, and I want to smooth my fingers over the crease to relax them.

"Absolutely. Come in!" I cheer, bringing the girls into the living room.

Finn runs his fingers through his hair and clears his throat. "Sorry we're late. I wanted to stop and get some snacks and drinks." He sets a canvas bag on the counter and starts pulling things out of it. Goldfish, a bottle of wine, fruit snacks, oranges, vanilla wafers, and granola bars. He places them in a neat line and shrugs. "I let Ave and El pick out most of it."

"It's perfect." I pat his arm before I can stop myself. My brain seems to be stuck on a record scratch after this morning, where all it does is repeat, "Touch him, touch him, touch him."

Micah walks into the kitchen, shakes Finn's hand, and helps get bowls for the snacks, while I take Finn to make introductions.

The girls are already sitting on the ground with Lena, diving into the Legos.

Emil stands and pats Finn on the shoulder. "Nice to meet you. Good thing you showed up. We're about to start Catan, and Micah always destroys us. We need a new competitor."

"I'll see what I can do." Finn chuckles, pulling pieces out of the box to help us set up.

Micah places a few bowls of snacks on the coffee table before he sits beside Diego to teach him how to play.

Pepper's nails click on the wood floors as she shuffles down the hallway, finally up from her nap in my bed.

"Finn?" I lean closer from the seat next to him. "How are the girls with dogs? Pepper's an old lady, and she's great with kids, but if they don't like dogs, I can put her up."

His lips tip up as he looks my way. "They love dogs. They've been begging for one for months. I'll have to double-check my car before we leave to make sure they didn't sneak her in there."

"Honestly, she would love that."

I call her over, and she sits right between us, immediately dropping her muzzle into Finn's lap.

The little traitor.

He cups her face. "Pepper. It's very nice to meet you." He smooths a hand over her back. "Such a soft pup." Her tail thumps against the ground while she looks up at him with complete adoration, a perfect depiction of the heart-eyes emoji. He kisses the top of her head. "What a good girl," he coos at her.

I bite the inside of my cheek.

Am I jealous of my dog right now? Have I stooped that low?

Damn it.

Standing, I pat her side and nudge her toward the living room. "Let's go meet the girls."

Avery's and Eloise's eyes light up when they see her. She sniffs their faces and makes herself comfortable between them, rolling over and arching her back for belly rubs.

Once the pizza arrives, we eat around our game of Catan. The laughter and banter at the table have distracted me from realizing that Finn is a few points ahead of everyone else, but then he sets his final piece down with a sturdy thud and announces he's won.

A collective gasp fills the room.

"No way," Micah says, scanning the board and tracking the scores. Finn flips over three cards in front of him, revealing his extra points. "Well, damn. Good job." He claps Finn on the shoulder.

"So, Spock." I nudge him with my elbow as he helps put his pieces away. "Seems you've played this game before."

He adjusts his glasses before turning to me with a raised eyebrow. "Spock? Really?" he asks, his stern voice making me grin.

"I like it." I shrug.

Finn wears a playful scowl as he says, "Well, Cookie, if you must know, I was the Catan champion for Wilhelmina University. I held the title all four years of undergrad."

His use of my so-called stripper name sends a bubbly thrill up my spine. "Is that a real thing?"

A pink flush creeps up his cheeks as he says, "I take board games very seriously. I'd never lie about that."

"You mean to tell me I thought you were *here* on the Nerd Scale." I hold my hand flat just above the table. "But you're actually *here*." I stand and put my arm up as high as I can.

Finn laughs and shakes his head. "I could tell you things that would make my rating even higher."

I lean my elbow on his broad shoulder. "Oh, do tell."

He's so deliciously tall that, in this position, our eyes are almost level. His are like the dark blue sky that lingers before sunrise. His hair is in disheveled waves, and I wish I could run my fingers through it.

"I have to keep *some* secrets," he says softly, his voice like velvet on my skin as his eyes connect with mine. My pulse skitters, and the air between us settles hot and heady.

When Finn and I lock eyes like this, I have the dizzying feeling that I'm lost and home all at once. I'm in unfamiliar territory and yet completely safe.

I realize the game cleanup has paused, and I drag my attention away from Finn to find everyone staring at us. Lena wears a satisfied smirk like she knows exactly what's going on in my head.

Diego looks between us quizzically. "This"—he points to Finn—"is your . . . boyfriend, Millie?" he questions with his strong Spanish accent.

Chills flash over my heated body. I drop into my seat with a falsely bright smile. "Oh, no, just friends." I shake my head incredulously. "Not together at all. Gosh, nowhere *near* anything like that. Like, we could never be!"

Surely I can make it true if I keep saying it. I can put us back on the safe side of that line I was sticking an arm over. I can remind myself we are *just friends*.

I glance over at Finn, finding him biting his lips between his teeth to suppress his smile.

Lena shakes her head with a delighted grin, and Micah won't make eye contact with me, his hand covering his mouth and cheeks. Emil snickers into his cranberry vodka.

Their expressions register, and my throat dries. It seems that after everything I just said, my best friends are acting like I just declared that he *is* my boyfriend.

My pulse pounds so loudly I can hear it booming through my body.

It feels like I just revealed every perfect thought I've ever had about Finn. I don't know where I went wrong, but I need to put it all back and undo it.

The first thing I think of blurts from my lips.

"I have a date on Saturday."

Finn's head snaps in my direction, dark eyes searching my face. He wears his trademark Finn scowl that used to be the only expression I got from him, and my breath stalls in my lungs.

"With . . . Finn?" Diego asks.

I bark a laugh to cover my tracks. "No. Not with Finn. Someone else."

Shit. Shit. Shit. I don't want to dig this hole deeper, but my mouth keeps moving before my mind can catch up.

Lena puts her chin on her hand and blinks at me across the table. "Who do you have a date with?"

"Someone I met. You weren't there." I cringe deep inside my brain.

A low rumble creeps from Finn's chest, but I try my best to ignore him as I announce, "We're going to Nacho Mama's."

Lena folds her arms over her chest and leans back in her seat casually. "How wild is that? I have a date there Saturday too." Her smile is full of mischievous danger.

My expression is as casual as I can muster in light of the lies I'm drowning in. "Perfect. Maybe I'll see you there."

Finn abruptly shoves his chair back with a loud scrape and trudges to the kitchen, muttering something under his breath.

Lena meets my eyes across the table and winks.

Chapter 15

Finn

*M*y knuckles are bleached white from squeezing the granite counter. I'm trying to rein in whatever is happening right now, but it's like a waterfall of jealousy washing over me, pelting my shoulders, and I can't get out from under it.

I made it all the way to Millie's kitchen before I realized I couldn't make myself the drink I was craving. A couple of shots sound good right now, but I settle for a swig of cranberry juice so I can drive the girls home safely.

Everyone at the table is back to talking and laughing, but all I can do is stand here, forcing my breath to return to normal while my jaw aches from how hard I'm clenching it.

When Millie opened the door this evening with her dazzling smile, realization collided into my heart like a freight train.

I want to be around this woman every day. Her presence feels like the storm clouds are parting. Like the sun is finally shining over me, brightening my day. And these sporadic moments together aren't enough.

I've loved watching her laugh and talk trash with her friends this evening. They're so welcoming that it almost feels like they're *my* friends.

But then she announced she has a date on Saturday, and everything in my brain froze like a computer glitch. I couldn't even refocus on the conversation because my mind was stuck on an image of some lucky asshole watching her across a candlelit table while she smiles for him and teases him with her smart mouth.

I hate it.

Fuck this guy.

"Uncle Finn?" Ave appears next to me and yawns as she leans her head on my hip. "I'm weely sleepy."

I lift her into my arms, and she drops her cheek onto my shoulder. "Sounds like I need to get you to bed, *piccola*."

The term of endearment always reminds me of my sister. My grandparents called Clara "little one" in Italian even in the hospital after she'd had her own little girls.

I walk into the living room and look toward the Legos, but Eloise isn't there. Instead, I find her curled up in Millie's lap, sound asleep with her face pressed into Millie's neck.

My breath catches for a moment because Eloise looks so *right* there. Comfortable enough to go to sleep without me, safe in Millie's arms.

Millie must feel me watching her and meets my eyes, a soft smile on her lips. She pulls El closer and whispers, "She's so sweet, Finn. I can't even take it."

I can't either.

Instead, I say, "I'm going to pack up and get these girls home to bed."

Emil jumps up from the table. "I'll get your stuff. You have precious cargo there." He rubs Avery's back as he passes and walks into the kitchen.

I glance over the mess the girls left on the floor and move to set Ave on the couch to clean it up, but Millie's voice stops me.

"Don't worry about it. I'll get it all later," she assures me before she stands with a groan and carries Eloise to the front door. It's almost comical watching someone a foot shorter than me carry a kid the same size as the one in my arms.

A quiet, clear night greets us as Millie, Emil, and I walk to my SUV in the driveway. Emil drops my bag in the front, and Millie and I put the girls in their booster seats on opposite sides of the car before we shut the doors as quietly as possible.

Emil reaches his arms out for a hug. "Come back soon. Micah needs someone to take him down a notch."

"Will do. We had a great time."

Then Emil returns to the house, leaving Millie and me standing quietly at the back of my car.

Her gaze drops to the dented fender, and she bites her lip. "You should get that fixed."

I visually trace the damage she left when she collided with me a few weeks ago. It felt like such a damning day, in more ways than one, and I haven't wanted to erase the evidence.

She left a similar indentation on my heart, and I haven't been able to erase that evidence either.

"I'm glad we came, Cookie," I say lightly, trying to make her smile. A burst of joy fills my heart when she does.

"Me too, Spock." She beams up at me. "I'm bringing my A game next time, though. I need to bring down the king of Catan."

Every muscle in my body screams for me to wrap my arms around her in a hug and never let her go. I could innocently press our bodies together in a normal, friendly embrace. There would be barely any physical contact, and it might satisfy my need to touch her.

But Millie backs away, and I've missed my chance.

"Have a good evening," she says, taking backward steps toward her house while her eyes stay on mine. Something tightens in my chest as the distance grows between us.

"Good night, Millie," I tell her reluctantly.

On the way home, El's and Ave's deep breaths keep me company. I look in the rearview mirror at their sleepy faces, and Clara floods my mind.

Sometimes Avery's laugh sounds so much like Clara's that my heart stops. And Eloise has her mama's untamed, wavy hair that I can't find the motivation to brush. It reminds me too much of my view as a kid, when I followed my big sister around like a shadow.

She was my best friend for thirty-three years of my life. We were a team, conspiring against our parents any chance we got. She read me bedtime stories and tucked me in, like I'm doing for her girls now. All we had was each other.

When she got pregnant, her boyfriend at the time decided he didn't want any part in it. He left her the day she told him about the babies, and she immediately called me in tears.

Those little girls have been my favorite people ever since.

Would Clara be okay with the bond they're forming with Millie? Would she be happy they have someone they trust and like spending time with? Or would she feel replaced?

Millie's company feels like warm embers settling into my soul. They're glowing and radiant, and they give me the motivation to keep digging out of the hole of grief that consumes me sometimes. And I know the girls feel it too. They get excited to see her, with bright, enthusiastic smiles that have been hard to come by the last few months.

The girls will never stop missing their mama, but hopefully, Clara would be happy that Millie's presence is soothing the sting a little.

Chapter 16

Millie

This dating app is pointless. Why are all these men either holding fish or posing shirtless on a motorcycle?

I tilt my head, considering one. He's not so bad, and his tattoos are sexy, but he's more Tessa's type. I take a screenshot and send it to her.

With a sigh, I pull my feet onto my desk chair and continue swiping mindlessly through profiles. I have no idea if anyone believed me about my date tomorrow, but I need to find one for myself, to prove these thoughts of Finn can be extinguished. He can't be the only person who makes my heart pound and my cheeks hurt from smiling.

Micah strides into the office from his lunch break. "Hey. Emil and I just went to that sandwich shop that opened down the road. Bubs and Subs?" He groans as he drops into his chair. "That sandwich changed my life."

"Oh yeah?" I reply, eyes still on my phone.

"I got their Knuckle Sandwich, which is a twist on a Reuben, where they add pickled red onions and cream cheese."

"Mmm." I'm still focused on my screen when Tessa responds with eight panting and drooling emoji.

"And Henry Cavill was there." That breaks my focus, and I flit my gaze up to find Micah with a questioning look. "What's wrong with you?"

Groaning, I set my phone on my desk. "I did a bad thing yesterday, and I don't know how to undo it."

His brows pinch. "I'm your most sensible friend, right?"

I tilt my head back and forth. "You tie with Emil."

"Fair, but he's not here. You've got me." He rolls his chair up beside mine. "Tell me what happened, and I'll try my best to help you fix it."

I take a deep breath before admitting, "I lied. I don't have a date tomorrow."

Micah's roaring laugh practically shakes the building. He throws his head back and cackles at the ceiling, way longer than is appropriate in this dire situation.

Crossing my arms, I glare at him. "Are you done?"

"We all knew you were lying." He pats my leg with a sympathetic smile. "You're the worst liar on this continent."

I glare harder, giving my best impersonation of Finn's grumpy scowl. Honestly, I don't know what's worse. Everyone believing me or no one believing me?

Micah shakes his head and grins. "But let me tell you the best part. Dr. Finn Ashford did believe you and, honey, he did *not* like it."

"How do you know that?"

"He had the look of a man going out of his mind thinking about you on a date with someone else."

My stomach flips uncomfortably. "I . . . I don't know . . ."

Micah is excellent at reading people, and I would usually take his word for things like this. One time, he was giving a tour through the butterfly vivarium, and by the end, he had played matchmaker with two of the guests and they got married there a year later. So we frequently tease him about being able to see a potential couple before anyone else.

But this is different. This is me. And Finn. There's no way he cared that much.

The room feels a little like it's spinning.

"Trust me—he may not exactly understand it yet. But he'll get there. And you will too." He gives me a cheeky smile and rolls his chair back behind his desk. "Want to take me on a date tomorrow? I'm available, and I happen to love Nacho Mama's."

This might be a cheat code, but I'll take it. I nod.

"Perfect. I'll tell Emil he's sharing me for the evening." He picks up his phone to send a text.

My phone vibrates with a message, and I pull it from my bag, thinking it'll be a group text from Micah.

But it's not.

> **Kyle:** I've been trying to talk to you, and it's bullshit that you won't answer me. If you keep ignoring me, I'll have to find some other way to get a hold of you.

My hands shake and my heartbeat whooshes through my ears as I read the message again.

His texts have gotten progressively worse over the last few weeks, and I don't want to know what they might escalate to. But it feels like he wins when I spend so much time thinking about him, so I shove my phone away.

* * *

A WARM BREEZE blows my hair in my face as I sling the bag of cookie ingredients over my shoulder and trudge up the steps to Finn's house.

He answers the door with a small, conspiratorial grin. "The girls want you to find them," he says, pulling the door open wide for me to come inside.

"Oh, okay."

Taking the bag from my shoulder, he leans in and whispers against my ear, "If you listen for a second, you can probably hear them giggling in anticipation." Shivers race over my neck and shoulders as his breath tickles my skin.

He pulls back and winks, and I decide it should be illegal for handsome men to wink. It might give an unsuspecting woman a heart attack.

Finn carries the cookie ingredients into the kitchen, while I tiptoe around the living room. I listen for a second, and sure enough, snickering echoes from the dining room.

But I don't want to find them too quickly, so I pick up pillows on the couch and move blankets around, talking to myself.

"I bet they're here. Oh, no . . . Here? Darn it, not there either. Where are they?" The more I strike out, the louder their giggles get.

When I reach the edge of the couch, my gaze lands on Finn. He leans against the wall, watching me search the room. His arms are crossed over his navy blue shirt, and the muscles in his shoulders and arms bulge against the fabric like they could bust through if he flexed too hard.

His dark eyes scan me from my white eyelet tank top and down my flowy rust-colored skirt, before stopping on my strappy sandals.

My body pulls toward him like I'm a fish on a hook, and he reels me in with little effort.

I stop a foot from him, and he licks his lips. "Hello, Millie." His voice is like molten chocolate running over my skin, and my body hums with how delicious it sounds.

He lifts a finger, and my breath stops as he touches my shoulder. "Sometimes I think about those butterflies on your dress the day you spilled coffee on me." He leisurely glides his fingertip along my collarbone, and the featherlight touch leaves a flushed trail of heat in its wake.

When he reaches the hollow of my throat, he makes a soft circle there. My whole body instantly reacts, my mouth popping open and warmth pooling low in my belly. A powerful ache swarms through my veins, and I find myself wishing and hoping he would keep touching me. Keep making me burn like this.

I'm pretty sure my whole body just jumped so far over the friendship line that I've lost sight of the boundary.

But I can't find it in myself to look for it right this second.

His teeth dig into his bottom lip, and a knowing smile blooms on his mouth, like he can see all my thoughts in the air between us.

"Millie," El shouts from the dining room, her voice bouncing off the walls to reach me. "Are you still looking for us?"

Finn's concentration on my throat breaks, and he meets my gaze, his eyes sparkling with something I can't identify. His focus drops to my lips for a beat before he steps back and swallows.

I blink a few times, trying to clear whatever just happened. Forcing a deep breath through my tight lungs, I sneak into the dining room.

Excited whispers sound from under the table, but I want to draw out their suspense, so I start opening drawers in the buffet. Avery and Eloise snicker like they believe I think they're hiding in a drawer big enough to hold only a few tablecloths.

When I get to the bottom drawer, I close it slowly and whip around. I meet Avery's wide eyes under the table—and both girls shriek at the top of their lungs, so loud and shrill that I'm sure the neighbors are wondering what's happening.

I nearly fall over laughing as they crawl between the dining chairs and launch themselves at me between fits of giggles.

"Why'd you scream so loud?" I ask when I finally manage to take a breath, the girls sprawled happily across me.

"You surprised us," El squeals.

Squeezing the girls closer, I whisper, "Want to make some cookies with me?"

"Yes!" they both cheer, jumping up and running to the kitchen.

I brush my skirt down, straighten my shirt, and run my hands over my hair to compose myself. When I make it to the kitchen, I find Finn standing with his back to the island. Avery and Eloise sit on the counter on each side of him, barely containing their excited smiles.

"We got you something," Finn says suspiciously, adjusting his glasses.

"It's a present," Avery squeaks, wiggling her little body like she can't stand to hold this inside much longer.

Finn twirls his finger in the air. "Turn around."

My body follows his orders before I give it permission. As he steps closer, I sense his presence right behind me, the heat radiating from him warming my back.

"I'm going to cover your eyes. Is that okay?" he asks gently, and I'm sure it's not supposed to sound sexual, but that's where my mind takes it anyway.

When I nod, he brings his hands over my eyes, and time stops. His scent wraps around me like a woodsy blanket, and I hope it soaks into my skin and stays on my clothes so I can inhale it later. Because right now, the temptation to lean back into his hard body is so enticing that I force myself not to take a breath in case it brings me in contact with his chest.

"Okay, turn back around," he whispers, and I shuffle my feet toward the counter.

"Now open," Eloise tells me.

Finn's hands glide over my face as he pulls them away to reveal a hunter-green KitchenAid mixer on the counter between the girls.

I step up to it and glide my hand over the cool top. "This is beautiful, girls," I whisper.

"We didn't buy it. Uncle Finn did," Eloise corrects me.

I chuckle under my breath and turn around to see Finn watching us. "Why?"

He shoves his hands into his pockets and lifts his shoulders in a shrug. "You wanted one," he states simply. "And I wanted to do something nice after everything you've done for us."

"I haven't done anything for you." The backs of my eyes burn as I try to convince him I don't deserve this.

He looks down at me with knitted brows. "You've done . . . everything. So much more than you know."

Chapter 17

Finn

Standing at the entrance to the kitchen, I watch Millie as she helps the girls measure sugar into the bowl of her new mixer. Ave and El sit on the counter on either side of the mixer, dancing and singing along with the Disney music that fills the house.

No matter how hard I try, I can't take my eyes off them. There's nothing that can hold my attention like Millie and the girls. They've put some sort of spell on me.

I went to three different stores looking for that mixer yesterday before game night, trying to find some way to thank her for everything she's done for us.

Maybe I wanted to be the one to put that beautiful smile on her face.

I think I'm addicted to it.

Add it to the ever-growing list of things about Millie that I'm addicted to.

The sound of her laugh, her teasing, her magnetic energy, the tilt of her lips when she's feeling sassy, her lemony scent, and the feeling of her lips on my neck from yesterday.

I'm starting to think the list will never end.

And I'm so fucking done trying to convince myself I want it to.

El drops an egg on the ground with a *splat*. "Oopsie," Millie sings. "I wish Pepper was here to clean that up for us."

"You should bring her next time," Avery says, licking her finger and dipping it in a pile of spilled sugar on the counter.

Millie wipes the egg up with a towel and helps El crack the next one into the bowl. "That's up to Uncle Finn. When I'm cooking at home, I drop a lot, so Pepper's always right by my feet."

"Uncle Finn likes dogs. He'll say you can bring her every day," Eloise says as she watches Avery's sugar method and mimics it.

I *wish* Millie could be here in our house every day.

That thought crashes into my chest, and I can't breathe around it.

Millie's eyes catch mine in the doorway, and I force myself to say something before she realizes I'm standing here watching them like a lovesick puppy.

"Let's order some dinner. What sounds good?" I ask, approaching their spot at the counter.

Millie licks her finger, hips swaying to the beat, and dips it in the sugar on the counter. "We're having cookies for dinner." She pops her finger into her mouth and smiles around it.

Fuck me. I want to be that finger.

My jaw clenches, and I have to school my face to remain neutral.

Eloise raises her arms in the air and chants, "Cookies for dinner, cookies for dinner!"

They're conspiring against me, and I can't even find it in myself to care as I narrow my eyes at the three of them. "Let's make a deal. I'll order some fried rice, and you can each have one cookie before it gets here, then more after you eat your dinner."

Millie leans in toward Avery and Eloise, and they whisper behind their hands. I fight a battle with my eyes, willing them not to wander over her mouthwatering curves.

But I lose.

The girls nod and make a few sounds of approval before Millie turns with a serious expression, acting as the ambassador for their trio.

"Deal." She offers her hand, and I shake it, a few grains of sugar gritty on her fingertips. The girls giggle behind her. "Thanks for doing business with us." She nods and then winks at me conspiratorially.

* * *

"This is a great house. It seems perfect for you guys," Millie says, sitting on the counter by the oven as she waits on the timer for the first batch of cookies.

The girls have distracted themselves with coloring books and crayons in the living room while we wait for dinner to arrive. I finish wiping down the counter and rinse the rag in the sink, trying to keep my hands occupied with cleanup. The busier I stay, the less likely I am to give in and touch Millie. Lust has been running rampant through my veins since my fingers grazed her collarbone, and I don't know how much longer I can avoid doing it again.

"Has it always been just the three of you here?" she asks.

"Yes. I'd recently broken up with my girlfriend when I bought it. We'd been dating for a few months, and we were starting to talk about buying a house together, but she didn't like the direction my life was going. She didn't want to sign on to live with two little girls." I turn to lean against the counter and take a deep breath, realizing it still makes me angry to think about that conversation. "Blessing in disguise. I found this house a few days after she left. It all worked out the way it was supposed to."

She twists her lips before asking, "Have you dated anyone since then?"

"No."

"Why? I mean, if you feel comfortable telling me." A blush stains her cheeks, like she's embarrassed to ask, and it's so fucking cute.

I rub my jaw and let my eyes trace her delicate freckles, emerald eyes, and those beautiful, full lips. "I haven't wanted to."

Until you.

"Oh." She dips her fingers into the bowl of cookie dough, bringing a clump to her mouth, and her tongue darts out to catch it. I'm completely riveted as her pink lips wrap around her fingertip before she glides it back out.

I clear my throat. "How's the dough?"

She takes another chunk from the bowl and *moans* at the taste this time, and I go light-headed.

Fuck.

"It's so good," she says, completely oblivious to what she's putting me through.

It's torture, yet I can't pull my gaze away from her mouth.

She picks up another chunk of dough, and all my restraint dissolves in an instant.

Fuck it.

I take two steps toward her, my hips bumping into her knees. My hand shoots out to grab her wrist, and her eyes dart to mine.

Holding her gaze, I pull her cookie-dough-covered thumb to my mouth and wrap my lips around it. Her eyes flare and her jaw falls open. I slide my tongue down her finger, catching the sweet dough and letting it melt in my mouth.

"Mmm." The sound is raspy, scraping out of my chest.

Millie stutters a breath, and I let my tongue swipe over her sweet skin one more time. Her pupils are blown wide, a thin ring of forest green around them as I slip her finger out of my mouth with a *pop*. A scarlet blush floods her cheeks, and when I follow the color down her neck, I find her chest rising and falling quickly.

My focus narrows to her lips, and I drift closer, desperate to taste her—

Beep. Beep. Beep.

Chapter 18

Millie

*T*he timer rings through the air, startling us both. Finn steps back, and I jump down to open the oven. I start to stick my hand in to grab the baking sheet but realize at the last minute that I forgot oven mitts.

"Where the hell are the oven mitts?" I turn in a circle, wiping my forehead with the back of my hand, completely frazzled.

Finn calmly opens the drawer beside me and slides his hands into them. "I can get it."

"Okay." I turn in a circle again. "I'm going to run to the bathroom," I blurt as Finn sets the cookie sheet on the stove.

Behind the safety of a closed bathroom door, I stare at my flustered reflection. I take in the thin layer of sweat dotting my forehead, my wild eyes, and the wavy strands of hair flying in every direction around my pink cheeks.

I look way too aroused for a woman baking cookies.

Maybe I need to give myself another pep talk. That seems to be a trend lately. It was only a handful of weeks ago that I was wiping coffee from my dress and trying to convince myself to put on blinders and ignore Finn's rude behavior.

But this time, the lecture is for my hormones.

Get it together, ladies.

Am I ovulating or something?

That cookie-dough-licking moment was hotter than any other event in my life. My body said, *Drag him to a bed.* Naughty Millie is on my shoulder, whisper-shouting terrible, wonderful things in my ear.

I mentally read through the list of reasons I'm supposed to stay far away from finger-licking and blushing and thinking about him constantly.

This guy is my coworker.

I'm trying to secure my dream job, and people are going to think I slept my way there if this goes *any* further.

I'm still healing from a bad relationship.

I pencil in one more item: he just said he doesn't want to date anyone.

Looking back into the mirror, I find my eyes are still heavy and hazy. How is my reaction to this man so quick and unavoidable? He looks at me, and lust races to the surface, regulating every movement and thought.

It's nearly painful to stop wanting him at this point. I've drawn the lines and held fast to the limits, but tonight feels like a disaster. Like I've just thrown it all away because the temptation is more than I can resist.

Remember why, Millie. Remember how important this job is to you and why he can never be anything more than your friend and coworker.

A knock pounds on the front door, presumably our dinner delivery, so I wash my hands and cross my fingers that I can maintain control of my libido for the remainder of the evening.

* * *

"IF I COULD be any animal in the world, I'd be a shark," Eloise says, shoveling a scoop of fried rice into her mouth. "Then everybody would be scared of me."

Finn snorts a laugh. "Most people already are, *piccola*," he teases.

She shoots him a dark glare that she must've learned from her uncle.

"What would you be, Ave?" I ask.

"A horse because they're pretty and they run fast," Avery answers.

"I'd probably eat you, then." Eloise shrugs.

"No." Avery shakes her head. "I could run away."

"But my teeth would bite your leg before you started running."

"But you can't chase me on land. You can only swim."

"I could jump really high out of the water and land on top of you. With my teeth." Eloise snaps her teeth together to punctuate the point.

"Geez, this is getting violent." I wince.

Avery sets down her spoon, giving this her full attention. "Then I won't stay by the ocean. I'll only drink out of rivers and lakes."

Eloise nods, seemingly stumped by how to win that one.

"Why are we talking about eating Avery?" Finn wonders, glancing between the girls.

Eloise waves this off. "I don't want to eat Avery. But if I was a shark, I wouldn't know she was my sister, so I would eat the horse because I was hungry. Sharks are super hungry."

Finn nods. "They don't tend to eat many land mammals—unless you are a seal or sea lion."

Avery shakes her head. "No, just a horse."

"Pretty sure you're safe, then," I say with a giggle.

Eloise stops eating and leans to wrap an arm around Avery. "Don't turn into a seal or a sea lion, okay? Promise?"

"Promise," Avery confirms.

I stifle my laugh with a sip of water.

Avery scans Finn's face. "Uncle Finn would be a wolf," she finally decides.

He straightens his shoulders. "Because I'm strong and protective?"

"Nope. Because you sounded like a wolf when you smashed your fingers in the car door last time. You howled, remember?"

He shakes his head, but there's a playful smile dancing across his lips. "You're gonna get it for that one."

Both girls drop their spoons like those are the code words to jump into action. They leap from their chairs to tickle him as he scoots back and traps them both in his arms with an evil villain laugh. Avery and Eloise squeal as they try to fight against him, and Finn scoops them up under his arms and carries them to the couch, dropping them in a fit of giggles.

When he makes it back to his chair, his cheeks are rosy, his eyes bright.

"Those girls adore you," I tell him.

He glances over his shoulder toward the living room. "I adore the hell out of them."

"Did they get to sleep okay after game night yesterday?"

He nods. "They didn't even wake up when I brought them to their beds. They want to come back for another one."

I smile. "You're all welcome back to the next one. We had a blast."

Finn's gaze scans my face, drops over my shoulders, then runs across my collarbone, and I shiver at the phantom feeling of his finger there earlier. Silence stretches between us, and I wonder if he's remembering that moment too.

A muscle pops in his jaw. "You have a date tomorrow," he says, low and gravelly.

Heat burns in my cheeks. "I think so."

"You think?" A crease splits his brows.

I nod, squirming in my seat. "I'm going on a date." This feels like a lie since my "date" is with Micah, but I'm not sure how to change it at this point. My palms sweat from the intensity of his stare, and I want to simply breathe out the truth. Let the words cleanse the air between us and reduce the pressure on my lungs.

But this is a definitive reason to stay away from each other. It's already laid out there for me because I accidentally blurted it. I can't fall any further into his charm because I have a date. Therefore, no more fingers in mouths. Period.

He runs a palm over his beard and shakes his head. His mouth is a tense line as he thinks through something. Finally, he pushes his plate to the side and leans his elbows on the table.

"Go on a date with me instead." His voice is so sure. So clear.

My eyes flare as my stomach flips. That statement is nowhere near the list of possible responses to what I said. "What?"

One side of his lips kicks up. "Go on a date with me. Please."

That *please* almost melts all my resistance, but I take a deep breath and strengthen my resolve. "I can't."

He stands, grabs the back of his chair, and slides it around the corner of the table to set it beside mine. He sits facing me and drops his elbows to his knees. "Why?"

The confusion in his eyes has my shoulders slumping. "I just can't. We work together, and we're friends. And I thought you said you didn't want to date anyone."

Grabbing the outsides of my knees, he turns me ninety degrees until I'm facing him, his thighs bracketing mine. It's a little cocoon, like in the coffee shop. Protective and comforting, in our own little world.

"Millie, I want to go on a date with *you*. Not *anyone*. Just you."

The idea of going on a date with him fills my stomach with butterflies. It sounds way better than Chad from Tinder with his two-foot catfish, and I'd momentarily considered wasting my time with that guy.

But Finn is different. The rules here are worlds apart.

If he was just a random person I bumped into, I could consider saying yes to him. I could enjoy the fact that he's asking me out. He'd be the kind of person that—I'm scared to admit—might mean something to me. Going on a date with him might change the trajectory of my life.

But he's *not* a random person I met somewhere else. He's a man who sits on the hiring committee for a promotion to my dream job. And while I've avoided thinking about that as we've become friends, we definitely can't be more than that while he is in charge of my job prospects. It's not right.

"I've been wanting you since I saw you in that elevator the very first time," he whispers. "Then you came here and lit up our house and our life, and I think I'm addicted to it." His grip on my knees tightens, like he can't help it.

"Finn." I sigh, clenching my hands into fists. "You can't say things like that."

He clasps my fists in his, and I glance down at them—his big, strong hands holding my smaller ones, and his thumbs rubbing little circles on the backs until they relax. The motion blazes a searing path straight to my core. "But I mean it."

I shake my head. "It makes my brain fuzzy, and I can't remember why I was trying to stay on this side of the friendship line I drew."

He pulls a hand away from mine and cups my jaw in his palm. "Well, every word is true." My eyes fall closed at the light graze of his thumb over my cheek. His fingers slide into the hair behind my ear, and I can't stop my head from leaning into his touch. Tingles race up my neck and into my scalp. "And I want to make you feel the same way you make me feel."

I already know I have to tell him no, but his touch feels so good. I want to hold on to this moment where I feel warm and safe and close to him. Hide it in my heart for days when I'm feeling like the world is dark and lonely.

When I open my eyes, I find him watching me with so much raw honesty that I almost throw away all my convictions. My chest aches to lean forward and press my lips to his.

But I regain control of myself.

"I can't date you. As much as my brain and body are screaming at me to say yes, I can't give in. You know how important this promotion is for me."

"Yes, but—" he starts, but I silence him with my fingers over his lips.

"No *buts*." Finn grins behind my fingers, but I ignore it to trudge on. "I'm also putting myself back together after my last relationship, and I don't think I'm ready for something new. I'm scared I'll get lost again."

He nods, eyes searching mine, and I drop my fingers from his mouth.

Taking a deep breath, I steel myself before admitting the last bit. I look down at my lap because it'll be easier if I can't see his eyes. "I don't have a date tomorrow. I made it up because I was so anxious about everyone seeing us together last night. I didn't want them to know I can't stop thinking about you."

His warm, deep laugh encircles me, and I lift my gaze because I can't resist seeing how it lights up his face. His eyes sparkle with mirth, smile lines accentuated around them.

"Do you know how jealous I was?"

I scoff. "You aren't je—"

"Hell yes, I was. You feel like mine, and the thought of you with someone else was driving me out of my mind."

You feel like mine.

Those words hit my heart like lightning, singing through my veins.

He places a finger under my chin and tips it up gently. "Did you say you can't stop thinking about me?" When I press my lips together and nod, the intensity of his smile steals my breath. "It's okay. I'm patient. I can wait until you're ready."

* * *

Oaks Folks

Mom: Wanted to let you all know that I put together an Amazon wish list for my birthday coming up. Here's the link.

Tess: You think we need a wish list?

Mom: Just want to make sure you have some gift ideas.

Tess: I can't afford to get you this $300 dog DNA test.

Fabes: And I refuse to get you a shirt that says, "I'm not like a regular mom. I'm a cool mom." Have you even seen Mean Girls?

Mom: Is that a movie? I just liked the shirt.

Tess: <GIF of Mean Girls scene>

> **Millie:** I call the mug that says, "My favorite child got me this."

> **Tess:** Too bad, I already ordered it.

> **Dad:** This will go down in history as your mother's most beloved day: when her daughters battled to be the favorite.

* * *

"How DID THE cookies turn out last night, Mills?" Lena asks, dipping a chip in our guacamole and popping it into her mouth.

Lena didn't *actually* have plans to come to Nacho Mama's, but Micah and I pulled her and Emil along with us for a double date.

"Good." I take a sip of my sparkling water and squirm in my bright orange chair.

I've been bursting to tell them every detail of what happened last night.

Probably best if I just rip the Band-Aid off.

As the soft Latin guitar music ends, I just say it. A little too loudly. "Finn licked cookie dough off my finger."

Heat spreads over every inch of my skin as everyone in the cantina turns my way. Lena chokes into her elbow. Micah spews margarita out of his mouth, hitting the appetizer plate in front of him. And Emil's glass clatters to the table, barely keeping its balance.

The next song comes on, a little livelier, and Lena regains the ability to speak first, her eyes wide. "I'm sorry. Finn? Licked? Your finger?"

"Yeah, those were the main parts of that sentence." Micah nods as he brings a napkin to his lips.

Emil waves his hands in front of his face. "Start at the beginning."

I tell them about the mixer—which I left at his house for now because I couldn't wrap my head around taking home such an expensive gift—how nice it felt to have Ave and El next to me making cookies, and every vivid detail of Finn's warm mouth around my finger. I also admit to hyperventilating afterward.

Lena fans herself with her hand. "Wow. For once, I'm speechless. Does he still think you're on a date right now?"

My shoulders slump. "I told him the truth." I dig my teeth into my bottom lip before adding, "And then he asked me to go on a date with him."

Micah smacks his hand over his chest and coughs, "The hits keep coming."

"He wants to go on a date with you, and you're out with us?" Lena's shrill voice rings in my ears. "We love you, but none of us are going to drop to our knees for you like that man would."

My cheeks flame. "I still can't date him."

"Why?" everyone choruses at once.

"Two reasons." I hold up a finger. "One. He's on the hiring committee for my promotion. I'm not sleeping my way to that job."

"Millie," Lena interjects with a devious grin. "Everyone loves a forbidden relationship." She wiggles her eyebrows up and down.

I ignore her and continue, adding a finger to my count. "Second, I don't know if I'm ready to date after Kyle. You were all there for the aftermath of that, and sometimes I don't know if I have my head on straight yet. He ruined my self-esteem so badly, chipping away at it until I had lost who I was. What if that's just how I am in relationships? What if I don't notice it when it happens again?"

The mood around the table shifts, sobering to a calm quiet. And in the silence, the sound of *his* voice echoes in my brain.

You've put on some weight.

If you stop by my office, you need to wear one of the outfits I picked out.

You're crazy if you think I'm taking you somewhere looking like that.

Why do you need to see your family again?

Oh, stop crying. I was just having a little fun.

I always brushed it off. Disregarded the words because he said he loved me. I convinced myself that's just what boyfriends do sometimes.

But slowly, I couldn't find myself anymore. I lost track of all the things that made me *me*. Everything I did was to please him, and even when I gave it all my best effort, there was always something else he wanted to change.

My friends and family were all searching for the wound, trying to figure out what was wrong, but I couldn't tell them where it was, because I didn't even know how to find it myself.

Emil covers my hand with his. "Has Finn made you feel that way? Like you're losing yourself?"

I shake my head, wiping a tear that falls down my cheek. "Never. Not at all."

Lena stands and wraps her arms around me. "How you felt in your relationship with Kyle is on *him*. It wasn't you in any way."

"She's right," Micah agrees. "I wish that shithead was here so we could all take a swing at him."

Emil nods. "A hard knee to the balls."

Lena kneels next to me, her jeans hitting the gummy linoleum floors. She grabs my cheeks in her hands and turns me to face her. "His manipulating and gaslighting and control issues didn't break you, Mills. You are strong in spite of him—in spite of everything you went through. And wouldn't it be the best retribution to get your own happily ever after one day? Because you will. Whether it's now or in ten years, you'll be in a healthy, loving, stable relationship, and he'll still belong in a dumpster with the rest of the trash." She wipes away the tears dripping from my eyes, her fierce expression holding me captive.

"But what if I'm not tough like you? You're the one graced with all the bravery and strength."

"You don't have to be the loudest in the room to be the strongest. You're as brave and strong as me—you simply don't believe it yet. But we'll show you. We'll cheer for you and encourage you until you realize what we've always seen."

I nod, trying my best to believe her.

"Can we do an experiment?" Lena asks, putting her hands on my knees.

"What kind of experiment?" I ask skeptically.

"Just a visualization exercise." She gives a casual shrug.

A collective groan resounds from Micah, Emil, and me.

"You and your visualizations," I grumble.

Lena smiles. "I think you'll like this one."

"Fine." I let my eyes drift closed, already knowing exactly what she's going to tell me to do. Lena believes in the power of visualizing and manifesting much more than I do, but I humor her occasionally.

"Take a deep breath," she whispers. "And then you're going to picture your future. Don't think too hard about it—just let whatever comes up flow naturally through your thoughts. Don't fight it either. I know how you are." She pokes my knee, but I keep my eyes shut.

"Okay," I mutter, almost nervous to see what future my subconscious is dreaming up.

"Go ahead. See what comes to mind," she encourages.

I take a deep breath and let the sounds of the cantina become static in my ears as I try to concentrate on summoning an image of what I want in the future.

Immediately, my mind betrays me by giving me a picture of Finn and me in bed.

My shoulders tense, and I almost open my eyes to end it, but Lena soothes her hands over mine and whispers, "Keep going. Let it happen."

Swallowing the urge to argue with her, I recenter my thoughts. It feels like I'm trying to focus a pair of binoculars on a distant view, and when the image finally clears, I can't breathe.

Finn and I are under a navy duvet, waking up slowly to the morning sunlight trickling through white curtains. My head rests on his bare chest, my leg slung over his and his arms wrapped around me. It's the safest place in the universe—our own little bubble away from the chaos of the outside world.

A quiet "good morning" whispers against my hair, and a kiss brushes my forehead. It's a kiss of reverence and love, like we've done this a million times, but it's still as special as the first. I look up into his eyes, the same deep blue of our duvet, and rub my hand over his short beard, feeling it tickle against my palm. He hums and pulls me closer.

The door bursts open, and Avery and Eloise jump right on top of us, giggling as Pepper hops in after them. The girls beg for pancakes, and Finn convinces them to go downstairs and wait for us in the kitchen. He drags me out of bed and kisses my lips and cheeks and neck, hands roaming all over me for a stolen moment before a busy day.

A soft hum echoes on each side of me, breaking me out of the visualization.

The fantasy I didn't know I desired.

The perfect dream I'm heartsick over leaving.

Lena smiles and sighs. "I think you have your answer."

* * *

THAT NIGHT, AS I'm brushing my teeth, my phone chimes with a text. I rinse out my mouth and grab it from the end of my bed, excitement tingling through my fingers when I see Finn's name on the screen.

> **Finn:** I can't stop eating these snickerdoodles. They're addictive.

> **Millie:** I stuck some dough in your freezer.
> ☺ That's my favorite way to eat it.

> **Finn:** My favorite way involves your fingers, so I'll have to wait until you're here.

Chapter 19

Finn

*M*illie's face as I stuck her finger in my mouth has been replaying in my mind constantly for days. The memory of her plush lips popping open on a gasp has me stifling a groan as I lower myself into my desk chair. I wave my computer mouse to wake the monitor and spend the next few minutes responding to emails.

While reading a particularly long message from a museum guest who's grumpy about not being able to rent out the planetarium for a movie showing, something tickles my hand. When I glance down, I squeak loudly—and very masculinely, of course—and whip the unsuspecting spider off my desk.

Once my heartbeat returns to a normal rate, I compose an email.

TO: Millie Oaks
FROM: Finn Ashford
SUBJECT: Afraid For My Life

Millie,

A frightening, albeit small, spider has taken up residence near my desk. I thought you might be able to identify the specimen and inform me of the future safety of my office. If

I must evacuate, it'll take a while to move everything into a secure location.

If you have time this afternoon, I would be relieved to have your assistance with this matter.

If you hear anyone mention a squeal that erupted from my office, please know that it was a different person in my department. Being the proud and dedicated feminist that I am, I call on my heroic female entomologist to save me from this peril.

Sincerely in need of a gallant rescuer,
Finn

TO: Finn Ashford
FROM: Millie Oaks
SUBJECT: Re: Afraid For My Life

After laughing until my abs were sore, I have recovered enough to inform you that I do have time in my schedule to save your office from said spider. The image in my mind of an impressively strong and sturdy man jumping and screeching because of a spider has given me a great deal of joy this morning.

I do think I heard that squeal you mentioned all the way on my side of the museum, and I thought it was the elevator malfunctioning.

Have you contained the offender? Hopefully you have not started vacating the office yet, because it's likely harmless.

Your gallant rescuer,
Millie

TO: Millie Oaks
FROM: Finn Ashford
SUBJECT: Re: Re: Afraid For My Life

Peter Parker is contained inside a coffee cup on my desk. In full disclosure, I should clear up some confusion. The "impressively strong and sturdy man" was, in fact, me.

I will also mention the spider was gently, carefully tossed away upon initially finding him or her on my hand. However, I quickly apologized and have since given them a pleasant coffee-scented home for the morning. Since he is contained, I will bring him to you. Maybe he can find a nice home in entomology to continue his life.

Your malfunctioning elevator,
Finn

* * *

Armed with a pastry bag from Maggie's and the coffee cup containing Peter Parker, I walk down the hall toward Millie's office. When I reach it, her brows are furrowed in concentration as she types something on her keyboard.

The surprise package crinkles as I slowly pull it out, and her eyes snap from the monitor to laser focus on the brown paper. "Is that what I think it is?"

There was one almond croissant left when I got to Maggie's this morning, and I bought it without thinking twice. Because, apparently, I have a weakness for seeing Millie's face light up.

"That depends. Are you thinking it's a spider in a coffee cup?" She huffs and purses her lips.

"Oh, this thing?" I hold up the pastry bag. "Mmm, this is mine.

I just wanted to show you I got one." I bring it under my nose and inhale the sweet, almondy aroma. "I think you have a little drool." I point to the corner of my mouth and nod toward her.

She shakes her head with a glare. "That better be a joke, Spock."

I narrow my eyes, dropping the package into her waiting palm. "I liked it better when you were comparing me to Kylo Ren."

"Too bad." Her eyes turn greedy as she pulls out the croissant. "You're amazing," she says, eyes on the pastry as she takes a big bite. She looks up at me, nodding and chewing. "And you're amazing too. Pull Micah's chair over here, and we can share it."

I slide into the seat and roll over to her desk. "You don't have to share with me," I say, setting the spider coffee cup beside her keyboard.

"I know, but you said you were addicted too. I don't want you fiending for it all day. You might resort to biting a museum guest."

I press my lips together to keep from saying the thought that comes to my mind.

You're the only one I want to bite, and it's not because I'm hungry.

She pulls the croissant apart down the middle, oblivious to my thoughts, and hands me the bag with the bottom half.

As I take my first bite, I soak in all the details of her office. It looks like an outward expression of her personality. She has happy plants on every surface and a few on the ground around her desk. The walls are covered in framed insect art and a picture of Millie with what I assume is her family. A sweater that looks like butterfly wings adorns the back of her chair.

Millie lifts the lid of the coffee cup, peeking at the spider inside. "Harmless wolf spider. Your office is safe."

I nod. "So I should have that moving crew put all my stuff back?"

She laughs. "Definitely okay to return your things. We can take him out to the pollinator garden, and he can track down a good lunch for himself."

Leaning back in her chair, she stretches her arms out to her sides with a low moan. The movement pushes her breasts against the yellow-and-white-striped fabric of her dress, drawing my eyes there like a magnet.

Fucking hell.

Save my poor soul and stop doing that.

I search her office for anything to distract me, and my gaze lands on the empty desk that used to be Calvin's. It sits in the corner, awaiting the new department director.

Millie has never mentioned her job interview to me. She has never asked me a single question about it, and I admire her for being able to shut those thoughts down around me. But I've been dying to talk to her about it. I tried to the last time she was at my house, but she put her fingers over my mouth to stop me.

"How are you feeling about your second interview?" I ask, and her eyes snap to mine.

She swallows her bite. "Well, I have my week in charge in like"—she clicks the button on the side of her phone to bring up the date—"ten days. I need to get ready for that first."

"Ah, yeah. I forgot about that step." I nod, waiting for her to continue the conversation.

But her eyes look anywhere except at me, and her knee bounces rapidly, making me think she doesn't want to talk to me about it. So I change the subject.

"Do you have plans tomorrow?"

Her leg stills and she lifts her brows. "Pretty sure I leave my Fridays open for you now."

My heart swells. "Well, I have a surprise idea if you're interested."

"Perfect. I miss my girls."

And that's all it takes. My heart reaches the point where it won't fit in my chest anymore.

Chapter 20

Millie

*T*he sun stains the sky a deep purple as it sets over Wilhelmina's city park. The grassy slope toward the amphitheater is full of families for an outdoor movie, and *Moana* has just begun from the projector.

Finn laid out a pale yellow blanket on the lush grass and spread a picnic out around me and the girls. He has a cooler with sparkling water and juice, along with containers of fruit, cheese, lunch meat, crackers, and some chocolate-covered strawberries for dessert.

"This is perfect," I tell him as *Moana*'s first song starts playing through the park while Avery and Eloise devour their snacks.

"I've been meaning to bring the girls to this, but I haven't felt brave enough." He grabs two jackets out of a bag and helps the girls into them then pulls out a woven blanket and wraps it around my shoulders.

Watching him fuss over us like a mother hen is almost too much for my heart.

"Thanks," I murmur, reaching for a grape and popping it into my mouth, flooding my tongue with its tangy sweetness. Finn positions a pillow behind me, and I sigh at the immediate relief when I lean back into it.

"Comfortable?" he asks, reclining on his own pillow with a sparkling water in his hand.

"Completely." A smile tugs at my lips, my answer meaning so much more than he knows. I'm absolutely at ease here with all three of them. "Do you want a plate?"

"No, thanks. I'm just going to drink some water for now." He winces and rubs his fingers across his forehead. "My head's hurting, but I'm probably just dehydrated."

We settle next to each other and the movie plays on, but I will have no recollection of it. *Moana* could turn into *Gladiator*, and I wouldn't know because I'm utterly distracted by the man beside me.

My weight against the pillow is making me slide toward Finn a millimeter at a time until it feels like I'm leaning on him, and if I tilted my head a few inches, I think it might be resting on his chest.

Finn hasn't moved at all. He's a firm stone wall beside me, heat bouncing off him in waves. It's a welcome warmth on this cool evening, and I could stay here forever, pressed against him like this.

Beds? I don't need them. Finn's body is much more comfortable.

We're reaching the end of the movie when I realize his steady breaths have turned into quiet snores. Every time he exhales, a small puff of air moves the hair on my forehead, and my shoulder settles into him more firmly.

A loud scene from the movie cracks through the air, and he twitches. His snoring stops, and he breathes, "Millie?" against my face.

"Yes, sleepyhead?" I turn to look up at him.

"Do you have any pain reliever in your purse? For a migraine," he says, his voice pinched with discomfort.

"Oh, yes." I fumble as I sit up and clumsily reach for my bag. Finn rises with a groan, dropping his face into his hands.

I shove aside my wallet, ChapStick, emergency apple, phone,

and fifteen receipts to find the ibuprofen and turn to see him in a full-body shiver. When he lifts his face, it's pale in the light from the movie screen, with dark circles under his eyes. I hand him the pills and his water. "Can I feel your head?"

He downs the medicine quickly and leans his forehead toward me. I rest my palm against him, and my heart stumbles.

He's burning up.

"I think you have a fever," I whisper. He leans back against his pillow and tosses his arm over his eyes.

Working quickly, I pack up the picnic. By the time the credits roll, I have everything in the cooler, and poor Finn still hasn't moved. Ave and El grab their things when I tell them we need to get him home. I nudge Finn's shoulder and softly tell him we are taking a load of things to the car and will be right back for him.

"Keys . . . pocket," he mumbles. My eyes drop to his pants, and I see the outline of them against his upper thigh.

Holding my breath, I cautiously slip my fingers into his pocket until the warm metal touches my skin. His whole body tenses as I push in a little deeper to grasp and pull them out as quickly as I can.

My breath comes back in a rush. "I'll be right back."

Ave and El help with the pillows while I try to balance the rest under my arms with the cooler in one hand. We're slow going, but we finally arrive and load everything into the trunk. When we make it back to Finn, he's in the exact same position.

"Girls, if I get Uncle Finn up, can you grab the blanket?"

They nod, even though Ave is yawning and Eloise is rubbing her eyes. I start the task of pulling Finn up. He's conscious enough to help with getting himself upright, and I wrap my arm around his waist as he leans on my shoulders all the way to the car.

The girls climb into their seats, and I try to shove Finn into the passenger side. He manages to help me get his legs in the right spot, and I lean across him to buckle his seat belt.

He drags in a deep breath. "Mmm. Lemons," he sighs, then leans forward until his face is buried in my hair. "Why do you always smell so good?" he whispers, lost in the haze of a fever.

I don't want to laugh at the man, but he's already growing un-inhibited, and it's adorable. What else can I pull from him in his fragile state?

I guess that's not nice, but my greedy heart wants it anyway.

Shutting the door, I jog around to the driver's side. I have to hold down the button to move the seat forward for no less than five minutes since a giant sat here last. When I turn to check the girls are buckled, Avery is already asleep in her seat.

"Is he okay?" Eloise asks, her voice wary.

I pat her leg. "He's going to be fine, sweetie. We're going to take good care of him."

* * *

I'M ALREADY WINDED from carrying two sleeping five-year-olds up the stairs and tucking them into bed, but getting a grown man out of a car, into the house, and up the stairs is a workout.

Apparently, I should be doing more cardio.

Pausing at Finn's closed bedroom door, I peek up at him. His eyes are shut, but I know he's slightly coherent because he's been helping me get him up the stairs.

I scan his dark lashes resting against his flushed cheeks. He's stunning, even in sickness.

"Can I open your bedroom door?" I whisper, trying not to star-tle him with too many loud noises.

"Always," he breathes, and it sounds rough with meaning.

I slowly turn the handle and enter his dark bedroom, where only an outline of the bed is visible. I make my way there, nudg-ing him to sit on the side. With a *snick-click*, I turn on a lamp on the nightstand, bathing the room in a dim golden light. It illuminates the space enough to see the room is painted dark green, with warm wood tones in the furniture, and a crisp green duvet across the bed.

My fantasy about life with Finn is still fresh in my mind days later, and being in this room with him makes my ache for that dream burn a little hotter. I'm slightly devastated I can't just slide into bed with him right now, because I'm exhausted.

Careful not to startle him, I pull his glasses off and leave them folded on his nightstand. The act feels surprisingly intimate in the privacy of his room. Much more intimate than co-workers should be.

"Not how I wanted to bring you to my room for the first time," he mutters, tilting to the side.

"Wait. Hold on. Stand up one more time so we can get you under the covers, okay?" I wrap my arms around his waist to pull him up. Once he's standing, I keep an arm in place and tug the covers over.

But when I try to sit him back down, he plants his feet and stands solid. He blankets his arms around me until we're in a secure hug. His chin drops to the top of my head, and for the first time, I'm completely embraced in his arms.

"Millie." He breathes out a sigh and hums contentedly as his body relaxes into me, and all my worries evaporate for a moment.

I fit perfectly here, in this place I've dreamed about. Like this spot was made for me. He's so warm, and I know part of that is his fever, but I have a feeling his arms would be this cozy and secure anyway.

How could I not come back to this now that I know how right it feels?

His arms tighten around me before his legs give. I reluctantly sit him on the sheet and steady his shoulders. Once he's holding himself up, I kneel to remove his shoes.

A miserable groan bleeds from his chest. "Not how I wanted you on your knees for me either." Heat flashes up my spine in a fiery wave, and my fingers still over his laces like they've forgotten how to move. My head snaps up, but his eyes are closed, his face etched with pain. Willing all my focus back to his shoes, I force my fingers into movement and work as quickly as I can. I'll analyze what his words are doing to me later.

I slip the shoes off his feet and stand between his knees. With his eyes still shut tight, he reaches up to undo the top button of his shirt. He gets the first one open but fumbles on the second, so I nudge his hands away and undo it myself.

Never in the plans for my day did I think I'd be undressing Finn Ashford in his bedroom, but here I am. I get the first few undone with a clinical focus on my movements, but the lower my hands get, the more his breathing picks up. I can't stop my gaze from wandering to his bare skin and the muscles I'm revealing on my path. My fingers accidentally brush the hot skin on his stomach, and he hisses.

"I'm sorry," I say, trying not to touch him again.

"Don't . . . be sorry," he grinds through clenched teeth.

As I get the final button undone, Finn leans his brow against my collarbone. I slide my hands across the scorching skin at his shoulders to slip the shirt down his arms. His warm breath coasts over the swell of my breasts, making me lose track of what I'm supposed to be doing.

He's weak with sickness, and he needs my help. But his gravelly voice and exposed skin are muddling my thoughts and sending heat rushing through my veins.

Mustering every ounce of my willpower, I drag myself away and lean him over on his pillow. I'm not emotionally prepared for removing pants, so he's going to stay in those. Lifting his legs onto the bed, I get him settled and tuck the blanket over him.

His eyes open briefly, hazy and cloudy as they focus on me. He lifts his hand to rest against my cheek, and the wonder in his eyes unravels something tight in my chest. He looks like he's not sure if the fever fog is making him hallucinate me.

"*Grazie, stella mia,*" he whispers as his eyes drift shut and his hand drops to the bed.

* * *

Oaks Folks

> **Millie:** Can anybody send me Dad's chicken and rice soup recipe?

Mom: Are you sick? Need me to come down there?

> **Millie:** No. Thanks, though. I'm making it for a sick friend.

Mom: Oh, okay. I'll send you a picture of his recipe.

Fabes: I want some soup, Mom. *cough, cough*

Fabes: You don't have to drive an hour to make me some. I'm just upstairs. 😊

Tess: I'll take some. It's soup-er delicious.

Dad: I'm a real soup-er star for making that recipe.

Fabes: He really soup-ed in and saved the day.

Millie: Thanks for the recipe.
It has soup-er powers.

Millie: Miss you guys. Can't wait to come visit.

* * *

"YOU'RE THE BEST," I tell Lena, pulling groceries out of the bags she brought.

I couldn't find any medicine in the downstairs bathroom, and I don't want to rummage around in Finn's. So I asked Lena to go to the store for a few things and the ingredients for my favorite soup when I'm sick.

"I *am* the best." She nods, dropping a bag of overnight clothes near the stairs and looking around the room.

Finn's kitchen is magnificent. Dark gray lower cabinets support white granite counters. Exposed beams run along the ceiling, and big windows give a view of the backyard. The front of the fridge is covered in pictures drawn by the girls, and my dark green mixer adds a beautiful pop of color in the corner.

"You look good in here," Lena says with a wink.

I duck my chin, not wanting her to see what that comment does to me. I don't think I'm ready for anyone to know how comfortable I am in this house.

"Okay, I see you need to sit with that thought for a little while before you accept it," she teases, coming around the island to kiss me on the cheek. "Text me if you need anything else."

She slips out the door quietly, and I lock it behind her before walking back into the kitchen to start the soup.

I spend the next few hours checking on Finn and the girls

in between making chicken-and-rice soup. It feels like I'm house-sitting downstairs by myself with a cup of tea and the smell of chicken and herbs simmering. I find a blanket in an antique chest in the living room and curl up on the couch with my Kindle.

When the soup finishes, I take a break from my book and make a fresh cup of tea for Finn. Once it's done steeping, I tiptoe upstairs and open the girls' bedroom door. They're sound asleep, curled toward each other. I press my hand to their foreheads to see if they're getting fevers too, but so far, so good.

Next, I peek into Finn's room. He's still under the covers, but his jeans are lying in a clump next to the bed. I set the cup of tea on the nightstand and lean over to check his forehead.

His skin seems pale in the dark room, and his hair is damp against his brow. He looks so peaceful with his lips parted in sleep and deep, sighing breaths escaping them.

I have no idea how he feels besides the migraine he mentioned. Maybe a stomach bug? Or a sinus infection? I won't know until he tells me more symptoms.

His eyes blink open and focus on me. "You're still here?"

"Yeah. Wanted to make sure you were okay. The girls are asleep."

He breathes a sigh of relief as I sit on the edge of the bed near his hip.

"How are you feeling?"

"Like two planets have collided in my skull," he groans, pushing himself up to lean against the headboard.

"Does anything else hurt?" I ask, picking up the tea and handing it to him.

He takes a slow sip and closes his eyes with a hum. "My whole body aches. All my muscles weigh a ton. And my stomach is cramping." He takes another drink and opens his eyes. "I'm sorry about our evening. This wasn't the plan."

I set my hand on his blanket-covered leg. "Don't worry about it. I've had quite a nice time snooping through all your secret drawers and searching the cabinets."

"I wish I was doing it with you. That sounds more fun."

"It does." I nod. "I haven't found your blow-up Princess Leia doll yet, but I'm not ready to give up."

He manages a weak smile and stretches to set the mug on his nightstand. "What time is it?"

"About one in the morning."

"Oh." He sighs, squeezing his eyes shut. "You should go home. You've done so much already that I don't know how to repay you."

"Then don't. I'm happy to help."

He blindly wraps his hand around my forearm. "It's too much," he whispers as his fingers slowly move up and down my arm in a soothing, light touch. I close my eyes and breathe in the sage scent in his room. The feeling of his calloused hand gliding along my arm is tugging directly on the thread in my heart, and I let it.

It sweeps me away into an imaginary world, where I'm not just house-sitting, and we can be together without the fear of what it means for my job.

I let myself get completely lost in thoughts of *more*.

He does the movement once more before his fingers pause and his chest lifts with the steady, deep breaths of sleep.

Chapter 21

Finn

*D*amp sheets cling to my clammy skin as I drift back into consciousness. I feel as though I might need a crowbar to pry my eyes open. Once I manage it, I blink a few times, assessing my aching head.

Fuck, it still hurts, but it's better than last night's migraine.

I roll over, groaning into my pillow at the ache in my whole body. But as I take a deep breath, the smell of fresh espresso calls to me. It rejuvenates me enough that I trudge to the shower.

Clean and wearing fresh clothes, I descend the stairs, clutching my sheets to start in the wash.

Giggles float toward me from the living room, and the sound of their voices brings a smile to my face before I've even seen them. I find Millie, Avery, and Eloise in the living room, kneeling around a board game on the coffee table. Millie is in a pair of black leggings and a white T-shirt with Wilhelmina Astronomy Club written across the front.

My shirt.

She looks like she was meant to wear it, and the thought of seeing her like this every morning jostles something deep in my chest. The primal urge to pick her up and claim her lips washes over me, and I have to clench my fists to stop myself.

Her eyes lift from the game and spot me. "Look who's up." She smiles, and the girls jump to greet me with hugs.

"Are you feeling okay?" Ave asks from my hip.

"Much better, *piccola*," I say, smoothing my hand over her head. She and Eloise both have two French braids this morning, and I'm in awe that Eloise let Millie tackle the task.

The girls return to their game, but Millie stands to walk to me. My shirt almost reaches her knees, and I hate that I can't see how those tight leggings look on her thighs and hips.

She catches me staring, and her hands fist the front of the shirt. "I found this in the dryer. Lena brought me leggings but forgot a shirt." She rolls her eyes like she's exasperated with her best friend. "Is that okay?"

I can't lie. "It's *perfect* on you," I whisper, running a hand over her shoulder.

An adorable blush floods her cheeks.

"Did you sleep?" I ask, nodding behind her to the quilt and throw pillow on the couch. I don't even know everything she did for me last night, but she must be exhausted.

"A little. How are you feeling?"

"Better this morning." I take a deep breath through my nose. "Is that espresso?"

Millie nods as she leads the way into the kitchen. "Full disclosure, I had to watch a YouTube video for the espresso contraption. You'll have to tell me how I did." She starts to reach for a cup in the cabinet but pauses. "Should you have some after not feeling well?"

My stomach is still unsettled, so maybe it's not the best idea. "I'll just inhale it for now and look for something safer first." I glance at the clock on the stove. "Is it really noon?" I ask, shocked that I've slept that long and that she has been able to keep the girls quiet for me.

Millie takes a seat on her barstool. "You needed the sleep, and we've been fine. We made pancakes for breakfast and have been coloring and playing games since then."

"Can I get you anything?" Opening the fridge to look for something safe for my stomach, I find a large container that wasn't there yesterday and turn to Millie. "Did you make me soup?"

"I did."

"Do you want some?" I set the container on the counter and take out a pot to heat it up.

"Yes, please." Millie watches me as I start the soup and put some bread in the toaster.

While it heats up, I lean my elbows on the island across from Millie. "You took care of me, made sure the girls were well, and made me soup."

She shrugs. "We're friends, right? That's what friends do."

I let my eyes trace over her, let them memorize every detail. From the dusting of freckles across her cheeks, to her plump bottom lip, to her glowing, bright eyes.

Fuck being friends with this woman. I want so much more.

I want her here every day. I want to finally run my fingers through her waves like I've been fantasizing about. Wrap my hands around her hips and feel how perfectly they fit in my grip.

I exhale a deep breath and shake my head. "Oh, Millie. I don't want what friends do. I want much more than that with you."

Her eyes flare and her cheeks pinken before she looks down at her lap. Her focus stays there for a beat, and I watch the flicker of emotions play across her face as she tries to decide how to respond.

I fully expect her to lift her gaze and tell me firmly not to say things like that.

It's the right thing to do.

But instead, when her eyes meet mine, they're a fiery green, and she watches me through her lashes as she whispers, "Like what?"

The floor is ripped out from under me with those two syllables. My throat goes dry, and I swallow a few times, trying to wet it.

Her teeth drag over her bottom lip, and I don't know if she's doing it on purpose, but it's fucking torture.

I wait for her to take the words back, but she doesn't. She just lets them land between us like a ticking bomb.

Tick-tick-tick.

She wants to know what I want to do to her?

Fucking *everything*.

The words tumble from my lips. "I want to sink my fingers into your hair and kiss you. Taste your lips after months of wishing I could."

She leans in, setting her forearms on the counter. Her throat bobs as she swallows, and her eyes drift closed slowly like she's savoring the idea.

When she opens them again, they're glossy and heavy with arousal as she whispers, "I want that too."

Fuck. Fuck. Fuck.

My fingers twitch like they have a mind of their own. Like they're about to follow through with my words.

I clench my fists and force myself to stay on this side of the counter.

"Then what would you do?" she asks.

This doesn't feel real. Maybe I'm still asleep in my bed, having a fevered fantasy about her.

I bite the inside of my cheek, trying to wake myself up, but it doesn't work. I'm still here, in the kitchen, with the woman of my dreams asking what I want to do to her.

Taking a deep breath, I whisper, "I would run my hands up that shirt and finally feel your warm skin on mine. Find out if you're wearing a bra, or if my fingers will get to slide over your nipples."

She goes perfectly still, and regret fills my chest. That was too far. I shouldn't have said it.

With our gazes locked, she presses her teeth into her bottom lip so hard that it turns white. Then she releases it and whispers, "No bra."

My legs go weak, and a low groan seeps from my throat. Fuck whatever this fucking sickness is. I'm straining against the front of my sweatpants, and I want to pull her into the pantry and follow through with everything I said.

Voices rise from the living room, the sounds of the girls arguing over their game flooding the space between us with reality.

"I'll go." Millie pulls her hands back and flees from the room like it's on fire.

Well, it fucking *is*.

I listen to their muffled conversation while I dish the soup into two bowls. Taking a deep breath, I dig my fists into the counter, hoping the situation in my sweatpants will deflate.

When Millie returns to her barstool, her cheeks and eyes are back to their normal color, like she's contained everything that just happened in this kitchen.

I'm having a harder time controlling that beast, but I force myself to ignore its rattling cage and serve her a bowl of soup and a plate of toast.

"This is delicious," I say as the first spoonful of chicken, rice, and vegetables hits my tongue.

She dips a chunk of toast into the broth. "My dad taught me how to make this. Most of my cooking skills come from my mom, but this one is my dad. He's not as good at the medicine and fretting part of having sick kids, so he always made the comfort soup." She picks up a spoonful and brings it up between our faces. "I don't really like celery, so he always cuts the pieces so tiny they're almost invisible."

"When I was sick as a kid, Clara would heat up Campbell's for me. I loved the hell out of that soup, but I think it was mostly because she made it for me."

"What was she like?" Millie asks.

The weight that always presses on my chest when I think about my sister shifts a little. "She was . . ." My voice comes out hoarse, so I clear my throat to reset. "She was the kindest person I'd ever met. She had this way of making everyone around her comfortable, even in the most awkward situations. And she was so selfless. Took care of me better than our own parents."

Millie nods. "Do the girls have some of her personality?"

I rock my head from side to side, thinking. "Both girls are a little like her. She was outgoing like Eloise and could talk to anyone she met, and she was compassionate and self-aware like Avery. And they both laugh exactly like her. Sometimes it haunts me when I hear it." That grief-filled weight feels a bit lighter with every word, like discussing Clara with Millie is releasing some of the heavy load that has been burdening me.

Millie leans her cheek on my shoulder and wraps her hand around my arm. "She sounds wonderful. I wish I could've met her."

"Me too."

Chapter 22

Millie

A familiar ache beats between my thighs as I writhe and twist through soft sheets. Fingers move from the warm skin on my stomach, down my hips, and over my leggings. My body melts into the feeling, and Finn's familiar scent engulfs me. The pressure increases, sliding smoothly over the thin fabric, and pleasure—

The distant sound of a door closing jolts me from sleep, and my eyes shoot open.

My hands burst out from under the covers, and I sit up to let my eyes adjust, baffled when I realize where I am. That's Finn's teacup on the nightstand and his shoes by the bathroom door. My head drops back to the pillow with a *whoosh*.

Reality hits me like a splash to the face.

Oh. My. God.

I was fantasizing about Finn.

In his bed.

Bloody hell, Millie.

I'd say fantasizing about your coworker in his bed is absolutely on the wrong side of the friendship line.

Fuck.

I yank the covers over my face with a groan, but that backfires when Finn's scent surrounds me. These sheets are pale green, a different color from last night, so I'm pretty sure they're clean. But somehow, they're covered in his scent, and I can't stop myself from squeezing my eyes shut and inhaling it like I'm an addict. The sage aroma must have magic powers over my brain. It feels like it infiltrates all the little corners and pockets, soothing my nerve endings and calming my thoughts.

How did I get to this point? I've let Finn so far into my heart that even his smell calms me?

Squeezing my eyes shut, I remember everything that happened a little while ago in the kitchen, and regret burns in my chest. I let that conversation get so much further than I should've. Everything logical in my brain says to stay away from him for all the reasons on the list.

Yet, no matter how many times I go over that list, my heart has other ideas. My heart is a needy, wanton floozy who craves Finn's attention. She aches for it.

The girls' voices filter through the walls to reach me, so I rouse myself from bed and remake it behind me. I find my phone on the nightstand and text Lena, begging her to come pick me up. Hopefully, I can make it to the front door without Finn reading everything all over my face.

I use Ave and El's bathroom, attempt to smooth down my frizzy, post-nap hair, and descend the stairs.

Finn's filling a water cup at the fridge when he comes into view, and his eyes flick to me. "You okay?" he asks with a tense brow. He leaves the cup in front of Avery and approaches me, brushing a hand over my cheeks and forehead. "You're all red."

Shit. He can totally tell what happened. I trip back a step as my ears get hot.

Leave, Millie.

"Oh, I'm fine. Just thirsty. Lena's here to pick me up," I say, shuffling toward the front door and grabbing my bag of clothes from the living room floor.

"Uncle Finn carried you upstairs after the movie, and we had to be soooo quiet," Eloise explains, following on my heels as I try to escape.

Finn hands me a glass of ice water at the door. "Are you sure you're okay?"

"Yeah," I squeal too brightly, gulping down a few sips and shoving it back to him. "Lena's just in a hurry."

Finn's brows are tight, his lips parted like he is trying to find the right words.

God, my cheeks are on *fire*.

I swing open the door, and luckily, Lena is waiting at the curb. I scurry down the steps, waving my goodbyes, and flee the scene of my amorous crime.

* * *

WHEN I GET to work on Monday, a pastry bag from Maggie's, a coffee, and a folded note sit atop my desk.

The light gray stationery has a beautiful galaxy of stars around the border.

Millie,

I have a special plan for Thursday if you're free. I know . . . it's not Friday, but it was the only available night for this particular event. It would just be you and me, but we don't have to call it a date. We don't have to go at all if you don't want to. I want you to feel comfortable.

Yours,
Finn

Dropping into my seat, I read through the note one more time. My wanton, floozy heart begs me to say yes. To ignore the fact that I ran out of his house just days ago trying to hide that I'd been fantasizing about him.

We can still be friends after that, right?

Chapter 23

Finn

"This way," I tell Millie, placing a hand on her back to guide her toward the door of Maggie's.

In the setting sun, this street is a completely different world. The cafés and shops illuminate their patios with candles and dim lanterns, and twinkly lights hang over the road, giving the whole area an undeniably romantic feel.

She stops as we reach the door and grins up at me, her eyes sparkling with the reflection of the lights above us. I scan the slopes of her cheeks, the freckles across her nose, the rich pink of her lips, and the slightest bit of cleavage above the neckline of her Neptune-blue dress.

She's fucking breathtaking.

We haven't seen each other since Lena picked her up last Saturday, and the craving to be near her has been a constant ache in my lungs.

"You are so beautiful," I whisper, unable to stop myself.

Her eyes widen in surprise. "Thank you."

I nod and keep my lips pressed shut before I say something more. This isn't supposed to be a date, and I don't want to push her past her limits.

Pulling open the door, I bring us into the dark dining area. Chairs are stacked on the tables, and the usual whir of the espresso machine is missing. I steer Millie to the swinging half door that leads behind the counter. The coffee shop closed a few hours ago, but we have an appointment with Maggie this evening.

Her feet pause on the threshold like she's hit a barrier. "We can't go back there."

"We're super special guests tonight." I wink and pull her hand until she starts moving again.

Millie gasps when she sees what's waiting for us through the kitchen door—stainless steel worktables and Maggie with a whole slew of things we're going to get to work on. Millie looks over her shoulder at me like I've produced her personal version of paradise.

"Good evening," Maggie greets us with a grin. She pauses from rolling out some sort of pastry dough to dust her hands down her espresso-colored apron.

"Do we get to see your process?" Millie asks, turning in a circle to examine every nook and cranny of the kitchen. Open shelves fill one wall, covered in endless baking ingredients I could never identify. A few commercial ovens and refrigerators line the sides, along with shelves full of supplies.

"You're doing it yourself." Maggie laughs, stepping around the table to hug Millie. "Where have you been? I haven't seen you in weeks."

"Oh, just busy," Millie says with a hint of evasiveness. "I miss it here, though."

Surprise flickers through me. I didn't know she hadn't been here in weeks. I haven't seen her here since the time she saw her ex.

Is that why?

Laying my hand on her lower back, I make a mental note to ask her about that later.

"Well, I'm happy to see you." Maggie waves around the kitchen. "I heard you've been trying to make almond croissants at home, and it hasn't been working." She moves to a rolling shelf of baking trays and pulls out two of them.

Millie looks at me with mock betrayal. "You told her that? Can't tell this guy anything," she grinds out and bumps me with her hip.

Maggie chuckles. "Well, be happy he did, because he's hired me to teach you while I prep for tomorrow."

* * *

"THEY'RE PERFECT!" MILLIE claps as Maggie pulls the tray of croissants out of the oven.

Maggie has been so patient and kind for the last hour while she taught Millie as much as she could about making croissants. She had prepared a few different stages of the dough ahead of time so that Millie could do an expedited version of the steps. I had no idea making croissants was a multiday process.

As they work, Millie has been entertaining Maggie with details of my own kitchen disasters, but that's alright.

She can tease me all she wants when she looks at me with *that* smile. The one that illuminates the whole room and melts me from the inside out.

"Now, while these cool for a few minutes," Maggie says, carefully picking up the first almond croissant and setting it on a rack, "you two go enjoy your dinner." She nods toward the door to the front of the shop.

In the dining area, we find a table in the middle, lit by candles that Maggie snuck out here and set up a few minutes ago. The strings of lights from outside shine through the windows, and the shop's perpetual coffee smell fills the air. I didn't ask for this romantic setup; I only hired her for the croissant-making. But I have to admit it's perfect.

Millie drapes her apron and purse over her chair and slides into the seat with her back to the window. She scans the meal in front of her before taking a spoonful of tomato soup.

A little moan escapes her as she closes her eyes and savors it. "So good." I take my own bite as she asks, "Want to play a game?"

"Always." I nod.

"It's called Game of Firsts. We take turns asking each other about our firsts of something, and for every answer, you get a point. If you don't want to answer, you lose a point. Winner makes the loser do a dare."

I smile as my mind conjures a list of dares I could request of her. "I can't wait to win."

Her eyes narrow on me. "Then you'll be sorely disappointed."

I drum my fingers on the linen tablecloth, already feeling my competitiveness moving through my veins. "You go first."

"I'll start off easy. First girlfriend?" She poses the question and dips the corner of her sandwich in her soup.

"Kelly Watson. Sixth grade."

Millie squints at me. "And . . ."

"You want details?"

She lets out an exasperated sigh. "Of course I want details."

"She was very nice, did well in math, which was important to me at the time, and she ended up breaking up with me because she had a crush on Chad Michael Murray and needed the free time to work on meeting him."

Millie winces in sympathy. "That's tough," she says, biting her lips to hold in her laugh. "I have to tell you, though. I wasn't *great* at math and definitely had a crush on Chad Michael Murray. So I don't know if it'll work between us," she teases with a raised brow.

The fact that she's even joking about an *us* makes me grin from ear to ear. "Well, math abilities are no longer on my list of relationship criteria, so you're off the hook with that one. But the

Chad Michael Murray thing may be a deal-breaker for me. I'll have to think about it."

She nods understandingly.

"First job," I prompt.

"Does working at the farm count? I helped with every chore my parents would let me. Then I worked as a lifeguard at the city pool after senior year. That one summer was enough for my lifeguarding career. I never wanted to be in charge of babysitting teenage boys in a pool ever again."

"Hmm. Millie in a lifeguard suit, rescuing teenage boys who are pretending to drown," I grumble. "Did you have to give them mouth-to-mouth?"

"No. Thank goodness for that." Her attention dips to my mouth before she asks her next question. "First kiss?" She sets her soup spoon down beside her bowl like she needs full concentration for this one. "Was it with a Princess Leia poster?"

"Ha ha," I deadpan, rolling my eyes. "Picture those English sheepdogs, with long hair all over, hanging in their eyes. They have these big tongues sort of lolling about all the time. Imagine one of those licking all over your face and inside your mouth. And you're trying to be a good person and not say anything, but it's a lot of slobber, so you try to last as long as you can."

Millie smiles, shaking her head.

"Kayla Jones told me that was how I kissed her the first time."

Millie throws her head back with unbridled laughter, and I can't help but join her, even though it's at my own expense. When she looks back at me, she wipes a tear from her eye. "Oh, no. I'm hoping you've gotten better since then."

"Undeniably." I nod. "Tell me about your first kiss."

"Middle school dance with Shane, my first boyfriend. My friends had warned me that he was going to kiss me at this dance, so I'd prepared myself as much as I could. I only had a little fruit punch and no snacks. I even wiped my lip gloss off so the kiss wouldn't be slimy. Then 'Angel' by Shaggy came on, and Shane asked me to dance. And he kissed me. It was just a peck, but then I had the terrorizing thought that if I opened my mouth, our braces might get stuck together."

She looks at me with big eyes, and I'm already laughing. "How did no one mention that?" she continues. "I was so terrified someone was going to call my parents and we'd have to sit in the car with our faces stuck together while we drove to the orthodontist to get pulled apart. So I shut my lips tight and put my head on his shoulder for the rest of the song." She takes a sip of tea and shrugs. "He kissed another girl on a bus ride two weeks later and dumped me."

"Asshole."

"Totally." She puts a hand under her chin, thinking of a new question. "First foreign country you visited?"

"I was going to Italy to see my grandparents since before I can remember. We went every summer for at least a month when I was a kid."

"Have the girls been?"

"Yes. Clara and I took them when they were three. My grandparents had already moved to America before the girls were born, but I do have some aunts and uncles in Italy. So we rented a little home with a lot of outside space. We had a blast and ate ridiculously good food. My aunts, uncles, and cousins are better company than my parents."

I sigh, remembering how happy Clara was there. "Clara wanted to start the process of moving there, actually. She asked me to come with her, but she began not feeling well soon after that." I take a deep breath before continuing because my next thought stings to think about. "She told me she wanted her ashes spread there one day, and I haven't had the nerve to go back and do it yet."

A rush of air leaves Millie, and she says, "It could be healing to bring the girls there and show them some places and people their mom loved."

I let that thought sink in, picturing the girls with their extended family, adventuring on Zia Sofia and Zio Filippo's property and eating as much pasta and bread as their little tummies can handle.

My thoughts are interrupted by a soft ring from Millie's phone. She pulls it out of her purse and groans. "My mom is Face-Timing me."

"Go ahead." I motion with my chin for her to take the call.

Her eyes scan me before she swipes to answer it. She holds it in front of her and smiles. "Hey, Mama."

"Millie, sweetie. Where are you?"

Glancing around the shop, she assesses what her mom can see and hesitates a little too long. "Maggie's." She looks as suspicious as a kid caught with their hand in the cookie jar.

"It's a little dark there." I can't see her mom's face, but I can hear the uncertainty in her voice. She's onto her.

"Yeah, Maggie is trying out this new vibe to see how the customers like it."

I take a sip of my tea a little too quickly and choke when it slides down the wrong pipe. I cover my mouth and bend over to muffle the sound of sputtering, but it's no use.

"Honey, there's a reflection in the window behind you. Does that handsome man at your table need help?"

Millie shifts her face to look at me, her cheeks flushed with embarrassment. "Oh . . . yeah, my friend Finn is here."

I've contained my coughing enough to offer a silent "Sorry."

"Finn," Millie's mom practically squeals. "Move your chair around and join our conversation."

Millie rolls her eyes, but she's grinning. My chair scrapes on the floor as I slide it around beside hers, and she adjusts the phone to include my face.

"Hello, Mrs. Oaks. Nice to meet you."

Millie's mother is beautiful, with gray hair framing her round face and glasses perched on her nose.

"Oh, call me Mary," she says, grinning from what looks like her kitchen table. "It's nice to meet you too. How's your evening going?"

"Perfect," I say, turning to smirk at my coworker turned friend turned maybe-date.

"Looks like it," Mary coos. "Millie, is this the man you were telling me about whose twins were in your summer camp?"

"Yes. Avery and Eloise."

My chest warms at the thought that she told her mom about me. That must mean something, right?

"That's so sweet," Mary says. "I won't keep you long. I was calling about your trip out here this weekend. Do you mind picking up a few things from one of those big-city grocery stores you go to before you make the trek to Fern River on Saturday?"

Millie nods. "Just text me a list."

"Of course. Thank you." She smiles at Millie before her eyes shift like she's looking at me now. "Finn, it's my birthday, and I think you and your girls should come. We have so much for them to do. They could collect eggs and help Dave in the garden. Oh, and swim in the pond and feed some animals. It's like a personal petting zoo over here."

Millie stays silent beside me, and I'm not sure what to say. "I don't want to intrude on a family weekend," I try.

"Don't worry." Mary waves off the idea. "My best friend from next door and her son are coming. The more, the merrier at our house. Dave and I always believe that. Besides, it would make my heart happy to have some kids out on the farm."

My chest tightens at her kind invitation. She's so unlike my own mother, and a wave of sadness crashes over me that I didn't grow up with someone this welcoming and gracious.

"Thank you. I'll discuss it with Millie and see what she thinks about us following along."

"Okay, I'll let you get back to it. Millie, I'll see you in a couple of days. Love you."

"Love you too, Mama." She smiles before ending the call.

* * *

MILLIE SITS QUIETLY in the passenger seat, a box full of our perfect croissants in her lap. She requested to come home with me to see the girls before I put them to bed and then have Lena pick her up, and I'm more than happy to oblige.

I tentatively put my hand on her knee at a stoplight, encouraging her to look my way. "Why haven't you been to Maggie's recently? It looked like there was a story there."

She tilts back to the headrest and closes her eyes. "I don't want to say it out loud because I've been avoiding thinking about it," she whispers into the dark car.

"You can trust me with it. You can trust me with anything." I squeeze her leg once in reassurance.

She lets out a deep breath and looks to the window beside her. "I haven't been back since I saw *him*." Her hands fidget with the hem of her dress. "That was my place, and it doesn't feel like mine if he's there. It doesn't feel safe." She says the last part so quietly I almost can't make it out.

My hand on the steering wheel squeezes tight as I try to control my rage, but I force the one on her knee to stay relaxed. She should always feel safe. I hate that she has to worry about whether he'll be somewhere.

"He's still texting every once in a while, and it's scary to think about seeing him." She sighs. "I wish I could take every hurtful thing he said that still echoes in my mind and shove it back down his throat. I don't know if I'm strong enough to get through it, though."

My teeth grind at the news that he's still messaging her. I can't even imagine what he's saying, but if it makes her this uncomfortable, it can't be good.

"Millie." She finally looks back toward me, and her eyes are red around the edges. "How about we go back sometime together?"

Silence hovers between us as I pull into my garage and turn off the car. I shift in my seat and reach for her hands, cradling them between mine on the console.

"I have no doubt that if you saw him or had to talk to him, you could stand up for yourself all on your own. But if it makes you more comfortable, I could come with you the first time and be your cheerleader. Or your bodyguard. Or your coffee-cup holder while you punch him. I'll be anything you want."

A tear rolls down her cheek, and I brush it away with my thumb.

"I'd like that," she whispers. "Can you be all the above?"

"Always."

* * *

"I want Millie to read our bedtime story," Avery requests from her snug position under the blanket.

I turn to the doorway and raise an eyebrow at Millie. She puts her hand over her chest. "Me?"

"Of course, you." Eloise giggles, scooting all the way to the edge of the bed to make room for her.

"I'd be honored." She crawls between them and opens the book.

My mind wanders as I watch Millie read their bedtime story while the girls cuddle into her arms. Ave and El have completely fallen for her in only a few short weeks. Her presence has created this spark in the girls that I haven't seen in months, and I don't ever want it to end.

When she closes the book, she lifts her arms, and the girls rest their heads against her sides.

"Uncle Finn, will you sing us 'Twinkle, Twinkle, Little Star'?" Avery requests, her eyes already drifting closed.

Warmth hits my cheeks, but I force myself to sing anyway. Millie watches me through the first and second lines, Ave and El drifting off to sleep at her side.

But as I start the last half of the lullaby, Millie's gentle, bright voice joins my rough, low one in the most beautiful harmony I've ever heard.

Chapter 24

Millie

*T*he door clicks shut as Finn leaves me snuggled between the girls. I offered to stay with them until they fall asleep, mostly so I could steal a quiet moment to untangle my twisted jumble of emotions.

Finn designed an entire night based solely on something he knew I wanted to do. He set it up with Maggie, bought me an apron, and laughed while we rolled croissants together.

And I loved every minute. But I can't stop the overwhelming feeling that something has shifted tonight.

When Ave's and El's breaths are steady and deep, I slip quietly from the bed and down the stairs. I search for Finn in each empty room until I find one I've never seen open. A pair of French doors off the living room are spread wide, leading to a study lit by a single lamp.

Bookshelves line three indigo walls. The last wall holds a large window overlooking the moonlit front yard, and a broad wood desk sits in front of it.

My gaze flicks to the ceiling, and I smile up at the black surface sprinkled with hundreds of tiny white stars.

When my attention moves to Finn, my smile falters. He's all confident, relaxed masculinity as his broad shoulders cover the entire back of the plush armchair he's seated in. His sleeves have been rolled up to reveal forearms corded with muscle. Shadows hide his eyes, but I can tell his gaze is on me as he lifts a glass tumbler to his lips.

Right now, the invisible thread feels like a tug-of-war rope, yanking me toward him while I dig my feet into the dirt and try to pull back.

I force my voice to say, "I'm going to call Lena to come get me."

He tilts his head, and a wave of dark hair falls over his forehead like it refuses to be tamed. "Can we finish our game first? We got interrupted earlier."

"Okay." I drop into the chair across from him, and the soft velvet seat caresses my skin. The tension in this round has already escalated, and we haven't even started yet. This version is completely different from the one at Maggie's: Game of Firsts After Dark.

He swallows a sip of his drink. "First thing you thought when you met me." His eyes are a dare, like he knows I might resist answering this one. He has a smug grin that tells me he thinks I'll miss a point here to keep my secrets.

But he doesn't know how competitive I really am.

I think about that first day, when I saw him charging toward the elevator with a tight expression, like a sexy-professor fantasy come to life.

"I thought . . . I thought you were a grumpy asshole who wouldn't get into the elevator with me. You looked like the idea of sharing a small space was offensive."

His eyes stay glued on me, unchanging as he brings the glass to his mouth for another drink before placing it back on his thigh. "I knew that if I got on that elevator, I'd either ruin your day with my mood or have a miserable time not flirting with you."

My floozy heart thumps heavily in my chest. The *ba-dum-bump* blasts through my body, shooting warmth to every square inch of skin.

"Finn," I whisper. "You can't say things like that to me."

His brow furrows with confusion. "Why?"

I throw my hands in the air like the reason should be obvious. Why do I have to say it out loud?

"Because you're one of the people hiring me for the promotion I've worked toward for months." I shake my head. "You'll judge my interviews and decide if I deserve the job. I don't want to be a person who slept her way to the top, and as a woman, even *looking* like I did is damning." I sigh out a deep breath before adding, "And my traitorous heart is already so far past the friendship line, that if we went any further with this conversation, I'm scared of how it would end."

He shrugs. "I'm not."

A scoff bursts out of me. "Of course you aren't scared. No one blames the man in situations like this."

"No, Millie. Listen." He leans forward to rest his elbows on his knees, the nearly empty tumbler hanging between them. "I'm not in charge of your job. I'm not one of the people deciding who gets it and who doesn't. I dropped out of the interview committee."

My breath halts in my chest. "What? When?"

A muscle flickers in his jaw. "The Monday after you taught me how to make pizza."

My stomach drops to my feet. That was almost four weeks ago. Nearly a month that I've spent hating myself for wanting the man I couldn't have.

"Why?" I whisper the words, almost afraid to hear the answer.

His lips kick up in a devastating smirk. "Because when you looked up at me after we spilled your coffee, with those little butterflies on your shoulders and your bright, sparkly eyes, I wanted to slide my hands into your hair and drag you to my mouth."

I shiver at the thought, flashing back to the memory of the spell I was under in that moment.

"And when you crashed your car into mine, I couldn't stop myself from scouring your body for any injuries, even though *you* ran into *me*. Then you fucking bent over to check my bumper." He lets out a dark chuckle, and the devious tone sends a thrill up my spine. "And my fingers literally flinched to touch you."

My heart pounds unsteadily as he runs a hand through his hair before he continues.

"However, I could've pushed all that to the back of my mind and made a logical decision about who to hire. But then"—he shakes his head—"you came to my house and lit the whole place up like a fireworks show. You laughed and had a dance party with my girls and made me smile until my cheeks ached."

His words soak through all the layers I've put around my heart, and the protection dissolves like sugar in hot water.

My rational brain has been raging at my heart for so long, trying to deny my feelings for Finn and his girls. I've fought against that tug-of-war rope until my fingers might as well have bled from the pressure.

But now I want to abandon all the resistance. I want to fall into the feeling in my floozy heart and let it lead the way.

Maybe she knows what she's doing.

Finn's eyes haven't left mine. He watches as I drag in a deep breath.

"Does that scare you?" he asks.

Bravery pumps through my veins. "No."

"Does it change anything?"

"Yes."

He licks his lips. "What does it mean?"

"It means we tied our game."

Amusement dances over his face. "I'll let you claim your prize anyway. Dare me to do something."

I shake my head sadly. "I sure wish you didn't kiss like a sheepdog, because then I might be tempted to try it."

He straightens. Clears his throat. "I've gotten much better. I promise," he says, his gaze dropping to my lips.

I let the words slip out. "I dare you to prove it."

He keeps his intense focus on me as he slowly swallows the remaining liquid in his tumbler. This is my chance to backtrack, and I think he's giving me time to reconsider my words.

But I don't want to.

Instead, I give him a subtle nod, and that's all the permission he needs before he rises to set the tumbler on the desk. Then he stalks to my chair and drops to his knees in front of me.

Silence stretches through the heavy air between us, and my lips practically buzz with sparks as he watches them like he wants to consume them.

His face is a portrait of desire, and I file it away under "Man who intends to kiss a woman until she forgets her own name."

He doesn't look like he kisses like a sheepdog. This man knows exactly what he's doing and has the confidence to prove it.

As he inches closer, heat pools between my thighs. He grips my knees, his fingertips sliding under the hem of my dress and parting my legs easily, as though my muscles can't find the strength to resist that light pressure. My thighs take up residence on either side of his waist like they were meant to. Like they choose to live there now.

I lick my lips and watch my fingers grip the silky fabric of his shirt. "We aren't very good at being just friends. I drew a line, and we weren't supposed to cross it."

"Millie." He rubs his thumb gently over the seam of my lips, then his fingertips move along my jaw, under my ear, and envelop the side of my neck. "Pretty sure I was erasing that line as you were making it."

His eyes are as dark as the night sky, and I'm falling into them, drifting through space without oxygen or anything to tether me. I'll be completely lost there forever, and I'm still longing for it.

"Is this okay?" he whispers, muscles tense like a predator holding himself back for the perfect opportunity to strike.

I nod, leaning into the warm hand branding my neck. "Kiss me."

He breathes a sigh of satisfaction before removing his glasses and setting them on the floor. Then he draws close, and I stop breathing. I stop thinking.

Velvet soft lips brush against my jaw, and heat swarms to the point of contact. They drift to my cheekbone, the coarse hairs of his beard scraping against my skin, leaving my nerves sizzling. Moving to my ear, he bites lightly at my earlobe, and it sends a bolt of lightning straight to my core.

I try to suck in a breath, but it sounds more like a needy moan. His lips must be drugged, because I'm helplessly slipping into a lust-filled trance, and my muscles have turned to mush with the slightest touch.

He pulls back with a devilish smile. "Look at you, already melting for me."

Those navy eyes dip to my mouth, and I lick my lips, desperate for them to earn more of his attention. At this point, he really could kiss me like a sheepdog, and I'd tell him he was a good boy. I'd worship at the altar of sheepdogs everywhere.

I'm breathless as he leans toward me with a singular focus until his lips coast over mine in a chaste kiss. Violent flames ignite in my heart. A gritty growl rattles from his chest, and I savor it. I embrace it. I *drown* in it.

Running his tongue across the seam of my lips, he requests entry, and I immediately grant it. Moans leave both of us when his tongue reaches mine, the taste of whiskey and mint invading my senses.

His movements are slow as he kisses me thoroughly. Greedily. One hand cups my neck and jaw as he tilts my head the way he wants it and consumes me like I'm the oxygen needed to sustain life.

My fingers dig into his hair, and I run my nails over his scalp, urging him not to stop.

A needy protest bleeds from my throat as he releases my mouth, and his lips move to my neck. Teeth graze my flesh. Groans fill my ears.

I'm coming out of my skin with the sensations he's creating. How can this feel so overwhelming and wonderful at the same time?

"Fuck, Millie," he rumbles before his lips come back to mine.

The desperation in his voice spikes my confidence. I twist my fingers in his hair and kiss him back without restraint. Our tongues slide against each other, and I sink my teeth into his lower lip.

Grasping my hips, he yanks me forward. My dress hitches up my legs as they spread wider to accommodate his torso.

Shivers rack through me as his hands run up the outsides of my thighs, and his fingers squeeze the skin there deliciously. "You're so perfect, *stella mia*."

The only sound I can make in response is a shameless whimper.

I circle my arms around his neck, his skin hot to the touch. I kiss him like I'll never get to do it again or like I'll do it forever—I'm not sure which.

Finn slides his hands out from under the hem of my dress and runs them up my back, pulling me closer until my breasts press into his hard chest and the heat between my thighs rests flush against him.

I try not to whine as he releases my lips and dives for my neck again. He growls as he scrapes his teeth over my pulse point before soothing the spot with his tongue. His lips float back to mine, and we kiss in a whirlwind, alternating between soft, languid strokes and demanding, fierce ones.

Eventually, his grip loosens, and his kisses dwindle to lingering pecks on my lips and neck before he drops his face on my shoulder with a sigh. I lean into the back of the chair, pulling him with me.

He tries to hold his weight off my body, but I need all of it.

I want to beg him to crush me. Steal my breath. It's his anyway.

"Stay here tonight," he whispers, lips brushing my neck. "Sleep in my bed. Nothing more has to happen. I just don't want you to leave yet."

He can't see my smile, but it beams for him anyway. "Okay, but I have to be on time tomorrow. Future department directors can't be late."

"How about you take my car home in the morning to get ready for work and then come pick me up? I'll make sure you get there on time."

* * *

FINN LEAVES ME in his bedroom with a T-shirt that says, "It's okay, Pluto. I'm not a planet either."

After I change into it, I steal a chance to text Lena and beg her to take care of Pepper for me.

> **Millie:** Are you home?

> **Lena:** Yep. Just got back from my date. He was a bore. And he smelled like he bathes in grape jelly. 🤮

Lena: Where are you? How was your surprise?

> **Millie:** Perfect. We had a private croissant lesson with Maggie. I'm bringing home all the tips and tricks.

Lena: No way. Finn is nothing but green flags!

> **Millie:** I know.

> **Millie:** Do you think you could let Pepper sleep in your room tonight?

Lena: Of course, but where will you be?

> **Millie:** At Finn's. I'll be back early tomorrow before work.

Lena: I'm sorry, WHAT?

Lena: You explain right now, woman.

Lena: Don't do this to me. You know how nosy I am.

Her last few texts come in a flurry, and my fingers freeze over the screen as I try to decide what to say back. How do I wrap everything up in a quick text?

The realization that Finn has nothing to do with my interview process is an immense relief. I can step into my trial run next week with the knowledge that I've done nothing to negatively impact my chances.

I'm still going to make him pay for not telling me sooner, but at least I can move forward knowing that I'm not doing anything wrong.

Finn opens the door, and I drop my phone to the bed like he just caught me doing something suspicious. He's holding two glasses of water and an extra phone charger as he pauses in the doorway, and his eyes land on his shirt hanging over my body. His gaze tracks over every detail before he clears his throat, hands me the water, and plugs in a charger for me.

The bedroom carpet is soft under my feet as he leads the way to his giant bathroom and pulls out a new toothbrush.

We do a sequence of mundane things together: We brush our teeth, Finn turns on the lamp, I plug in my phone, and we both lift the duvet on our own sides to slip between the cool sheets.

But none of it feels mundane at all when it's across from the person who stars in all my daydreams and fantasies.

Finn leans against the headboard, shirtless but still wearing his glasses, with his hair a little mussed, and I can confirm that it's the sexiest thing a man could possibly do.

I can't keep staring at that view, so I focus on the ceiling. We're in bed together, Finn's bare skin inches away from me, and we literally just made out like the world was ending. But suddenly everything feels like too much. My view shifted too substantially over the last hour, and I can't process this new reality. I wiggle my feet, and my hands twist on my stomach as I try to control my breathing.

"Are you nervous?" he asks.

Those are the same three words he said to me in that meeting weeks ago. The same three words that I assumed he meant with mockery.

But it's just Finn, checking on me because he's worried about me, not because he's coldhearted.

In fact, he's completely the opposite.

His hand finds mine under the covers, and he brings it out to his lips, kissing the back once before setting it on his chest. "Tell me what's on your mind. We can figure it out together."

That gentle reassurance soothes my nerves a little. "I'm scared. About a lot of things, really."

He sets his glasses on the nightstand and scoots down to lie next to me. Then he turns on his side and nudges my arm until I do the same, and we face each other with our hands between us. "Let's go through them one at a time," he says.

Explain what's raging through my anxiety-ridden brain? Where do I even start?

"What are we doing?" I ask.

A small grin curves his lips. "What do you think we're doing?"

"Well, we've been trying not to fall toward each other for months, and I've been beating myself up over wanting a guy I shouldn't have, and then we *just* got to the point where we're talking about it, and I'm already in your bed."

He lets out a satisfied hum. "Yeah, I love that part."

I shove his shoulder lightly. "This is serious."

He schools his face until only a little humor peeks out. "Okay. My honest answer is that I've been hoping we would get to this point ever since I asked you on a date and you rejected me." He narrows his eyes playfully. "But nothing has to be decided tonight. I just like your company, and I don't expect anything more."

"Why didn't you tell me sooner that you had dropped out? I could've stopped beating myself up a long time ago."

He huffs a laugh. "I tried to tell you the night I asked you on a date, but you slammed your hand over my mouth before I could."

"I did not *slam* my hand over your mouth." I roll my eyes. "And you could've told me after."

"It wasn't the only reason you mentioned. You also said you needed time after your last relationship, so I was waiting until you felt more secure in that way."

There's a comfortable safety in this little cocoon we've made in his bed. It feels tender and gentle, and it pulls the truth from my lips. "I'm still scared of being in a relationship. I don't know how to be in a healthy one, and I'm afraid I'll get lost. I want to be able to trust you, but I also want to be able to trust *me*."

Finn nods. "I want all of that too. How can I help you?"

"I don't know," I say with a sigh.

His hands wrap around mine, and they rest together between our bodies. "I've never done this. Never had a relationship like the one I want with you, and I don't have healthy examples in my life to learn from. But everything in me wants to make you happy. Make you proud. Keep you safe. I may not know all the answers to everything in our relationship, but I know you can trust me to try. You can trust me to be respectful and kind." He slides a hand through my hair. "You can trust me to work with you to solve anything that makes you uncomfortable." He brings my fingers to his lips and kisses them softly. "I'm not here to stifle you or control you or shape you into something else. I'm here to help you shine."

A tear slides out of the corner of my eye and drips across my nose. For months, my emotions have felt raw and fragile, but with every moment in Finn's presence, they gain a little strength.

He draws me closer until I'm nestled against his chest. "I promise you can trust me."

Chapter 25

Millie

*W*e may have fallen asleep last night with innocent intentions, but the pulse pounding between my legs tells me something has shifted.

When I open my eyes, the sky outside is still shrouded in darkness. The soft fabric of Finn's pillowcase caresses my cheek, and his arm is slung over my hip, his body molded against my back. As he sighs in his sleep, his warm breath dances through my hair.

I feel like a dam broke after our conversation last night. Like the pressure of my feelings for him was building and growing, and when he finally told me he'd dropped out of the interview, the dam burst, and everything poured forward in a deluge. And now all the thoughts and wishes I had smothered and pushed aside are threatening to drown me.

He's not forbidden anymore, and it makes me want to push my hips back into his and see what happens.

Finally, my floozy heart cheers.

I shut my eyes as I tentatively press my hips into Finn.

His breathing stops. Every muscle in his body freezes.

"Millie?" he whispers against my ear. He lifts his arm to move it off my hip, but I wrap my hand around it before he can pull away.

Turning onto my back, I meet his dusky eyes and sleep-rumpled hair.

Finn first thing in the morning is a delicacy I didn't know I was missing. And I want to *devour* it.

He studies my face as his hand settles against my stomach. "What is it?"

The timbre of his voice is deep and rough in my ears, and his eyes are hazy with disbelief, like he can't decide if he's still dreaming.

I loop my hand around his neck and drag his lips to mine. He stays perfectly still against my mouth, but I move mine anyway. I kiss the corners, trying to tell him how greedy I am for his touch. His palm presses into my shirt like an anchor to my core, hot and solid.

My desperation rises to the surface, but Finn still hasn't moved to kiss me back. So I pull his bottom lip between my teeth and run my tongue over it.

There's a beat of shocked silence before his restraint snaps, and his lips part over mine. His hand wraps around my waist, and my entire world narrows to that point, where his fierce grip is keeping me from floating away on an ocean of need.

He tastes and explores my mouth with his tongue while his fingertips slip under the hem of my shirt, and I whimper at the sensation of his rough hands against my skin. My fingers surge into his hair, tugging him closer until his hardness nudges my hip, and a satisfied moan vibrates from his mouth to mine.

Heat floods my veins, turning me into a soaked, writhing mess for him. I want Finn's hands on me more than I want my next almond croissant. I'd give up years of them for him to travel up my shirt and touch me.

He must be able to read my mind, because his warm hand slides up my stomach, and I focus on every millimeter he gains.

He leaves a blazing trail over my skin until he stops right when his fingertips hit the underside of my breast.

"What do you want?" he whispers against my lips.

How can he expect me to speak right now? My brain is a bowl of alphabet soup, and I can't form the letters into words.

I wrap my hand around his forearm, and the coarse hairs scratch against my palm as I slide up to his wrist. His eyes are nearly black as I guide his hand up until his warm skin settles over mine, encompassing my breast and sending a needy ache all through my body.

"Millie." He sighs as his eyes fall shut. He kisses me again, drawing my tongue into his mouth and groaning as he pinches my nipple between his fingers. They drift lazily over me, teasing and making me tremble.

"Yes. Finn." I nearly whine as he releases my breast, before his fingers squeeze my hip. He flashes me a questioning gaze, and I nod so quickly I might've pulled a muscle in my neck.

A low hum of approval leaves his throat, and his hand wanders to cover where I'm burning for him. Anticipation builds as he slides over my underwear and down between my thighs. "You're so wet already," he breathes, fingers poised to destroy me at any moment.

"Please," I beg softly, even though I want to scream it.

He deftly pulls the fabric aside and dips one finger into my warmth. The slight pressure intensifies the fire raging inside me, igniting everywhere I'm needy and aching.

"Oh, Millie," he moans, pressing his lips to my neck.

Air hisses between my teeth as his fingers drift up to circle my bundle of nerves in leisurely movements, exploring and learning.

"That feels so good," I whisper, pulling his hair until he lifts his head from my neck.

"Yeah, it does." He circles again, and my hips twitch as his eyes lock with mine, cataloging every detail. "Tell me what else you like."

"I like . . ." I lose my train of thought when he touches my clit again.

Warm breath coasts over my cheeks as he chuckles. "What do you like?"

"Slow and teasing," I say, my voice breathy and needy. "Then harder when I get close."

"Mmm. Perfect." He grinds against my hip as he pushes a finger inside me. "Fuck."

I kick the covers off and wrap my hand around his forearm, desperate for as much contact as possible. His muscles ripple and shift as he adds another finger and plunges deeper. I can't stop my hips from pressing up into his strength, drawing him in closer.

"Look at you fucking my fingers. That's it. Take what you need."

Pleasure builds in my core at his praise and the way he watches every move I make like he doesn't want to miss a single detail.

"I need . . ." I trail off, completely consumed by the riot of sensations he's causing. It's so hard to think when I'm burning like this.

"Tell me," he encourages, low and husky.

"No more teasing." I gasp for breath.

"Alright." He smirks like he's savoring my torture. "But I love watching you squirm."

His pace picks up, and he applies more pressure against my clit as he hits deep inside me with his fingers, my rapture soaring closer and closer.

Everything is overwhelming and uncontrolled, but I focus on the feeling of Finn's skin against mine and look into his eyes as I crest the mountain and shatter.

I can't breathe while the fire spreads through my whole body, and I clamp around him.

"So beautiful," he groans as he carries me through it, and my body dissolves back into the sheets.

***

Oaks Folks

Mom: Sorry to interrupt your date last night, Millie. Hope you had a great time!

Tess: DATE? Was it with that tattooed Tinder guy you sent me a screenshot of?

Dad: When are you bringing him home to meet us?

Mom: I invited him for my birthday while I was talking to Millie.

Mom: He's quite handsome.

Fabes: Is he the one with the tiny hands in that pizza picture you sent?

Dad: Is he the one who was sick? Did he get you sick?

Millie: I don't know if you know this, Mom, but it IS possible to text one person individually instead of announcing everything to the whole family. 😳

Millie: Finn was the one who was sick, and he did not infect me, Dad.

Tess: But does he have tiny hands?

Millie: His hands are perfect.

Tess: Like, perfect size to cover just your nipple or the whole boob?

Mom: Tessa Oaks. That is inappropriate.

Millie: Tess, see above message about texting individually. And they are normal six-foot-something man hands.

Fabes: Mmm. That's the size I like.

Dad: How do I remove myself from this text chain?

The sound of Finn's low murmur pulls my attention from my phone. The man who had his fingers inside me this morning is acting completely casual, humming a *Moana* song as he drives us to work.

Luckily, I managed to sneak out of his house before the girls woke up. I rushed home and got ready, then picked him up to drive to work together.

It all feels very . . . domestic. Surprisingly normal.

Maybe that's why I ask, "Do you want to come home with me tomorrow?"

His humming pauses. "I'd love to, if you're comfortable with it."

The thought of Finn and the girls in Fern River makes a wide grin play over my face. They could spend time in my childhood home, run wild on the farm, and meet my family. Play in the treehouse my dad built, meet my favorite horse, and dance through the flowers I helped plant last spring.

I think I want that more than my brain will let me admit.

"The girls will need swimsuits and clothes you don't mind getting dirty. And we have goats. Sometimes goats can chew on clothes or shoelaces, you know? I'll give my mom a few ideas of foods the girls like. I don't want them to be hungry the whole time. Oh, and I don't know what the sleeping arrangements will be, but I'll let you guys have my old room. There's a full-size bed in there, and we can blow up an air mattress for the girls. I'll crash in Fable's room." I suck in a deep breath to calm my rambling.

His grin is amused. Tender. "You seem nervous to bring me home."

"I think so. Maybe."

Finn rests his hand on my thigh, and his thumb makes a slow circle. "It'll be perfect. I want to meet your people so they can be my people too."

Chapter 26

Finn

*R*ocks crunch under the tires as we roll down Millie's childhood driveway and a white two-story farmhouse comes into view. The house is surrounded by a green blanket of grass sprinkled with wildflowers and two massive hemlock trees.

Pepper perks up in the backseat between the girls, tail wagging as she looks out the windows.

"Are we there?" Eloise asks from her booster seat.

Millie's legs bounce as she takes a deep breath. "Yep. This is it." She points for me to park next to an old gray truck.

A cheerful greeting from outside the car has her opening the door before I've even turned off the car. Millie clings to a young woman in a sun hat, and Pepper leaps through the front door to escape the car.

As I open the back to let the girls out, Mary approaches with a kind smile that's identical to Millie's. "Welcome!" She wraps her arms around me in a motherly hug that instantly reminds me of my nonna. It's been years since I had a hug like this. "I'm so glad you're here." We pull back, and her palm lands on my shoulder with a squeeze. "I've been wishing to meet you."

"Thanks for having us. Your property is beautiful."

"Oh, thank you." She squats in front of the girls. "I'm Millie's mom, Mary. I'm so happy you're here to visit our farm."

Eloise smiles immediately. "I'm Eloise. Can I pet your goats?"

"Absolutely. They would love that," she coos. "Is there an animal you want to pet, Avery?"

"Horses," she says simply.

Mary nods. "That can be arranged. They're my favorite too."

Millie brings the young woman over and introduces us to Fable. Her sister is slightly shorter than Millie and looks right at home on the farm in a pair of denim overalls rolled up over her work boots and two honey blonde braids on her shoulders.

When I reach out to shake her hand, she clasps it and then turns our joined hands to look at mine like she's inspecting it. She narrows her eyes and says, "Good-sized hands."

That's the oddest greeting I've ever received. "Um . . . thank you?"

Dropping my hand, she winks before kneeling to speak to the girls. "Know anyone who want to help me collect eggs?"

Avery nods, and Eloise jumps a few times. "Me! Me!"

Fable grabs their hands—not inspecting them at all—and turns to lead them toward the chicken coop.

As Millie and her mom are catching up, a tall, broad man in jeans and a flannel shirt catches my eye. He's walking out of the barn when Pepper bounds up to him, and he runs a hand over her back before continuing our way.

"Well, Millie finally came back home," he says, wrapping her in a tight hug and rocking her back and forth.

When she pulls away, she gives him a stern glare. "You're the one who didn't come to visit last time Mama did."

He ruffles her hair like I do with El and Ave.

I offer my hand, and he shakes it firmly. "It's nice to meet you, Mr. Oaks. I'm Finn Ashford."

His face creases all over with the strength of his smile. "Call me Dave."

Millie grins as she watches us, the apples of her cheeks rosy, like they're already sun-kissed.

"Okay"—Mary loops her arm through Millie's—"let's show Finn around so he feels right at home."

* * *

THE ONLY THING more excruciating than Millie in a bikini is not being able to *touch* Millie in a bikini. The forest-green fabric is stretched across her perfect tits, giving enough of a tease to draw my attention constantly. She sits on the edge of a small dock in her jean shorts, feet dangling in the pond as the sunshine dances across her strong shoulders and delicate collarbones.

I watch her from where I'm swimming behind the raft that Eloise shares with Avery. Millie's practically glowing, and I want to lick every inch of exposed skin. And every hidden one too.

"Come on, Millie," Eloise cheers. I note the streaks of sunscreen on her cheeks from where she wriggled away from me before I could rub it all the way in. "It's not scary. You just have to jump in."

"I'm not scared." Millie laughs. "I'm warming up in the sun before I hit that cool water."

"Should we pull her in?" I whisper to the girls, pushing their raft closer to the dock.

Avery's eyes go wide as she nods. Eloise covers her mouth with her hand to stop herself from spoiling the surprise, but it only makes her look suspicious.

As I kick us closer, I spot some pink on Millie's shoulders, even though I saw her apply plenty of sunscreen.

I only watched to make sure she covered everything.

For sunburn prevention.

No other reason at all.

When we approach the dock, I can barely touch my toes to the muddy bottom. I inch toward Millie until I can reach her foot and quickly slide my hand around it and tug.

"It's cold," she cries, scooting out of my reach. I spot her phone on the wooden slats next to her, so I know it's safe.

Keeping one hand on the girls' raft, I hold the other up like a truce while I creep closer. When she glances at the girls, I have just enough reach to grab her around the waist and toss her into the water next to me.

She shrieks the whole way, and the girls cackle. We tumble into the pond together, a wave of water crashing over us as our arms and legs tangle, and we try to right ourselves.

When we surface, she pulls the hair out of her eyes and gives me a wicked grin. She treads water as she undoes her shorts, and they make a wet *smack* when they land on the dock.

"You think you're so funny, Spock." She shoves me back with both hands, and it surprises me enough that my feet slip out from under me. My head falls back under the water as Millie grabs the float and kicks away.

Once I regain my footing, I swim in their direction.

"There are some big fish in here," she tells the girls when I catch up with them.

"As big as an alligator?" Avery asks, pulling her feet in tight to her body as I join Millie in pushing the girls.

"Not that big. But one time, I was fishing right there with Tessa, my big sister." She points to a spot under a big spruce tree. "I caught a fish as long as your arm. My dad cooked it for dinner that night, and I learned that I don't like the taste of fish."

As if on cue, Millie lets out a sudden squawk and launches herself onto the raft next to Avery. She stares at me with wide eyes, her face as white as a sheet. "Something slimy touched my leg."

I burst out laughing as she scours around the float for the offender. "Here I was, impressed by your outdoorsy skills," I tease.

Her eyes narrow with a benign threat. "Some people scream about spiders," she says pointedly. "And some people scream about fish." Then she kicks water into my face, and the girls follow her lead.

* * *

"DRAW FOUR, UNCLE Finn," Eloise says during what feels like my seventy-fifth round of Uno with the girls, Mary, and Dave.

After drawing my cards, I scan the room around me. The difference between this house and my childhood home is night and day. Where my house was sterile and tidy, and the evidence of children was erased from every surface, this home welcomes those intimate signs of life. It brings me right into the warm memories like I was there.

Millie probably did her homework and ate every meal on the old farm table where our game is being played. Family pictures line the living room walls, full of vacations and Halloween costumes and swim meets.

Fable walks in and leans over her dad's shoulder, her fingers looped around the straps of her overalls. "You kicking this big guy's butt?" she asks Eloise and Avery.

"He hasn't won a single game yet," Mary says, laying down a yellow six.

Fable shakes her father's shoulders. "Are you letting them win? You never let us win when we were kids."

"I wouldn't dream of it," Dave says decisively, laying down a draw-two for Avery. She scowls at him but takes her cards from the pile.

Fable starts toward the stairs before pausing to look over her shoulder. "Are the Nikolaous coming for dinner?"

"I think so," Mary answers, eyes still on her cards. "We invited them."

"Great," Fable grumbles, dragging out the word as she disappears up the stairs.

During our next round of Uno, the front door opens behind me with a creak, and boots hit the hardwood floors. I look over my shoulder and find a man, probably a little taller than me, wiping his shoes on the mat in the doorway.

He slides off his Fern River Volunteer Fire Department cap, hanging it on a hook by the door and smoothing a hand over his clean-shaven jaw. He's followed by a curvy older woman with a kind smile and warm brown eyes to match his.

A flash of auburn hair and jean shorts whizzes by as Millie runs toward him from the kitchen and launches herself into his arms. Heat creeps up my spine, and my body tenses, but I force myself to stay in my seat.

Holding her off the ground, he spins a few circles, her arms around his neck and face against his green flannel. I wish I could hear what their muffled voices are saying.

"Uncle Finn," Eloise nudges beside me. "Your turn."

I play my red four and turn back to see the man lower Millie to the ground and tug the braid in her hair.

"It's been too long, Mills. Good to see you." His voice is soft and fond, and my teeth grind together.

Mills. I hate that he calls her the same name her friends do.

"What's this?" Millie asks with a laugh, standing on her toes to rub her hand over his hair. "You forget how to drive to the barber?" She moves to hug the other woman as Avery pulls my elbow, bringing me back to the game.

I lay down a blue six and meet Mary's eyes across the table. Her mouth is set in a knowing smirk as she looks over my shoulder where Millie and the man are.

"Theo and his mom, Eva." She nods toward them. "He and his sister grew up with the girls."

That information does little to relax my stiff jaw.

Millie looks so comfortable with this Theo guy. She just threw herself at him with no second thought. I want that level of familiarity with her. I want her to jump into my arms without overthinking it.

I catch myself evil-eyeing him and turn to lay my cards facedown on the table, trying to smooth out the crease I've made. Dave lets out a small, deep chuckle.

"Uno," Avery calls out.

A hand slides over my shoulder as I play my next card. "This is Finn," Millie says, pulling me to turn around.

Begrudgingly, I stand and reach my hand out to Theo. Forcing my jaw to unclench, I attempt to look as pleasant as I can under the circumstances. "Finn Ashford. I'm Millie's . . ."

I pause, wanting to stop there. I'm Millie's. Period.

A possessive urge to claim her trickles through my veins, making my fingers twitch to wrap around hers.

Millie's eyes bulge as she dons a bright smile. "Friend," she says to finish for me. My attempt at looking mildly pleasant must not be working, because she sends me an accusing glare.

Theo seems unaffected by my grimace. "Theo Nikolaou. Great to meet you," he says, smiling wider than I ever have in my life.

I resist the urge to roll my eyes.

This fucking guy, with his movie-star smile, must be everyone's favorite.

"I win," Avery shouts from her seat, drawing our attention.

Millie walks around the table and kisses the top of her head. "Good job, Ave. My parents are hard to beat."

While she introduces Theo and Eva to the girls, I catch Fable out of the corner of my eye.

She struts across the living room in a low-cut burgundy dress, her hair in golden waves behind her as she walks with an icy confidence she didn't show before. Theo freezes where he's talking to Dave, lips parted and eyes wide as he tracks Fable's movement across the room. She never looks his way as she strides straight for the kitchen, hips swaying and chin high.

Theo clears his throat and sputters as he tries to refocus on his conversation with Dave.

For some reason, seeing a little agony creep into Theo's expression gives me a hint of pleasure. The tension between my brows releases slightly. "Is there anything I can do to help with dinner?" I ask Millie.

"Can I trust you not to burn anything?"

"Maybe give me an easy job?"

* * *

As it turns out, I have a gift for struggling with easy kitchen jobs. I've been given the task of making a salad, which sounded pretty straightforward. But somehow, Tessa has already told me that the lettuce pieces are too big, and Fable informed me that I added more cucumber than I should've.

"Fabes, I love your dress. You sure got fancy for dinner," Tessa says from the stove, stirring green beans. Her brown hair is in a neat French braid that I wish I could replicate for Avery.

"You've seen this dress a hundred times." Fable presses the masher into the potatoes with a tight jaw.

"Sorry. I thought it was a compliment." Tessa smirks over her shoulder, a hidden meaning dancing through her eyes. "You look nice is all I'm saying."

"Are you going out later?" Millie asks, her tone attempting innocence as she cuts the garlic bread into perfectly symmetrical slices next to me.

Fable drops the potato masher on the counter with a *clang*. "No. I wanted to look nice for our *mother's birthday*." She slams her hands down on her hips, daring anyone to contradict her.

"Mm. Okay." Millie meets Tessa's eyes, and they share a knowing look.

Tessa wipes her hands on a kitchen towel. "Theo sure looks good. He's all rugged and charming tonight, and I like it." She moves to the sink and starts washing a bowl.

"Well, you've always had a thing for unkempt lumberjacks." Fable glares at her sister's back.

Tessa doesn't let the insult touch her as she laughs heartily. "Yeah, I kind of dig it on Theo."

With a low growl, Fable places the bowl of mashed potatoes on the counter beside my salad and stomps out of the kitchen.

"You poked the bear, Tess," Millie says, sneaking the heel of the bread to a patient Pepper between us.

"That's the job of the oldest sister." Tessa shrugs.

"True," I chime in. "My older sister knew exactly where to poke to make me the angriest." I drop the last bit of tomato into the salad and open the croutons.

"How much older was she?" Tessa asks. The way she phrases her question lets me know Millie has already told her about Clara, and the relief of that relaxes my shoulders.

"Four years. Luckily, we were never in high school together, or she would've made my life a living hell."

Millie's eyes flick to Tessa's. "Been there. Tessa wasn't too bad, but she had her moments."

"Usually after you borrowed my clothes and didn't return them," Tessa grumbles.

"One time, when I was in middle school," I say, "Clara told me I needed to practice how to talk to girls in the bathroom mirror. She said that's how all the boys in high school learned. I believed her and stayed up late having an entire conversation with my-self." I shake my head, my cheeks heating. "Turned out she was recording the whole thing from the shower and played it for my friends the next day."

Their bright laughter rings through the kitchen as I clean up my salad-making mess. Memories of Clara seem so cloudy in my mind sometimes, like I can't concentrate on them, because if I do, the pain of missing her will sharpen. But watching Millie with her sisters makes me want to clear the haze and pull them into focus. I *want* to remember what I had with Clara, because every time I do, my chest feels a little lighter.

Chapter 27

Millie

There might not be anything hotter than two tall, handsome men hunched over the sink together, hand-washing the dinner dishes. I shamelessly watch them from the doorway as Finn hands Theo a pan to dry.

Finn seems to have recovered from whatever put him in a terrible mood when Theo arrived. Now he's answering questions about the logistics of the planetarium like they've been friends forever.

Walking toward the sink, I loop my hand into the crook of Finn's arm. "I have a little surprise to show you after the girls go to bed." I catch Theo's eyes behind Finn's back, and he winks at me. "My mom said she would listen for the girls in case they wake up."

"Surprise, huh?" He hands a clean plate to Theo. "Should I be scared?"

"I promise you'll like it. No spiders involved."

He shoots me a playful glare. "Okay. I'm in."

I let go of Finn's arm and find Tessa at the table sliding the Catan game board pieces into place. "Who's playing?" I ask.

"Fable, me, you, Finn, and maybe Theo, if Fable lets him." Tessa grins conspiratorially. My poor little sister's been hiding in her room, avoiding the man since Eva went home after dinner.

My dad yawns from the couch where he's sitting with Avery and Eloise on either side of him while Mom reads the girls a book. It's the sweetest thing I've ever seen, watching the two of them live out their grandparent dreams. They've doted on the girls all day, catering to their every need and want. My mom even let them blow out the candles on her birthday cake.

"Think Finn wants to play?" Tessa asks, setting the bags of pieces around the table.

"He definitely does," I tell her, peeking over my shoulder to make sure he can't hear me. "But he's really good. So we need a plan."

* * *

"It doesn't make any sense," Finn says, eyebrows puckered as he scans the game board. "One, two, three different people could've blocked you from getting the points for the longest road and didn't. It's almost like they wanted you to win." He studies me suspiciously.

"I kicked your ass, Spock," I brag, taking a victory lap of high fives around the table. "You're just jealous."

His eyes narrow as I drop back into my spot, and Tessa and Fable snicker. Did I ask everyone to secretly gang up on Finn with me? Absolutely. Was it worth it? One hundred percent.

I shrug, grinning at his pinched expression. He's so cute when he's worked up over a board game. "I've dethroned the king of Catan."

He shakes his head. "Does it still feel like a victory if you had to steal it?"

"Heck yeah. That look of grumpy confusion on your face makes it all worth it."

Finn reaches for my waist, but I manage to escape my chair just in time. I sneak to the living room to check on the girls and find them sleeping on either side of my dad, his snores so loud between them that I don't know how they can stay asleep through it.

After walking back to the table, I lean over Finn's shoulder. "Want to help me get the girls upstairs? Then we can go to your surprise."

I guess he forgives me for the Catan win because he says, "Sounds good."

We trudge up the stairs to my childhood bedroom, each of us carrying a sleeping child. The walls are still bright yellow from the time I read that yellow rooms make people happy and convinced my dad to help me repaint it. I had painted it poppy red the year before, so he wasn't pleased with the sharp turn in an entirely different direction, but he worked on it for two straight days anyway.

The dim fairy lights hanging from the ceiling greet us as we deposit the girls onto the air mattress my mom set up for them. Finn gets the bed I slept in as a teenager, complete with sunflower sheets.

When Eloise is tucked into her spot, I stand to find Finn scanning my wall of books.

"No judging my book choices," I tell him.

His eyes snap to mine. "*Twilight*?" he questions, brows almost to his hairline.

"Of course I have *Twilight*," I whisper-yell, crossing my arms.

"Team Edward or Jacob?"

Never in my life would I have guessed that Dr. Finn Ashford knew even an ounce of information about *Twilight*. "Team Edward, but I have a very special place in my heart for Jacob."

"You think sneaking into a girl's room to watch her sleep is okay?"

"Maybe I do, given the right circumstances. Like, is he a sexy vampire? Then, yes. Does he sparkle? Then, yes." I turn on my heel and walk out the door.

"I didn't take you for a girl who likes stalkers," he says, following close behind me and pinching my hip lightly.

"I didn't take you for a guy who knew anything about *Twilight*, but I guess we all have our secrets."

* * *

"It's just up here," I assure Finn as Dad's old truck climbs up the steep hill on my parents' property. He has a death grip on the passenger door handle, with his other hand clasped around my thigh. "The view is worth it. I promise."

At the top of the next hill, I stop the truck right before the flat, grassy overlook and turn it off. Finn helps me spread out a striped blanket, and I take off my sandals and lie down on it. The grass is long enough to push the fabric up, so it feels like a cushion under the cloth. I pat the spot next to me, and Finn slips off his shoes to lie down.

Our pinkies loop together on the blanket as we both take in the view. A clearing in the trees up here grants us a good bit of sky to see the stars. Away from the city, they shine so much brighter, and I spent many nights watching them from this spot as a teenager.

"You're happy in Fern River," Finn says, turning his head toward me.

"I love it here."

A long, weighted sigh leaves his chest. "I can't imagine growing up in a house like that. It's so different from what I had."

I wrap my hand around his. "What was your house like?"

"Silent. Sterile." He clears his throat. "You know how at dinner tonight everyone was laughing and talking, like a family?"

"Yeah," I say, remembering how Eloise held everyone's attention with her detailed explanation of how raptors hunted.

"We had none of that growing up. My parents wanted us to be quiet or talk about what they designated as appropriate conversation. Most of the time, though, it was only Clara and me at dinner, and those were my favorite nights. But your family is so . . . *lively*."

"You mean loud?" I chuckle. "My mom used to wear earplugs on the days we were particularly wild. We fought over everything you can think of. Clothes, shoes, boys, hair clips, who got to use the car. Be glad you weren't around for those parts."

"That's what I have to look forward to, I guess. One day, I'll be breaking up fights over who gets to wear the purple hair clip?"

"Well, Eloise probably doesn't want that hair clip." I laugh. "But, honestly, they seem nicer to each other than we were at that age."

"Who knows what they'll be like when they're thirteen, though. I'm slightly terrified."

"I have a feeling they'll be best friends for life. It may be rocky through a few hormonal years, but then it gets better."

We fall silent for a few moments, our gazes tracking all over the sky.

I thread my fingers through his, pressing our palms together. "Where's the best place you've seen the stars?"

"New Zealand. The whole sky was filled with stars, so many you couldn't pick out individual ones." He points to a group above my head, outlining their shape. "That's Lyra, Avery's middle name." He moves a little lower. "There's a small cluster right there. That's Delphinus, the dolphin. Eloise's middle name is Delphi." His voice cracks on the edges as he adds, "Clara surprised me with that the day they were born."

My chest feels unbearably tight as I look over the constellations he pointed out. Releasing his hand, I scoot closer, cuddling into his side. "I love those names." He rests his palm on my hip and takes a deep breath, his chest rising and falling beneath my cheek.

The moon peeks over the trees behind my parents' property, making a few dimmer stars disappear in its light. We watch the sky for a while, listening to the sound of the crickets in the grass and an owl calling in the night.

Finn's fingers slip under the hem of my sweater, and he draws hypnotizing little circles on my waist. "You and Theo . . . Did you ever . . ."

I slide my hand over his stomach, a knowing smile on my lips. "Date?"

He lets out an affirmative grumble.

"No. And I never wanted to. His sister and Fable are best friends, and our moms are also. They live down the road, so they were around a lot growing up." I smirk against his soft shirt. "He's sexy, though, don't you think?"

Finn makes a low sound, deep in his chest, and it rumbles against my cheek.

"I've never met someone so muscular," I say, trying to rile him up. "His voice is so deep, it gets my heart racing. And those forearms . . ."

In one swift movement, Finn flips us and leans over me, pinning me down with his leg shoved between mine. My breath picks up when I see his knowing grin.

"I like you jealous," I whisper. "But Theo only has eyes for Fable."

"He better." He presses a soft, lingering kiss to my lips. "Have you ever brought a date here?" he asks.

"What kind of girl do you think I am? I don't reuse make-out spots."

His eyes narrow. "This is a make-out spot?"

I shove his shoulders and use all my strength to roll us over until I straddle his waist. The blanket scratches against my palms as I plant them beside his head. "Yes. I brought you here to show you the stars and kiss you until you forget them."

His hands find my hips, and he pulls me lower on his lap, right where he wants me. "Better get to it, then."

With heavy-lidded eyes, he watches as I pull his glasses from his face and set them beside us. I slide my fingers through his hair, and he hums in pleasure.

Soft skin brushes against the pads of my fingers as I trail them down his neck and under the collar of his blue shirt. "I like this color on you. It makes your eyes the deepest shade of navy."

"I'll get rid of all my other shirts, then." He grins, sliding his hands up under the hem of my sweater and curving them to my waist. "I like this color *off* you." I raise my arms as he lazily lifts the fabric over my head and drops it beside us. His eyes feast on all the skin he's uncovered—the swell of my breasts and my pebbled nipples straining against the white lace of my bra. "It was fucking agony seeing you in that bikini today."

He sits up close to my body, a few inches from my mouth.

"I was about to tell you I'm sorry, but the truth is, I'm not," I whisper before I press my lips to his.

His mouth opens for me, his beard tickling my cheeks as I grind my hips against his hard length.

"Are there any neighbors close enough to see or hear us?" he asks, dipping his head to my neck. He kisses my collarbone, and his tongue leaves a warm, wet trail as it skates over the tops of my breasts.

"No," I gasp. "Only an abandoned A-frame. But I can be quiet."

"Can you? That feels like a challenge," he teases, pulling back to meet my eyes as his fingers dance over one strap of my bra. "This looks constricting."

"It is." I nod, and he slides both straps down my arms. Anticipation blooms in my chest, and my heart pounds against my ribs. Finn reaches around my back, bringing his lips closer to me as he fumbles to open the clasp.

When my bra drops between us, the chilly night air brushes over my peaked nipples as he sucks in a breath. "You're exquisite."

His eyes shine in the moonlight as he studies me, looking over every inch of skin. Then he finally cups his hand to one achy breast and squeezes gently. It's so satisfying that I let out a pained whimper. He does the same with his other hand, and it feels like they were made to fit over me.

His grip moves to my back, holding me in place as he trails his lips over my breasts. Then his tongue lands warm and wet over my nipple, and he sucks it into his mouth.

My strangled cry completely ruins my promise to be quiet.

I grab his face and pull him back until my nipple slips free. "Shirt. Off," I order, too impatient to make coherent sentences.

A smirk crosses his lips as he slides it over his head, and I shove him flat on his back.

Chapter 28

Finn

I'll never forget this view. Millie's curves in my hands as she straddles me, stars sprinkled across the universe behind her. Her rosy-pink nipples tease me as she leans forward, bringing them achingly close to my mouth but just out of reach.

"Have you thought about this? Touching me?" she whispers.

"Every fucking day." A smug grin blossoms on her lips. "I've thought of endless things I want to do with you." My hands caress her hips as they roll against me. "Have you thought about me, *stella mia*?"

She bites her bottom lip and nods.

My blood pumps faster. "While you touched yourself?"

Her lashes fall to her cheeks, and she whispers, "Yes."

Fuck. That image will be seared into my brain forever.

"Can you show me?"

Her eyes flash open, and a playful grin takes over her lips. I love how comfortable she is with me—like she trusts me enough to be herself.

She sits back, and I watch her movements like a hawk as she palms her breasts and rolls her fingers over her nipples. Moonlight dances over her cheekbones as she tilts her face to the night sky and grinds her hips against my aching erection.

"Finn," she moans to the stars.

I'm breathless as her hands wander teasingly down her stomach, and she flicks open the button on her jean shorts. The zipper makes a resounding buzz as she lowers it to reveal a small patch of her green underwear.

She slips her fingers inside, but I can't see what she's doing. It's the sweetest agony to watch her arms squeeze her tits together as she dives deeper and grinds against her own hand.

"Look at me." I grasp her chin and guide her face down. Her eyes scan mine, and she smiles as bright as the moon. "You're so fucking stunning right now. I wish you could see yourself." Her attention dips to her body, and she shutters a breath. "I want to make you come. I need it—need to taste you and hear you moan again. Can I? Please?"

She drags her teeth over her bottom lip and nods. "Yeah. Yes," she stammers, lowering herself onto the blanket beside me.

I catch the slight tremble in her body and pause. "We can stop here if you want to."

A snort-laugh bursts out of her. "If you stop, I'm going to scream."

Dropping my lips to her ear, I whisper, "Oh, I'm going to *make* you scream." The sound of her tiny whimper brings a smile to my face. "Mind if I remove these?" I ask, running my fingers over her shorts.

"Please."

God, I want to listen to her beg me to touch her for eternity.

I loop my fingers into her shorts and underwear and slide them down her body, tossing them aside. A hum of approval falls from my lips as I glide my hands up her legs and across the silky skin of her hips.

I've fantasized about having her bare under me more times than I can count. My Millie naked, wanting me, with a greedy smile of impending pleasure on her face.

And I finally don't have to imagine it anymore.

She softens as I crawl up her body, looping her arms around my neck and fusing herself to me. I leave a trail of kisses from the corner of her mouth to her neck, down her collarbone, and over her nipples. Her little moans and sighs are music to my ears as she writhes against me.

I continue the path of my lips down her stomach and skim over her hip. Her legs drift open wider for me, like she's discarding every vulnerability. Letting me see all of her.

I don't know what I've done to deserve this, but I now have the privilege of knowing her this way. It's rewriting my DNA. Making my heart beat just for her.

She runs her hands over my head, and I meet her eyes, admiring the look of impatience on her face. "I'm getting desperate," she grits out as her grip tightens in my hair, steering me closer to where she wants me.

I can't stop my loud groan as I finally give in to what both of us are craving and slide my hand between her thighs.

"Mmm." I sigh as her wetness coats my fingers. "You're so needy for me," I whisper, moving up to circle her clit. I slide back down and press a finger inside.

"I'm not sorry for that either." She laughs breathlessly.

Satisfaction burns through me as I pull my fingers away, because apparently, we've fixed the apologizing problem.

But her humor ends abruptly when I lower my head and press my tongue against her sweet, swollen clit.

Finally. Fuck, I needed her like this.

She gasps as I glide and lick in lulling, soft movements, knowing it won't be enough. I want to drag it out because watching her squirm beneath me is my favorite form of torment.

"Fucking hell," she hisses, grabbing my hair and pushing herself against my tongue.

My blood turns to lava as I cling to her for dear life, gripping her thighs so tightly that I might be leaving marks. I can't help rolling my own hips into the blanket, seeking any pressure I can find.

Her fingers scrape over my scalp, and the movement has my eyelids dropping shut from the ecstasy of having her all over me. Every part of me is invaded by her. All my senses are engulfed in her pleasure.

Releasing one leg, I glide two fingers inside her, twisting and curling them until I hit a spot that makes her cry out. Her thighs twitch around my head while she pants and writhes under my movements. When I can tell she's getting close, I suck lightly on her clit, and she releases a guttural moan into the night. It echoes in my ears as she wiggles and pulses, and I suck harder, gliding my fingers in and out with steady pressure.

Her heels dig into my back as she holds me against her desperately. I look up to her face and take in the devastating view of her while I'm pleasuring her like this. Her tits bouncing as her breaths heave in and out, green eyes locked on me.

She lets go of my hair and snaps her hands over her mouth to muffle her scream as she detonates. The muscles around my fingers clench and throb, and she shakes beneath me as her orgasm takes over, my focus glued to every detail of it.

She's so goddamn perfect that it hurts.

As she calms, I slow my movements and pull my hand away. Her eyes are shut tight, breasts heaving, with a content smile on her face.

"I won that challenge," I tease. "You were nowhere near quiet."

She lifts her head and glares at me before letting it fall back again.

I huff a laugh and kneel between her thighs. She rises onto her elbows and looks to where the outline of my dick is pressing very obviously against the front of my jeans. Her tongue darts out to lick her lips, and the pressure gets worse just watching her.

When she reaches for me, I almost stumble to bring myself closer to her, picturing her full lips wrapped around me like I've been fantasizing about for so long.

But we both pause at the distant sound of her phone ringing. She freezes, hands poised over my jeans, and meets my eyes.

Fuck. That could be Millie's mom calling about the girls.

She must see where my mind goes, because she lets her hands drop and starts gathering her clothes. I throw my shirt on as she runs toward the truck, still pulling her shorts up her thighs.

"Hey, Mama," she answers, trying not to sound out of breath but failing miserably. "Yeah, we'll be right there." Holding the phone in the crook of her shoulder, she slips her sandals on. "Sounds good." She hangs up as I set the folded blanket in the truck. "Avery woke up and asked for you. My mom is sitting on the couch with her."

Guilt slices through me like a hot knife to the stomach.

* * *

I'VE BEEN A sullen grump this morning on the drive home to Wilhelmina. Millie and the girls are giggling and talking like nothing's wrong, but I can't get last night out of my head. I want to laugh with them and join their conversations, but my mind is spinning on a loop of shame after leaving the girls last night.

Avery was snoring in Mary's lap when we got back to the house, completely content. When I picked her up to carry her to bed, she opened her eyes and groggily asked me where I had gone.

They were okay, but I should've thought about the fact that I was leaving them in a new place. Of course they wouldn't sleep well in a foreign house. It may have been only a restless night this time, but what could it be next time?

I was on that overlook, enjoying Millie's company and body when I should've been with them. They are my primary responsibility, and this isn't what Clara wanted when she left me the most important people in her life.

Somewhere in the last few weeks, my priorities got skewed. I'm lost, not knowing how to balance everything the right way. The way Clara would want me to.

We pull up to the stone pathway in front of Millie's small, cottage-style home. She gives me a wary look, like she knows something's on my mind but doesn't want to push me about it.

She opens the back door to tell the girls goodbye, and Pepper bolts toward the house. We silently unload her things, and when I shut the rear hatch, her hands twist anxiously in front of her jean shorts.

I know I'm the reason she's feeling unsettled, but I don't know how to fix it.

Or if fixing it is even the right thing to do.

"Millie, I . . . I need a few days to think." I can't touch her, or I might kiss her, so I shove my hands into my pockets.

"Because of last night?" She tilts her head.

"Yes." I run a hand through my hair, hating how I sound.

Her shoulders hitch as she takes a deep breath. "Okay. I have a busy week ahead of me anyway."

I feel like a piece of shit right now, leaving her on the curb with no information. But I have no idea what to say or how to handle everything on my mind.

A strand of hair blows across her lips, and I force myself not to tuck it behind her ear.

"I understand." She picks up her bag and flashes me a falsely bright smile that guts me.

Chapter 29

Millie

*M*aybe he hasn't recovered from the raging hard-on you left him with." Lena shrugs behind her bottle of sparkling water.

I roll my eyes, running my hand over Pepper on the couch between us. "Maybe he didn't like it?"

After he had me literally seeing stars on that overlook, Finn barely spoke to me on the way home from the farm. It's unsettling—not knowing what shifted between us so suddenly.

Today was my first day as the temporary director of the entomology department. It was close to a normal day, aside from a few phone calls I had to make and emails I responded to. This week I'm focusing on a new collection plan for the lab room that I'll present at my interview. Then tomorrow I have a meeting with Sharon and all the department heads in the museum, so hopefully that will give me a chance to shine.

Even though Finn will be there.

Which is awkward, but I guess that's what we signed on for by sort of starting something up and then letting it fall apart. We will just have to take a swift jump back into the coworker realm.

Lena nudges me with her foot, snapping my attention back to her skeptical glare. Her dark curls are up in a bun today, and she's wearing the hell out of a workout set like she's going to the gym soon, but we both know she'd have to be dragged by a hot guy or gal to ever set foot in there.

"I can tell you for certain that he *liked* what happened on that overlook," she says sternly.

I sigh. "I mean more generally. Maybe he doesn't want a physical relationship like that with me."

My insecurities are like an exposed wound this week, leaving me riddled with anxious uncertainty, and not hearing from Finn is only exacerbating them.

Lena sets her drink on the coffee table. "We could host a game night to invite him to something back in the friend zone." When I don't answer right away and just stare into the ivy hanging in our window, she says, "You don't like that idea."

"I don't want to go back to friends," I whisper, giving voice to what's been floating around in my mind all day. "All these thoughts and feelings were coaxed out of me, and I don't want to put them back. I don't even know that I could." I lie down next to Pepper, and she lifts her nose to rest it on my shoulder with a long groan. "It's sad that I'm coming around to the idea as he's pulling away."

My phone chimes with a text notification, and I sit up to reach for it, a bubble of excitement filling my chest at the prospect of a text from Finn.

But that bubble pops against my ribs when I see the name.

> **Kyle:** This is fucking ridiculous. Quit acting stupid. I need to talk to you, and you're being a bitch.

My arms drop to my lap as my stomach twists in knots. Lena bends until she draws my eyes to her. "What is it?"

"Not Finn." I hesitate, hating that I didn't tell her about this sooner. But it would be even worse to continue avoiding it. I hand her my phone as a dark cloud forms over my heart.

"I'm gonna kill him," Lena rages, scrolling up to his past messages. "I'll do it. Oh my god. He has no right to treat you like this."

My chest constricts like someone's fist is wrapped around it, squeezing all the air out. "He . . . he came into Maggie's one morning."

Her gaze sharpens. "Shit. Mills. Why didn't you tell me?"

"Because you shouldn't have to fix everything for me."

"I don't *have* to. I *want* to. I could've been helpful."

"Finn was there, so I hid behind him until Kyle left." I try to straighten my shoulders to let more air into my lungs, but they still feel tight.

Lena's forehead pinches. "Kyle lives thirty minutes from here."

"I know. It freaked me out so much that I haven't been back to Maggie's other than the croissant lesson with Finn."

She shakes her head. "Did Finn know what was going on?"

"I told him. He said he'd go back to Maggie's with me if I wanted him to."

"You know I would too, right? I can be your right-hand bitch, ready to do anything necessary. Cut off his balls, bury a body . . ."

A small laugh bursts out of me. "Finn said something similar, except not quite as gruesome."

Lena shrugs. "Maybe we double-team it, then. Finn does the wimpy stuff, I do the hard-core stuff?" She covers my hand with hers. "First, though, you block this asshole. You shouldn't have to read shit like that or expend any mental energy on him."

* * *

Oaks Folks

Mom: Found a pair of blue, little-girl socks under the couch. Want me to send them to you, Millie?

Tess: Have you really not cleaned under the couch since we were little?

Mom: 🙄 I assume they belong to Avery or Eloise.

Dad: Don't mail them. Make Millie and Finn bring those sweethearts back. We didn't get enough time with them.

Fabes: True. I want to see them again!

Tess: Yes! Please!

Mom: Bring them back!

I stare at the phone, searching for the right response, but it never arrives. Things with Finn are still in an awkward holding pattern, and reading the sweet messages from my family makes the pain in my chest burn hotter.

I miss him. I miss the girls.

* * *

THE MEETING STARTS at ten in the morning, but I land in my chosen seat at nine thirty, determined to be there before anyone else.

Well, okay, I want to be there before Finn. That way *he* has to choose where to sit based on where I am. If he picks a seat right next to me, I'll take that to mean things might be okay eventually. If he sits as far away from me as possible, that probably means things I don't want to think about.

As the minutes creep closer to ten, other department heads filter into the room. Jamila from the local flora and fauna exhibit takes a spot next to me, but my other side remains open. I manage to make small talk while keeping one eye on the door, waiting rather impatiently for the moment of truth.

With one minute until ten, the door swings open, and Finn's broad shoulders invade the room. Heat creeps up my neck, and I drop my gaze before he can see me watching the door. I fiddle with my sparkly orange pen on the table and studiously avoid his eyes while I wait with bated breath for him to choose a seat.

But he never comes to my side. A chair squeaks across the table as Finn drops into it. Peeking up through my lashes, I let my vision lift just enough to see his tie.

It's plain black today. No astronomy flair.

Dr. Black Hole is back, arms crossed over his chest as he leans back in a seat on the other side of the table, three spots down.

That pretty much counts as "far away" in my book.

My shoulders slump. I had secret hopes, way down in my heart, that seeing each other in person would fix something. We could either go back to friends, or he could see me and want to talk.

But instead, he's gone back to ignoring my existence.

Sharon joins us, and I try my best to pretend everything is fine. I act as if I'm the director of the entomology department, and judging by the way Sharon includes me and asks my opinions, I think I'm doing well. It's my best impression of "fake it 'til you make it" while deliberately avoiding ever looking at Dr. Finn Ashford.

The responses he's forced to give are short and grumbly. And when my eyes accidentally land on him, his dark blues are full of annoyance as he grimaces and glares at every person in the room.

Except for me. He never looks my way.

His arms remain crossed over his chest until the moment the meeting ends, then he escapes the room as quickly as he can.

* * *

SWEAT BEADS ALONG my hairline as I trail my eyes over the butterfly vivarium's large, transparent panels and gray steel frames. The massive palms and vines growing up the sides of the building make me feel like I've been transported somewhere else. To a humid jungle oasis, far away from the confusion in my life.

I've spent more time here than normal this week, hoping to keep my mind off missing Finn and the girls. This is like a meditation space for me, where I can let go of everything else in my life and just be with the butterflies.

Yet, despite the peace this sanctuary brings me, it hasn't been able to block all thoughts of Finn from creeping into my mind.

I've had no word from him. No message, no call, no note on my desk.

And, for the most part, I've held it together. I just have to make it through one more day of my week in charge. My idea board and mock-up for the butterfly exhibit I want to pitch are nearly done, and I feel prepared for my committee tour of the vivarium tomorrow.

I've managed to stay busy at work.

But once I arrive at home every evening, my heart aches.

That visualization of my life with Finn and the girls plays on a loop in my head, and I can't turn it off. Over and over, my throat tightens as I feel those kisses brushed across my forehead and hear that laughter ringing through the bedroom. And I hate how the possibility of that fantasy was ripped away before I ever had a chance to enjoy it.

Chapter 30

Finn

I've been a goddamn asshole.

I know I have.

Everyone at work knows it, Gabriella knows it, and the girls probably know it too, even though I have tried my best to hide it when they're around.

And, worst of all, Millie knows it.

I walked into that meeting on Tuesday with every intention of pretending to be a pleasant person, but she wouldn't even look at me. She wouldn't let me see those mossy-green eyes that have become my favorite color in the world.

So I couldn't force myself on her. I couldn't sit next to her, because if Millie won't smile at me, she must think I'm an asshole. And the world is a dim, dark place without that smile.

Plopping onto the couch in Dr. Kline's office, I survey all the whites and creams in the dreary morning haze streaming through the window. This couch is soft enough to be comfortable but not enough to tempt me into a nap.

Sometimes it's hard to know how to sit here. Do I spread my thighs and slouch the way I naturally would? Do I sit up as straight as I can like this is an interview?

Dr. Kline crosses his legs as he settles in the chair across from me and tucks his gray cardigan under his notebook. He clears his throat and opens his pen, eyeing me as I fidget into a relaxed position.

Slouching and comfortable it is.

"How have you been since our last visit?" he asks with a warm smile.

"Well, things were going okay until this week, honestly. There are a few big changes I wanted to talk about if that's okay." Our last visit was two weeks ago, so a lot has shifted since then in terms of my relationship with Millie.

"Anything you want to talk about is perfect. I don't have an agenda," he reassures me.

I have no idea why I'm nervous to bring up Millie. He's never given me any reason to believe he's judging a single thing I say.

"I've been starting a relationship with someone," I start as he nods.

"That's great. How is it going?"

"I think I'm struggling to balance my time. Things with Millie changed over the last couple weeks, and I'm worried about neglecting the girls in the process."

"Has something happened to make you feel like there's an imbalance?"

I recount the events of the night on the overlook, being as honest as I can without divulging all the details, but I'm sure he can read between the lines.

"I see." He makes a note before setting his pen down. "What do you think Clara would say if you were asking her for advice about your relationship with Millie?"

I try to imagine calling my big sister for relationship advice and almost laugh at the absurdity of it. "That wasn't something I did normally, but I think I could talk to her about Millie. Clara would like her." Dr. Kline's eye contact encourages me to continue. "She would be excited for me and probably tease me about it as much as possible."

"I agree. I think she would be happy for you."

Nodding, I fold my hands in my lap. "How do I learn to balance my time between Millie and the girls? How do I let go of the guilt I feel when I spend time away from them?"

He tilts his head. "Did Millie give you any reason to believe she's upset about the division of your time?"

"No, never. She has spent a lot of time with all three of us and frequently talked about how excited she was to see the girls."

"Do you think that if you spoke to her about balancing your time, she would be supportive?"

The answer is as clear as the window in front of me. Obviously, Millie would be supportive. "She would be helpful and understanding."

"It sounds like she's someone you can trust with a conversation like this," he says. "Do you think your frustration with yourself has anything to do with the amount of attention your parents paid you and Clara as children? I believe part of your fear here might be that you will become the kind of caregiver your parents were."

The reality of those words makes my stomach sour. "Yeah." I sigh, running my fingers through my hair. "Clara left me responsible for her girls, and I would never want to disappoint her by acting like our parents."

He hums in understanding. "Let me start by saying that worrying about how you're doing as the girls' caregiver already makes you a good one. You'll be able to handle this because you're concerned and talking to people to solve it. Clara knew you well enough to know you would do that. She didn't trust you with her girls because she thought you would be perfect. She trusted you because she knew you would do your absolute best. That's all we can offer anyone in our lives—not perfection, but the promise of doing the best we can."

His words are echoing the ones I told Millie almost a week ago. I said she could trust me, not because I could promise to be perfect, but because I could promise to try my best.

Why is it so hard to do the same thing for myself?

I let out a long breath and nod. If I had been in Clara's shoes, with children I needed to leave in her care, what would I have expected from her?

The best she could.

Dr. Kline continues, "I also believe she wanted you to have a life beyond the girls as well. She didn't intend for you to shut everything and everyone else out to take care of them. In fact, you might find that you can be a better caregiver if you are getting time away to rejuvenate. And that doesn't mean at work. It's time outside of both, to be yourself, whether that's a relationship, a hobby, or alone time."

I can't even remember the last time I did something alone, completely for myself. My days of cycling and hiking are long gone since the girls came to live with me, and sometimes I wish I had time between work and making dinner to do something like that for myself.

"So, what should I do?" I ask.

"You start with an honest conversation with yourself. Sit somewhere relaxing and try to picture what you want moving forward. What will give you the most joy in life? Then have an honest conversation with Millie about what a future together would look like. Last, you should practice having time away from the girls, even if it's not with Millie. It's good for them to spend time with other people, and it's good for you as well."

* * *

THE TICKING OF my watch reminds me it's nearly time to go home and make dinner. Gabriella deserves to leave on time after the grumbling and scowling I've done this week, but I need to push it for just a handful of extra minutes.

A few keystrokes later, the planetarium view soars toward the Butterfly Cluster.

I need my sister's advice, and while some people would go to a loved one's grave to talk something through, I feel closer to her in this room. In the stars.

I drop to the ground and lie flat on my back against the scratchy carpet. The vulnerability of this position makes my hands twitchy, but it feels necessary. How can I move forward if I don't make myself a little uncomfortable first?

Taking a deep breath, I whisper, "Hi, Clara." I scan over each star in the cluster and clear my throat. "It's me." I shake my head. "Obviously. I assume no one else is talking to you like this." I swallow thickly. "I met someone . . ." I breathe, my throat tight with emotion. "And I wish you could meet her."

As tears gather at the edges of my eyes, I pour out every whispered word I wish I could say to my sister and hope that, somewhere in the vast universe, she hears me and knows that I'm still trying my best to make her dreams come true.

Chapter 31

Millie

Jojo, our giant jungle nymph, has been sitting with me since I gave the interview committee a tour of the butterfly vivarium this morning. Her bright green body is about the length of my hand, and it's important that she's comfortable with being held, so Micah and I take turns during the week. She's a great silent companion that hasn't judged me for talking to myself for the last hour.

My computer dings with a new email, and a squeak of excitement bursts out of me when I see it's Sharon scheduling my second interview for almost two weeks from now. She has a few time options for me to choose from, so I email her back, thanking her and picking the earliest time slot. I'd rather get it over with first thing in the morning than dread it and feel anxious about it all day.

This means I have twelve days to prepare myself to convince a hiring committee that I'm the right person for this job.

I'll still have to endure the other applicant having their time in charge next week, but I can handle it. I will be the picture of civility, even if I'm screaming on the inside, because I'm a professional. And I have to prove it.

My phone buzzes on my desk, and my stomach jumps when I see Finn's text on the screen.

Finn: Hi, Millie. Would you be willing to meet me at Maggie's for lunch?

My mind floods with the millions of things I want to say to him, but none of them should be said over a text.

Millie: Does one o'clock work?

* * *

As I ROUND the corner toward Maggie's, Finn's hunched shoulders come into view through the raindrops in my vision, and my heart rate picks up just seeing him there. He stands under the awning, hands shoved in his pockets, while rain pelts the sidewalk and splashes onto his black shoes.

The fact that he waited for me spreads a soothing warmth through my limbs. I haven't been back here since our date, and having someone with me will make it easier.

"Thanks for waiting." I join him under the awning and unzip my raincoat.

Finn reaches for the strap on my arm and pulls my bag to his shoulder. "No problem. I'm sorry it took so long to get back here." He places his hand flat against my lower back and opens the door with his other. The warmth of his palm stays there, but he doesn't push me inside. It's a stabilizing comfort while he waits for me to feel ready.

The smell of roasted coffee and warm, fresh bread hits my nose as I scan what I can see through the doorway: a few people waiting in line to order and a barista walking by with a tray of food.

I can do this. Even if Kyle is here, I have a buffer. I have Finn in my corner, and I may not know what's going on between us, but I trust he would do anything I needed him to.

I cross the threshold, Finn following close behind me. My gaze darts around the restaurant as I take off my coat. I don't see Kyle's blond hair or hear his voice over the others. When I get into line, I breathe a sigh of relief, and Finn squeezes my shoulder.

"Remember when you thought you could hide me from your mom's FaceTime call?" His breath kisses over my ear as he talks, intimate and secret. "But you forgot about the reflection in the window?"

A bubble of laughter breaks through my anxiety, and I peek over at him. "Remember when I found out you kiss like a sheepdog?"

His eyes narrow into thin slits. "I proved I didn't."

"Did you, though?" I needle him.

Finn stays right behind me while we order, like a bodyguard in case I need it, and then we make our way to a table. I take a seat and pull my warm coffee mug in front of me, cradling it between my hands like it's a Drink Protection Wall guarding me against any devastating news he may present.

"How was your week?" he asks.

Everything I want to say pushes and shoves at the gates of my mind.

I missed you. You kissed me senseless, then haven't called me in days. I don't know what's happening to my brain and my heart, but it wants to be around your brain and your heart constantly.

"Long," I say, giving him the simplest, least revealing answer.

He adjusts his glasses. "Everything going okay with your week in charge?"

"I think so." I nod and take a sip of my coffee, but it's too hot, and I can practically hear my tongue sizzle.

An awkward silence hovers in the air between us. Screw this small talk. I need answers. But he doesn't seem to know where to start. His hands cradle his coffee mug, and he stares into it like he might find the answers there.

Finally, he takes a deep breath and begins. "I want to apologize for the mood I was in on the way home from your parents' house. There's no excuse. I just didn't know how to put into words what I was thinking, and I didn't want to say the wrong thing."

"You were in a pretty bad mood at the meeting too," I remind him.

"Yeah," he sighs, rubbing a palm over his beard. "I'm sorry." There's another stretch of silence. "When we were up on that overlook," he starts, and my mind flashes back to that picture-perfect moment. To the stars over my head, his face between my legs. He smirks, probably seeing the blush heating my cheeks. "*That* was fucking perfect. I've thought about it every day since."

"Me too," I whisper, unable to filter myself.

He bites his bottom lip and turns serious again. "But when your mom called, I felt guilty, like I was being irresponsible. Clara left the girls with me because she believed I would take care of them, and on the overlook, it felt like I'd chosen you over them. If something had gone wrong, I was with you, distracted."

My spine stiffens. "That's not what I intended when I took you up there."

He reaches over and wraps his hand around one of mine, trying to breach the Wall. "I know. But I have this huge responsibility, and I'm still trying to figure out the right ways to handle it."

A waitress steps up to our table and sets my chicken Caesar salad and Finn's roast beef sandwich in front of us.

When she leaves, Finn continues. "My therapist helped me sort things out yesterday, and I think it's important to explain to you before we continue building a relationship. Because that's what I want, Millie. I want to be together, in front of the girls and everyone else."

Little bubbles of happiness gather in my chest as Finn reaches for my hand again.

"Clara and I were raised by two people who always put everything else before their own children. Hell, they went to a dinner party on my eighth birthday, and I pretended to blow out a candle over a bowl of cereal with Clara." He shakes his head. "So I'm having a hard time finding the right balance between the example I was shown throughout my childhood and the kind of parent I want to be for Ave and El."

He sighs and shakes his head. "I'm trying to trust that Clara knew I wasn't going to behave like our parents, and I have to believe in myself enough to trust the decision she made. But I need you to know that Ave and El will always be there. You and I being in a relationship will mean the girls are a part of it. I have to make sure you want that."

As he explains his fears, I remember what he told me about his ex. How she broke things off because she wasn't willing to share him with his nieces. Something twists and strains in my heart. I could never give him an ultimatum like that.

It's Finn *and* his girls. A package deal. I would never want it any other way.

The decision is effortless. "I want to be in a relationship with all of you, but what if this ends badly? I hate the thought of things going wrong between us and never getting to see the girls again."

His eyes soften. "I don't think that's going to happen. But I also think that if, for some reason, we don't continue our relationship, we're both mature enough to handle it well for them."

I press my lips together, feeling a wave of sadness crash over me at the thought. "They've already lost so much. They don't deserve to lose more."

"I know," he whispers, brushing a circle over the back of my hand. "We won't let it happen that way."

I nod, tears springing to my eyes. "I've missed them this week."

His head tilts. "You missed us?"

A snort of a laugh leaves my throat. "No, I said I missed *them*. Not you. Did you see your Grumpy Spock scowl at that meeting?"

We both know my words are a lie. I missed him every day.

He gives me a wry look. "What are you doing tonight?"

"Um." I raise my eyes to the ceiling and pretend to think over my schedule. "I have plans with a guy who isn't grumpy and doesn't scream at the sight of spiders."

His mouth twitches in amusement. "He sounds boring. Come out with me, instead."

Chapter 32

Finn

*M*illie's eyes light up as we pull into our destination. She reads the lettering over the doors and flashes me a knowing grin. "Is this a nerd date?"

I park in front of the modern gray building lined with huge windows. "Absolutely. It seemed like the perfect place for two nerds to spend the evening together."

Dionysus Games is full of every board, card, or dice game in existence. The inside is connected to Muses Books, a local bookstore catering to every kind of reader.

I can't keep my eyes off Millie as she gets out of the car. Her red-brown waves frame her glowing pink cheeks, and her tight jeans and tan sweater reveal enough of her curves to make my mouth water.

Sliding my hand against hers, I intertwine our fingers. She squeezes tight, and when I look down at her, she's beaming up at me.

"It feels good to be on a date with you," she whispers.

"Better than that boring guy you had plans with?" I tease.

"I don't know. He smiles a lot more than you."

I picture Theo's movie-star smile and try to emulate it, plastering on the biggest one I've ever worn, my cheeks pinching from the force of holding it. But if Theo can do it, I can do it.

Millie cracks into bright laughter and pats my cheek. "Don't force it. I like this, but I like you grumpy too."

I turn and kiss her palm, and we enter through the game-store doors. Shelves and racks full of games surround us, and Millie's eyes are wide as she looks around the room like she's landed on a new planet.

"This is nerd heaven," she says as she runs her hand along a shelf of games and picks one up.

I settle an arm over her shoulders. "Let's pick one out."

"Only one?"

"As many as you want."

"Are you trying to sweet-talk me?"

"Possibly."

"It's working." She shrugs.

Millie spends a while browsing through shelves as I follow behind her. I've always loved games. Clara and I played so much Yahtzee growing up that my nonna bought us our own personalized set for Christmas one year.

When Millie has filled my arms and her own, we walk to a table at the back and set them down to look through our choices. I sit in a chair, and Millie stands across the table from me.

"Okay, I picked out a few things that looked good for us to try," she says, putting her hands on her hips and surveying her stack. By "a few" she means seven games. I have three in my pile.

"This first one is a twist on the classic Catan with a *Game of Thrones* flair." She holds it under her chin for me to see.

"Trying to find a different version so you can beat me?" I tease, narrowing my eyes.

"I've already beaten you."

"Fair and square?"

She bites her lips and sets the box down, avoiding my question. "Yes pile," she says definitively.

"My first option is Wingspan." I hold the game under my chin like she did and press my cheeks into a wide smile like I did outside. "Board Game Geek says this is excellent."

She bites back a grin. "A generous wingspan is excellent."

I look at the box in my hands. "What do you mean?"

A snorting laugh bursts out of her. "I wish Fable or Tessa were here. They'd get it."

She can tell I'm lost and slides into the chair next to me to lean my way. "Okay, there's a popular fantasy-romance series where the sexy heroes have wings, and they use the term 'wingspan' as a euphemism for a man's . . ." Her gaze drops to my lap suggestively. "The size of his wingspan relates to the size of his . . ." Her eyes flare with meaning.

"The size of his pants?" I ask, feigning innocence.

She leans closer and sets her hand on my thigh. "No. The size of his—"

"Do you all need any help this evening?" a cheery voice asks from beside our table. We both glance up to find a tall young woman surveying our stacks of games.

"Hi, Deanna," Millie greets her, noting her name tag. "We were discussing the importance of a good wingspan. Don't you agree?" Millie stands with a wily grin.

I don't know how she's pegged this woman as someone who knows whatever language she's speaking, but Deanna's eyes sparkle with understanding, and she nods emphatically. "But sometimes the wingspan is more of an energy, you know? An aura about a person."

"Totally agree." Millie points to the game before me. "I say yes pile for that one."

Deanna gives me an assessing once-over and sets her hand

on Millie's shoulder. "You better put him in the yes pile too, honey."

"I'm considering it," Millie says, and warmth zings from my chest, spreading through my body.

Millie, Deanna, and I discuss the rest of our selections, and Deanna has great insight for the games we've never played. By the end, we have ten games in the yes pile and a nonexistent no pile. Millie even picked out three games for the girls because she saw them and claimed she couldn't help herself.

"We're going to have to whittle this down," she says, looking over the games fondly as Deanna steps away to help another customer.

"No whittling. Let's get them all." I ignore Millie's protests and carry the stack to the cashier to check out.

Between the two shops is a coffee house, making that our next stop. We order our drinks, and once they're ready, we venture into the bookstore.

"Here's the plan," I tell Millie as she takes a sip of her coffee. "You pick out your favorite book for me to read, and I'll get my favorite book for you to read."

She slams her free hand to her chest with a loud gasp. "That's blasphemy. You have *one* favorite book? Out of the millions of books in the world, you can narrow it down to *one* favorite?" She steps between two romance shelves, and I follow her into the aisle as she runs her fingers over the colorful spines. "There are so many good ones. How could I pick?"

Stepping in front of her, I place a gentle hand to her stomach, pushing her back until she's pinned against the shelf of books. My shoe tips bump hers, and she's forced to lift her chin to meet my eyes.

I bring my lips a hairbreadth away from hers. "How about this one?" I ask, pulling a dark book covered in flowers from the shelf above her head. When I bring it into her line of vision, her cheeks turn rosy.

"Mmm," I hum. "You've read this one. Did you like it?"

She nods, and her gaze drops to my mouth.

My lips graze over her cheek as I whisper, "If I get it, will you read it to me?"

She whimpers a yes, and I have to force myself to back away. I leave her red-faced and breathless in the romance aisle before I'm tempted to ravish her against the bookshelves.

By the time I've gathered three series from the fantasy section for Millie to choose from, I spot her with a basket full of books looped over her arm. She approaches the tables and heaves it up onto the surface.

"You have a lot to pick from," she says as I approach the table. "But first, I have to run to the ladies' room." She points a finger at me sternly. "No peeking."

Millie finds me a few minutes later at the front of the store with several bags of books in each hand. She stops with her arms crossed over her chest, a deep line marring the space between her brows.

"Finn Ashford. What did you do?"

She tries to summon a stern look of fire and steel, but it doesn't work on me. In my eyes, she'll always be sunshine and wildflowers.

I drop a kiss on her temple and turn to lead her out of the store. "I checked out. We're ready for step three of our date."

Chapter 33

Millie

*F*ry jacks?" I shout, grabbing Finn's big biceps in both hands when I notice the Belizean food truck. "We have to get, like, ten of them, because they're also delicious for breakfast," I say, pulling him toward the bright orange truck.

Picnic tables run through the middle of the food-truck park. The whole space is bathed in a golden gleam from the sunset, and patio lights hang above the tables. Finn has never had a fry jack, so I really do order ten of them. He gets pad kee mao and mango sticky rice from a Thai food truck, and we also get Greek gyros.

"Where do we start?" Finn asks, sliding onto the bench next to me and gazing over our smorgasbord of food.

I carefully unwrap the foil around a fry jack and reveal the dough filled with refried beans, chicken, and cheese.

"I'm going to let you have the first bite because I'm *so* nice," I tell Finn seriously, holding it up to his mouth. He takes a giant bite and nods his appreciation as he chews it. "I lived off these things when I did a summer abroad in Belize and Guatemala. There was a woman who made them in a cart right outside our rental, and I think we kept her in business through the summer. She'd have them waiting for us when we came downstairs every morning, and during our last week there, she taught me how to make them." I take a bite and grin as the savory flavor hits my tongue.

"What you're saying is, I could've had these already, and you've been withholding them?"

"I keep these a secret until I know I truly like the person." I shrug. "And I don't know if I like you that much yet."

He flashes an impish grin. "You seem to like me when my tongue's between your legs."

I choke on my bite and hunch over coughing. Finn rubs my back while he laughs until I've swallowed my food and can breathe again.

"Well, you're not wrong," I admit, rolling my eyes. "I guess I'll make them for you."

Finn opens his container of pad kee mao and scoops up a bite. "Are you ready for next week?"

A lump forms in my throat. "I don't know how ready I can be to meet the person I'm competing against for a promotion."

Finn nods. "Do you want to talk about it?"

"Are we allowed to?" I ask, my brows pulling together. "I've managed to get this far without prying information from you, but I can't deny that I'm curious."

He shrugs. "I'm not on the panel anymore."

"It feels like cheating, though. I don't want any special treatment."

"Well, I won't give you any information you're uncomfortable with. But I'll answer any questions you have as honestly as I can if you want."

I pull my lips between my teeth as curiosity swirls through my mind. The questions are endless. But as I filter through them, one thought seems to encompass most of my concerns.

I'll allow myself that one question and his one answer, and I'll leave it at that.

"Are we evenly matched?"

Finn sets down his drink and meets my gaze. "You are," he says in a soothing tone. "You each have different skills and abilities to bring to the position, but both of you are very passionate and would make great department directors."

I bite the inside of my cheek and try to let the sharp sting steal my focus from the pain his words are causing.

But it doesn't work well. I try to remind myself this is not a betrayal. Even if I don't like his words, I asked for his honest answer, and he gave it.

My tongue burns to ask follow-up questions, but I won't let them out. I refuse to allow my relationship with him to impact my promotion. I've worked too hard to taint this experience with secrets and insider information.

"Okay. That's all I want to know," I tell him, and he nods, rolling us into a new topic.

As we dive into the rest of our food, the sun completes its final show of the day around us. I block out all thoughts of next week, and the conversation flows easily as we talk about our high school and college experiences and what we've done in life since then. We end the feast with ice cream cones, Finn's arm around my shoulder the whole time we savor our treats.

"When do you need to be home for the girls?" I ask as we walk back to his car.

"I told Gabriella I'd be home at eleven tomorrow morning," he replies, completely nonchalant. He turns to catch my questioning gaze and chuckles softly. "We have the whole night to spend together."

"Are you serious?"

"Yes. Dr. Kline ordered me to practice taking time for myself away from the girls, and I want to spend it with you." He laces our fingers together. "That does not mean we have to do anything you're uncomfortable with. You get to choose. We could just sleep next to each other and wake up together tomorrow morning and I'd be thankful you let me."

I flash him a bright smile. "And if I want more than that?"

* * *

Oaks Folks

Dad: Wishing Avery and Eloise were here to play Uno with me. Your mother's out with Eva and I'm bored.

Millie: Maybe Fabes will play with you.

Fabes: He hasn't asked me. Probably scared I'll beat him.

Tess: From what I hear, he was going pretty easy on Ave and El. He must not be as sharp as he was when we were little.

Fabes: Maybe all that homemade beer killed too many brain cells.

Dad: Stop hiding in your room and find out, Fabes.

> **Millie:** Wish I was there to see
> the showdown in person.

> **Dad:** <photo of Fable and Dad playing Uno>

* * *

FINN'S HAND STAYS plastered to my thigh for the whole drive to my house, and he keeps a firm grip on my hips while I unlock the door. The steady contact has kept the tension between us on a low simmer, but as soon as Finn kicks my front door shut and slouches against it, everything escalates to a boil.

"Where's Lena?" he exhales as I step between his legs, and he guides my lips closer.

"Visiting her brother this weekend."

His hands drop into the back pockets of my jeans, and he yanks me firmly against him, burying his face in my neck. The hot slide of his tongue has my head falling back to expose more skin for him.

But we're interrupted by a soft whine and Pepper's nose nudging between our thighs.

"Hey, Pepper girl," Finn says adoringly, taking his hand from my pocket and petting the top of her head.

She's been inside for a while, so I reluctantly pull myself from the warmth of his body to let her outside. She creeps toward the back door, leveling me with a side-eye the whole way, like she was hoping for more time with Finn.

When I get back to the living room, Finn has settled on the couch, arms over the back and thighs spread wide. His head tilts, glittering blue eyes assessing me behind his glasses.

I have this insanely attractive man spread out on my couch,

and my body buzzes to be near him. To slide onto his lap and kiss him. And I could. We could do anything we wanted.

But the prospect makes me nervous for some reason. I know I'm safe with him, but I'm also suddenly overwhelmed.

This isn't a one-night stand to throw myself into, free of strings and attachments. This feels so much bigger than that.

I wring my hands in front of my jeans, and Finn's eyes drop to catch the movement. His brows stitch together, and he unfolds his body from the couch to walk toward me.

"What's on your mind?"

"I'm anxious and jittery," I tell him honestly.

"Okay." He scans around the living room like he's looking for an idea. "What would you do if I wasn't here? What does a normal night at home look like for you?"

A book, a bath, and a toy from the drawer in my nightstand. That's what I'd do if he left right now.

I bite my bottom lip, hesitant to tell him the truth.

"Tell me," he urges. "I want you to feel safe with me, and the only way I can do that is if you communicate with me." He wraps his arms around me in a tight hug, and I exhale against his chest.

My shoulders nestle perfectly between his arms, and his chin rests against the top of my head. It's my spot.

Safety and understanding and acceptance.

Home.

"I would read a book. Maybe take a bath." I clear my throat. "Probably get in bed with a vibrator and think about you."

Finn pulls back, eyes huge and muscles tense at the words that came out of my mouth. They twirl in the air between us like sweet, smoky incense.

Long eyelashes flutter against his cheeks as he blinks a few times before his pupils return to their normal size. He puts his lust in a box and pushes it away until only a bit of desire shows through. "Let's start with the book. I'll go get our bags from Muses out of the car, and you go get into something comfortable."

At the door, he pauses, handle in his grip as looks me up and down. "Don't think I'm going to forget about that last part, though."

Chapter 34

Finn

"Am I supposed to like the villain? I'm so confused," I say, shutting the book Millie picked out for me.

"You'll have to keep reading, Spock." She nibbles on her bottom lip, trying to hide her smile. Her head lies across my thigh, auburn hair fanned out over my jeans, as her eyes travel across the pages of the book I chose for her.

She came out of her room earlier in a matching light pink pajama set that looks so silky smooth that it's painful to keep from touching her. Every fiber of my being wants to wrap my arms around this woman and kiss every inch of her.

Hell, it feels like I've been craving that since the beginning.

With a huff, she snaps her book shut and looks up at me.

"Would you like to take a bath?" I ask, running my thumb over her cheek.

"No." She sits up to kneel beside me, taking my book and setting it aside.

"What would you like then?"

My eyes widen as she lifts a leg over mine and straddles my thighs. I dig my fingers into the couch to force myself not to touch her yet. I want her to be in control of things tonight.

She pulls my glasses from my face and places them on the arm rest. Then she wiggles her hips a little, getting settled closer to where I'm straining against my jeans already. Her eyes sparkle with mischief before she lowers her mouth to my neck.

"Are you trying to torture me?" I whisper as she leaves warm, wet kisses along my collarbone.

"Maybe," she breathes against my skin. She leans back and clutches the bottom of her tank top, lifting it over her head excruciatingly slow.

She reveals her silky waist, the round curves of her perfect tits, and then finally—*fuck*—she's topless on my lap, her peaked rosy nipples just inches away.

"I'll take it. This form of torture isn't so bad." My hands shake with the need to touch her, so I squeeze my eyes shut and clench the couch cushion.

She huffs a laugh as she pries my hands from the couch, placing them on her ribs, and it forces my eyes back open.

"I love watching the agony on your face," she says, tilting her head back. She shakes her long hair behind her, tormenting me further when the movement arches her breasts closer.

"You're a wicked little temptress," I groan in a gravelly voice.

She looks back at me, as she grinds her hips against me once, the pressure right where I want it.

My thumbs move up an inch to the underside of her breasts. Her eyes darken, and her lips part.

"There's a little agony on *your* face." I smirk.

"Then do something about it," she tempts me, raising the ante. No more bluffing. She's all in.

I don't hesitate. My mouth immediately clamps down on her nipple, sucking it between my lips. She moans loudly, losing her balance and tilting back, but my arms are there to catch her, and she melts against their support.

My hips press up into hers, and I use my grip on her back to hold her still as I move to her other breast. I let my teeth graze her skin as I release it, and she whimpers.

When I meet her gaze, she lunges for my mouth. Our lips haven't touched since the overlook, and when they do, sparks ignite between them. This kiss is pure, burning heat. Lips, tongues, and teeth move against each other as my hands slip over as much of her as possible. They graze the swell of her hips, the velvet skin of her stomach, and her strong shoulders.

She pulls back, and her hands cup over my beard as my heart races in a fog of lust. "Take me to bed," she orders.

Chapter 35

Millie

*F*inn is kissing me tonight like he's losing his mind. Like he's been holding back every other time, but the last bricks of protection around his heart have tumbled down, and he's ready for *everything*.

The hardwood floors squeak under his steps as he carries me down the hallway.

"Left," I direct him, and he turns to step through my bedroom door.

Stopping at the end of my bed, he lowers me down his body, my hardened nipples grazing over the smooth fabric of his shirt as I slide to the ground. His glazed eyes are locked on mine as one corner of his mouth lifts in a small grin.

"Is this okay?" he asks.

"Perfect." I slip my hands under his shirt, following the ridges of his muscles with my fingers as I pull the fabric off and drop it to the ground.

We're equals now, topless and aching for each other in the glow of the lamp beside my bed. Finn's hair is completely disheveled from my fingers, his eyes like twin flames, sparking and flaring as they take in every inch of me.

I want to open a new Finn file in my mind to store every detail of this evening. I need to remember exactly how our skin feels against each other and the way his eyes squeezed shut as he tried to hold back from touching me on the couch. And how he looks at me like I'm his favorite dessert and he can't wait for the first bite.

"Millie." He shakes his head with disbelief as he cups my jaw.

His gentle touch brings my head toward him until our lips meet. He tastes like the vanilla ice cream from our dessert tonight, and I sigh against his lips. Our bodies collide as we tangle our arms around each other and stumble back until my thighs meet my bed.

He breaks the kiss with a question in his eyes.

I nod and fall onto the mattress, leaning back on my elbows and letting him scan every inch of my body.

The bed dips beneath his hands as he leans toward me to press a kiss between my breasts. "I want to see you like this for eternity." A soft lick above my navel. "I want to memorize every freckle." A scrape of teeth along my hip bone. "Tell me you want me too."

His eyes meet mine, hopeful and earnest while he waits for my answer.

And my response slips from my lips without pause. "I want you. It's excruciating."

"Yeah, it is." He grips the waistbands of my lounge pants and underwear together and pulls them down, his knuckles grazing my thighs, leaving a trail of burning skin behind.

Once I'm completely uncovered, he steps back to admire his work. "Look at you," he says, shaking his head as his eyes dip to the junction of my thighs. "Show me how wet you are, Millie."

This version of him makes me light-headed. Everyone else sees buttoned-up, professional, stoic Finn.

But I get this Finn in secret—undone and amorous.

And I want it to be just for me, forever.

I scoot up on the bed and let my knees fall wide, baring everything for him.

"So goddamn perfect," he whispers, muscles tense across his shoulders and arms like he's barely holding back.

His gaze burns into me, taking every detail in with a hungry expression that gives me the courage to tease him a little bit. I let my hand drift over my stomach and down to my core.

"Mmm." I sigh, keeping my eyes on his as I move my fingers over my clit. He watches with rapt attention, hands clenching at his sides. I'm drenched already, my arousal coating my fingers instantly as I slide them down to my opening and slip two fingers inside, moaning at the pressure.

"That's it. Just like that. Fucking flawless." Finn licks his lips, prowling up the bed toward me.

I bring my fingers back up to touch my clit, and tingling pleasure shoots down my thighs. "I need you," I whimper.

Having his eyes on me while I touch myself is intimate as hell, but I'm not scared at all. The way he's watching my every move is only making the ache for him sharper.

"I know, *stella mia*." He runs a hand over mine as it moves between my thighs, like he's memorizing everything by touch. "But you're doing so good."

God, his words make my thighs tremble.

"Finn, please."

He lowers his head and breathes out a chuckle against my inner thigh. "You're impatient tonight."

I pause my movements as he gets closer, anticipation flooding my veins. My hand falls to the sheet beside me in hopes he'll finally take over. But his fingers dig into my thighs, and he still just watches me.

"I want you to touch me," I huff as he presses a kiss to my hip.

His eyes are nearly black as he lowers them between my thighs, and his hot breaths drift like silk over my skin. "Oh, I know what you want. I just like watching you writhe and beg for me." He nips a small bite on my inner thigh, and my back arches off the bed, my nails digging into the sheets.

Then his mouth descends, and I'm in another world.

The sweeping movements are intoxicating, and pleasure blooms through me, reaching every corner of my body. He licks my clit and dives into me as my hands pull his hair and guide him closer. He chuckles, and the vibrations of his laugh send sparks through my nerve endings.

I slam my eyes shut to focus on the expert movements of his tongue. The cotton sheets against my back are a stark contrast to the cool air over my nipples, and it heightens everything happening to my body. He keeps moaning against me, and the buzz makes my hips jump.

My orgasm pushes higher and higher, reaching for the surface like a tsunami that'll crash over me any minute. I'm almost scared of the intensity I feel building in my spine and hips, and for a moment, I think it might be too much.

But Finn's fingertips dig into my thighs, holding me tightly in place. And when he twirls over my clit again, the release rushes over me, forcing my legs straight and my back to arch as I cry out.

Wave after wave crashes over me, flooding my body with warmth and stealing my breath.

When I pry my eyes open, Finn's watching me, one corner of his lips tipped up in an arrogant smirk.

I want to wipe that smugness right off his face.

He crawls up the bed and leans next to me on one elbow as I sit up to start unbuttoning and unzipping his jeans. Wordlessly, he watches me as I get on my knees and slide his pants down.

"What are you thinking?" I ask, slipping my palms over his hips, right above his tight black briefs.

He brushes a hand through my hair. "How beautiful you look right now. How much I love the taste of you on my tongue. How fucking badly I want you to keep taking my clothes off."

I grin, lowering my hands to his waistband, and he sucks in a breath as I pull them down. His cock springs free between us, and my eyes widen. "Holy shit," I whisper, my voice laced with lust.

He barks a laugh, but it dies in his throat as I kneel between his legs and run my hands up his thighs.

"Millie," he sighs as he tucks my hair behind my ear, his eyes wild with desire.

"It's my turn to watch *you* writhe and beg," I tell him, tickling my nails over his hips until his cock twitches between us. My thighs quiver with anticipation.

He falls back and covers his face with his hands. "I guess I deserve that."

I lean forward and press a kiss to the warm, silky skin at the head of his cock, then run my tongue over the same spot.

"Fuck." He gasps as his hips jump. With a sigh, he wraps my hair in his hands, his nails scraping over my scalp and sending shivers down my spine.

I slide my lips up the length of him in a feathery movement, tempting him to lose composure. I want to see Finn on the edge. Want to witness him completely coming apart for me.

"Tell me what you like," I whisper, my lips brushing him as I speak.

"Fucking anything, Millie. Anything . . . you do." He stumbles over his words as I dip my head and bring the smooth, velvety tip into my mouth, sucking gently.

His legs tense beneath my hands with the force of holding himself still. I do it again, earning a groan from the back of his throat and the tightening of his hand in my hair. Then I slide him into my mouth as slowly as possible, letting the salty-sweet taste coat my tongue.

As I swallow his length as far as I can, his hips vibrate against my palms.

"That's it," he says, smoothing a hand over my cheek. "That's perfect."

I slide him out and push back in, relaxing my throat to take him a little deeper this time.

"Fuck. Yes, Millie." He gasps, stumbling over his words. "Just like . . . fuck."

I try to keep a steady rhythm as I focus on his eyes. They're ravaged, blown wide so there's no blue left at all. That edge of control I was striving for is right there. He looks desperate, and I love the power it grants me. It's so heady to be in charge of his pleasure—to know I did this to him.

"That feels so good," he groans, lifting his hips slightly to thrust into my mouth. I add my hand below my lips and pump them together.

He makes a choking sound, and his fist tenses in my hair. "Come here, *stella mia*," he whispers, pulling me back until he pops out of my mouth.

I move up the bed toward him, and his warm lips land on mine as he presses his body completely against me. He kisses my lips and throat and breasts like I'm the treasure he's been scouring the earth for.

"Millie," he whispers against my neck, sending goose bumps skating over my shoulders and arms.

"I love when you"—my breath hitches—"say my name."

"I love when you moan mine," he replies, peppering kisses over my collarbone.

When he settles his weight over me, the pressure is so perfect. My legs slide out to fit around his firm torso until his hardest part lines up perfectly against my softest.

"Are you sure?" he asks against my mouth.

"Positive." I thrust my hips up, grinding myself against him, and he growls into my ear. "There's a condom in the top drawer," I say, motioning to the nightstand.

He reaches across the bed and pulls out the small package. The foil crinkles as he opens it and slides the condom over himself as he meets my eyes.

His are defenseless, open and raw. He kneels between my thighs completely naked, but the look in his eyes feels the most intimate.

I was right. Being with Finn is not something I can just fling myself into and then fall away from one day. This feels permanent and inevitable, like we've been hurtling toward each other all along and are finally about to reach the point of impact.

But there's not a single part of me that wants to change direction. I hitch my legs around him, drawing him closer, and he leans forward to meet me.

Our gazes hold, and I memorize every detail of him shuddering with satisfaction as he pushes the tip of his cock inside me. He breathes raggedly, eyes scanning over my face, lips parted in shock. All I can do is swallow thickly and nod, encouraging him to keep going.

He presses his hips forward, inch by brutal inch, and I suck in a breath. I feel so full, almost to the point of pain, but the sting never comes. Just a satisfying, heavy pressure that spreads pleasure through my body.

"Oh, *fuck*. Millie," he groans as he reaches the hilt and buries his face in my neck.

My nails dig into his shoulder blades, and he shakes with the effort it takes to hold still inside me. His hot breaths dampen my neck as his chest rises and falls against mine.

A burning sensation ripples through my chest as my lungs constrict, and tears sting the edges of my eyes at this feeling of *rightness*. This feeling of being exactly where I'm supposed to be.

It's astonishing how quickly someone could transform into such a fundamental part of my life. How they could become so ingrained in every little bit of my soul that I can't even fathom how painful it would be if they left it.

That's how this feels. Like Finn is burrowing into every corner of my soul, and not even a divine being could remove him.

When he pulls out the slightest bit and thrusts back into me, we moan in unison.

He lifts his head and drags his heavy eyes to mine. "You feel perfect. Like we were made for each other," he whispers before he pulls back and presses in.

Wrapping my legs tighter around his hips, I urge him for more pressure, and he groans as he grinds harder against me.

The pull-and-push movement brushes his chest over my peaked nipples, barreling me toward another orgasm. I yank his lips to mine, and our mouths and tongues move against each other at the same tempo as our bodies. He thrusts deeper and brings his fingers between us, moving them in soft circles over my clit.

Sweat coats our skin, and my body feels feverish with heat as he picks up his pace. He presses his other hand to mine, squeezing our palms and lacing our fingers together, and the connection between them feels as powerful as everywhere else we're touching.

An electric current zaps through my body from our joined palms, doing irreparable damage to my heart. It will never recover from this.

The ache builds and races through my nerves until I detonate around him, his wild eyes holding mine the entire time. Seismic waves pulse and throb through my body, and his thrusts become erratic as he buries his face against my neck and loses his restraint.

"Millie," he grinds out as he spasms inside me, huffing breaths against my skin. His lips graze my neck and my jaw and, finally, my lips as his thrusts slow.

We collapse together, our skin slippery as we tangle our arms around each other and attempt to catch our breath.

My eyelids are drooping heavily when Finn pulls away and brings back a warm washcloth for me. He helps me clean up and gets us glasses of water while I use the bathroom.

When we climb back into bed, we intertwine our arms and legs between soft kisses. And as I drift off to sleep, every sweet detail finds a cozy spot in my heart, made just for Finn to live in forever.

Chapter 36

Finn

*M*illie's breathy whimpers ring through my ears as she writhes above me. My hands dig into her hips, and I grind up into her wet warmth, all of her swollen softness wrapped tightly around me. She looks down at me with a knowing smirk before she twists her hips and—

Pepper's loud whines from outside the bedroom door wake me from the best dream of my entire life.

Damn it.

The pressure in my dick is tenting the sheet over me, and there's no hiding it. Millie's soft, even breaths puff against my chest, and she has an arm and a leg thrown over me like she's an octopus wrapping me in her tentacles so I never get away.

Like I would want to be anywhere else right now.

What happened last night between Millie and me was earth-shattering. It was a cataclysmic event that there's no going back from.

And I never want to.

I coast my fingers over her arm, not wanting to wake her, but needing to feel her warm skin again. Her hand shifts and lands right over my heart, palm pressed into my chest, and I feel like the luckiest man in the universe.

She's done something to my heart that I wasn't expecting, yet somehow it feels like it was the plan all along.

Her legs stretch out against mine, and she yawns as she lifts her head.

"Hey, you," I whisper.

"Good morning." She smiles sweetly, pressing a kiss to my lips.

"How are you feeling?" I run my hand over her bare hip, and she gives a contented sigh, stretching out on her back across the bed. My body automatically follows, like a magnet drawn to its opposing force. I'm still hard from my dream and ready to re-create it with her.

Her eyes sparkle with amusement when I lean closer and leave a kiss over her heart.

"I'm feeling"—she bites her lip—"hungry."

I suck her nipple into my mouth, the firm peak pressing into my tongue as she rolls her fingers over my scalp.

"Well, we can't have that." I kiss her lips, coaxing them open for me. A deep groan rumbles through my chest as I tilt my head, desperate to consume more of her.

As I'm about to dip my hand between her thighs, her stomach grumbles with a loud, hungry moan.

Her cheeks pinken with embarrassment, and I laugh as I kiss her stomach. "Oh, you meant *hungry*?"

"Yes, I'm starving, apparently. Let's eat a breakfast fry jack and then pick up donuts to surprise the girls."

If I wasn't already obsessed with this woman, that right there would've sealed the deal. She wants to bring Avery and Eloise a treat, and they're going to love her for it.

* * *

"I WANT THE one with pink icing and sprinkles," Eloise demands, eyeing the blue box of donuts as she follows me into the kitchen.

Gabriella greets us from the sink, where she's washing out the espresso percolator. "I didn't expect you home so early." She purses her lips and squints in my direction.

Setting the box of donuts on the kitchen island, I lean in to kiss her cheek. "Millie wanted to bring the girls a treat."

"Ah, I see." She nods. "She must've worked up an appetite," she murmurs with a sassy wink.

I chuckle as I wrap an arm around her shoulder. "Thanks for staying the night."

Leaving them overnight was easier than I thought it would be. It felt good for me to get a bit of distance and spend some time out of caretaking mode. I'm sure I'll have to keep psyching myself up for it, but a short break has brought me back refreshed.

Millie makes it into the kitchen, dragging a leg the whole way with Avery clinging to it.

"How were the girls?" I ask Gabriella, making them two cups of milk.

"They were good. Weren't you, girls?" She opens the box of donuts for Eloise and hands her one on a plate. "They helped me bake a cake last night, and then they went to bed easily. They were perfect little angels."

I ruffle the top of El's head and kiss her cheek. "I'm glad you guys had fun." I bend to pry Ave off Millie's leg. "Are you only excited to see Millie? What about me?" I ask, tickling her sides until she's laughing and forced to release her grip. Then I swing her over my shoulder and set her on a barstool.

"How was your date?" El asks in a singsong tone, with pink icing smeared across her cheeks.

Grabbing a chocolate donut, I lean against the counter and flash Millie a grin. "It was the best date I've ever been on."

Millie steps next to me, and I offer her a bite. "My favorite part was the bookstore. I even snuck a few books in the basket for you two," she tells them.

I shoot her a questioning look. "That was your favorite part?" Leaning in so only she can hear, I ask, "Out of everything we did last night?"

She hip-checks me and lowers her voice to murmur, "My favorite part—"

"Are you getting married now?" Avery wonders.

I choke on my breath, and Gabriella snickers as Millie tries to hold back a laugh behind her hand.

"When two people love each other, they get married. Then they can kiss and have babies," Eloise chimes in.

Millie splutters, bending at the waist in a coughing fit.

I pat her back as I bite my lips to keep from laughing. "Thank you, Eloise. That's helpful."

Once her breathing returns to normal, Millie straightens and pastes on a bright smile. "I have something fun we could make today. Do you girls want to do a craft with me?"

The art of distraction. Perfect.

*　*　*

I WOULD BE happy to never set foot in another craft store again in my life. As soon as the doors slid open, irritability prickled up my spine. I'd never been to a land ruled by glitter and yarn and stickers, and the longer we were there, the more pressure I felt escalating into a headache.

Who knew there were so many different types of paper? And why do they need five aisles to choose from?

Fortunately, Millie could sense my rising frustration. She simply patted my hand and told me to follow her as she navigated through the aisles of bright colors and patterns without losing me or the actual children. She tossed white T-shirts and socks, tie-dye kits, a package of kids' gloves, and a bag of five hundred rubber bands into our basket.

Then, to my immense relief, we left the craft store of chaos and went in search of burgers for lunch before turning our backyard into an explosion of tie-dye. All of our shirts and socks are now soaking until tomorrow when we can rinse and wash them.

"How are my girls doing?" I ask as I approach the three of them playing their new card game at the kitchen island.

I don't miss how Millie's eyes flare at the words "my girls," and I make a note to use it more often. Because she damn well is my girl, and maybe if I say it enough times, she'll believe it.

"We're great." Eloise beams at me. "I won the last round, and I'm probably going to win this one too." She does a little dance of excitement in her seat.

"Remember what we talked about, *piccola*? Nobody likes a bragging winner." I narrow my eyes at Millie.

She lifts a shoulder with a smug grin. "I don't know what you're talking about. I would never brag about winning."

"Sure, Miss Victory-Lap-Around-the-Table."

"Mmm, I like *stella mia* better. It's easier on the tongue."

Fuck, she's laid it right there for me. It's so tempting to make a retort about how easy she is on my tongue, but little ears are present, so I press my lips together and make a mental note to tell her later.

Avery swoops in to win the game, and we all help get the cards back in the box. El and Ave run upstairs, and I slide my arms around Millie, kissing her warm neck. She melts into my body, and we breathe each other in for a stolen moment.

"I'm making you dinner," I say, pulling away from her and dropping a tender kiss on her lips. "You take a bath or read, or whatever you want, and I'm going to make us a feast."

"Really?" She sounds a little skeptical.

"I've been your apprentice long enough," I say with a wink. "I want to make something for you, and I want you to relax while I do it."

She nods as I kiss her again, and a little chorus of *ooohhhs* erupts from the top of the stairs.

* * *

SLIDING THE TOASTER next to the oven, I lean my phone against it and find the YouTube channel of the dad I've been watching cooking videos from. His kids usually join him, and it's adorable listening to their Australian accents as they cook. In this lesson, he's showing us how to make steaks, scalloped potatoes, and steamed broccoli.

I'm wary of the girls liking this meal, but if all else fails, I have some chicken nuggets in the freezer for them.

I slip my apron over my head, and get to work, the girls drifting in and out the whole time. They help me by sprinkling a little too much salt on the steaks and dropping a few potatoes on their way into the dish, but in the end, I'm impressed with the dinner we've made together.

As I'm setting the potatoes on the table, Millie appears at the bottom of the stairs in my black sweatpants and Catan Battles 2009 shirt. She's swimming in them, the fabric of the sweatpants bunched at her ankles and rolled at the waist, but she looks perfect.

One side of her lips kicks up. "Hope this is okay. I didn't want to put on the same clothes, and I found these in your drawers." She holds her arms out and does a spin.

I approach her and slide one finger into the waistband, feeling her silky skin warm the back of it. "Does that mean there's nothing under these sweatpants?" I whisper, and the blush across her cheeks gives away her answer. I wrap my arms around her shoulders, inhaling the scent of my soap on her skin. *God*, I could get used to this. "I love seeing you in my clothes. Wear them every day."

"I'm pretty sure Sharon wouldn't be promoting me if I showed up to work in this."

"Then wear them every moment you're not at work," I tell her as I guide her to a spot at the table and pull out the chair.

"This looks amazing," she says, taking her seat.

"I burned a bit of the cheese on the potatoes."

"Well, I believe burnt cheese is an underappreciated delicacy," she says, eyeing the dish with a brown scar across the top.

Eloise approaches the table with a wary look. "Do I have to eat that green stuff?"

"Broccoli is good for you, so I think you should give it a try," I tell her as I sit down.

"When I was little, my sisters and I pretended they were trees," Millie says, serving herself some potatoes and passing me the dish. "We used to talk about the fairies that lived under them and what they did for fun or what they were eating for dinner." She holds up a piece of steamed broccoli and squints at it. "Can you imagine how tiny the fairies would have to be if these were trees?"

Eloise and Avery follow her example, putting a piece of broccoli in front of their noses to examine the imaginary fairies. They're likely still reluctant to eat it, but maybe playing with it is a good first step.

Millie cuts into her steak and closes her eyes around the first bite. "You did so good." She shakes her head in disbelief. "You've come a long way from your cooking disasters a couple months ago. You nailed this."

"Thanks," I say, appreciating the sight of her enjoying the meal I made for her.

Throughout dinner, I can't keep my eyes from drifting to her. We've had a handful of meals together in this room, but today it feels completely new. Like I'm seeing things clearly through a new pair of glasses after years of blurry vision.

And I want to see this view forever.

Chapter 37

Millie

The final drop of hot glue cools against my fingertip, and I release the small string. The chrysalis sways as I let go, but the hot glue and string keep it in place. Twenty-three new Blue Morpho chrysalises adorn the rack that will hang in our containment room until the butterflies emerge in about six days. I set the rack in the frame where it belongs and walk back to our room of offices.

Today is the day. The other applicant should be here any minute, and I'm not quite sure how to prepare myself for it. Micah is at a library outreach program all day, so it's just me, waiting for fate to bring my competition down the hall.

Maybe it'll be a kind old woman who has been obsessed with insects her whole life and can teach me how to crochet a sweater. Or maybe someone my age, who's just so incredibly wonderful that I can't help rooting for them to get the job. A new best friend might be popping around the corner at any moment.

I drop into my desk chair and open my email. As I scan a message from Reva, footsteps thud down the hallway. The deep sound is rather menacing, but I'm sure it's just a trick of the acoustics. I sit up straighter and will my smile not to break as my new friend approaches.

But when the visitor rounds the corner and enters the doorway, the temperature in the room drops to freezing. A fist squeezes through my ribs and constricts my lungs until my vision darkens from a lack of oxygen.

I blink a few times, trying to clear the mirage before me.

Splash of blond hair.

Sharp, smooth jaw.

Beady eyes.

This is not real life.

No possible way that Kyle Marks is the other applicant.

But that's Kyle's arrogantly lifted eyebrow and smarmy grin.

And that's Kyle's cavalier voice grating over my nerves when he says, "Cat got your tongue?"

He saunters to the empty desk and drops into the seat, kicking his heels up on the surface and crossing his arms over his chest. "Is this my new desk?"

My hands shake in my lap, and I hide them in the flowy sections of my skirt.

"Maybe you wouldn't be so shocked right now if you'd answered my messages," he sneers.

Take a breath, Millie. I have to keep breathing. The alternative is not good.

I force a small intake of air past my lips, but it does nothing to make my limbs move or my mouth form words.

Kyle's feet drop to the floor, and he spins in his chair like he's a child on a playground without a care in the world. Meanwhile, I'm over here suffocating as an anxiety attack clouds the edges of my vision.

"Do you remember how to speak? If not, it's going to be a little complicated being your boss this week."

Another breath, Millie.

I lower my eyes to my desk and find the green Post-it note

that still has Finn's handwriting on it from the coffee he left me weeks ago. It has lost its stickiness, but I've taped it beside my office phone. I trace his letters with my eyes, trying to calm myself through the visual focus.

But my spotty vision does me a disservice. I can't see that Kyle has approached my desk until it's too late. His fingers rake through the tips of my hair, and I cower away from him.

He laughs cruelly. "Damn. If you had that haircut when we were together, I might still be around."

The words hit me like a blow, and my muscles spasm as I shrink back from him. My heart rate can't be in a normal range right now. The strength of its beat is rattling my skull.

Kyle huffs a dark chuckle, apparently amused by my reaction to him, then glances at his watch. "I have a meeting with my new boss. I just wanted to say hi before I dazzled her."

My desk rattles as he knocks his knuckles on the hard surface before strolling out the door.

Darkness creeps into the edges of my vision, and I crumple to the ground and lean against the wall as the room closes in around me.

* * *

SEVENTEEN TILES SPAN one direction of this room, and twenty-nine the other. That's 493 tiles that I have counted six times.

I think that means my vision is doing better. The room doesn't feel so dark and small anymore, and my lungs have almost reached the point of expanding to their full potential again. I can feel my fingers and toes, and the sound of the air conditioner whirring through the room is louder than my heartbeat in my ears.

So many emotions have exploded through my system in the last hour. Rage. Shock. Denial. Humiliation. Confusion.

How did I not see this coming? As far as I know, Kyle has a

job as an entomologist with an environmental biology company. Working in a museum isn't the kind of job he ever mentioned being interested in. Actually, he knew this was *my* dream job. I've been talking about it since we met in college.

He isn't meant for a job like this. I am.

But even *Finn* said he was a good applicant. Betrayal burns hot through my veins as I remember his words.

You each have different skills and abilities to bring to the position, but both of you are very passionate and would make great department directors.

A sharp pain stings my throat as I try to understand. Now that I know it was Kyle he was talking about, the words feel like treachery.

How could he like someone who hurt me so badly? Who treated me like trash and apparently still finds it entertaining to do so. How could Finn not see through the orchestrated version of Kyle that he must've presented in that interview?

Well, I spent years falling for his manipulations.

The air squeezes out of my lungs in a harsh, forced breath.

I need a plan before *he* gets back to this office. I can't spend the rest of the day hiding in the corner.

Pressing my palms and fingers into the cool tile floor, I try to think through what to do.

There are a few tasks that would keep me out of the office, but I have no idea what Kyle's day will look like, since he doesn't actually work here. Where will he be and what will he be doing all day? And most importantly, how can I avoid him?

Before he can make it back in here, I lift myself from the floor and bring up the library outreach event email. Then I shut down my computer, grab my purse, and flee the office to join Micah for the afternoon.

* * *

I'm NOT PROUD of the fact that I called in sick to work this morning.

I'm also not proud that I lied to my best friend about being sick and then watched *Gilmore Girls* all day without her.

And I'm not proud that I've completely ignored every one of Finn's worried calls and texts.

But I have no idea what to say to him. I've processed enough over the last twenty-four hours to logically understand that Finn is not the bad guy here. I can't blame him for something that isn't *actually* his fault.

It's Kyle's fault.

I had to tell Micah yesterday afternoon when I found him at the library since he also has to deal with the work situation, but I swore him to secrecy.

So today has been wasted in bed as I wallow in self-pity. I'm now surrounded by an empty bowl of salsa, a half-finished bag of tortilla chips, an iced coffee that I didn't drink before the ice melted, and a considerable dusting of powdered sugar from the almond croissants I had delivered. And in the back of my mind, I'm telling myself to buck up and get it together. Maybe shower and eat some not-junk food. Go for a walk and get some sunshine on my face.

But I just can't find the enthusiasm. I can't find the *will* to go back to work tomorrow and face my worst nightmare.

My phone chimes with a text, and I lift it from my nightstand.

> **Finn:** Just dropped off some soup at your front door. I didn't knock in case you're resting, but go get it when you wake up so a raccoon doesn't steal it. I hope you feel better soon.

A deep breath rushes out of me. He bought me soup because he thinks I'm sick, and I'm lying about it by omission. Guilt sours my stomach.

Clutching my phone to my chest, I jump into motion. The bag of chips tumbles to the floor, but I ignore it, jogging through the silent house. Maybe I can catch him before he leaves and tell him the truth right now. He doesn't deserve to think I'm sick. It's not his fault.

When I open the door, a small cooler sits on the doormat, but I don't see his car in the driveway. I take a few steps out and see he's not on the street anymore either. My shoulders droop, and I reluctantly grab the cooler and lug it into the kitchen.

My phone rings in my hand, startling me, and I place the cooler on the counter to look at it. An image of my mom and dad sticking their tongues out greets me, and I swipe to answer the FaceTime before I can think better of it.

"Hey," I greet them, holding the phone up so they can see my face. The tiny image of me in the corner reveals my hair sticking in every direction and a lovely salsa stain on the collar of my pajama shirt. I drop my chin and try to rub it away, but the evidence remains.

"Sweetie," Mom coos. Her face fills most of the screen, with only about a third of my dad's in view. "We heard you're sick. How are you feeling?"

I roll my eyes. Lena must've called them. "I'm okay." As the guilt of my lie burns in my throat, I decide now seems like a good time to start being honest with people before the news spreads any further. "It was more of a mental-health day, really."

Mom sticks her bottom lip out. "Oh no. What's going on?"

I abandon the cooler and walk to the couch, tucking myself into my favorite corner and pulling my weighted blanket over my lap while I tell them about yesterday.

By the end of my explanation, my dad is pacing through the kitchen behind my mom, working himself into a tizzy. "We're going down there, Mary. I don't want that bastard around our daughter." He stops with his hands on his hips, scowling into the phone. His dark, protective eyes remind me so much of Finn that my heart aches.

"I'm going to handle it," I tell them. "I just needed today to recuperate. Tomorrow I'm going to show up to work with the best attitude I can muster." I nod, trying to pump myself up for that.

Mom's arm must be tired, because she sets her phone on the table and sits in the chair in front of the screen, cutting off the view of the top of her head in the process.

"Millie, listen to me," she says, pointing toward the phone. "You've come a long way since you left Kyle, and we're proud of you *every day*. But that doesn't mean you don't need help sometimes. You have so many people who would be by your side in an instant if you needed them. Don't forget that."

My chest tightens, and I bite the inside of my cheek to stop my lips from twisting with emotion.

Dad walks up behind Mom and sets his chin on her shoulder. "You're better than he makes you feel. He's a liar and a snake and he *will* get what's coming to him."

Two tears drip from my eyes, and I try to wipe them away before they can see. They might get in the car to drive down here if they know the raging emotions battling inside me right now.

Mom's lips press into a firm line. "Honey, does Finn know about this?"

I shake my head silently, afraid that if I open my mouth, more tears will fall.

She sighs. "Yeah, he didn't mention anything."

My breath freezes and my body stills. "You talked to Finn?"

Dad nods. "We got off the phone with him about an hour ago."

Regret bubbles through me. He's so worried about me that he got me soup *and* called my parents to tell them I didn't feel well?

My chin quivers. I'm the worst. I can't believe I let him think that.

I look between my parents, trying to sort through how to fix this.

Dad's brows stitch together, and he tilts his head. "Who did you think taught him how to make the soup?"

Chills creep over my body, prickling the hairs on the back of my neck. I inhale a shaky breath as two more tears fall, but I can't move my hand to wipe them away this time.

Who did I think made the soup? The café around the corner, obviously.

"Well, shit." Dad sighs, kneeling on their kitchen floor beside my mom's chair. "Doesn't look like she knew about that yet."

Several quick, short breaths fill my chest, but my body doesn't feel the oxygen.

The soup. *The soup.*

I spring into action, running the few steps to the kitchen. I set the phone down on the counter, giving my parents a great view of the ceiling while they whisper to each other.

As soon as I lift the lid of the cooler, the herby aroma of Dad's chicken-and-rice soup fills the air, and more tears fall without permission. I pull the glass container out and unsnap the lid.

Chunks of chicken, rice, diced carrots, and celery chopped so finely it's almost invisible. It looks exactly like my dad's.

Sniffling, I pick up the phone and find my parents' soft gazes. The small image of me reveals how red my eyes are. I actually *do* look sick now.

"How did the soup get here, Dad?" My tone makes it sound like an accusation because I already know the answer in my gut. I just need him to confirm it for me.

"I imagine Finn dropped it off," he says with a shrug. "We

spent an hour on the phone with him, walking him through all the steps. Does it seem like he got it right?"

"It seems like he got it perfect," I whisper, trying to hold back the flood threatening to pour from my eyes.

"Well, take a bite," Mom encourages.

The silverware drawer squeaks as I open it and grab a spoon. I scoop up a bite of soup, and the moment it hits my tongue, the chicken and herbs meld together perfectly, soothing my soul.

"It's exactly like yours, Dad."

He nods approvingly. "Finn's a good one. I like him."

"I like him too," I whisper.

"Then you better tell him what's going on." Mom's voice is firm. "Because I like him too, and I want to see those girls again."

My parents keep me company while I eat two bowls of soup, fussing over me through the phone screen, before they hang up, demanding I talk to Finn.

I settle back into my spot on the couch to text him. Everything is still too raw to hear his voice and explain my thoughts right now.

> **Millie:** You went so far beyond what you had to with the soup. Thank you. You have no idea how much it means to me. Can I come by your office tomorrow?

> **Finn:** You're welcome. And you can always come by. Are you feeling better?

> **Millie:** A little bit. I'll tell you more about it tomorrow.

> **Finn:** I wish you were here. My bed is cold without you.

> **Millie:** Same. Your blanket is warmer than mine.

Finn: That's the only thing you like here?

> **Millie:** Also the morning espresso. ☺

Finn: Is that really it?

> **Millie:** Oh! I forget about my
> mixer! I like that too.

Finn: You're still a wicked little temptress.

> **Millie:** Yeah, but you like it.

Finn: So much, stella mia. I'll see you tomorrow.

> **Millie:** Goodnight.

The front door bangs open as I send the last message, and Lena storms in, with Emil and Micah hot on her heels.

"Millicent Phoenix Oaks." Lena stops in front of me with her hands on her hips. "Are. You. Sick?" she demands with a tight jaw.

My eyes flick to Micah, and he winces. "Sorry, Mills."

I purse my lips, and that's all the confirmation Lena needs.

"Damn it," she huffs. "You needed us and didn't tell us." She turns to jab a finger in Micah's chest, and he flinches. "And *you* should've told me the second you knew." She narrows her eyes at Emil. "How long have you known?"

He lowers his eyes, and Lena growls in response.

"Completely ridiculous," Lena shouts, throwing her hands in the air. "Are we even friends if we don't have each other's backs?"

The guilt is burning through my veins again, threatening to make me sick.

"Well, Millie only told me—" Micah starts.

"Don't even," Lena cuts him off. "You should've told us immediately. Our girl needed us."

Micah scratches his cheek and nods in understanding.

I swallow the lump in my throat and tell Lena, "Don't be mad at him. It's my fault. I forced him to keep it a secret."

"Well," she says with a satisfied smirk. "Apparently, it only takes one margarita for him to spill it. He also admitted to giving Finn my number so I could give him your dad's." She grins knowingly. "How was the soup?"

A sad smile lifts the corners of my lips. "It was delicious."

"Good." Lena drops to the couch next to me. "Now, tell us what happened yesterday."

Micah and Emil join us on the couch, and I finally tell the truth about everything.

Lena blows out a long breath as I finish, shaking her head. "We need a plan."

I shrug. "I have one. I just endure it. I refuse to quit my job, and I refuse to pull out of the running for the promotion. He doesn't get to watch me completely ruin my life because of him again." All three of them nod. "I'm going to fight tooth and nail to earn it." I cross my arms over my chest, feeling better already just by saying all of that out loud.

Lena squeezes her arms around my shoulders, swaying me back and forth. "I'm so fucking proud of you. I had a whole pep talk planned, but it sounds like you didn't need it. You thought it up yourself." She smacks a kiss on my cheek. "Now let's bake cookies and learn how to make voodoo dolls to hex him with."

Chapter 38

Finn

"Good afternoon, Mom," I answer as I drop into my office chair. Her set ringtone echoed three times from my pocket before I decided to answer.

"Well, you finally speak to me. That's so kind of you," she says, sarcasm dripping from her words like acid.

"What can I do for you?" I set my glasses on my desk and press my fingers to my forehead, hoping to release some of the tension.

"I was wondering if your father and I are ever going to get to see our granddaughters. It's been nine weeks."

I roll my eyes. Of course she would be counting. She probably has a fucking calendar to keep track.

"I'm sure we can work something out soon."

"That's great to hear. I've scheduled a dinner for next Wednesday. I expect you and the girls here."

"Is it a dinner party or just the five of us?"

"The five of us," she scoffs. "You're insane if you think I can put together a dinner party for my friends in that amount of time."

There's a brief pause where I consider moving to a new state and changing my phone number so I don't have to go to this dinner. But I also feel a responsibility to the girls and my parents to help them retain some sort of relationship. They'll never have that grandparent-and-grandchild bond that the girls see in movies, but deep down, I feel obligated to try. I want the girls to have nearby family in their lives besides me, and my parents feel like the only option.

"Okay."

"Wonderful. What do the girls like to eat? I'll have Beatrice make them something."

"They love any kind of kid food. Macaroni and cheese, pizza, hot dogs. But honestly, they would also be happy with a roll or a peanut-butter-and-jelly sandwich too."

"I'll see what we can do," she says, and I practically hear her curled lip through the phone.

"If I need to pick something up for them, I can do that," I say with a sigh.

"That won't be necessary."

"Okay. We'll see you next week."

"Six o'clock, sharp. Be on time, Finneas. You know how your father likes to eat his dinner hot."

Like I could ever forget the screaming match of 2017, when he sent our chef running away in tears because his dinner was lukewarm.

I can't even come up with a kind response to her remark, so I end the call and drop my head to my desk.

Why the fuck does she make it so hard to talk to her? Every sentence holds some form of manipulation or control, and I leave the conversation feeling more broken than when it started. And that's just a phone call. Actually *being* in their toxic presence exhausts and drains me even more.

Sometimes I think they enjoy stomping into those grief-shattered pieces of my heart, grinding them into dust beneath their heels.

A quiet knock hits the wall beside my open office door, and the sight of Millie's beautiful face evaporates all thoughts of my parents. She's wearing that dress with butterflies on the collar again, and it reminds me of when we collided at the reception desk.

The day that started all of this.

"You're a sight for sore eyes. Come in. Are you feeling better?" I ask as she pads through the doorway. I turn my chair and reach out my arms in anticipation of her coming over to me, but my brow tenses when she stops on the other side of my desk and takes a seat.

My shoulders tighten as I notice her eyes are rimmed in red. I lean my elbows on the desk, scanning her for any sign of what's on her mind, but I can't find any. "Are you okay?"

She presses her lips into a firm line. "Thank you so much for making me soup." A hint of blush colors her cheeks. "That was . . . It was really nice of you." She swallows. "But I wasn't physically sick. It was more like I needed a mental-health day."

"What's going on?" Realization tickles at the back of my mind. "Is it the other applicant?"

"Yes, actually."

I offer her a sympathetic grin. "I really meant what I said the other day. He's a good option." She flinches slightly. "But he's not *better* than you. I wish you didn't have to worry about it."

Millie nods, biting the inside of her cheek. "But I do have to worry about it." My brows press together, but she continues. "Can I be honest with you?"

"Always."

"You have to promise not to say anything to anyone on the interview panel."

A knot twists in my stomach. "Okay. I promise."

Her shoulders droop, hunching like the weight of the world sits atop them. "The other applicant is . . . He's my ex-boyfriend. The one I saw at Maggie's that day."

My lips part as confusion swoops through my head.

No. There must be a mistake.

The other applicant was a nice guy. He was professional and polite. He complimented Sharon's necklace and told me he liked my tie.

Millie looks like she wants to throw up. She's a pale husk of my Millie.

She's not okay.

My chest pinches tight, and the crease between my brows deepens to the point of a headache. I'm trying my best to reconcile the person I met in that interview with the person I know Millie's ex to be. But the two are not blending in my head. I can't picture it.

"What happened?" I ask.

In my gut, I know the answer before she says it, because the pain is etched so clearly in her eyes.

"Well, on Monday, he came in as the Kyle I knew. He was awful, and I basically had a panic attack on the floor after he left." She scoffs a laugh like she's trying to make the whole situation seem less than it is.

"Fuck. Are you okay?" Red tints my vision as I round the desk and kneel beside her chair.

I was in the same building and had no idea, and I hate myself for it.

"I wasn't at the time. So I left on Monday, then called in sick yesterday." She sighs a deep breath. "And today he's been what I imagine he portrayed in the interview. The masked version he shows everyone else."

The fucking bastard. The lying, manipulative asshole. I can't believe I thought he was a good candidate. I can't believe I thought he seemed like a decent enough person to work here.

He's absolutely worthless.

"We have to tell Sharon," I say.

There's no doubt in my mind. I'm on Millie's side unquestioningly.

Her body tenses. "No."

"How could we not? She doesn't know what kind of person he is."

She jumps from her seat and shakes her head. "I don't want to interfere, and I don't want you to either."

I stand. "But Sharon would want to know. She doesn't want someone like that working at the museum."

Millie thrusts her hands into her hair and pulls at the roots. "I want to earn it, fair and square."

"You will earn it. But don't you think Sharon would want to factor this in?" I walk toward her, but she backs away.

"No. I won't let you tell her."

"I can't let him trick and manipulate people into thinking he's a good person."

She waves this off, walking to the window overlooking the front of the museum. She touches her fingers to the glass and sighs. "If he gets the job, I'll just quit."

I run my hand over my face. "You don't deserve that. I could tell her anonymously. I could leave a note under her door or something."

She turns back to me and stands tall, face firm. "No. I want to be chosen because I'm the right person. I'm not going to run to Sharon and tattle. I have to earn my job the right way. Not because I slept my way to the top, and not because I told on someone else for demeaning me."

God, I want to kiss her. I want to kiss this stubbornness right out of her, but I understand. I do. She needs to know that she is the right person for the job, and the knowledge that maybe *he* would've gotten it would sour everything.

A sad smile stretches across my face. "You're incredibly strong, you know that?"

I step toward her, and she lets me get close enough to wrap my hand around hers. When she looks up at me, her eyes are glassy, and the pain in my chest is so tight I can't breathe. "I want to prove I'm better than him."

Stretching my hand across her jaw, I whisper, "You already are, even without the job."

"I know you want to protect me, and I wish you could." She leans into my palm, a tear slipping from her eye to hit my skin. "But I can do this. I just need you to trust me that I can do it."

I pull her toward me until she's pressed against me, our arms around each other and my cheek resting on her head. "Of course you can do this. There's not a doubt in my mind."

Her shoulders hitch up a few times and then finally settle. She breathes out a deep sigh, and we stay there, in my favorite hug, until her tears have dried.

"I can't believe you called my dad for his soup recipe," she whispers against my chest.

"I can't believe you think I wouldn't."

Chapter 39

Millie

I'm going cross-eyed from looking at my computer screen for too long, attempting to type up some bullet points I want to mention in my interview. I need to focus, but I'm too busy trying not to think about Kyle doing his tour of the butterfly vivarium right now.

In college and in his last job, he focused on aquatic insects, so I'm not sure when his passion turned toward pollinators and museum education. But I suspect it started swinging that way when he was looking for a new way to control me.

The last two days of work have been miserable. They've done nothing but confirm that if Kyle gets the job, I'll be looking for a new one. He has schmoozed and lied through his teeth in every interaction I've witnessed. I've run from the room any time he entered and feel no shame in it.

The memories of the way he treated me had dulled over time, but being around him this week has sharpened the edges. Now I can remember every detail of how he made me wilt under his words.

It has taken a concerted effort to remain upright this week. To keep breathing and moving and thinking instead of fading back into my past self.

Luckily, Micah has been a buffer. If I stick close to him, like right now, Kyle can't act like a piece of shit. When Micah's here, Kyle puts on his manipulator face. His lying-to-the-world face.

He's not aware that Micah knows it's all a ruse.

Speak of the devil. Kyle's irritating face draws my gaze to the doorway. I snap my eyes back to my computer as he saunters in, just like five days ago.

I keep my focus on my screen as he walks up beside me and leans his hips against my desk, right beside my seat. He kicks his feet out in front of him, and I feel his stare on my face like a burning laser.

Without looking, I growl, "Get off my desk."

He breathes a small laugh through his nose. "Is that the way you talk to your boss?"

I pull my gaze from my computer and meet his small eyes. "You are *not* my boss."

His lips curl. "*Yet*, Millie. *Yet* is the key word."

"You ready to leave?" Micah calls, his loud voice breaking through the tension hovering between Kyle and me.

I turn to find Micah, almost a head taller than Kyle, looming over him. His eyes are firm, almost like he dares Kyle to say something else.

Kyle snorts like he finds all of this ridiculous, and Micah's nostrils flare as he takes another step closer. The air is thick and heavy as we all freeze, waiting for what could happen next.

Without another word, Kyle lifts himself from my desk. He bumps Micah's shoulder on his way past and leaves the room.

I've never seen this look on Micah's face before. Gone is the gentle giant he normally is. This version is menacing and ready to fight a battle in my honor.

"Hey," I whisper. "He's not worth it."

Micah's eyes soften as they meet mine. "But you are."

I inhale a shaky breath, those words calming my soul more than he'll ever know. I press my lips together as I stand and thread my fingers through his. "Let's go."

He schools his features, relaxing his fingers around mine, and we escape the office for the rest of the day.

* * *

"HIGHER," ELOISE SQUEALS as she swings up to the sky. When she drifts back my way, I put a little extra force into my push, and she inches higher.

I'm staying with the girls for a little while so Finn can have some alone time. I had to talk him into it, but he finally realized I wasn't giving up. He eventually came down the stairs in a skin-tight cycling jersey and shorts that were completely impossible not to stare at. Then he pulled his bike down from its hooks in the garage and dusted it off for a ride.

The girls begged for homemade pizza again, so once Finn left, the three of us made it together. After a week of not seeing the girls or Finn outside of work, I'm loving this time with them. The tense moment with Kyle and Micah this afternoon is still burning in the back of my mind, but these sweet girls have a way of being a happy distraction to keep me from wallowing in the stress of my job.

"Can Pepper have the rest of my crust?" Avery asks from her spot in the grass next to us.

I brought Pepper over with me for the night, and she's living her best life with Avery and Eloise spoiling the hell out of her.

"It's probably not a great idea," I tell her as I push Eloise again. "She got enough treats when we dropped all that cheese earlier."

Avery nods and finishes it herself.

"You can stop pushing now," Eloise groans. "I'm getting swing-sick. It feels like carsick."

Grabbing the swing near her hips, I slow her to a stop. She tips out of it and drops onto the ground next to her sister.

"I totally get it. I get carsick sometimes." I sit in the grass next to the girls and stretch my legs out straight. "Lying down might help," I tell Eloise, patting my thigh.

She turns, lays her head on my leg, and pulls my arm across her. "Is this what homesick feels like too?"

I tilt my head to the side and watch her dark eyelashes lift as she looks at me. "Usually, homesick feels like you're sad and miss something."

Eloise fiddles with my fingers on her stomach. "Do you get homesick?"

"Definitely."

Avery comes to my other thigh and lays her head next to her sister's, their bodies stretched out perpendicular to mine. Her chest lifts with a big breath before she whispers, "Sometimes I get mama-sick when I really miss Mama."

Something claws its way into my chest and squeezes my entire heart, and I can't breathe through the pain of it.

"Me too," Eloise murmurs.

Tears sting my eyes, and I have to work to control the hiccup that wants to creep out as I try to inhale. I don't want to give away how much this hurts, because I know it's exponentially worse for them.

I've spent the week mourning my job and being afraid of running into my ex-boyfriend. But these girls have lived through something *so* much worse. Problems like mine seem inconsequential compared to theirs.

Avery runs her fingers over my forearm in a soothing motion.

I have no idea what to say. I don't know the right or wrong things. I'm completely unprepared. No one has coached me for this sort of situation, and I'm frustrated I never Googled it. How do I find the right words?

"It hurts to miss someone, doesn't it?" I whisper.

They nod against my thighs. Pepper rises from her spot a few feet away and drops herself right beside Avery's hip with a sigh.

"Do you think Uncle Finn gets mama-sick like us?" Eloise asks.

"Oh, I know he does. He misses your mama every day. But he's so happy he gets to see you guys, because the two of you are part of your mama."

There's a long, thoughtful silence before Avery whispers, "He says we laugh like her."

"And he says her hair is like mine," Eloise adds.

The ache in my chest burns hotter listening to the pain in their voices. "That means we get to remember her all the time through the two of you," I say, running a hand over their cheeks.

* * *

FINN'S "HELLO" ECHOES through the house from the garage door. He shuffles into the kitchen and drops a few things onto the counter. Then he appears in the entrance to the living room with red cheeks, messy hair, and sweat coating his skin.

He looks at our craft supplies spread out on the coffee table and smiles wide, limping a little as he walks toward us, like his muscles are already sore. "What are you all up to?"

"We're making cards for Mama," Avery says, holding hers up for him to see.

When my grandmother died, I was around their age, and we wrote her letters as a way of dealing with our grief. I'm crossing my fingers Finn is okay with me doing something similar with them.

I watch his face closely as he scans her card. The edges of his mouth twitch in a sad frown, and he blinks a few times. "I love it," he whispers. "It's perfect."

"Millie's making one too," Eloise adds.

He gives us a small grin, and I hope I'm not intruding, but after my conversation with the girls outside, I felt heartened to write my own note. I'm becoming a tiny part of Clara's girls' lives, and I want her to know how special they are to me.

Finn hands Avery's card back to her and kisses the top of her head. He walks to Eloise and does the same. Then he squats behind me and wraps his arms around my shoulders, kissing my cheek. "Thank you," he breathes. "For everything."

* * *

"Do you think Uncle Finn is handsome?" Avery asks, toothpaste creeping out of the corners of her mouth as I supervise toothbrush time so Finn can shower.

"Very handsome." I nod, smoothing her hair down her back.

She spits her toothpaste in the sink and rinses out her mouth. "Are you having a sleepover?"

I snort a laugh. Where do these girls get their probing relationship questions? If I didn't know any better, I'd think my mom set them up with the questions she wants answers to.

"Is it okay with you if I do?" I ask, handing her a towel to wipe her mouth.

"Yeah. I like when you're here. Uncle Finn is always smiling."

I've seen that smile a lot lately, and the memory of it makes my own lips lift in a grin.

Avery drops from her stool and leads me to the bedroom. She slides under the covers next to Eloise, and I sit on the edge of the bed while I wait for Finn to arrive.

After a few minutes, he walks into the room, carrying the scent of his sage soap with him through the air like a woodsy breeze. He kneels beside the bed, damp hair hanging over his forehead.

My cheek warms beneath his lips as he plants a quick kiss before rasping, "Thanks. I'll be down in a minute."

While Finn gets the girls to sleep, I wander around downstairs like this house is mine, Pepper's quiet paws walking behind me as she follows my path. I take a sparkling water out of the fridge, pick up the board game the girls played tonight, and put all the craft supplies back in their containers.

The girls had made their notes, and then we all shared them with each other. Eloise had drawn a picture of one of her favorite memories—when she'd practiced jumping into Clara's arms in the pool. Avery had drawn a picture of Clara reading to her in her hospital bed. It was painful to hear their stories, knowing they have so few memories they get to keep of their mom. But they were smiling, so I forced my own teary one.

My path through the house leads me to Finn's study. I've been dying to snoop through his books and find his guilty pleasure stash. Surely he has something in there he's trying to hide.

By the time Finn comes downstairs, I've made it through three shelves and have absolutely nothing to tease him about.

"Looking through my things?" He slides his hands under my shirt and around my waist.

"Looking for ammo. Like your secret monster romances or something."

His lips skate over my pulse point. "Hmm," he hums against my skin. "I don't have any of that yet, but if it's something you're into, I can make room for it."

I lean my head back on his chest and scan the tiny stars painted on the ceiling. "How much free space do you have?"

"For you, I'd make room for anything. Everything," he says, his voice suddenly serious, like it conveys so much more than a shelf of books.

I turn and stand on my toes to wrap my arms around his neck. "Those words, the soup, all the sweet things you do without even meaning to . . . It's all melting me."

Finn's hands grip my butt and lift until my legs wrap around his waist. "Perfect. I want you warm and melted for me." He kisses me with a contented sigh. "Let's go to bed," he whispers against my lips. "I've been missing you all week."

"Do you think the girls are okay with me staying here?"

He leaves kisses along my jaw and cheek, and a hum of pleasure slips out. "Those girls are planning a wedding and babies already. I'd say they're on board with a sleepover."

Chapter 40

Millie

*T*aylor Swift breaks the silence suddenly as my phone rings, her voice filling my bedroom with lyrics about new beginnings. Finn's image appears on my screen—a picture I took of him lying in the grass in his backyard with Pepper a few days ago.

When not at work for the last week, I've spent most of my time with Finn and the girls, playing games and going to the park and cooking together. They've taken up almost all of my brain space, forcing thoughts of Kyle and my interview tomorrow to drift to the very back of my mind.

But tomorrow is coming quicker than I want it to, and I don't know if I'm ready for it.

I swipe to answer the call. "Good evening."

"How's my girl?" Finn asks, a smile in his voice.

God, I love when he calls me his girl. I'm a grown woman and a badass feminist, but for some reason, that term of endearment makes me feel silly with happiness.

I answer honestly. "Tired and anxious and really fucking sad that I didn't—"

"Millie said a bad word." Eloise gasps through the phone.

"Forgot to say you're on speaker," Finn mumbles guiltily.

I drop my face into my hand. "Sorry, girls."

"That's okay. We've heard Uncle Finn say that word," Avery informs us.

"Yes, you have, but kids still shouldn't say it, right?" Finn asks the girls. They hum in acknowledgment, and he continues. "We wanted to tell you good luck tomorrow."

"Yeah," Avery says. "You're gonna be awesome."

"You're my favorite person at the museum," Eloise cheers before filling the earpiece with her boisterous laugh.

"Hey," Finn snaps playfully. "What about me?"

The girls giggle uncontrollably, and for some strange reason, it floods my eyes with tears. My chest hurts from missing them so much. Sure, I'm thoroughly addicted to Finn and constantly counting down the time until I see him again. But I feel the exact same way about the girls. On the days I don't see their sweet faces and hear their bright laughter, my heart aches.

My voice shakes when I say, "You all are my favorites."

The rowdiness on the other side of the phone quiets. "Did we make her cry?" Avery asks.

"Don't worry. I'm okay," I tell them. "They're happy tears because you guys made me feel so special."

"Ohhh," Avery says.

I sniffle and try to make my voice even when I ask, "Can we celebrate together after my interview?"

Finn groans. "I wish. We have dinner with my parents tomorrow evening."

"Do you want me to come? Need a bodyguard?" I ask, desperate to plan something to distract me after my inevitable post-interview spiral.

He huffs a laugh. "More like I need my Millie."

A warm, cozy feeling spreads through my limbs at the way he says *my Millie*.

"I'll be there." A yawn takes over my body before I can contain it. "I better rest up for tomorrow. Thank you all for calling."

"We love you, Millie," Avery says into the phone, and my heart skips a beat. They've never told me that before, and my arms ache to hug them.

"I love you all too." *All three of you.*

I know the words are true as soon as they pass my lips.

Being in love isn't a familiar feeling for me. I never felt like I truly reached it with Kyle. I felt like I *needed* him to make myself happy—like I feared what my life would be without him. There was an undercurrent of feeling so bad about myself that I needed him to make me feel good.

Once I had the clarity of being away from him, I realized it didn't feel like love. It felt like a trap.

But I've taken the wasteland Kyle left, all barren soil and no sunshine, and I've tended to it. I've watered it. Planted seeds. Worked to grow myself back.

Then Finn came along and encouraged the progress. He amplified my light, and he and the girls have brought an abundance of new blossoms and bright colors and sweet smells.

And something has settled into place. A realization that this is what love looks like. It's mutual respect, where I can stand on my own, and he encourages me to do so. It's the feeling that we're fine without each other, but a million times better *with* each other. It's blooming and thriving with someone else and caring for the person next to you because seeing their flowers grow makes your world even more extraordinary.

"Can we have ice cream?" Eloise asks, releasing the quiet tension and making all of us laugh.

"You all enjoy your ice cream," I tell them.

"Good night, Millie. See you tomorrow," Finn promises.

My shoulders slump as I end the call, wishing I could be at

their house right now. I want to laugh with the girls and absorb their sweet innocence instead of thinking about tomorrow. I want to let Finn's body tire me out before his deep, calm breaths lull me to sleep.

But as I get ready for bed, thoughts of Kyle blaze to the front of my mind. Anxiety about what I'll do if he gets the job and fear that I'm not good enough to get it myself play on a loop as I try to fall asleep.

* * *

Oaks Folks

Tess: Good luck today, Mills. No matter what happens, we're proud of you.

Millie: Thanks, Tess!

Fabes: It's so rude to send group texts at 5:06 a.m. It should be illegal. I'm going to call my local representative about it.

Fabes: But also, you're going to do amazing today, Millie. You're my favorite sister.

Tess: Who's rude now? You know you were about to get up anyway. Wouldn't want to miss shirtless Theo on his morning jog.

Mom: Girls, you're adults now. Be nice.

Mom: Millie, you show those interviewers how amazing you are. We're so proud of you.

Dad: You were made for that place, and
they're lucky to have you. Call us later.

* * *

I'VE BEEN A nervous mess since four this morning, when I woke up
and couldn't get back to sleep. And I want to say that I've used that
time to prepare for my interview, but I haven't. With the image of
Kyle's irritatingly smug face circling in my mind all night and this
morning, I haven't been able to concentrate on anything else.

So I've put all my anxious energy into getting dressed in the
perfect outfit—a pair of fitted slacks, a bright white blouse with
little flower details, and a pair of heels that are tall enough to give
me a boost of authority without being so high that I'm going to
fall in the interview.

When I walk into the kitchen, Lena is in her pajamas, hair
wild in every direction while she pours coffee into a mug.

"Boss bitch energy," she mumbles as she surveys my outfit, trying to sound a lot more awake than she looks.

"Sleepy bitch energy." I laugh, waving my hand in her direction.

"Of all seven dwarfs, I identify most as Sleepy. Maybe Grumpy
this morning." She pours about a cup of creamer into the mug and
gives it a stir before taking a sip. "This'll help me rally, though.
Want some?"

"No, thanks. I think I need Maggie's today." I grab my bag and
reach my arms out for her.

Lena sets her mug down on the counter and wraps me in a
hug. "You look great, your outfit is perfect, and your ass is fantastic." She smacks it for emphasis before clasping my face between
her hands. "Remember who you are. You're Millie Oaks, and you
deserve that job. You're a badass butterfly who has emerged from
her chrysalis, fucking stunning and ready to fly."

* * *

MY HANDS SHAKE with nerves as I join the line at Maggie's. She spots me from behind the espresso machine and waves me over to the pickup area, pulling a bag out from behind the counter.

"Finn called right when we opened this morning," she says with a sparkly grin. "Said today was an important day and we needed to make this special for you." She slides the pastry bag my way.

My lips part as I unfold the top of the package to peek inside. The golden-brown almond croissant is still warm in my hands.

Maggie grabs my Americano from the barista at the espresso machine. "He also said you might need this." She pulls an apron off the kitchen door and hands it over the counter to me. "And I say you need *this* while you eat so you don't mess up that gorgeous outfit."

After thanking Maggie profusely, I make my way to an empty table and sit down. My stomach fills with flutters as I absorb the fact that Finn went through all the effort of calling this morning. I'm not quite sure I deserve it.

Even with everything looming this morning, I force myself to think of Finn and the girls while I enjoy my breakfast, wishing they would come in the door any moment to join me.

Once my croissant and coffee are gone, I return the apron to Maggie, extremely grateful not to have crumbs all over me. Sticking a pair of headphones on my ears, I start a Girl Power playlist Lena made and walk to my office, soaking in as many motivational lyrics as I can.

Micah greets me from his desk as I enter. "You're looking like an entomology department director today." He beams.

"Well, thank you." I drop my headphones into my bag, and my eyes land on a bouquet of flowers and a wrapped package on my desk.

I look to Micah, and he shrugs. "They were here when I came in."

The small, delicate blooms of purple, pink, yellow, and blue look like they've just been plucked from a field of wildflowers. I bend forward and close my eyes to inhale their soft, sweet scent, letting it transport me to the fields I grew up on, where I spread wildflower seeds and ran through the blossoms.

When I open my eyes, they land on the small envelope and two pieces of paper.

I pull out the first picture, which has Eloise's name at the bottom and a woman with Ariel-red hair surrounded by bugs of every color and shape. Some are near-perfect renditions, and some have a distinct creative license that makes them look more like monsters. My eyes squint with the force of my smile. When I pick up the second picture, it's from Avery. This one is a woman with the same red hair, holding the hand of a man with black hair and glasses, and a little girl on each side. Tiny, pink hearts adorn the top of each person's head.

My vision blurs with unshed tears, and I bite my lips to stop them from quivering. I have to read the letter before so many tears flood my eyes that I can't see.

I flick open the envelope and pull out a small piece of galaxy stationery.

Dearest Millie,

There were two missing pieces in your office. I hope you like them.

    I'm so proud of you.
    I'll be there waiting when you get out of the interview.

Astronomically Yours,
Finn

I trace my fingers over where he's written "astronomically yours," feeling it seep through my skin and into my bloodstream, before I set it on my desk.

My hands shake as I pick up the rectangular package wrapped in brown paper. I slide my fingers through the opening and pop the tape. Pulling away the paper, I reveal two frames, one small enough to sit inside the other.

My breath stalls as I scan the small, framed image of me and the girls. Finn must've taken this picture a few days ago from behind us as we walked to the park, Avery and Eloise on each side of me, holding my hands.

I have to press my thighs against my desk to keep my body steady. Micah walks toward me and places a warm palm between my shoulder blades as a show of silent support. With a reassuring nod for myself, I lift the small frame out of the larger one, setting it on my desk and revealing the image in the second frame.

I suck in a sharp breath, covering my mouth with my free hand as I take in the details of the painting.

A deep purple galaxy of sky surrounds a majestic butterfly. *Hamadryas laodamia*, more commonly known as the Starry Night Cracker butterfly, has nearly black wings with white flecks that make it resemble the night sky and the Vincent van Gogh painting it's named after.

My head shakes slowly as I notice the small, curvy LS in the corner—Lena's signature.

Tears overrun my eyes until I can't see the painting anymore. I set it gently on my desk, and Micah's big arms wrap around me. I turn in his embrace and let the tears fall against his chest. He rubs slow, soothing circles on my back until I've calmed down enough to lift my head, and he wipes the tears from my cheeks.

"Do I look like a raccoon?" I sniffle.

His coffee-and-cream eyes dance with amusement as he helps me wipe a bit of mascara away. "Not at all," he says, dropping a kiss to my brow. "You look perfect. Now, go get 'em, tiger."

He gives me one last tight hug before he walks back to his desk. I take a deep breath, letting it out through pursed lips as I set the picture of me and the girls next to my computer monitor and look over its placement with a watery smile.

One hour until my interview. One hour to wipe my damp cheeks, touch up my mascara, and hardwire my brain to memorize everything I want to say. One hour to give myself the pep talk of the century. To muster every ounce of confidence I've built up over the last few months and channel it into today's interview.

Kyle may have the deceptive ambition and the cunning personality, but I have the unending passion and the genuine heart for this job. And if I can calm my nerves enough, I know I can show that today.

I think back on Lena's words this morning and shake my shoulders, lift my chest, and spread out my invisible wings.

Ready to fly.

Chapter 41

Finn

I blow out a deep breath as I lean back on the bench around the corner from Millie's interview, my leg bouncing with tension.

My heart is a wreck today. I've been itching to have Millie in my arms, craving her touch and wanting to calm the nerves I knew she must've been experiencing. Waiting here for the last hour has been miserable. I'm pretty sure I scared the poor woman who walked by a few minutes ago with the force of my scowl.

A door shuts down the hallway, and heels click toward me. When Millie rounds the corner, she has a shining, self-assured smile on her face that grows even bigger when she spots me.

My shoulders can finally relax, and I stand, wrapping my arms around her and burying my face in her hair. "You look amazing." The tension seeps from my body as I inhale her lemon-and-vanilla shampoo.

"Thank you." She exhales a long breath against my chest, her arms encircling my waist. "Thank you for everything this morning."

I pull back and give her a quick kiss. "You're welcome. How did it go?"

"I feel good about it. Everyone seemed to respond well to my answers, and it was very conversational, so I was able to relax a bit once we got going."

"Fantastic." I drop my forehead to hers and run my fingers into her hair.

"Jamila took your spot on the panel," she says. "And she didn't glare and grumble like certain other people." She laughs, poking a finger into my chest. "She actually smiled instead of being a pest the entire time."

"But did you crash into her car on the way in?" I tease, wrapping her hand in mine as we walk toward the stairs.

"No, actually. I only run into people who—"

Millie jerks to a stop on the landing, her blank stare targeted on Kyle ascending the stairs. He's dressed in a light gray suit and red tie as he strolls up the steps, cold eyes on Millie the entire time.

Her hand shakes slightly before she drops it from mine.

As he reaches the landing, his gaze leers over her like she's a piece of gum he's stepped on. "Guess it's my turn," he says, curling an eyebrow at us.

Stinging pain lances through my heart. I fell for his act. I opened the door for him to come back into her life. The man who spent years abusing the woman I love is now digging away at all the hard work she's put in.

Fuck. I *love* her, yet I did this to her.

My skin vibrates with rage as I put my hand on Millie's lower back to encourage her to keep going, but she doesn't move. She seems to steel her spine, pulling her shoulders back and lifting her chin.

I slide my hand up higher, and Kyle's attention swings to me. "Is this your new plaything?" He chuckles darkly, looking at where my arm disappears behind her back. "This must be how you got a second interview. You fucked your way into it?"

Millie flinches, and a pounding fills my ears. Hot adrenaline rushes through my body, and my hands shake with the need to punch that arrogant fucking smirk off his face.

But as I step forward to respond, Millie beats me to it. "Do not speak to me." Her voice is more lethal than I've ever heard.

"Aw, come on, I was having fun." A malicious grin contorts his lips.

A growl rumbles out of my throat, predatory and protective. "She said don't speak to her."

He laughs coldly. "I'll do whatever the hell I want when I'm her boss."

Millie straightens and takes a step toward him, looking every bit the warrior I hope she sees herself as. "Get the *fuck* out of our way, Kyle. I won't take this from you anymore." She shoves a finger into his chest, and it's enough to make him lose his balance and shift back. Millie steals the step from him and gets right in his space again. "Get out of my museum."

A sinister laugh creeps from him, the sound loud in the staircase. "Is this your museum?" He tilts his head to look around. "We'll see about that."

"Let's go," I say, putting my hand on her waist and pulling her toward me. A breath rushes out of me when she shifts her feet so we can move down the stairs beside him.

"You should probably get my desk ready," he snarls from behind us.

On the bottom step, she plants her feet, turns to face him, and spits her next words with venom. "I regret every day I spent with you, and I refuse to waste even one more thinking about you."

With that, she grabs my hand and walks toward the museum entrance. She keeps her footsteps steady until we reach my car.

When she swings into the passenger side, she slams the door behind her and seems to deflate into the seat.

My throat feels tight with helplessness as I get in the car. I turn and take her fidgeting hands in mine. "Millie—"

"I can't do it right now," she mumbles, eyes on the parked cars out the windshield.

I nod, turning the key until the engine roars to life. "Okay, what sounds good for lunch?"

"I want to go home," she says robotically.

"Alright, I think I have something there I can make you."

"No. My house." Her hollow, cold voice sends chills down my spine.

"Millie," I try.

"Finn." She finally meets my eyes, and hers are glassy with tears ready to fall. "Just let me process, and then I'll be ready for this evening."

She rides silently next to me, staring out the window. Her fingers pick at the skin around her nails, so I settle my hand over hers to stop the anxious movement.

I want to hold her. I want to remind her that he means nothing, and she means everything.

I want to tell her I love her.

But as we reach her front door, my chest caves in. She doesn't invite me inside, and she shuts the door before I can kiss her goodbye.

I sit in her driveway and order a lunch delivery, hoping she'll be awake long enough to answer the door for it. And then I drive home, nausea churning in my stomach at the reminder I'm one of the people who brought Kyle back into her life.

Chapter 42

Millie

Oaks Folks

Dad: Let us know how your interview went, Mills. We're waiting anxiously.

Dad: Your mother baked a cake for you even though you're not here.

Mom: Nervous baking. You know how it goes.

Fabes: I'll definitely benefit from that cake tonight.

Mom: I invited Eva and Theo over for some as well.

Fabes: Nevermind. I'm busy.

Tess: I'll be there. Maybe Millie can FaceTime us and tell us how it went.

Fabes: We love you, Mills!
Call us when you can.

* * *

FINN'S CALL WAKES me from a deep sleep, and I blink my eyes open, groggily reaching for my phone. The time says I've slept for four hours, and I'm supposed to be ready for dinner at his parents' right now.

My voice is hoarse when I answer, "Hey."

"Hi. We're outside. Are you ready?" His tone is gentle, like he's talking to a frightened animal.

"No, I'm so sorry. I forgot to set an alarm to wake up. I'll let you in."

I slip some leggings on underneath my T-shirt and stop in front of the mirror. My perfect waves from this morning have gone frizzy and wild. I brush a hand over them as I head for the door.

When I open it, Finn, Avery, and Eloise are clad in their adorable tie-dye shirts. I force a smile across my face as the girls wrap their arms around me.

Finn shrugs with a bag from the café around the corner. "I guess this got here after you'd fallen asleep."

A flash of guilt sinks into my stomach. "I'm sorry."

"Don't apologize for needing rest," he says firmly.

I nod and put my hands on the girls' heads. "Thank you both so much for my pictures and flowers. I found them this morning, and they brightened my whole day."

"You're welcome," Avery says.

"Will you wear your tie-dye like us?" Eloise asks. "I want to show Nonna and Nonno what we made."

"I'd love to. We'll be a tie-dye team, won't we?"

The girls smile wide and nod before running into the living room to find Pepper. Finn steps closer, wrapping me in a hug that needed desperately.

Sage.

Strong arms.

Safety.

I bury my face into his soft shirt and breathe him in as he kisses the top of my head. "If you want to cancel, you can. We could come pick you up for the fun part later."

"No, I want to go. I can't be left out of this tie-dye team."

When I lift my chin, concern etches his face. "I'm so sorry, Millie. Sorry I thought he was a good enough person to bring in for a second interview. And sorry I brought him back into your life. I never would've done that if I'd known. I hate myself for it."

I press my fingers into the pinched crease between his brows and smooth it out. "I know you wouldn't. I'm not upset with you at all. He tricked you like he tricks everyone else."

His jaw tightens, but he nods. "Would you think less of me if I kind of want to kill him?"

A smile cracks over my tired face. "No. You'd be in line right behind me. And Lena."

* * *

As HE DRIVES to his parents', Finn sets his hand in my lap, a steady weight over my thigh. A grounding reminder that he's right there if I need him.

The view outside the window changes to a neighborhood of extravagant houses. Colossal structures, each with its own design aesthetic, line the road, surrounded by perfectly maintained grass. Sprinklers click in the front yards, and a few women run down the road ahead of us in the workout gear of suburban royalty.

Finn pulls his car into the driveway of a three-story, Italian-style mansion, with stucco walls and a tiled roof. The house has an almost untouchable beauty, like it's a little too perfect to be real.

We park next to a carved fountain that's lit by the warm glow of spotlights. Dressed in our tie-dye armor, we exit the car, and the girls' wide, unsure eyes stare at the building.

Finn's expression softens when he notices their apprehension. He kneels in front of them and puts a hand on each of their shoulders.

"We can leave whenever you all are ready, okay?" They nod like they've gone through this conversation before. "I love you both so much." He kisses their foreheads, and we hold hands as we make our way through the courtyard to the front door.

Finn pushes the doorbell, and it echoes through the house. A petite older woman answers the door, nodding to Finn and giving the girls a familiar smile. They offer a small grin back.

"How are you ladies this evening?" she asks in a kind voice.

"Good, Miss Sally," Eloise answers.

A woman with long jet-black hair appears in the corridor behind Sally, her heels beating against the tile floor as she approaches. Her beauty gives a subtle hint of plastic surgery, and I know from Finn that it hides a nasty interior. Like a shiny candy coating over a raisin.

Her dark eyes assess all of us with her mouth set in a tense line. "You're late. I told you to be on time."

Wow. What a way to greet your son and granddaughters.

Finn's hands slide around the girls' shoulders, and he pulls them slightly toward his legs. I want a little of that protection, but he only has two hands, and the girls need it more.

"Yes, we're a little late, but we're here now," Finn says firmly.

Eloise pulls the hem of her tie-dye shirt out and says, "Do you like the shirts we made, Nonna?"

Finn's mother finally looks at her granddaughter and gives her a belittling wince of a grin. "They're very special, dear."

Eloise's face pinches with confusion, and she grabs Avery's hand for support.

"Mother, this is Millie," Finn says, nodding toward me.

She meets my eyes with a critical stare. "Serena," she says with a nod. "Are you here to help with the girls while we eat?"

"No. She's my guest. My girlfriend." Finn's voice is tense, like he's barely holding himself together.

He's never called me that before, and although it's been a rough day—and seems it will continue that way—that small word sends a thrill through me.

He catches my eye and winks.

Serena claps her hands loudly, making the girls jump. "Well, dinner is ready."

We follow her through the entry hall and turn left into a dining room the size of my entire house. A long table that could seat an army is surrounded by ornate chairs and intricate place settings at the far end.

At the head of the table sits an older man taking a sip of amber liquid in his tumbler. The color of his eyes matches Finn's, but even from across the room, I can see his father's are dull and void of personality.

He tips his chin to us as we all take our seats, Serena on his left, Finn on his right, and the girls along the table next to Finn.

Serena snaps toward Sally and tells her to bring another place setting. She instructs her to set it up on the other side of the girls. Ave, El, and I are left to feel like outcasts spread out along the edge of the table while the "adults" form the end. Finn casts me a look of sympathy, but the alternative is to sit by Serena, and that doesn't sound fun either.

"Dad, this is Millie, my girlfriend. Millie, this is my father, Richard," Finn says, waving a hand between us as he sits down.

Richard doesn't respond to my smile or our introduction. He just looks like a king at the head of the table, surveying the people below him. I ignore his dismissal with my own, moving to help Avery and Eloise get settled in their seats.

Serena places a napkin in her lap. "Well, tell me about yourself, girl. I should probably know the person my granddaughters spend time with."

Girl. It doesn't sound sweet when *she* says it.

"Finn and I work together. I'm an entomology curator at the museum."

Serena snorts and rolls her eyes. Heat warms my cheeks.

"She had an interview today," Eloise adds, smiling in her grandmother's direction.

"Lovely." Her eyes dip to my tie-dye shirt. "I hope you didn't wear that."

Her dig doesn't go unnoticed. "Mother," Finn growls.

But I try my best to brush it off, just like I always did with Kyle. "No, I didn't wear this. Although the interview panel would've thought this shirt was so fun, right?" I nudge Eloise with my elbow, trying to send her a little bit of reassurance.

Sally pours red wine into Serena's glass before coming around the table to serve mine.

Serena's voice drips with judgment as she says, "Well, I also hope your hair didn't look like that."

A gasp leaves my throat without permission. Everyone's eyes flick to mine, even Sally's. A little wine drips onto the tablecloth when her hands fumble.

As I stare into Serena's icy gaze, my vision blurs, and her face contorts until Kyle's cold stare peers back at me.

Kyle hated my hair in waves. He told me it was too frizzy. Too messy. Too *crazy*.

So I straightened my hair. I wore the clothes he picked. I faked a smile when he told me to be happy. I believed him when he said I was crazy.

And it destroyed me.

I run a hand over the top of my head self-consciously and turn to Finn. His gaze on his mother is deadly. "That is completely—"

"Millie's hair is pretty," Eloise interrupts with a big smile. "It's like mine and Mama's." She runs her fingers through the strands on my shoulder.

Her bright blue eyes connect with mine, and hers are filled with comfort. My chin dips, and I give her a watery smile. Her sweet innocence casts a spell over my sorrow, drowning out all the terrible things I've heard today and replacing them with her heartfelt sentiment.

Sally and the chef interrupt the thick tension in the room, carrying dinner plates to the table. I pull my attention away from Eloise to thank Sally as she deposits mine in front of me.

The chef stands behind Richard and introduces her dinner to us. "Ms. Serena has requested a seared duck breast with tamarind-sesame sauce this evening. Along with that, we have a chilled sprout soup with pancetta, sous vide egg yolk, caviar, and yuzu hollandaise."

I don't know what most of that is, but the savory herbs smell delicious, so I paste on a gracious smile. Sally sets the same plate in front of Avery and Eloise, and I have to stifle a laugh at their bewilderment.

"Mother, were you planning one of the foods we discussed for the girls?" Finn asks tightly.

"They can eat the same thing as the adults, Finneas. If they don't like it, they can go hungry."

He clears his throat. "That's not how I'm raising Avery and Eloise." Finn's voice is stern as he levels his mother with a glare. "They're encouraged to try everything, but they are always offered at least one safe food that I know they like."

She gives him an identical look, and the room chills as they stare each other down in a battle of wills across the table.

Serena breaks eye contact first, flicking her gaze in my direction. "Is this something you put in his head?"

Finn sets his glass down with a *thud*, sloshing a few drops of wine across his fancy dinner. "This is something Clara requested. And I will uphold her wishes."

Serena rubs her crimson-tipped nails across her forehead. "Oh, this again. You take every chance to bring up being the guardian of *my* grandchildren. Who's taking care of them while you're with *Millie*?" She spews my name like it's sour milk.

The words hit Finn with an almost invisible flinch, but I catch it. Knowing his worries about being a good caregiver for Avery and Eloise, I'm sure that cut him exactly how his mother intended it to.

Richard finally joins the conversation. "Maybe if Clara had left them with us, like she should've, they would be able to eat like sophisticated children. Instead of sitting in these ridiculous tie-dye ensembles, expecting junk food."

The entire room freezes for a brief moment. No one breathes.

But then the words land. Finn's chair scrapes against the wood floors at the same time as mine, the sound like nails on a chalkboard as it grates in my ears. Both of us stand to defend the girls, who look terrified and disgusted by their grandparents. Fury laces Finn's features as he bends to stare down his parents, his fists clenched on the ivory tablecloth.

"How sweet." Serena's mocking voice makes my ears ring. "Your little nanny is trying to pretend she's a part of this."

"Millie," Finn keeps his eyes on his mother as he says in a low voice. "Please take Avery and Eloise to the car."

I nod and help the girls out of their chairs. They walk quietly toward the door, and Sally is there with her arms out for them. She wraps them in a hug, hidden around the corner from the view of Serena and Richard. Ave and El rest their cheeks on Sally's shoulder while she whispers something to them with a sad smile.

Serena snips, "At least she listens. I could never get you and Clara to do that." I whip my head back in their direction.

"This"—Finn pokes a finger between the two of them—"is exactly why they don't live with you. I don't care how much money you have or how big your house is. None of that matters more than love and compassion and kindness." He looks like a dangerous shadow looming over their fancy dinner. I've seen many dark glares from him, but I would never want to be on the receiving end of *that* one.

His voice is a lethally low tone as he adds, "I don't care how you decide to live your lives at this point, but we will not be a part of it, because none of us deserve this treatment."

"Really?" Serena brushes imaginary crumbs from the tablecloth. "Are you going to run off with that *girl*? She gets to see our grandchildren, and we don't?"

I flinch back from her patronizing tone, fire blazing through my veins.

Finn's fist bangs against the table, and the wineglasses teeter. "Shut your *fucking* mouth about the woman I love. We're done." His chair crashes to the ground as he turns to leave.

* * *

MY STOMACH CHURNS in the car, sweat accumulating on the back of my neck. I can't get the image out of my head of Serena's face morphing into Kyle's.

Her words, her sneers, her casual dismissals. It's all *just* like him.

And I want to believe they're both wrong. I want to focus on the people I care about in this car with me and leave everything that just happened in their stuffy, oversized prison of a house.

But her words echo in my ears nonstop until they're all I can hear.

Chapter 43

Finn

*T*hanks for taking us for pizza." Eloise smiles, her hair fanned against her sage-green pillow.

I love those wild waves. I'm obsessed with them, and I hope she never feels like she has to change them.

"Anytime, *piccola*." I climb onto the bed between the girls, wrapping an arm around both of their shoulders. "I'm sorry about Nonna Serena and Nonno Richard tonight."

"They weren't very nice," Avery says, looking up at me with a crease down her brow.

"No, they weren't."

"I don't like when they're mean." Eloise bunches up the blanket between her fingers.

I pull them closer, like I'm hoping to squeeze the hurt out of them and absorb it into myself. "I love you both so much. I'm so proud of you, and I want you to have the best of everything. Sometimes that means we don't need to spend time with people who make us feel sad and treat us like that."

"They were mean to Millie too," Avery reminds me, the empathetic soul she always is.

"Yes, they were. And she doesn't deserve that either. But I want you to know that how they act has nothing to do with you. They have sad hearts, and when someone's heart is sad, they can be mean to other people around them. But that doesn't make it okay. They still shouldn't treat anyone that way. It doesn't mean anything is wrong with you or me or Millie. You are both perfect." I lean in to kiss their heads.

"It made *my* heart sad when we were there," Eloise says, handing me tonight's book from her nightstand.

"It made my heart sad too," I reply.

Once the girls are asleep, I creep out of their bedroom and find Millie in a plush armchair in my room, knees tucked close to her chest, staring out the bedroom window.

"Hey, beautiful," I say, kissing her forehead and sitting in the matching chair beside hers. "You doing okay?"

"Not really," she whispers distantly.

My chest burns with anger at my parents. "I'm so sorry about everything."

She drags her eyes away from the window and faces me with splotchy red cheeks. "Don't apologize for them. It wasn't your fault."

I reach for her hand and pull her toward me until she concedes, sitting in my lap. "They were completely disrespectful to you."

She shakes her head with a furrowed brow. "I'm more worried about the girls."

"I talked to them a little tonight, but I have a feeling we'll do it again tomorrow." I run a hand over her hair. "Everything my parents said was utter bullshit."

Millie's mouth twists, but she doesn't respond.

"Do you believe me?"

She blows out a breath. "I spent years with someone like that. *Years.* And it wasn't constantly as bad as tonight, but everything she said still felt so familiar. It was so hard to remind myself that I'm not stuck in that cycle of abuse anymore." She presses her lips together. "I've been sitting here going over everything she and Kyle said to me today, and I don't think that I can endure any more of it."

"You shouldn't have to. We never have to go over there again."

She gives me a sad smile. "But *you* shouldn't have to choose between us."

"What do you mean?" Dread churns in my chest at her words. She sounds like she's already decided she's not worth the choice.

"They're your parents and the girls' grandparents. It's not fair to make you pick one or the other."

I shake my head. "It's the easiest choice I've ever made."

She blinks as tears gather in the corners of her eyes.

"I grew up in their house and lived with that every day, and I can tell you with absolute certainty that they're not the kind of people I want the girls around." I cup my palms around her cheeks. "But *you* are. You mean more to us than my parents ever have."

Her voice cracks as she says, "You wanted the girls to have grandparents."

"I do. And I'm pretty sure your parents are obsessed with the idea."

A small grin seeps through her sadness, and I want to beg her to let it spread. Let it shove all her worries to the side and wash us clean of every bad thing that happened today.

But her grin falters. "Didn't Clara want them to have a relationship?"

I search her green gaze. I've experienced countless dinners and visits with my parents in the last eight months to maintain a relationship with them. I've put up with their toxic comments and manipulations to give them time with their granddaughters.

And they've practically spit in my face for it every time. But especially tonight.

They completely disrespected the three most important people in my life, and never seeing them again wouldn't destroy me like never seeing Millie again.

I *know* in my heart that she's the right choice. It's a simple decision.

And I know with absolute certainty that Clara would agree.

I gently nudge her off my lap and stand, grabbing her hand. "Come with me. I want to show you something."

Chapter 44

Millie

*F*inn tugs me down the stairs and opens the doors to his study in a rush. The room welcomes me with an old-book smell that soothes my shoulders when I inhale it. Warm golden light from a lamp bathes the room as he guides me inside. He shuts the French doors behind us and grabs a blanket from a chest in the corner, then spreads it out in the middle of the room.

"Lie down," he says, waving a hand over it. The thin fabric is smooth under my skin as I lie back and stare at the ceiling.

Finn clicks the lamp off, cloaking the room in darkness except for the ambient moonlight streaming through the window.

I've never been in this room without a lamp on, and I've apparently been missing out on the best feature. Because despite the lack of light, the ceiling glows with tiny bright stars.

Goose bumps creep over my skin as I take in the view. "Beautiful," I breathe. Finn joins me, and we lie below a sea of crisp white stars. My gaze bounces over every detail, and I have the dizzying feeling that I'm floating through space on a magic carpet.

Finn grounds me by looping an arm around my shoulders until my head rests on his chest.

"Did you paint them?" I ask.

"I did." His voice cracks on the words. He takes a deep breath and sounds steadier as he says, "I spent a long time painting them after Clara died. Every night, pretty much."

My chest is tight, barely letting me breathe as I picture Finn in here, painting stars across the ceiling while he grieved the loss of his sister.

"It's amazing. I feel like I'm looking through a telescope."

He lifts his free arm and points to a group of stars to the left. "Remember what Lyra looks like?"

I nod, tracking the constellation he points to.

Of course my nerdy astronomer would paint real constellations on his ceiling.

He lowers his hand a little to another group of stars. "And there's Delphinus." He squeezes his arm around me, pulling me closer to his body.

"And that"—he points to a small grouping of stars— "is the Butterfly Cluster."

My body goes completely still, the sound of my heartbeat whooshing through my ears.

"That was Clara's favorite part of the galaxy."

I suck in a deep breath as my eyes ping between each star in the cluster.

Finn moves his finger in an arch. "The butterfly shape is hard to see—"

"I can see it," I interrupt. My eyes burn, threatening to spill tears. "It's magnificent."

He breathes a sigh of relief and sets his free hand over mine on his chest. "Every time we went outside at night, she'd ask me to look for it. And often it wasn't visible, but when it was, she made a wish on it. Sometimes I go to the planetarium and send the view to the Butterfly Cluster, and I sit there talking to her. I pretend she's listening to me ramble, and occasionally I laugh at the absurdity of it."

Finn shifts, and I turn onto my side with my head on my elbow. He does the same, facing me until we're a mirror image of each other. Only our outlines are visible in the dim light from outside, but I can feel his gaze warm and steady on me.

"But what if it's not absurd at all?" he says. "I painted you here months ago. The same stars Clara wished on every chance she got." He tucks a lock of hair behind my ear as a tear drips from my eye and seeps into my arm. "Millie, she pointed me right to you."

My chest aches and my lips quiver from trying to hold back my sobs.

"I wish you could see how much you've done for us," he whispers. "I've laid all the shattered pieces of myself in front of you over the last few months. All the broken fragments I've been trying to glue back together on my own. The grief and the pain and all my flaws and insecurities." He cups my face in his palm. "But you weren't afraid of it. In fact, you've been helping me put it all back together in little ways since I met you."

I scoot closer to him until my cheek rests on his biceps and my nose brushes his soft cotton shirt. His scent fills my lungs as I breathe in to say, "You've done the same for me. You and the girls have healed my soul in countless ways."

Finn squeezes his arms around me, surrounding me in his warmth and safety. "That's because we love you."

My heart stutters on its next beat. "You do?"

He nudges me onto my back, and our gazes collide as he leans over me. My eyes have adjusted to the lack of light enough that I can see the sparkle in his navy blues. He's outlined by the glowing stars behind him, but his eyes shine brighter. I smooth my hands up his arms and let the hair tickle my palms as he shivers under my touch.

"Of course I love you." He bends and touches his lips to mine. "Could you not tell when I bought you an entire shelf of books?" A kiss to my jaw. "Or by the way I'm obsessed with basking in every one of your smiles?" Another kiss to the hollow of my throat. "Or could you not tell by how you draw endless smiles out of me?" His lips come back to mine. "Or how I let you beat me at Catan that one time?"

My vision goes blurry as tears gather in my eyes.

His palm settles over my chest, right above my heart. "I don't need the sun when you're here, *stella mia*. You're the brightest star in my universe, and I've been orbiting around you since you poured coffee all over me. I could spend the rest of my life watching you shine."

His words slide over me like a second skin before they settle into my soul, completely warping my view of the future and replacing it with a movie montage of years to come. An image of Finn and me flashes by, our hands clasped as we walk down the aisle between rows of family and friends. Jubilant smiles cover our faces, with two flower girls following behind us. Then the picture glitches to a bedroom—to tired eyes and messy hair as we lean together over a baby with navy blue eyes. The next image is Avery and Eloise trying to push a stroller through the park together while Finn wraps his arm around my shoulder and kisses my head.

A tear slips down my temple as I whisper, "I didn't pour coffee all over you."

Finn runs his thumb over my bottom lip. "You did. You also broke my nose and my car."

"But you still love me," I say through a watery laugh.

A smile tugs at his mouth as he removes his glasses, setting them next to the blanket. "They're some of my favorite things about you."

My heart bursts right through my chest. Maybe she wasn't a wanton floozy all this time. Maybe she just knew how impeccable it would feel for Finn to hold her in his palm. How safe it would be there, exactly where she was meant to land.

My voice comes out hoarse as I whisper, "I love you too." Then he glides his lips over the corner of mine, and I seal our mouths together in a kiss that could blind the universe.

Chapter 45

Finn

A groan rolls from my chest as our tongues collide, dancing in a sensual rhythm. Millie wiggles her hips beneath me. Her soft whimpers fill the room as I leave a trail of kisses on her neck and suck at her sweet skin.

Pulling back, I study her glistening eyes and already swollen lips. It feels impossible to memorize every part of this moment, but I want to try. I'll absorb every little detail through my hands, eyes, ears, and mouth, until they're branded into my memory forever.

Millie watches me as my gaze roams over her body, my Catan shirt loose over her torso and tight black leggings covering her hips and thighs. Soft cotton brushes against my skin as I settle my hands on the hem of her shirt, and she sits up to help me remove it.

Her skin is blazing beneath my palms as I slide them around her waist and over her ribs, pulling the shirt up as I go. A quiet gasp seeps from her lips when my thumbs graze her nipples. The hard peaks beg for my focus, but I continue my path up until she's completely uncovered, creamy skin and full, round tits on display.

The room falls into a stark silence as she waits for my next move. Fuck, she looks like a dream come true right now. Every fantasy I've ever had wrapped up in a beautiful woman who cares about me and makes me smile and *loves* me.

"Why did I wait so long to tell you you're everything to me?" I ask, shaking my head.

"I've been wondering the same thing," she quips.

Placing a hand between her breasts, I gently push her back until she's lying below me again. I drop my lips to her chest, teasing her with small kisses and licks, avoiding her nipples, just to see her lose it a little. It's torture for me, honestly, but her stuttered breaths tell me she's getting desperate too.

She digs her fingers into my hair and attempts to steer me toward her rosy peak. "Finn. Please," she pleads in a raspy moan.

A dark laugh bubbles out of me before I give her what she wants. I finally pull her pebbled nipple into my mouth and suck hard, laving it with my tongue. Her groan of satisfaction makes me smile around her delicate point, and I let my teeth dig in just a tiny bit. She hisses a breath, and her hips buck beneath me.

As I move to the other breast, I let my hand follow the curve of her waist. The fabric of her leggings glides smoothly under my fingers as I trace a path down until I reach the junction of her thighs. Even through her leggings, I can feel the warmth radiating from her core as I grind my palm against her clit. The need to make her come, to feel her heat and wetness coat my fingers, is driving me wild.

"Finn," she bites out as she pulls my hair until I meet her lust-filled gaze. Licking her lips, she eyes me up and down before ordering, "Strip."

This confident version of Millie is so satisfying to hear. It makes my heart sound like a racehorse in my ears. "Yes, ma'am."

Her gaze never leaves me as my shirt hits the floor in record time, and I stand at her feet to strip my pajama pants and boxers from my body. I let her look her fill, completely bare before her.

From this view, I can watch every flick of her eyes over my body, every twitch of her thighs as she seeks some relief for the pressure between them, and every movement of her breasts as she takes shuddering breaths.

Her eyes land on my cock, and it twitches in response, making her lips snap into a knowing grin. She slides onto her knees, and my breath stops. The intention is clear on her face as she crawls the two steps toward me and rises until I can feel her hot breath on my cock. My eyes widen as she tilts her head back and forth over the glistening tip, spreading my arousal on her lips.

The entire world stops on its axis as she tips her chin, looking up at me through her lashes, and teasingly licks the tip once.

Fuck. She's going to ruin me.

My knees go weak. I don't think I can hold myself up anymore.

She scrapes her nails up my thighs, and my abs tighten as I try to keep myself under control. When she reaches my hips, her full lips part, and she takes the tip into her warm, wet mouth.

"Fucking hell," I grind out. She groans with pleasure, the vibrations shooting straight up my spine. The silky strands of her hair glide between my fingers as I grip them, needing something to hold on to.

She watches my reactions closely in the dark room as she coaxes me into her mouth agonizingly slowly.

"Jesus Christ, *Millie*." I don't even recognize my own husky, raw voice. My fingers clench in her hair like it's a lifeline, and I force myself to relax them a little.

Her eyes drop closed as she sucks, grazing her teeth lightly over my skin as she comes up and dives back down, pulling me in even deeper. My heavy breaths and groans mingle with the sounds of her wet mouth gliding over me, and it takes all my strength not to spill right down her throat.

I roll my fingers over her scalp, and she whimpers as her thighs press together and her hips squirm.

"Are you aching for me?" I grit out. Her eyes flick up to mine, and she nods. She slides back down my cock and—*fuck*—she takes me all the way this time, right to the back of her throat. "That's *so good*. Right there." I can't help the primal urge to press my hips forward just the tiniest bit.

My spine burns with an impending orgasm, but I don't want to come down her throat. I pull her hair back until my dick leaves her mouth with a *pop*.

Glittering eyes meet mine, and she licks her swollen lips. "What is it?" she asks, blinking and feigning innocence like the wicked little temptress she is.

"You fucking know what." I drop to my knees and grab her chin. "Your turn to strip."

The apples of her cheeks rise with the force of her grin, and she stands, giving me an eye-level view of her waist as she slips her fingers into her leggings and pulls them off.

She stands before me in her thong, looking down at me with smoldering eyes. I drag my knuckle up her inner thigh, watching the path it takes. A pained whimper comes from her lips when I glide my knuckle over the soaked fabric.

"These too, *stella mia*."

Following my orders, she tucks her fingers into the band, lowering the thong and letting it slip from her grip to drop to the ground.

She's fucking magnificent—every curve illuminated by the moonlight. This breathtaking woman is *mine*. I get to spend the rest of my life showing her how much I care about her and how much she means to me. And it's a goddamn privilege.

Her perfect tits rise and fall with her heavy breaths as I skate my hand up between her thighs. I dip a finger into her wetness and glide through her center. Her soft moans echo through the room as I reach her swollen clit and circle it.

"Oh, Millie. You liked having my cock in your mouth. You're

dripping," I murmur, my voice gruff and scratchy to my ears. "So needy and achy, aren't you? Lie down and spread your legs for me. I can help with that." Whimpering, she drops to the blanket and lets her knees fall wide.

I clasp her hand and press her fingers against her clit. "Touch yourself for me," I order, standing and reaching for my pants. "But don't come until I get back. I'm running upstairs to get a condom."

"No." Her free hand snaps around my ankle. "I have an IUD," she whispers. "I just want you."

I scan her face. "Are you sure?"

She sits up and pulls on my ankle. "One hundred percent. I was tested a few months ago and haven't been with anyone since."

Her unguarded expression has my heart pounding in my chest. "Same for me," I whisper.

"Then come back. Please."

Dragging in a shaky breath, I lower to my knees between her thighs and search her face for any doubts. Any second-guessing. Any chance she might have made a mistake and doesn't actually want to do this with a crumbling mess of a man like me.

But she looks completely sure, her expression confident and loving in a way I've never seen.

Relief courses through my veins, filling me with adrenaline and making my hands tremble as I bring them to her hips. Vanilla and lemon fill my senses as I claim her lips in a possessive kiss. Millie's nails dig into my back as her tongue brushes over mine, and I get to taste every one of her soft sighs and moans.

Leaving her lips, I meet her eyes again and watch her face as I press at her slick entrance. The sensation of touching her with nothing between us is already overwhelming. Skin to skin, I slide into her slowly, igniting every nerve ending.

Tingling pleasure races up my thighs and spine, and I can't stop the low groan that cuts through the room when I'm seated completely inside her.

Every soft curve of her tight, wet heat envelops me. Every glorious inch, filled with *me*. Nothing between us. I'm unable to move as she seizes every one of my senses. Her scent, her warmth, her breaths, her eyes.

"You feel so damn perfect," I murmur, pulling out slightly and holding my breath as I push back in. Fuck, I don't want this to be over too quickly, but I don't know if I can stop it.

Her eyelids flutter shut with my movement, and when she opens them again, tears glisten at the edges of her eyes.

I freeze, completely focused on those drops of moisture shimmering in the moonlight. "What's wrong, *stella mia*?" My thumb catches a tear as it slides down to her ear.

"They're called emotions, Spock." She laughs, deep and raspy, and her inner wall clenches.

It takes an act of extreme willpower not to move, but a small groan leaves my throat at the feeling of her tightening around me. "Are they good emotions?"

"The best ones," she sighs with a small smile.

I nod and catch a tear with my tongue, licking the salty moisture and absorbing the emotion into me. "I love you so much," I whisper against her cheek.

She stutters a breath as I give a tentative push toward her. "I love you too."

They're such simple words, but they completely restore every fractured bit of me.

Lowering my lips to hers, I breathe her in. I let her fill my lungs and my soul, and every shattered piece of my heart is finally gathered back together. Those fragments will never be assembled into the exact same shape they used to be, but she reconstructs them into a new version.

A better one. Millie's version.

She lifts her hips into mine as I pull out and press back in. I capture her moans with my mouth, sealing our bodies as close as possible. We move together in unhurried, deep strokes, the room filled with the sounds of our whispered promises and cries of ecstasy until we come together in a shower of sparks, panting each other's names.

Chapter 46

Millie

I could stay in this bed, in the shelter of Finn's arms, for the entire day.

Maybe a week.

Maybe forever.

Unfortunately, his alarm is chirping from his nightstand, signaling that I actually have to get up for work today. But the green duvet over us is so warm and cozy, begging me to call in sick.

Yesterday left me emotionally spent, and I desperately want to ignore the outside world while I just live in the glow of last night with Finn.

But I can't hide. I have to face everything at work and deal with it.

Or I'll never move on.

Finn reaches for the phone, trying his best not to disturb me. After he stops the alarm, he wraps his arm around me again.

"Good morning," I grumble, tilting up to catch his gaze.

His eyes crease in the corners as he grins down at me. "Good morning to you." He kisses my forehead. "I'll never get over how good it feels to wake up with you."

I sigh against his chest. "Let's never get up, then."

"Mm, that sounds good. But what about food?"

"That's what delivery services are for."

"They don't usually do bedroom deliveries." He laughs.

"We'll tip them extra," I say, burrowing closer.

"Good plan, but the girls will miss us."

"We've got plenty of room for them."

"You have a solution for everything."

I nod. "But maybe I also just don't want to face the world quite yet."

Finn hums in understanding, running his fingers through my hair as the bedroom door clicks open. Two little giggles echo from the hallway. "The wildlings are coming," Finn whispers into my hair.

Avery and Eloise squeal while running toward us, and Finn bursts up to surprise them. He wraps his arms around them, pulls their bodies onto the bed, and yells, "Cuddle puddle!" They wiggle and giggle above the duvet, kneeing me in the thigh, and Finn takes an elbow to the face.

Amid the joyful snickering, I suddenly remember my daydream. My fantasy: sweet touches and soft words and playful little girls asking for pancakes.

My throat clogs with emotion. I got it. I got the daydream and the fantasy all rolled together, and I can live in it forever.

I look to Finn over Eloise's wonderfully untamable hair. "Do we have time to make pancakes?"

The wattage of his smile blinds me. "Always time for pancakes."

* * *

AN EMAIL FROM Sharon pings into my inbox midmorning, asking me to meet her for lunch, and I have to force myself to remain calm.

This'll be fine. Even if she has bad news for me, she's a kind, understanding woman, and I trust her to deliver it well. I can smile graciously and thank her for the opportunity, then fall apart somewhere else.

My chest pinches when I look around my office and picture Kyle at the empty desk. My plants would be shriveled and dead, the office atmosphere a ghost of its past life.

Anxiety is already prickling through me, so I reply quickly, then fill a watering can in the lab room for something to do. When all the plants are happy, I decide the office floor could use a sweeping.

None of that actually lessens my anxiety, but thankfully, I've wasted enough time that I can start toward the café. My chest inflates as I take a deep breath and slowly let it out. I give the office one last meaningful look, shake out my imaginary wings, and walk toward The Buttered Bistro.

* * *

SHARON SITS AT a patio table under a dogwood tree that looks like the perfect oasis from the summer heat. She waves me over, her armful of bracelets jingling as she does.

I slide into the seat across from her. "Hi. Thanks for inviting me."

"Of course. Have you ever been here?" Sharon asks, pushing her menu aside.

When I tell her I haven't, Sharon goes through her favorite items on the menu. Then she leans into the table and whispers, "I'll let you in on a little secret. My husband is the chef, so everything is amazing." She gives me a saucy smile. "I like to eat here because it gets me food made by a sexy man, and it reminds him to stay on his toes." She winks, and it forces a light laugh out of me.

Once we've placed our orders, Sharon folds her hands on the table. "Let's get to business. I want to be straightforward with you about yesterday so I'm not holding you in suspense any longer than necessary." She tilts her head with a smile. "So let me start by telling you how wonderful you did in the interview."

"Thank you," I say, bubbles of confidence filling my chest. I lift my shoulders a smidge.

"It was refreshing to hear your ideas, and they align perfectly with my thoughts and the rest of the hiring committee's hopes for the entomology department."

I nod, my fingers tapping a rapid beat on my thighs.

"And I'm beyond excited to tell you that we've decided you'll be perfect for the position."

I breathe out a sigh of relief as my heart soars. "Thank you so much."

"You're welcome, my dear. I'm so proud of you."

I lift my chin. "I'm pretty proud too."

"You should be. As you left yesterday, we all looked at each other and nodded. We just knew you were the right person. You had this steady confidence and strong passion that we felt through every answer you gave."

Tears sting in my eyes. Damn, these emotions the last two days have me acting like a blubbering mess, but it feels so satisfying to know I got this job because I'm the right person. Because I deserve it.

"That being said . . ." She sighs, her tone dropping an octave. Her chin lowers as she levels me with a serious look. "Why didn't you tell me that you knew the other applicant?"

The blood drains from my face, and I swallow. "It . . . it didn't seem like the right thing to do."

She nods. "Well, I wasn't aware until he had a breakdown of sorts in his interview yesterday. He was shouting and making accusations about you and your merit as an applicant."

The sudden urge to throw up sweeps through me. If it wasn't for the fact she already offered me the job, I'd crumple to the ground with humiliation.

"And I was shocked," she continues, "because he seemed like a completely different person from the man I met in the first interview and last week while he was here."

"I'm so sorry," I whisper, because it's the only thing I can think to say.

"Millie, *I* am sorry. You have nothing to apologize for." Sharon reaches across the table to put her hand over mine. "Women in science need to stick together. I don't know your whole story, but I do know that man I met yesterday is not the kind of person I want working at our museum. And he's not the kind of person I want hurting one of my employees either. So I want to apologize for not seeing that sooner."

"Well, if it makes you feel any better, I didn't see it for a long time."

She shakes her head sadly. "You're very strong, Millie."

I scoff a laugh. "People keep telling me that, but I'm not. I couldn't even tell anyone what was happening at the time."

Her brows lower. "That doesn't say anything about your strength. You were strong every day of that relationship. You were strong last week, enduring being around him. You were strong yesterday, showing up for that interview. And you're strong today, having this conversation with me. Strength isn't always loud. Sometimes it's a quiet power that isn't so obvious to the world."

I bite my lips and nod, her words reminding me so much of what Lena's told me in the past.

"It's one of my greatest joys in life to prove idiots wrong—especially men," she continues, raising an eyebrow. "So I'm over-the-moon excited for you to prove that idiot wrong. While he was being walked out of the museum by security, spouting nonsense about some of my favorite employees, he was only solidifying my decision."

My chest is lighter as I take a deep breath. It feels so good to hear that someone finally saw his true colors.

We're interrupted by a dashing older man in a black apron, who approaches our table with a wide grin and two plates of food.

"I had a feeling this was for you," he says warmly as he sets Sharon's plate in front of her and kisses her on the cheek.

"This looks fabulous," she coos, then motions toward me. "Darling, this is my new entomology director, Millie Oaks."

The title hits me in the chest. Millie Oaks. Entomology Director. It sounds like a dream.

"Nice to meet you." He smiles. "How does everything look?"

Sharon's eyes rake over her husband seductively, and he blushes all the way to his ears. "Delicious."

He kisses Sharon's cheek one more time, and as he turns to go, she smacks him on the butt and bursts out in cackling laughter.

* * *

"I DID IT!" I barge through Finn's office door with a squeal, and he swivels his computer chair and jumps to his feet. Practically vibrating with excitement, I grab his tie and yank him toward me.

He wraps me in that safe, protective shield I love, and I let myself burrow into it. "Holy shit. I knew you could."

I shake my head against his chest. After weeks of worry and stress, a weight has been lifted from my shoulders, and I can finally breathe all the way in. My thoughts are all jumbled after lunch with Sharon, but gratitude pumps through my veins like adrenaline.

My arms squeeze tighter. "I know you wanted to tell Sharon about Kyle, but it feels so good to know I got the job on my own."

He presses a kiss to the top of my head. "You're perfect for that job, and I can't wait to watch you shine."

"Thank you." I pull back and meet his eyes. "Apparently, Kyle had to be escorted out of the museum after yelling at the panel that I was only interviewing because we were sleeping together."

"What?" he croaks.

A small grin plays on my lips as I remember my conversation at lunch. "Sharon said she never even entertained the accusations." I narrow my eyes. "She said *you* told her you had feelings for me when you dropped out of the interview process."

Finn's cheeks turn pink. "Maybe I did."

"You told our boss that you had feelings for me weeks before you actually told me?" I shake my head in disbelief.

He cups the back of my head and brings my lips to his. "Yeah, *stella mia*. I had to make sure she knew the truth and never thought we were trying to cheat the system." He nips at my bottom lip before he pulls back and adds, "She was all over that, by the way. Told me to go for it."

My chin quivers. "Thank you for supporting me even when you didn't know you were doing it."

"I always will," he says, his mouth coasting over mine and tickling the sensitive nerve endings.

He groans as I part my lips and let him claim my mouth. Our arms tighten around each other as he kisses me thoroughly and hungrily, and I wish we weren't at work right now. I force my movements to slow, and we settle into a languid pace before I pull my swollen lips away.

His voice is breathless as he asks, "How should we celebrate?"

"Want to go to Fern River with me?"

He smiles wide. "Absolutely. The girls have been begging to go back."

Pulling my phone out of my back pocket, I shoot off a quick text in our group chat.

Oaks Folks

> **Millie:** Any cake left from last night?

I peek up and find Finn watching me with a serene smile and soft eyes. I'll never get over how I used to only see scowls from him but now get to see *this*.

My phone buzzes with a response, and I drag my eyes away.

> **Dad:** You know your mom always makes twice as much food as necessary.

> **Millie:** Mind if we come visit?

> **Mom:** Only if you bring Ave and El.

Finn comes to stand behind me and drops his chin to my shoulder, laughing as he watches the replies come through.

> **Millie:** I'll bring them. Finn too, if that matters.

"Of course it matters," he mutters, nipping my earlobe.

> **Dad:** Good. I need his help with something in the barn.

> **Mom:** I'll go get some groceries the girls like.

"Your mom is the best," he whispers, wrapping his arms around my waist. "Serena couldn't even have her chef make something the girls would like, and your mom is going to make a special trip to the store for them."

I turn my head and kiss his cheek. "That's because they're worth it."

Fabes: I'll be there too. Can't wait to see you guys!

Tess: Does this mean the interview went well?

Dad: Hopefully, it's good news since she's coming all this way to tell us.

Millie: I'm coming for the cake I was promised.

Fabes: Too bad. Fucking Theo ate your piece.

Mom: Fable Oaks.

Fabes: Sorry, Mom.

Finn nuzzles my neck and squeezes me tighter in his embrace. "What's up with Fable and Theo? Why does she hate him so much?"

"Mmm," I hum, leaning my head back into him and letting him support me. "Have I really not told you about the video?"

He shakes his head against my neck.

"Well, I'll tell you the whole saga on our way to Fern River."

I shove my phone back into my pocket and turn in his arms.

His navy eyes search mine before he gives me a playful smirk. "Do we get to sleep in the same bed on this trip?"

"I was thinking a night out on the overlook might be fun. The ground is a little hard, but you know the views are amazing." I wink saucily.

He quirks a brow as his heated gaze travels down my neck and shoulders. Pulling back a little, he follows my curves down my body. "Yeah, the views are spectacular," he says, voice husky and warm. "I love every single thing about them."

My cheeks heat. "You must really like stargazing."

He shakes his head. "Fuck the stars, baby. All I see is you."

Epilogue

Millie

One Week Later

"These look fucking beautiful," Lena proclaims, setting the basket of homemade croissants in the center of Finn's patio table. I place a tray of espresso and two milk cups beside it.

There's a cool evening breeze blowing through the gaps in my crochet sweater and upbeat Disney music coming from the speaker in the corner. Stars are just twinkling into view in the sky as the sun dips below the horizon.

"Lena. There are children present. No bad words," Emil scolds with a dark look in her direction.

Pepper skirts around my legs to settle on the floor below the table with Moosey, who she's fallen in love with. The girls let her have the little stuffed animal, and she brings it with her everywhere, hugging it with her teeth until she finds a good spot to snuggle with it.

"It's okay," Finn says, wrapping his arm around my shoulder as I take the seat next to him. "I forget to filter myself all the time."

"Yeah, he said the s-word the other day," Eloise informs us, eyes wide. "He hit his toe on a chair and said, 'Stupid chair.'"

We all gasp on cue. The dreaded *s-word*.

"Oh, that *is* a bad one." Micah grins as the first few notes of "Kiss the Girl" from *The Little Mermaid* drifts from the speaker.

"If you remember, El, you weren't supposed to say it either." Finn flashes a sly look in her direction, and she just mimics it back to him.

"Can we please try them now?" Lena whines impatiently. "My mouth is watering. I might accidently curse again if we don't dig in soon."

Emil passes the basket around, and we all take one. I inspect the flaky, golden pastry on all sides. "They're beautiful, but they're a lot of work. Definitely a special-occasion thing."

Finn takes his first bite and shuts his eyes. "Oh my god," he mumbles with a full mouth.

The table erupts with a chorus of *ooh*s and *ahh*s and pleased sighs.

Micah swallows and smiles. "If you hadn't gotten that promotion, I would've told you to ask Maggie if she's hiring."

Finn leans toward me and whispers along with the song, then plants a buttery, sweet kiss against my lips. I laugh as he nuzzles into my neck, and Eloise takes advantage of the distraction by snatching a second croissant and escaping back to her seat.

When "Kiss the Girl" comes to an end, the introduction to "Let It Go" starts ringing through the backyard. Eloise, always the first to start a dance party, meets my eyes across the table with a knowing smile. I nod, which is all the signal she needs to abandon her croissant and bounce to the open area beside the table. She plants her feet, hands on her hips, and awaits my presence, drawing everyone's attention. I drop a kiss on Ave's head as I pass and flank Eloise on our dance floor.

She starts singing along with Idina Menzel, swaying her shoulders to the beat. I join the chorus, my cheeks burning a little with all these eyes watching us, but soon, Lena sets down her croissant to dance along with us. I wave to Avery, who pushes her chair back and links her hand with mine. Eloise sings to the audience, like she usually does, putting on a show with big dance moves. But Avery keeps her eyes on me, like she's singing and dancing just because I encouraged her to. That simple act always makes my heart feel like its bursting at the seams.

Emil drags Micah onto the makeshift dance floor, and when I meet Finn's eyes, love shines from their blue depths. He sits all alone at the table, but he looks so incredibly happy to be watching us. The connection between our gazes creates a swelling tug between us, and before I know it, he's rising. With his focus locked on me, he walks closer, his mouth moving quietly with the lyrics of the song.

When he reaches me, he holds my face between his hands and kisses me hard, right through the words. Everyone around us lets out a whoop of celebration, and Finn starts moving his body along to the beat, singing with us.

The seven of us finish out the song, jubilant smiles and loud voices and linked hands, and I know it's exactly where I'm meant to be.

I simply had to be brave enough to spread my wings and get here.

* * *

Finn

Two Months Later

"Is this really necessary?" I wonder aloud, tugging at the collar of my blue synthetic shirt. It's itchy and stiff, but I'll endure this costume for a few hours for Millie.

"Absolutely. You aren't Spock without the hair." Millie's brows knit in concentration as she runs a small black comb through the front of my hair, plastering it down against my forehead.

Grasping her hips, I pull her a little closer until she's standing between my thighs. The bright colors of her childhood bedroom fade away as I watch her teeth dig into her bottom lip. My hair must not be cooperating, because she lets out a frustrated huff before tossing the comb to the mattress beside me and smoothing it with her hands.

I let my gaze trail down the white fabric that flows smoothly and tantalizingly over her curves. She has two Halloween costumes this evening. One is a long white Princess Leia robe, complete with buns over her ears and a hood on her head. But the second costume is the real reason I'll put up with this silly Spock outfit. Because the second Princess Leia costume is just for me when we get back to our house later tonight.

Our house. Those words still feel surreal.

Millie moved in with us a few weeks ago, and I still can't get over the fact that I have the privilege of waking up with her every morning. She has fit so seamlessly into our world that it's like she was meant to be there all along. We were just holding the spot open for her.

"Okay, I think you're ready." She tries to pull back, but I keep a tight hold on her hips, so she drops to my thigh. "I know we've crossed two space worlds here," she says, pointing between us, "but I have to say, I think Spock and Leia would've gotten along great."

"There's probably a fanfic about it somewhere. We should read it later." Tucking my fingers into the fabric at her neck, I try to peek down the front of her dress, but it's too tight to grant me the view I'm hoping for. "Do I have to wait until we get all the way back home to see the second costume?"

She swats my hand away. "It'll be more satisfying if I draw out your suspense for a while." With a devilish smirk, she wiggles on my lap, grinding perfectly against where I'm already hard for her.

I tighten my grip to hold her still as I grit out, "Do that again and I'll tear this dress right off you and—"

"You kids hurry up," Dave calls up the stairs, a smile bleeding through his voice. "These girls are getting antsy." A short pause. "And I am too."

Millie snickers as she jumps up and looks suggestively at my lap. These thin black pants aren't hiding her effect on me. Closing my eyes, I try to think of something scary and Halloween-y to get my mind off tearing through that white dress.

Creepy clowns. A room full of spiders. Freddy Kruger mask. That should work.

Millie pulls me to stand and surveys my outfit. "Absolutely perfect."

I raise my hand in the Vulcan salute. "Live long and prosper."

Her mouth drops open and she fans herself dramatically. "Oh, Spock, you know what that does to me," she purrs, wrapping her arms around my neck.

By the time we've kissed again and made it all the way downstairs, our little girls are antsy by the front door, way past ready to fill their buckets with an obnoxious amount of candy.

This weekend will be the girls' first time staying overnight with Millie's parents, and all four of them have been looking forward to it for weeks.

Leaving the girls with them is a big step, but I have no doubts.

After a few difficult conversations with my parents, we are officially no-contact. I expected to feel a sense of sorrow or guilt, but instead it has felt like a relief. Like fresh oxygen in my lungs after a lifetime of breathing stale air.

Thankfully, Mary and Dave have stepped flawlessly into the role of grandparents. They were cheering louder than anyone else in the audience when Eloise finished her first dance recital. They were an hour early to the kindergarten art show last week, and then proceeded to stand beside Avery's watercolor painting the entire time, proudly informing everyone who walked by that their granddaughter was the artist.

Their love for the girls is so obvious, so unconditional, and I could never express to them how grateful I am for it.

"Let's go," Avery whines, her butterfly wings flapping as she bounces with excitement. Millie and I made her costume together, complete with giant, colorful wings that hang down to her feet.

"Sorry." Millie sighs. "Fixing Spock's hair took so much longer than I thought." She crouches to make a few last-minute adjustments to Eloise's astronaut costume that I'm proud to say is extremely accurate.

"You look weird, Uncle Finn," Eloise says, squinting at me over Millie's shoulder.

"It's Uncle Spock tonight," I inform her, plastering on a serious expression.

Millie kisses Eloise's cheek and stands. "I think he looks handsome."

"Then why don't you marry him?" Avery asks, her brows lifted in challenge.

My gaze collides with Millie's and the air pulls tight between us. Her lips curve into a secret smile that seems to speak directly to my heart.

I'd marry her right this minute—dressed as Spock and Leia—without a second thought. As long as my girls are here, that's all I need.

I've never been more sure about anything in my life.

All my focus narrows to my future wife as I promise, "Soon."

The word is barely above a whisper, but she hears it and her smile shines even brighter.

"Are we ready?" Mary asks, opening the front door.

A chorus of cheers bounces through the entryway, and Millie and I share one more intimate smile before we follow everyone out. Dave and Mary lead the way, with Ave and El between them, and I wrap my arm around Millie's shoulders.

"Thanks for making me the luckiest man in the world," I whisper, kissing her temple.

"Just the world?" She blinks up at me.

"No, the galaxy."

"Just the galaxy? There are billions of galaxies, Spock."

I chuckle. "You're right, *stella mia*. Luckiest man in the universe."

Bonus Epilogue

Millie

Three Years Later

The music is so loud that I can feel my brain vibrating.

I slam my fingers into the volume knob, cloaking Micah's car in silence.

Lena, who was singing at a higher decibel than the speakers, lets out a frustrated huff from the backseat. "I was enjoying that," she grumbles, leaning between me and Micah to send me a sharp look.

"I know, but I'm nervous," I whisper into the quiet as Micah turns into my neighborhood. "I can't think when the music is so loud."

Lena stretches forward to set her hand over my thigh. "Why are you nervous?"

"This." I lift my plastic-wrapped arm and let my hand flap around. "Remember when I got my first tattoo thirty minutes ago?"

Micah huffs a laugh. "I don't think either of us could forget your incessant giggling through the whole process. Who *giggles* while getting a tattoo?"

Me, apparently. I've hyped this evening up for six months, since I made the appointment with an artist I found on social media. For weeks, I had to talk myself into contacting her, then when I finally worked up the nerve to call, she was booked six months out.

But that was okay. It gave me time to plan the whole evening. Since I really wanted to keep it a surprise for Finn, I needed Lena and Micah to come with me, so I wasn't alone. And with Lena living two hours away now, getting together for a Friends Night Out took a good bit of organizing. Luckily, we have the Best Husbands Ever™ who helped us make it happen.

Hopefully, we're not going to return home to find Finn, Emil, and Lena's husband, Gavin, tied up and duct-taped while the kids raid the kitchen for cookies. The little sugar gremlins. Actually, knowing Gavin's sweet tooth, he might be in on that plan . . .

"Are you regretting the tattoo already?" Micah asks.

"Oh no. Not at all," I say, bouncing my knee. "I just feel excited-nervous, I think. Like my bones are jittery?"

Lena laughs. "Finn didn't know at all? Not even a hint?"

As I shake my head, Micah flicks his gaze over his shoulder to Lena. They share a momentary, weighted look that I don't understand.

"What?" I turn to glance between them. "What is that look for?"

Lena bites her lip and Micah pats my thigh twice before pulling into our driveway.

"We just know he's about to be obsessed with it, love," Micah assures me.

"So obsessed that we were telepathically asking each other if we should invite Avery and Eloise to stay with us tonight at Micah and Emil's house," Lena adds, her eyebrows dancing suggestively. "A little sleepover so you and Finn can have some alone time."

My cheeks heat. "Thanks for offering, but no. I want the girls to see it too. I'm going to do a grand reveal." I graze my fingers over the plastic, following the pattern that now has a permanent place on my skin.

"Well, the offer is open if you change your mind," Lena says.

I let out a breathy laugh. "I'll let you know."

Micah turns off the engine, and a comfortable silence blankets the car. Maybe we all know, without saying it out loud, that we need this little moment of peace before we enter what is sure to be a hectic house.

I visually trace the peaked roofline of our home. The windows are alight with a warm glow, and I watch as two silhouettes dance by on the other side of the living room curtain.

When I first pulled my old 4Runner up to this house three years ago, I never could've imagined everything that would take place inside those walls. Years of memories. Years of cooking together, dance parties, board games, busy days and loud evenings, cozy at-home date nights, and slow Sunday mornings.

This home has been filled with so much *life*, and after the emotional journey that Avery and Eloise endured in their first few years, I'm so grateful for the laughter and joy we've managed to bring them inside this house.

Sadly, though, we're outgrowing it. Finn and I have talked a lot recently about what the next phase in our life will look like, and the idea of moving is heartbreaking, but also exciting. This has been the perfect home for the four of us, but with only two bedrooms and the office downstairs, we don't have any extra space for guests to stay over.

Or for any additions to our family.

We've been discussing looking for a house with a little property around it, somewhere that Avery and Eloise can still attend the school they love. They would have freedom to run with Pepper, and I could build the garden I've been hoping for. There could be a room for the baby Finn and I have been dreaming about.

Bonus: The stargazing would be better a little bit out of town, which is always a plus with my husband.

Lena lets out a long, slow exhale. "Friends Night Out has come to an end."

"Think they've survived in there?" Micah asks, quirking his head.

"I'm sure Emil kept them in line," I say with a nod.

"Gavin might be passed out on the couch." Lena chuckles. "Eight o'clock is way past his bedtime."

"Honestly, mine too." Micah sighs.

"Why are we so old?" I shake my head with a laugh.

Lena shoves our shoulders playfully. "I'm not. I was ready to go clubbing, but you two wimped out." A beat passes. "Do people still go clubbing? Is that a thing?"

I turn to pat the top of her head. "Exactly my point."

She yawns and reaches for the door. "Fine. You might be right. Micah's guest bed is actually sounding really good right now."

I pull my sweater on to conceal my forearm, then we exit the car slowly, savoring the last few moments of quiet.

As we reach the steps, the kids spill out of the front door, a chaotic cloud of excited shouts and squeals. Eloise collides with me first, wrapping her arms tight around my waist. Avery helps Micah and Emil's two-year-old son, Ollie, down the steps to his dad, who kneels on the sidewalk with open arms, ready to scoop him up. Lena's heels click on the concrete as she jogs toward her daughter, Julia, who is holding her baby brother, Bowie, on her hip.

Everyone's talking at once, reporting on the pizza they ordered, the tower of blocks Ollie built, the cookies Gavin baked, and the dress-up party they had. Meanwhile, seven-month-old Bowie babbles incoherently while staring into his mama's eyes adoringly.

Micah, Lena, and I share a secret smile over all our children's heads.

Lena seems to say, *Look how much our lives have changed.*

Micah replies, *It's chaos. I love it.*

And I say, *Wouldn't trade it for anything.*

When we turn back to face the house, there are the men we love dearly. Finn, Emil, and Gavin are lining the top step, all smiling at us with secret messages of their own.

Finn mouths, "I missed you," with a wink that soars straight to my heart like a shooting star.

* * *

"WHAT TIME ARE we meeting at Maggie's in the morning?" Emil pauses on the path to the car while Micah buckles Ollie into his seat.

"Bowie and I will be up at five thirty," Gavin responds, stopping beside Emil with his son in his arms. "How early do they open?"

I snort from my spot on the porch. "No clue. I've never even considered being there that early."

"I'm sure they're open," Finn says, sliding his hand across my lower back. "But I don't think we'll make it by then."

Lena pats Gavin's shoulder. "Oh, fuck no—" Gavin tries his best to cover Bowie's ears and sends her a scowl without any real heat behind it. "I won't be up then. That's daddy-and-son time," she says, grinning. "But how about nine?"

"Deal. We can handle that," Emil confirms.

Micah shuts the back door of their car and shouts, "Someone warn Maggie we're about to raid all her pastries."

"Good idea," Finn says with a laugh. "I'll call in the morning to reserve some almond croissants." He tugs me in front of him, pressing my back to his chest and wrapping his arms around me.

We stay on the porch, watching our friends bundle their children into their respective cars, and then they pull away in a flurry of waves and smiles.

Finn presses his lips to the back of my head and murmurs, "Did you have a good evening?"

I lean into him, relaxing in his embrace. "It was perfect. Dinner and drinks and then . . . a surprise."

He dips his head and hums against my throat. "A surprise, huh?"

"Let's go inside. It's for the girls too," I whisper, grinning up at him as he pulls away from my neck.

Eyes dancing with curiosity, he guides me toward the open front door. "Think they've made any progress getting ready for bed?"

"I'm going to guess they've made it into their pajamas, but Eloise is probably going to forget to brush her teeth."

"Avery's probably already got *The Lightning Thief* open to tonight's chapter." Finn locks the door behind us.

Pepper follows me through the house as we make a quick sweep on our way to the girls, picking up little bits from the evening on the way. One baby sock on the floor by the couch, Ollie's cup tipped over on the coffee table, a coloring page that was clearly done with Julia's expertise beside one that was clearly done with Ollie's.

Finn steps on a Lego and emits a groan of agony like he's just taken a bullet to the foot. "Damn Legos," he grumbles before bending to scoop them all up.

When we've finally made it upstairs, the girls are waiting in the bed they share, and sure enough, Avery has their book poised and waiting for Finn to read it to them.

"Did you both brush your teeth?" I ask, sitting at the end of Eloise's side.

They both confirm they have clean teeth as Finn comes in to join us, crawling into the spot between them. The girls are still the cuddle bugs they were when I met them and spend most nights curled up toward each other in their sleep, with Pepper at their feet.

Nerves skitter through my stomach as I prepare to reveal the tattoo, but I shove them away the best I can. "I, um, want to show you guys something I did tonight."

"What is it?" Avery asks, tilting her head curiously.

Finn's navy gaze studies me as I pull the sweater off my arms. I feel the moment he spots the wrapping on my forearm and his attention lands there like a hot brand.

"I got a tattoo tonight," I tell them, mostly directed at the girls, who probably have no idea why I have plastic encasing my arm.

Ave and El lean forward, watching the movement as I unwrap it. Setting the plastic aside, I hold the inside of my elbow toward them so they can see what's tattooed there.

Finn sucks in a sharp breath. His searing gaze traces over every star in the Butterfly Cluster now etched into my skin. My freckles are dusted throughout the tattoo to create a little replica of the night sky on my arm.

The column of his throat shifts on a slow swallow. "Millie," he whispers like a quiet plea before grabbing my hand to pull me closer.

I crawl up the bed to reach him and settle between his spread legs, leaning back into his chest.

"Did it hurt?" Avery wonders, tracing her fingers over the dark lines.

"Only when she was getting really close to the inside of my elbow. The rest of the time, it actually kinda tickled."

Finn brushes my hair off my shoulder before setting his chin there. He cradles my elbow in his hand, tilting it side to side to see all the angles. "It's perfect," he murmurs.

"Space nerd seal of approval?"

"Sealed with a kiss," he says before grazing his lips over my jaw.

"Is it the Butterfly Cluster?" Eloise asks, leaning to inspect it.

My nose burns. My throat clogs with so much emotion that all I can do is nod.

The girls have learned the story of the Butterfly Cluster, how much their mom loved it and why it holds a special place in our hearts. Finn has spent many nights helping them find it in the stars. We took a trip to the observatory a few months ago to get a better look, and last year, the girls slept in the study for a week while we painted their bedroom ceiling to match.

This cluster has become a symbol for our family, a guiding light when the girls want to talk to their mama, and there's a palpable shift in the room as the girls realize what's now inked into my skin.

My voice cracks as I tell them, "This little cluster of stars is important to me because it reminds me how lucky I am to have the three of you in my life."

I feel Finn's lips smiling against my neck as he inhales, like he's breathing me in. "It pointed me right to you," he murmurs.

"Exactly," I whisper as my heart tries to swell past my ribs.

"I love it," Avery sighs, leaning her head on my shoulder.

"Can I get one?" Eloise wonders, blinking up to us.

Finn ruffles her hair. "Of course." Her face lights up. "When you're *legally* allowed to get one," he adds, and her smile falls into a scowl.

Avery lets out a loud yawn, and Finn takes that as a signal we need to get these tired girls to bed. He grabs the book from Avery's lap and guides it to my stomach to read over my shoulder, keeping me pinned against his body like he can't imagine letting me go long enough to finish this chapter.

* * *

AFTER GETTING THE girls to sleep and changing into my pajamas, I tread down the stairs to find Finn at the sink, washing the last few dishes from the evening. He peeks over his shoulder as I approach, his dark gaze heating as it travels up my legs, past my sleep shorts, to land on his Catan Battles shirt. I've worn it so much over the last few years that its seams are starting to fray. But it's now the softest T-shirt in the history of T-shirts, so I still gravitate toward it almost every night.

I hop up onto the island counter behind him and wait as he washes the last baking sheet.

"How long have you had that planned?" he asks, expertly lifting one eyebrow as he dries his hands.

"Six months."

Tossing the towel aside, he stands between my knees and grips my thighs firmly. "Six months?"

I skate my hands up his chest and over his broad shoulders. When I reach his neck, I graze my nails into the hair behind his ears and his eyes fall closed with pleasure. "I had to book the appointment way in advance. She's a busy gal."

His hands move up my thighs and slide under the hem of my shorts to grip my hips and pull me against him. When he meets my eyes, flames dance in his blue depths. "So, for six months, you've been keeping this secret from me, knowing full well that I was going to love it?" His fingers dig into my flesh with a needy pressure that pools warmth low in my stomach.

"Yeah, I did."

He pulls back enough to bring his mouth to the dark lines of stars on my arm. "*Stella mia,*" he whispers, his lips brushing lightly over my skin.

The endearment carries no less weight than it did the first time he said it. For a man who has grown up obsessed with stars, it's the highest compliment.

"What are you supposed to put on it to help it heal?" he asks, grazing his fingertips over the tender skin.

I point to a bag on the counter behind me. "We stopped at the store on the way home and picked up what she recommended."

He steps out from between my thighs to rifle through the bag, before returning and squeezing some of the moisturizer into his hand. With the utmost care, he glides it over my forearm. He concentrates on his movements as he makes slow, soothing circles over my skin, giving each star a layer of protection. The warmth of his touch spreads through the rest of my body, swirling in my chest and down to my core.

"Millie." He shakes his head. "You have no idea how much this means to me."

After making one final pass over the stars, he sets the bottle aside and his gaze meets mine. An ache burns in my throat as I take in the glassy shine in his eyes, the quiver at the corner of his lips.

Tears gather in my lashes. "I wanted to honor Clara and everything she brought to me. This whole life that I didn't know I was destined for."

A smile curls up his lips before he brings them to mine. "It was written in the stars all along," he murmurs against my mouth.

When I nod, a warm tear falls down my cheek.

He kisses it reverently before his lips slide to my neck. "I missed you tonight," he whispers, tucking his hands under my shirt to drift over my waist. His touch leaves a warm, sparkly trail over my ribs.

"Did you?" I ask, breathy and distracted.

I feel him smile against my neck. "I'm happy when I get to watch you, talkative and excited while people are here. But the whole time, I'm wishing I could sneak you into a different room and kiss you." He slides his hand up, brushing his thumbs over the bottom swells of my breasts. "Ravage you in secret."

My nipples tighten and I can't stop myself from arching toward his touch. "I could be available for ravaging." I squirm my hips, scooting closer to him, trying to satisfy the ache in my core.

"Oh yeah?" he asks, pulling back to flash me a devious smirk.

Then he leans toward where my nipples are pressing against the front of my shirt and sucks one into his mouth through the fabric. My hands drift into his hair, sliding through the dark waves as we groan in unison.

When he pulls back, his eyes are dark pools of night. "How would my Millie like to be ravaged?"

Looping my arms around his neck, I drag him closer until I can leave a soft bite on his earlobe. His body melts toward me, wrapping his arms tight around my waist until we're flush together. "On your desk," I tell him, and he shudders around me.

"Hold on to me," he says, and I hook my ankles together behind his back. Lifting me effortlessly, he carries me toward the study, flicking off the kitchen light on his way. Once we're inside, he shuts and locks the study door before setting me on the edge of his desk.

I giggle as he reaches behind me to clumsily slide away whatever is on the surface. Something clatters to the ground and we both freeze, holding our breaths to see if we woke anyone. Another giggle slips out, and I smack my hands over my mouth to muffle it.

With wide eyes, I stare up at Finn. A silent moment passes as we both strain our ears to hear anything. But when no sound follows, we both burst into snorts of laughter. He presses his face into my neck, his shoulders shaking until we both calm down enough to suck in a deep breath.

He pulls back, and I make a show of dragging my shirt up my body and tossing it aside. He studies me as I lean back on my palms and swing my legs playfully.

"Fuck. You look perfect there," he says, voice low and gravelly. He drags a hand down his face and folds it around the side of his neck. "I'll never get a single bit of work done in here now. I'll be too distracted thinking about my wife spread out on my desk, needy and aching for me, those pretty nipples begging for my attention."

I draw my shoulders back to push my chest out and he chuckles. Reaching behind his neck, he tugs his shirt over his head and drops into his rolling chair, gliding it toward me. He places my feet on his thighs and then grips the waistband on my shorts. "Lift your hips for me."

I follow his directions, and when he tosses the last of my clothing aside, he leans back to watch me again, his dark gaze dipping down my body. His thighs are spread wide, bare chest and stomach on display, and my mouth waters to touch him. I want to kiss every bit of skin I can see, along with every bit I can't.

A desperate growl crawls up his throat as he rolls his chair closer. I spread my thighs further to accommodate him and then suck in a breath as he throws my legs over his shoulders. He grabs my hips to drag me to the very edge of the desk before lowering his mouth to my center.

His tongue slides over me in one long, slow swipe that has me falling back onto my elbows. He pulls away with a soft, knowing chuckle, licking his lips indulgently. "So sweet," he murmurs before dipping his head again.

He takes his time, lavishing me with his tongue, sucking and pulling and caressing me as I writhe and whimper on his desk. My nails drag over his scalp and thread through his hair, and his contented moans vibrate through my clit.

When my orgasm crests, it ricochets into every bone and muscle in my body.

Before I've recovered enough to make coherent thoughts, Finn stands to yank his pajama pants off, flashing me a carefree smile. His muscles tense as he fists his erection and brings himself to my entrance, sliding through my arousal.

"Please," I whisper, and he sinks slowly into me, leisurely

watching our bodies meld together as a guttural groan rumbles from his chest.

When every inch of his length is inside me, he holds himself there. I relish the flickering movement of muscles in his neck and shoulders while he forces himself to stay still. Like it's the sweetest form of torture but also the perfect buildup.

"Finn, please," I beg, aching for friction. Aching to feel him all over me and inside and *everywhere*.

With a ragged breath, he folds his hands around my hips, and finally moves. He pulls himself almost all the way out, before pressing back in, slow and deliciously satisfying.

"You feel so fucking good." His grin is a little wild on the edges, and I want to savor that look forever, but I need to touch him. I need him closer.

"C'mere," I say, reaching for him.

He leans down with a tender smile, and I cup his jaw between my palms. One of his hands grips my elbow and he trails his lips down my arm in a path of adoring kisses until he reaches the edge of my new tattoo.

His gaze caresses the cluster of stars while his hips continue that slow, dragging pressure that sends sparks of pleasure up my spine.

When he finally brings his lips to mine, our kiss is hungry and breathtaking. Shivers cascade over every inch of my skin. He tastes like *me*, and it fuels the heat inside me to the point that I think I might burst into flames like this.

We kiss like two people who know each other by heart. Our deepest wishes and our biggest failures and every little moment in between. It's safe and reckless, new and familiar, and soft and untamed.

His lips trace a path down the line of my neck, keeping a deep, steady rhythm with his hips. He loops his arms under my back and holds me against his chest, protecting me from the hard surface of the desk with every thrust.

"I love you so much, *stella mia*," he murmurs in my ear, and an infinite number of stars dance in my vision as we shatter in the safety of each other's arms.

Millie's Snickerdoodle Recipe

Ingredients

- 1 cup (2 sticks) unsalted butter, softened
- 1 1/2 cups white sugar + 1/4 white sugar, divided
- 2 eggs
- 2 teaspoons vanilla extract
- 2 3/4 cups all-purpose flour
- 2 tsp cream of tartar
- 1 tsp baking soda
- 1/4 tsp salt
- 1 tbsp ground cinnamon

Directions

1. Preheat oven to 400°F/200°C.
2. Beat butter and 1 1/2 cups white sugar until fluffy. Then add eggs and vanilla extract and beat again until combined.
3. In a separate bowl, mix together the flour, cream of tartar, baking soda, and salt.
4. Add dry ingredients to butter mixture and blend until dough forms.
5. Mix the remaining 1/4 cup sugar and cinnamon in a separate small bowl.

6. Scoop and shape cookie dough into rounded balls, about 1 1/2 inches thick. Roll the balls in the cinnamon-sugar mixture, then place on a lined baking sheet about two inches apart. (Or stick them in the freezer for a cookie dough treat later.)

7. Bake 8 to 10 minutes, until the edges are a light golden brown.

8. While one batch is baking, feel free to snack on the dough. *wink*

9. When the cookies come out of the oven, cool them on a wire rack.

10. ENJOY!!

Acknowledgments

*D*eciding to write this book—my first book—is one of the bravest things I've ever done, and I'm grateful every day that I found the courage to do it. There are so many things in this book that I've pulled from real life, and it feels like I'm sharing a bit of my soul with you. Little pieces of Millie's and Finn's personalities and healing journeys have been influenced by my own, and I'm so happy I got to share them this way. It was a cathartic process, where I was able to make the characters in my book say and think things that I *want* to be able to say. And in doing so, I've given myself a boost of confidence and strength that I didn't know was possible.

To my daughters, who encouraged me to make my book-writing dreams come true. Your random conversations and interests have given me inspiration for Avery and Eloise, and I wish I could magic them into existence to be your best friends. I'll always be there, cheering for you and encouraging you, and I'm so damn proud to be your mom.

To my husband, who never doubted me for a second. Your confidence in me is unwavering. Thank you for being my biggest cheerleader, carrying me through every down day, and dragging me out of the house when my brain was mush. You believe in me without question, and everyone deserves someone who thinks of them that way.

To my mom, who I was nervous to tell I was writing a steamy romance book, but who was immediately proud of me and asked how she could help. Thank you for believing in me every single day of my life. I wouldn't be where I am without you.

April, thank you for letting me use your sheepdog first-kiss story as book content. I hope you enjoyed all the Easter eggs from our friendship sprinkled along the way. Thank you for bringing back my love of reading all those years ago.

To my editor, Priyanka, thank you for falling in love with Millie and Finn and all their nerdiness. It's such a relief to have my stories in your capable, encouraging hands. Finding a home for my books at Avon has been a dream come true. To the entire team at Avon—thank you a million times. You've taken this book and helped me polish it into the version that we get to share with the world, and having this team behind me is more than I ever could've hoped for.

To Lauren, my agent, thank you for always being there when I need you and for believing in me wholeheartedly. I'm so glad I have you by my side for this journey.

Brooklyn, you are a queen. This book would *literally* be nowhere near as wonderful without you. Thank you for fixing my loads of comma drama, being so patient with me, and offering me constant encouragement. You called dibs on Finn first, so here it is in writing: He's yours. ;)

Hannah Bonam-Young, the woman you are. The day you DMed me that you'd picked up my book will go down in history. Thank you for being my soul sister and for every heartfelt, wonderful piece of encouragement you've given me.

Ada, there aren't enough *thank-you*s in the world to properly show my appreciation for you. Your friendship, support, and guidance have held me together through this process, and I just adore you.

To my hype-woman extraordinaire, Wren, I'm forever grateful. You truly have been here since the beginning, and I couldn't imagine this journey without you. Your enthusiasm and love of my characters has carried me through many hard days.

My OG beta readers, Taylor, Heidi, Melinda, Abbey, Kim, Melissa, and Roni, this story wouldn't be the same without your dedicated attention to detail and fantastic feedback.

To anyone who read this book in its indie publishing journey, you are my rock stars. Thank you for taking a chance on a new author and sharing the hell out of my book. I wouldn't be here without you all and the fantastic community we've built together. Tears spring to my eyes every time I think about those first few months of my author journey and the support you all showed me. Thank you astronomically.

And finally, to myself. You did the damn thing and you didn't let any of the obstacles stop you. Sometimes strength is quiet, and that isn't weakness. You are strong, and I'm so fucking proud of you.

Read on for a preview of Jillian Meadows's
holiday romance . . .

WRECK MY PLANS

Chapter 1

Lena

*C*leaning puke off my new Christmas pajamas just isn't a part of my journey this year," I inform Millie as my tires screech on the pavement, trying to gain traction on the hill up to my mom's house.

"But if you come back here, we could be sick in a blanket fort together." My best friend's voice is laced with disappointment as it echoes through the car speakers. "We can hide in there and rewatch *Bridgerton* while Finn plays nurse for us."

"Mmm, being waited on by your boyfriend does sound tempting. Is he going to dress up? I might be willing to risk a stomach bug for that."

This was going to be the first year I spent the week of Christmas away from my family. *Ever.* But my plan to stay in Wilhelmina with Millie and her new family imploded this morning when Finn's niece, Eloise, threw up all over their game of Uno.

"I'll get online right now and order a costume as a last-minute gift," Millie says. "Think they make sexy nurse outfits big enough to fit him?"

Our combined laughter fills the car as I reach my mom's two-story cabin and park behind her SUV. "He's going to hate me for giving you this idea. I'll be subjected to even more of his scowls and eye rolls. It's a wonder he's not sick of me yet."

"If he was, we'd have to seriously reconsider our arrangements over here," she says. "He'd be sleeping in Pepper's dog bed from then on."

I snort a laugh as I unbuckle my seat belt. "I'm about to become an even clingier best friend just so I can see that." Pulling my keys from the ignition, I twist them in my grip. "I'm here, Mills."

A whoosh of breath crackles over the line as she sighs, the sound dousing me with the urge to hug her. "Okay. Everything is going to be great. They'll be so excited you ended up coming, and at least you don't have to spend your week with a stomach virus."

"I will pray to Santa and Mrs. Claus that everyone feels better soon," I promise.

"Thanks," she sighs. "Love you. Try to forget all the job stuff for a week. It can wait until you get back."

"Love you too, and I'll try. Kiss your girls for me. And sneak a picture if you get Finn in that costume."

When the call ends, I blow out a long breath, letting my gaze trace over the white Christmas lights trimming the house and the golden glow shining from the windows.

Millie's words echo in my head. *Forget about the job stuff.*

Is that even possible? It's been a constant weight on my shoulders since my dreams of being an art teacher crumbled around me two weeks ago. I'd hoped that spending the holidays with Millie's family would be a breath of fresh air, a chance for something different.

Millie and her family have been the perfect distraction from all the negative thoughts in my head lately. At their house, everything is loud, joyous, and carefree.

Mine, on the other hand?

It's too quiet now that Millie and Pepper have moved out. Too calm and boring and void of friendship.

Maybe I should look into adopting a dog.

Don't get me wrong, I'm happy for Millie and Finn. I want to scream from the top of the Wilhelmina Natural Science Museum that I was an integral part of forcing those two clueless scientists together.

When Millie and Finn make eyes at each other across the room, and his lips kick up like he's completely smitten with her, it makes my heart warm and fuzzy. And when my other best friends, Micah and Emil, hold hands in the car while we drive to dinner, it makes me grin like a proud mom.

But my own loneliness still hangs like a collar around my neck, reminding me I don't have what my friends do.

I can be happy for them and sad for myself at the same time, I think. I've spent my whole life feeling that way.

My role is "best friend support system." The one to help send that firmly worded text. The one who has their back against a bully. The one who pumps them up when they need a pep talk.

It's an honor to protect the people I care about.

But occasionally, I want my own person to help protect *me*.

I firmly believe I can make my way in the world without a partner, but that doesn't change the fact that sometimes I'm simply *lonely*.

Sometimes I wish I had someone to laugh at my ridiculous day and remind me to eat a real meal every once in a while. Someone to cuddle up to on the couch and have inside jokes with. Someone to lean on when I'm not feeling my strongest, and who can guide me in the right direction when I'm feeling lost.

And maybe some physical benefits too? Honestly, my lady bits might be amassing cobwebs at this point from the lack of contact with anything other than my vibrator.

Shivering at that possibility, I pull my rainbow beanie over my head. Then I slip on my sage-green gloves and stuff my arms into the sleeves of my puffy red jacket.

I take one more deep inhale for good measure before I get out of the car. Maybe the extra oxygen will relax all my tension-filled muscles.

My lashes are weighted with snowflakes when I finally make it to the front door, opting to leave the last-minute gifts I grabbed in the car so my five-year-old nephew, Jack, can't tear into them early.

When I push open the door, relief sweeps into my heart like a warm breeze.

I soak in all the little details. The garland twining around the banister, the phantom smell of sugar and vanilla, the faint Christmas music drifting to my ears.

Home.

I let my eyelids fall shut as I close the door behind me and drop my bags.

Despite the fact that I'd planned to stay away this year, I can't deny the comfort washing over me. I've missed it here.

"What the fuck, Lena?"

My eyes shoot open to land on my sister-in-law, Zara. A shocked smile brightens her blue eyes as she stands from the couch with her one-month-old son, Noah. "What are you doing here?"

"I heard it's Christmas." I shrug, grinning as we meet in the entryway.

"Did you have this planned all along?" Zara asks, tugging me into a quick, one-arm hug.

"No. Millie's family got sick, so I'm a surprise gift." My dark curls brush Noah's cheek as I lean toward him to leave a kiss on his forehead.

"Tia Lena," Jack screeches, his wild ringlets bouncing as he barrels toward me and collides with my legs.

Mama rushes in from the kitchen, hands waving excitedly. "Oi," she squeals. "You came! Merry Christmas, *amorzinho.*"

Letting go of Jack, I pull Mama toward me, a wave of calm coursing through me as she squeezes me tight.

As Mama releases me, my grandmother, who we call Luci, rounds the corner. With tears glistening in her eyes, she frames my face between her palms. "*Menina*, you scared the shit out of me saying you wouldn't be here." She shakes her head. "Don't do it again." Her blunt words have me nodding in her grip. "I'll make you hot tea. It's freezing outside," she announces in the lingering Portuguese accent from her childhood in Brazil.

I huff a laugh. "It's okay. I'm really not that cold. I have a heater in my car."

She waves me off as she makes her way back to the kitchen.

Zara snickers, her blond hair swinging as she shakes her head. "She's a force to be reckoned with today."

"Where do you think I got it from?" I shoot her a sassy wink as I strip out of my cold-weather gear.

Zara nudges Noah toward me, and I settle him into my arms, a snuggly little bundle against my sweater.

"You're stuck with him now," she calls over her shoulder as she jogs up the stairs. "Auggie's at the store, and I need a shower more than you want to know."

Carefully carrying Noah into the living room, I navigate around Jack's doll collection in the middle of the floor.

"Where's your sister?" I ask him, lowering myself to the couch.

"With Daddy at the store," Jack says as he stuffs his doll's feet into a plastic shoe. "They had to get more bread for dinner."

I hum in understanding as I focus on the little guy in my arms.

New addition to my running list of jobs to look for: holding snuggly babies all day.

"We've only met once before," I whisper to Noah's sleeping face, soaking up every detail of his rosy round cheeks and long dark lashes. "But I'm sure you remember me. I'm the one who told you the secret about your dad actually being an alien."

He lets out a sigh that sounds an awful lot like a moody teenager.

"I know, but if you ignore the green antennae, he's a nice one, I promise."

Luci approaches with a mug nestled between her hands. "Raspberry. Our favorite."

"Thank you." I grab the tea, and she lets out a groan as she drops to the couch beside me.

"How's my Lena?" she wonders, patting my thigh.

I take a sip of my tart tea, trying to gain control of my emotions. "Good. Great." The words come out too loud, and the corners of my lips quiver.

I've felt so . . . adrift lately. Like I'm lost in a turbulent ocean without land in sight. And for some reason, the concern in her voice feels like she's thrown me a life preserver.

It makes me want to pour out all my thoughts and have her sort them out with me.

Her brow furrows, but before she can respond, the back door squeaks open and a commotion rises from behind us in the kitchen. My brother's voice booms through the house in greeting before my niece, Penelope, shouts, "Tia Lena!"

Craning my neck, I try to see her, but I don't want to wake Noah, so I set the mug on the coffee table and wave her over. She bounds toward me and dives onto the couch beside me.

"There you are." I sigh, wrapping an arm around her shoulders. "I missed you, kid."

She grins up at me. "I missed you too. I'm glad you came."

"Me too." Pressing my nose to her chestnut waves, I breathe her in and grin. "Did you get the bread?"

"No, they didn't have the right kind for Gavin."

The last two syllables land like a bomb in my chest. I suck in a breath, but it does nothing to help me process the name she just said.

Gavin.

My stomach drops to the floor.

Anger and excitement swirl into a storm in my brain, mixing to the point that I can't distinguish them.

Pen's blue eyes blink up at me, and I must look as sick as I feel because she asks, "Are you okay?"

A tremor shakes my hands as I try to find the words to answer her.

It's not him. She must be mistaken.

But I can't confirm. I'm trapped on this couch, facing the wrong way, while unease churns in my gut.

In the mixture of voices behind me, one distinctive chuckle dances over my skin, raising every hair on my body. The deep, hearty laugh is a sound I've heard so many times, but not for the last three years.

They've been devoid of the man behind me.

Boots thud against the floors, ominously approaching. And suddenly, anger bursts out of my storm of emotions, and I know exactly where to direct it.

About the Author

JILLIAN MEADOWS writes cozy love stories that make you swoon, smile, and squeal. She lives thirty miles past The Middle of Nowhere, Texas, with her husband, four wild daughters, two unruly dogs, and her sparkling water addiction. When she's not writing, you can find her devouring a romance novel, playing board games, or enjoying the outdoors with her family.

If you want to learn more about Jillian and her books, please visit jillianmeadowswrites.com or find her on Instagram @jillianmeadowswrites.

Discover More By
JILLIAN MEADOWS

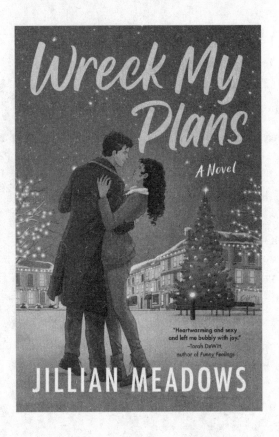

A sweet and spicy holiday romance between a spirited artist who returns to her small town for Christmas and her older brother's best friend, a serious architect who pushes all her buttons—but whom she can't seem to stay away from.